Praise for Susan Fleet's Frank Renzi crime thrillers

ABSOLUTION
Best Mystery-Suspense-Thriller of 2009 — Premier Book Awards
"Relentless tempo . . . sharp writing." — Kirkus Reviews
"Creole-flavored suspense." — Attleboro Sun Chronicle

DIVA
"Fleet subtitles *Diva* a novel of psychological suspense. That's an understatement." — Jan Herman, Arts Journal
"... an obsessed stalker lusts after his victim." — Tom Bryson, author *Too Smart To Die*

NATALIE'S REVENGE
Best Mystery-Thriller of 2014 – Feathered Quill Book Awards
"An amazingly great read! Fast paced and extremely challenging to put down." — Rebecca's Reads
"Frank Renzi has a new crime to solve. Natalie is a truly intelligent and seductive character. A tremendously great series." -- Feathered Quill Book Reviews

JACKPOT
"Thrilling and gripping. The writing is tight and builds to a tense climax." — Readers' Favorite
"Great character development, and an absolutely fascinating ending." -- Feathered Quill Book Reviews

NATALIE'S ART
"Compelling characterization and a surprising conclusion. That's fine art, indeed." — Midwest Book Reviews
"Non-stop twists begin on page one. A fast-paced, action-packed read!" — Feathered Quill Book Reviews

MISSING

"Fleet opens with a bang. A fast-paced, hard-hitting emotional roller-coaster ride far above the usual whodunit."
— Midwest Book Reviews

"[The] action never stops and the suspense is palpable." — Feathered Quill Book Reviews

"Surprise read of the year. I could hardly put it down." – Amazon reader

NATALIE'S DILEMMA

"There is no better place to begin a suspense thriller than on the gritty streets of New Orleans with Detective Frank Renzi. You will not see the end coming...and feel a roller-coaster of emotions when it does." – Feathered Quill Book Reviews.

"The gritty atmosphere comes vividly to life [with] characters who face difficult choices. *Natalie's Dilemma* will delight fans of intrigue and thrillers." – Midwest Book Reviews

"From Italy to New Orleans, this intense thriller will take you on the ride of your life!" – Amazon reader

SNIPER

"The Frank Renzi series is among the best in the crime fiction realm. Action at its finest, plot turns faster than the sniper's bullet. Fleet [is] a master at writing crime fiction." – Feathered Quill Book Reviews

"*Sniper* is delightfully unpredictable. A thriller that turns expectations upside down and weaves a far more sinister tale than that of a lone random sniper." – Midwest Book Reviews

"A fast paced thriller strewn with international intrigue and a veritable gumbo of characters. The story plays like a taut jazz combo trading eights in a dark and sweaty French Quarter nightclub. Detective Frank Renzi assembles puzzle parts in a race to see the big picture before it's too late." – Amazon reader

PAYBACK

A FRANK RENZI NOVEL

"May the road rise up to meet you,
and the wind be always at your back."
– traditional Irish blessing

"The best luck of all is the luck you make for yourself."
– General Douglas MacArthur

Dedicated to the families and loved ones of homicide victims
and the valiant police officers who solve these crimes

SUSAN FLEET

Music and Mayhem Press

Published by Music and Mayhem Press

No part of this book may be reproduced, scanned, or distributed in any printed or electronic form without written permission except in the case of brief quotations in articles or reviews. For information and permissions contact the author at: www.susanfleet.com

ISBN-13 978-1-7321301-1-1
ISBN-10   1-7321301-1-6

Front cover photograph used with permission from Fotalia:
Scary face in shadow © dundanim

Back cover author photo by Pete Wolbrette

Printed in the United States of America

CHAPTER 1

THURSDAY October 13, 2011 – 11:45 PM Eastern – Ray Brook, NY

Stretched out on his lumpy mattress, Brian Devlin watched the unsuspecting beetle scuttle along the wall toward the trap he'd set for it, a crumb of bread he'd saved from dinner. Almost there, it was. Another inch or so and the pest would be history.

Poised to strike, he grasped the heavy-soled shoe in his hand. *Whap!*

The beetle fell to the floor, it's thick shell crushed, it's spidery legs twitching. Done for. Soon Frank Renzi would be done for, too.

Not dead. Not right away at least. He had other plans for Renzi. That's what had kept him going all these years.

Fifteen years, two months and six days locked up in jail cells.

Some had been better than others. The federal penitentiary in Texas was the worst, a hellhole that required constant vigilance or his life could end in an instant, a shiv in the heart or a broken neck. It had taken his high-priced lawyer fifteen months to get him out of there, a hardship transfer to FCI Ray Brook, a medium security federal prison in upstate New York, because his worthless piece-of-shit father had a bum ticker and couldn't travel to Texas to visit him.

Not that Pa had ever visited him in prison.

Here at FCI Ray Brook life was safer, thanks to his sister. After he paid one of the guards to look the other way so Bridget could smuggle in Oxy during her twice-a-month visits, he had a cell with no roommate and protection from predators.

A piercing scream cut through the never-ending cacophony, some hapless inmate being raped by his cellmate no doubt. An ugly fate he no longer had to worry about, trading Oxy-pills for protection, plenty of hard-asses ready-willing-and-able to do his bidding.

But the deprivations continued. Not a ray of sunshine through the two-foot-by-one-foot window, encased in stainless steel wire-mesh to prevent the smallest inmate from escaping. Not a breath of fresh air, just

1

the stench of urine and feces, and the stink of sweaty unwashed men. The incessant curses, day and night, angry men enraged by the slightest perceived insult. Three times a day, eating food unfit for pigs.

Worst of all was the utter lack of privacy. Constant observation by low-IQ guards with a yen for power, eager to crack him over the head with their nightsticks for the slightest infraction and put him in the hole. Need to take a crap or jerk off? Someone was always watching.

But tomorrow he was getting out of here.

No more orders from guards. No more screams from raped inmates. No more shitty food. No more clang of a cell door trapping him inside a barren eight-by-six cubicle. Freedom at last!

Anticipating the perks that came with it, Devlin smiled. Food and sex topped the list. He might be fifty years old, but his dick was still in good working order. First he would savor a gourmet dinner and a bottle of fine wine with Sunny in her elegant apartment. Enjoy the peace and quiet. Have an intelligent conversation with a beautiful woman.

He hadn't seen Sunny for fifteen years. The worst deprivation of all. Lord, how he'd missed her.

Later, they would retire to a king-sized bed with silk sheets. Instead of indulging in sexual fantasies as he gazed at a picture of a half-naked movie starlet in his cell, he would once again enjoy the exquisite pleasures of making love to Sunny. His lover and business partner.

The next morning, he'd go for a run on Carson Beach in South Boston, smell the fresh salt-sea air, feel the ocean breeze ruffle his thick black hair. After a quick shower, he would stroll through Southie, greeting old friends and admirers.

His sister had warned him that the old neighborhood had changed. Soon he would see it with his own eyes. . Equally important, he would make sure his business interests were secure and his leadership of the Shamrock Gang was unchallenged.

Unable to sleep, he stretched out on the mattress, gazing at the black sky outside his window. Twelve hours from now he would be free.

But not free of observation. The feds would be watching, waiting for him to make one false move so they could send him back to prison. Stalking him like sharks pursued seals near Cape Cod beaches in the summer.But he would never go back to prison.

From this day forward he would live free or die.

Tomorrow he would set in motion the plan that had kept him sane all these years. Payback for Frank Renzi.

———

10:45 PM – Central – New Orleans

NOPD Homicide Detective Frank Renzi sat in his unmarked Dodge Charger outside the yellow police tape, assessing the crime scene. Both ends of the block had been barricaded to make room for police and emergency vehicles.

Cruisers with flashing blues were parked haphazardly along the street, an NOPD crime scene van, an ambulance with blinking red lights. Numbered orange evidence cones marked shell casings and spent cartridges on the street and sidewalk.

On the opposite sidewalk, a large crowd had gathered, weeping black women comforting one another, black men with hard eyes clocking the action. A scene fraught with tension, monitored carefully by several NOPD patrolmen, and the inevitable media gathering: reporters, photographers and TV cameras.

He took out his SIG and jacked a round into the chamber. Twenty years with Boston PD and ten more in New Orleans, he knew that two dead gangbangers didn't mean the shooting was over. Nine times out of ten, a drive-by was about retaliation. An endless cycle of violence.

He unbuttoned his jacket so he could grab the SIG fast if he needed it, left the car and ducked under the crime scene tape. Six-foot-one, lean and athletic, he purposely carried himself with the air of authority required at a crime scene, conveyed by his dark penetrating eyes.

Hank raised a hand to greet him, a black patrol officer with graying hair and a soul-patch under his bottom lip, an NOPD beat cop for twenty years, long before Frank had arrived in 2001.

"Yo, Frank, hate to say it, but this is gonna ruin your night."

"And my weekend, probably. What have we got?"

Hank pointed to a body sprawled on the sidewalk in a puddle of blood. A black male clad in dark running pants and a dark hoodie, surrounded by photographers and crime scene technicians. "One of the Hollygrove 'bangers. Recognized him right off. Took two in the chest, one in the face." Aiming his chin at the EMTs loading a gurney into the ambulance, he said, "The other 'banger might make it."

"Dispatch said there were two victims. Where's the other one?"

Hank scrunched his mouth like he was sucking a lemon and pointed at a one-story house with blue clapboard siding and a white picket fence.

3

SUSAN FLEET

Lights blazed in the windows facing the street. "In there. Ten years old. Poor kid got caught in the line of fire, never knew what hit him."

"Damn! What about the other occupants? Are they okay?"

"Just the parents. Not injured, but the mom is all tore up. I wanted to send her to the hospital, you know, but she wouldn't leave. The father's pissed. Can't say I blame him. Horrible thing, your only child gets shot while he's doing his homework."

"You got names?" he asked, an attempt to stay objective, but the senseless death of innocent children bothered the hell out of him.

"Noah Scott, age 51, manages a grocery store. Alvina Scott, age 50, teaches at a Catholic elementary school. The boy's name is Elijah."

"Black folks, right?" When Hank nodded, he said, "I'd get Kenyon over here, but he's out of town. Took four days off and went to Atlanta with his family." Kenyon Miller, Frank's closest friend in the District-8 Homicide office, was a former president of the Black Police Officer Association. Everyone knew Kenyon and respected him.

Intuiting his unspoken concerns, Hank said, "Want me to go in with you? Maybe pave the way, you know, tell the parents you're an experienced detective, clear a lot of homicides."

"Thanks for the offer, Hank, but let me give it a go first. If I need you, I'll call you."

He went to the front door, rang the bell and stepped into a small living room. Slumped in the left corner of a floral-print sofa, the mother sobbed quietly, clutching a wad of tissues. The father stood at the other end of the sofa, stiffly erect, six feet tall and slender in neatly-pressed trousers and a white shirt, his arms crossed over his chest, his chiseled face a mask of anger.

Frank's first impulse was to comfort the mom, but the fury in Noah Scott's eyes told him that would be a mistake. He showed his photo ID to the father and said, "Frank Renzi, NOPD Homicide Detective. I'm very sorry for your loss, Mr. Scott."

Scott's expression didn't change, but the mahogany-brown skin around his eyes tightened. "This was a wonderful neighborhood when we bought this house ten years ago, Detective Renzi. Not anymore. Now it's a gang-infested cesspool." Scott jerked his thumb at the window. "These punks are so brazen they sell drugs on the corner in the daytime! Children can't go outside to play. Can't ride a bike to the corner store. Can't even walk to school. And what have you done to stop it? Nothing!"

Maintaining a neutral expression, Frank said nothing. The man had a right to express his opinion, and he wasn't about to interrupt a grieving parent.

"It's not his fault," said Mrs. Scott. "Parents don't teach their children how to behave—"

"They don't deserve to *have* children, Alvina!" Scott's nostrils flared. "They don't know how to be parents. They don't want to work, they just want to collect their food stamps and housing vouchers and watch TV all day, while their drug-dealing offspring run around with guns!"

"I know you folks are distraught," Frank said, "and I don't blame you. But we need information to catch whoever did this. Can you tell me what happened?"

"We heard gunshots around nine o'clock," Alvina said, gazing at him with doleful eyes. "Noah and I were having coffee in the dining room after dinner. Elijah was in his room doing homework. He's an honor student at Our Lady of Mercy Charter School."

Frank went over and took her hands in his. "I can't imagine how terrible this must be for you, Mrs. Scott. I'm so sorry your son was taken from you in such a cruel way. It's inexcusable."

Her eyes welled with tears. "Elijah was a good boy, Detective Renzi. Smart, well-behaved. A happy child, always smiling."

Gazing into her eyes, Frank said, "I have a daughter, Mrs Scott. Maureen is much older than Elijah, but if something like this happened to her, I wouldn't rest until justice was done. I can promise you this: I will work just as hard to find whoever did this and get justice for Elijah."

"Thank you," Alvina whispered. Noah Scott just looked at him, stone-faced, and said nothing.

A crime scene tech walked through the room, headed for the front door. "We're done in the bedroom, Frank. You need to take a look, go ahead. The coroner will be here soon."

"Noooo," Alvina wailed. "Please God, no. Don't take my boy away."

Noah Scott rushed to her side, bent down and embraced her. "Stay here, Alvina. Before the coroner arrives I want Detective Renzi to see what happened."

Frank followed him down a short hall to a small bedroom facing the street. He'd seen his share of corpses: violent car accidents, suicides by hanging, stabbings, multiple shootings, dozens of victims survived by loved ones who cared about them. But young victims tore at his heart. Steeling himself, he focused on the details.

SUSAN FLEET

Elijah's short-sleeved blue shirt, the chocolate brown skin of his arms, his long slender fingers, fingers a jazz piano player might envy. To reconstruct what had happened, he looked at the window, then at Elijah. Unaware of what was about to happen, the boy had been seated at a small desk facing the window, working on a laptop. Pock-marked with holes, the wall behind him told the tale. Elijah had been blown back in his chair by a hail of bullets that shattered the window. Some had pierced his chest, leaving his shirt bloody, his body broken, his large dark eyes vacant and staring.

"Want to know what he was working on, Detective Renzi?"

Startled, he turned and faced Noah Scott. "Tell me."

"A project for his social studies class." Scott paused, his face working with emotion. "Before he started school this year, Elijah said, we hear gunshots every night, Dad. Why do so many people have guns? I told him to do some research and find out. So he did."

Frank said nothing, aware of the gun control arguments, many of them media driven, that erupted whenever there was a heinous crime like this.

Scott opened a closet door and took out a poster-board with a colorful map titled: *Guns Laws Around the World*.

"Ironic, isn't it? A ten-year-old honor student wants to educate folks about gun laws. He was all excited when he found some information on New Zealand. There, gun licenses are issued only for a valid reason, at the discretion of the police."

His face contorted in grief. "And now he's dead. My only child is dead." He turned away, his body shaking. "Elijah," he whispered, "what will I do without you?"

Frank left the room, knowing there was nothing he could say to ease the man's suffering.

What he *could* do was find the bastards who killed Elijah and bring them to justice.

CHAPTER 2

FRIDAY October 14 – 10:25 AM – Ray Brook, NY

When the metal gate clanged shut behind him, Devlin stopped short, paralyzed by a sudden rush of emotion. All those years ago when the judge imposed his sentence—20 years to life—he had kept up a cocky facade, telling Bridget and Sunny he'd be fine. But there had been long lonely nights in his cell when despair threatened to annihilate him, bringing tears to his eyes. Dangerous.

No tears allowed in club fed. Never show weakness or the predators will pounce. Now that he was free, he was fighting back tears, fearing he'd start bawling like a baby. Unacceptable. He bit the inside of his cheek and strode toward the black SUV idling at the curb, clutching a brown paper bag with his meager belonging in one hand.

Tank jumped out of the SUV and embraced him, saying in a deep raspy voice, "About fuckin time!"

Despite his resolve, Devlin clung to him, verging on tears, the faint smell of cigar smoke evoking a rush of memories. Tank was the big brother he'd never had, a five-foot-ten wide-body, his most trusted lieutenant.

"Let's get out of here," Devlin said gruffly, and got in the car. He was the boss, and a boss never shows weakness of any kind. No displays of heartfelt affection, certainly not tears.

"The faster the better," Tank said. The SUV accelerated, racing along a perimeter road lined with barbed wire, twenty-foot fences and guard towers. Loathing the sight of them, Devlin closed his eyes.

After they left the prison grounds, Tank said, "I brought the clothes you wanted, get you out of that jailbird crap." Jerking a thumb at the worn jeans and ragged T-shirt Devlin was wearing.

Devlin reached into the back seat and pulled them into his lap. Unlike Tank's loose-fitting sweatshirt, his outfit included a long-sleeved Armani silk shirt and black-leather Gucci loafers. Two minutes later the jailbird outfit was in the foot-well and he felt like a human being again.

"You hungry?" Tank asked. "Wanna stop somewhere?"

"No. I want to eat my first meal in Southie."

Tank grinned at him, his eyes mischievous. "With Sunny?"

The name conjured up her image: long blonde hair, brilliant blue eyes, the most beautiful smile he'd ever seen and a body to go with it. "Yes. How long will it take to get there?"

Tank held out a map in his meaty hand. "I marked the route. Go south through Vermont and New Hampshire, pick up I-93 south. Two hundred sixty miles, give or take. I figure it'll take us about five hours." He shrugged. "Wouldn't wanna get stopped for speeding."

"Why not? You didn't bring a gun?" He was only half joking.

Tank frowned at him, then started laughing. "You still got cojones, Dev, I'll give ya that."

The day I lose them is the day they put me in the ground.

Aloud he said, "You're in charge, Tank. I'm going to take a nap." Last night he'd been too keyed up to sleep.

"Okay. We get to Vermont, I'll wake you up and we'll stop for coffee."

With Tank at the wheel, he could relax. He would trust Tank with his life. He adjusted the seat and leaned back against the headrest, recalling the night they had met. Forty years ago, but the memory was vivid, a technicolor movie unreeling in his mind.

After another row with Pa, he had stomped out of their cramped North End apartment. Hurt and angry, he walked down Charter Street to the Copps Hill burying ground. But he got a bad feeling inside when he got there. Someone was leaning against the graveyard fence, underneath a streetlight. Irish by the looks of him, blue eyes, shaggy dark hair, and big. Almost as big as Pa. "What you doing out here this time of night, kid?"

"What's it to ya? It's a free country." Act tough, maybe the guy would leave him alone.

"Yeah, but kids your age belong in bed."

"I have to share a bedroom with Pa. He's in there now screwing some tramp."

"Who gave you the shiner?" Pointing at the purple bruise on his cheek, clearly visible in the glow of the streetlight.

"This kid was teasing my little sister. Kate's ... slow. The nuns at school have to help her with everything. He called her a re-tard, so I shut him up, busted his lip wide open."

"What kid?"

"Nicky Valenti."

"Jesus! You went after Nicky? That wop bastard is trouble. Only sixteen and almost as big as me! Him and his pals will come after you. Tell your Ma to talk to the nuns."

"Ain't got no Ma. She died when Kate was born."

The guy didn't say anything for a moment, frowning now. "Who takes care of Kate?"

"Pa, after he gets home from his shit job pumping gas. My sister mostly. She cooks the meals and looks after Kate. Bridget's eleven, a year older than me."

"You help Bridget?"

"I help when I can, but I've got a paper route after school. We need the money. When Pa was unloading cargo down on the docks, his arm got crushed, broken in four places."

The guy stuck out his hand. "Call me Tank, what's your name?"

"Brian," he said, and shook Tank's hand.

"Beat me to the end of that fence down there," Tank said, "and I'll get you a better job."

Brian took off running, beat him by ten yards. He figured Tank would be mad, but he wasn't. He was smiling. "Okay," Tank said, "you get the job. Meet me at the playground after school tomorrow. And don't let them wops follow you."

That's how he got into the North End Irish gang. He collected betting slips from street corners and ran them over to the gang office, got paid eighteen bucks a week, twice as much as delivering papers. He didn't tell Pa, didn't give him any money either. He gave most of it to Bridget. She didn't ask how he got it, had been happy to use the money to buy groceries.

Comforted by the memory and lulled by the drone of the wheels, he dozed off.

An hour later, Tank woke him up, poked him in the ribs and said, "Let's stop for coffee. I gotta take a leak."

They stopped at a Dunkin Donuts in White River Junction. Before he left the SUV, Devlin took a tattered photograph out of the brown paper bag and stuck it in his pocket. They put in their order, a large iced coffee for him, a hot coffee for Tank, and grabbed a booth beside a window.

He took the photograph out of his pocket and put it on the table. "Remember this guy?"

"Yeah, the fuckin' wop detective. Renzi."

"Correct. The wop detective that sent me to jail. Now it's payback time."

Tank shook his head, frowning at him. "You gotta lie low for a while, Dev. Check in with your parole officer twice a week, pee in a cup and stay outta trouble."

Rage bubbled up inside him, fueled by the injustice of it. The endless days, months and years he'd been locked up, while Renzi walked the streets as a free man, a homicide detective with Boston PD and, since 2001, in New Orleans.

Thanks to the news reports he'd found in the prison library, he knew all about Frank Renzi, had already identified his weak spots. Married, then divorced, his daughter living in Baltimore, his father living in Swampscott, not far from South Boston.

"Tank," he said grimly. "I'm not gonna lie low. I've got a plan."

Tank sipped his coffee and said nothing, expressionless.

Devlin raised his iced coffee in a mock toast. "But first we need to celebrate. You're the best, Tank. You're like a brother to me. Always have been. Always will be."

Smiling now, Tank raised his coffee mug. "Same here, Dev. You know that."

"Five hours from now I'll be celebrating with Sunny. Saturday morning we'll have a sit-down, just you and me and Sean Whelan."

Tank's smile faded. No surprise there. Tank didn't like Sean Whelan. Devlin didn't either, but he needed Whelan to execute his payback plan. After that, all bets were off.

———

9:30 AM Central – New Orleans

"The scumbags are already ragging on us," said Lieutenant Detective Morgan Vobitch, waving a copy of the *Times-Picayune* in the air.

Bleary-eyed from lack of sleep, Frank sipped his coffee, knowing it was pointless to speak until his boss finished his rant. Two weeks ago, Vobitch had returned from a three-month medical leave after open-heart surgery. Doctors had replaced one of his heart valves. Forced to recuperate at home, Vobitch was furious. Frank, his longtime confidant in the District-8 homicide unit, had listened to his complaints, diatribes sprinkled with F-bombs, incensed that he couldn't work.

"You see the picture?" With a sneer of disgust, Vobitch dropped the newspaper on his desk. "An innocent ten-year-old honor student, looks like an angel. They think we don't care about that? They think we don't work just as hard when a black kid gets shot?"

Vobitch took umbrage at any hint of racial bias directed at him. His Jewish parents had emigrated to New York City after being persecuted in Russia, and his wife was black. As an NYPD patrol officer, Vobitch had saved her from a mugger outside the theater after Juliana, a willowy ballerina with ebony-black skin, finished a performance.

Stubborn as a bulldog and built like one, Vobitch was a five-foot-seven force of nature who now weighed twenty pounds less than his previous 190 pounds, thanks to Juliana's persistent efforts after the open heart surgery.

"It sells newspapers," Frank said. "Gets people riled up for a few days. A week from now they'll be bitching about something else, a heavy rain storm and the pumps aren't working."

Vobitch glowered at him, his slate-gray eyes icy, and ran a hand over his thick silvery-gray hair. He glanced at a TV set mounted on the wall beside his desk, tuned to a local station, muted, a cooking show on now. Like every other NOPD supervisor, Vobitch constantly monitored the local news: print, radio and TV.

"So," Vobitch said. "You look like you been up all night. You get anything?"

"Got no sleep and no leads. We canvassed the neighborhood. Nobody saw anything."

Vobitch grimaced. "How the hell do they expect us to find the shooters if nobody will talk?"

"They're scared. Two 'bangers get shot, by a rival gang probably, folks don't want to be seen with us, never mind talk to us."

"Tell me about the parents."

"The mother's heartbroken. The father is too, but he's also pissed off."

"Pissed off enough to hire a dumb-fuck ambulance-chaser lawyer?"

"Hard to say. Maybe."

Vobitch glanced at the TV set, grabbed the clicker and upped the volume as a jingle sounded and a Breaking-News graphic appeared. "There you go," Frank said, eyeing the screen. "A news conference featuring the grieving parents and a rabble-rousing black lawyer."

Standing behind a bank of microphones, Rufus King, a local attorney known for his militant stance on black issues, addressed the cameras. "Any objective observer of crime in New Orleans would have to conclude that there is a certain lack of zeal when it comes to prosecuting perpetrators of crimes against African-Americans in this city. We have a police department headed by an African-American, but the NOPD clearance rate for murders in black neighborhoods is abysmal. Now we have a dead ten-year-old boy, an innocent victim of a violent crime, and no indication police have conducted any sort of rigorous investigation, much less identified any suspects."

"Christ on a crutch!" Vobitch exclaimed. "If we started pulling in suspects willy-nilly, this guy would bust us for profiling blacks. He'll spin any set of facts to fit his agenda."

"It gets worse," Frank said, gesturing at the television screen.

King held up a photograph of the young smiling victim. Standing behind him, Alvina Scott began to weep, dabbing her eyes with a handkerchief. Beside her, Noah Scott remained impassive, standing straight and tall, looking almost ministerial in a black suit and muted-gray tie.

In a voice full of outrage, King said, "Elijah Scott was an honor student at Our Lady of Mercy Charter School, the only child of parents who had great hopes for him." Gesturing at Alvina and Noah Scott, he said, "I invited them here to assure them that we in the black community will not allow Elijah to be another statistic. Elijah Scott is not a number. Not just another victim of black crime in New Orleans. His father would like to tell you about him."

Noah Scott stepped to the microphones and gazed into the camera. In a quiet sonorous voice, he said, "Alvina and I married later in life and feared we might never have a child. But the good Lord sent us a son. We named him Elijah. For ten years, he brought us great joy. We raised him to respect the law. To study hard and do chores around the house. Elijah rewarded us by becoming an honor student and now ...." Scott's face worked with emotion.

He paused for a moment, then raised his head in an angry motion and spoke in a firm voice. "But the police do nothing to protect our neighborhood. Decent folks like us can't let our children go outside because hoodlums sell dope on the corner in broad daylight! Every night we hear gunshots. Gang warfare, the newspapers say. Well, I say the police need to do something. Because our neighborhood is worse than Beirut."

"Worse than Beirut," Frank said. "Man, there's a soundbite. Wait till that goes viral."

"Yeah," Vobitch said. "Check the crawl-line at the bottom of the screen. Our favorite dickhead lawyer already organized a protest march for tomorrow." He picked up the phone. "I better call the Super and tell him to put extra troops on the ground in case some asshole decides to start a riot."

Frank rose to his feet. "I'll be there, for sure. Talk to you later."

He walked down the hall to the Homicide office, sat at his desk and his cellphone rang. He saw the Caller ID and smiled. Kelly O'Neil. He was tired and frazzled, but not too tired to talk to his fellow detective and lover. "Hey, Kelly, what's up?"

"Plenty! Did you see the news conference?"

"Yes, in Vobitch's office. Needless to say, he was bullshit. So am I, since I'm lead on the case."

"Lucky you. I guess we won't be having dinner tonight, huh?"

"Probably not." He lowered his voice and murmured, "But I might come over later and take a nap with you."

Kelly uttered a sultry laugh. "A nap. That'll be the day. But seriously, Frank, be careful. These thugs are armed to the teeth, got more weapons than the soldiers at Fort Polk, and they don't give a damn who they shoot, civilians or cops. I don't want it to be you."

"I don't either," he said, knowing she was right.

Then, picturing Elijah Scott's vacant eyes and bloody chest, he said, "But you didn't see the body like I did. That's what they should put on TV, pictures of Elijah, dead in his room. That would wake people up. But they won't. They'll be out there tomorrow to cover the protest march and mouth the usual platitudes afterwards, which solves nothing. I'm the one who's gonna find the maggots who killed Elijah."

CHAPTER 3

SATURDAY October 15 – 9:10 AM – South Boston

For the first time in fifteen years, the clang of a cell door didn't wake him. Quiet and still, he gazed at Sunny, lying beside him, admiring her firm breasts and well-toned body.

They'd met twenty-five years ago when Sunny was nineteen, an honor student at Brown University. He was twenty-four, an up-and-coming gangster. Now he was fifty. Sunny was forty-four, but looked years younger. A natural ash blond, she resembled Liv Ullmann.

Playing possum with him now, her eyes closed, a hint of a smile on her sensuous lips. He leaned down, inhaling her musky scent, and kissed her. "Stop faking. I know you're awake."

Her eyes opened, brilliant blue eyes, eyes any movie star would envy. She caressed his cheek. "Just enjoying the moment. I missed you, Dev."

"Same here. There were many nights when I fantasized about you. Fifteen years and you're as gorgeous as ever, Sunny. Curves in all the right places, a flat stomach. How do you do it?"

Clearly pleased, she said, "Hard work, that's how. You know me, Dev, better than anyone." She ruffled his hair. "I like the flecks of gray at the temples. Distinguished. And I still can't resist those emerald-green eyes of yours. Sexy." Stretching the word out in her sultry low-pitched voice. Another turn-on.

"I can't tell you how happy I am that you're back." She caressed his cheek and glanced at the clock on her bedside table. "Unfortunately, I have to get to work."

Sunny's apartment was on the top floor of the Seaview Inn, a stylish five-story hotel three blocks from Carson Beach. Only the top floor had ocean views, but Sunny never lacked customers. Businessmen and tourists rented rooms on the first two floors. In bordello-like rooms on the third and fourth floors Sunny's girls entertained their johns, women to suit every man's taste: hot-blooded Latinas, voluptuous Italians, ice-princess blondes, Asians for kinky threesomes.

Years ago after Sunny graduated from Brown, he had bought the Seaview Inn to help her start the business, not that his name appeared on the deed. She gave him a percentage of the profits every month.

"I've got work to do, too," Devlin said.

"So soon? Why not take some time off and enjoy yourself. Go for a run on the beach."

"I've got a new project." He smiled grimly. "Gotta make plans with Tank." He hesitated, knowing Sunny wasn't fond of his enforcer, and added. "And Sean Whelan."

Sunny's eyes grew colder than a Norwegian fjord in February. "I'd like to watch a piranha chew the bastard to bits and swallow him."

He didn't know why she hated Whelan, but he wasn't going to ask and risk ruining their reunion. He kissed her lips and smoothed away her frown. "Forget Whelan. We're together again, that's what counts. Thanks for the fantastic reunion, way better than the one I fantasized about."

Her sunny smile reappeared. "For you and me both, Dev. Come back soon."

———

10:15 AM – Plymouth, Massachusetts

Bridget sat at the dressing table in her bedroom, stroking a brush through her glossy black hair. During the week she wore it in a French twist, her prim and proper professor look. Only on weekends did she have time to pamper herself: sleep late, eat a leisurely breakfast, then shampoo her long black hair and rinse it with conditioner.

Working for Brian did have certain benefits. She'd spent last weekend in Las Vegas.

As a freshman at Yale she'd lost her virginity at a frat party to a boy whose name she couldn't recall. The devout Catholic girl who'd gone to parochial school discovered she liked sex. Now, she took lavish vacations as often as possible, some in Vegas, others in sunny California, staying at swanky hotels. If she met a man she liked, preferably a married businessman, she had a fling with him, no strings attached, and returned to her job, relaxed and sexually satisfied.

She set the brush down on the table beside her eye shadow and lip gloss and studied herself in the mirror. She was fifty-one, a year older than Brian, but people often took them for twins. Black hair, emerald-green eyes and high cheekbones, thanks to their Irish ancestors.

15

After she graduated from Yale, Brian had greased the palm of a greedy civil servant—twenty hundred-dollar bills from his ill-gotten gains—to certify a fake marriage certificate: the groom was Robert White, a non-existent man with an innocuous surname. Thus, at the age of twenty-four, she got a new name: Bridget White, and landed a college teaching job on Cape Cod.

At the time, Brian claimed he'd done it to celebrate her graduation, but she knew better. He'd done it so she could live a double life: college professor by day while secretly working for him and his Shamrock Gang. Truth be told, having a faux-husband came in handy if she needed to fend off some boring Lothario looking for sex. She had no interest in getting married for real or having a child. She'd spent far too many hours taking care of Kate while they were growing up.

Now she lived by herself and loved it. During her first semester of teaching, she went house-hunting and found a two bedroom cottage in Plymouth, not too far from the college, an easy drive to the group home near Boston where Kate lived. Brian had given her fifty grand for the down-payment, which left only a small mortgage, and had his lawyer do the closing. Slick as a whistle, an hour later the lawyer had presented her with a deed in Bridget White's name.

She left the bedroom, went down the hall to the kitchen and poured herself a cup of coffee. Brian was probably in bed with Sunny. His partner in crime. She grimaced and sipped some coffee. She hadn't seen Sunny since Brian went to prison.

Sunny was bad news, the bad-news bitch from hell.

———

10:30 AM – South Boston

The Shamrock Gang security tech swept the game room at the rear of the Leprechaun Pub every day to make sure there were no bugs. The technological kind. Seated at a poker table, secure in the knowledge the feds wouldn't overhear, Devlin regarded his two top lieutenants, Tank and Sean Whelan, his enforcer.

Born and raised in Southie, Whelan was Irish through and through: ice-blue eyes, a face plastered with freckles and red hair, with a temper to go with it. A five-foot-eleven explosion waiting to happen, massive shoulders and fists like granite slabs.

A man who always carried a gun.

16

His father had put him in the boxing ring when he was six. A natural, Whelan had quick hands and quicker feet. By the time he was sixteen he'd won several titles, but his hot temper defeated him. He used his fists to beat up kids outside the ring once too often, put one kid in the hospital with a fractured skull and wound up in juvy detention. End of boxing career.

"What's up?" Whelan asked, brushing frizzy red hair from his forehead. "You got something new going?"

Devlin glanced at Tank, who remained expressionless. Tank would never tell Whelan about anything without his say-so. "Something top secret," Devlin said. "No bugs in this room and no loose talk outside of it, understand?" Only three people knew the code to unlock the solid steel door to the game room. Whelan wasn't one of them.

Whelan frowned. "Of course. That goes without saying."

Maybe, Devlin thought, and maybe not. In the prison library he'd looked up the Gaelic name for Whelan and found out it meant wolf. Wolves were useful when you needed one to keep people in line, but Whelan was forty-four and ambitious. Useful, but not to be trusted.

"No pillow talk with your girlfriends."

Whelan spread his hands and grinned. "When I'm in bed with a broad, I let my dick do the talking. No complaints, so far."

A bully and a braggart. "I've got a job for you. A hit."

"Yeah? Anybody I know?" Whelan said eagerly, already champing at the bit.

"Salvatore Renzi."

"The name don't ring a bell. Who is he? Some wop from the North End?"

"He's a judge, works at the federal courthouse in Boston."

"Far out!" Whelan exclaimed, smiling broadly, exposing cigarette stained teeth. "Knock off a judge? No problem." He reached inside his jacket, took out a .357 Magnum and aimed it at an imaginary target. "Just say the word and I'll hit him outside the courthouse."

"Don't be stupid, Sean. Do you ever watch the news? Six years ago a prisoner killed two guards and a judge inside an Atlanta courthouse. These days they post cops around all federal courthouses, including the one in Boston. Use a gun, they'll put you away for keeps."

Whelan put away the Magnum and pursed his lips. "Okay, I'll use my Bushmaster then. Get on a roof across the street, shoot him and split before they can find me."

"No. No guns."

Whelan's cheeks flamed red, accentuating his freckles. "So how the fuck do I kill him?"

"It has to look like an accident."

"Definitely," Tank said, speaking for the first time. "No guns. A car accident maybe."

"I like it," Devlin said. "You know anything about cars, Sean?"

"I know how to put a bomb under one, that'd be easy enough."

"But it wouldn't look like an accident, would it?" he said. "Sean, didn't you hear me? What part of *accident* did you not understand?"

"Best thing to do," Tank said, "fix his car so the brakes will fail."

"How old is this guy?" Whelan said, pouting now.

"Seventy-eight," Devlin said. "Why?"

"What if he's got a driver?" Whelan shot him an impudent grin. "You ever think of that?"

Devlin clenched his fists in his lap. He hadn't, but he wasn't going to admit it.

Tuned in to his mounting anger, Tank said, "We know he lives in Swampscott. I'll watch his house Monday, see how he gets to work."

"Good thinking, Tank. Use one of the cars in the garage and put a stolen plate on it." They kept several vehicles in their service-station garage to use for certain clandestine activities.

"Better get there early," Whelan said. "Rush hour traffic into Boston is a bitch. Unless he's got a helicopter." Flashing another impudent grin.

"Sean, this is no joke." Devlin didn't raise his voice, but there was menace in it. And there was no mistaking the message in his eyes. *Don't fuck with me. Not now. Not ever.*

Whelan raised his hands as if to ward off a blow, no longer smiling. "Jesus, Dev, I didn't mean nothing. I never heard of this guy. How come you got a hard-on for him?"

"Never mind. Go see your friendly car mechanic and have him teach you how to fix the brakes so they'll fail at the proper time, you got that?"

"Okay," Whelan said, his face sullen. "I'll get started on that this after-noon."

"No," Devlin said coldly. "Get started on it *now.*"

Whelan left the table and went to the emergency exit door. Large red letters on the door said: EMERGENCY EXIT ONLY. ALARM WILL SOUND. It wouldn't of course. The alarm would sound only if someone tried to get *into* the game room, alerting the tech who swept the room for bugs.

Whelan turned and said, "I know you just got outta the joint, Devlin, but you need to ease up a little. I took care of business for a long time while you were in the joint."

"And got compensated handsomely for it."

"True. But a word of thanks wouldn't hurt."

"You'll get my thanks when you take out the judge and make it look like an accident."

Whelan said nothing, just opened the exit door and left.

After a moment, Tank said, "The guy's a snake, Dev. You sure you want him to do it? I could get somebody to fuck up the brakes, get behind him in a Hummer and force him off the road."

"No. I don't want you anywhere near this. You and I will be on Castle Island chatting with a friend of ours when the hit goes down."

Devlin massaged his temples. All the wine he'd consumed last night celebrating with Sunny plus lack of sleep had brought on the mother of all headaches. Whelan's smart-ass jibes made it worse. "What if he's got a driver?"

Tank waved a dismissive hand. "He don't have no driver, Dev. That's expensive and judges don't make that much dough. He don't use a fuckin helicopter neither. That's just Sean being a wise-ass."

"Okay, check out the house. Take some pictures with your cellphone." Devlin smiled. "I love these new phones. Imagine what I could've done with one fifteen years ago."

Tank grinned at him. "Yeah. Take a picture of Sunny … naked."

Devlin laughed. "That, too. We had a great reunion last night. How about you?"

Fifty-five years old and never married, Tank had long since given up on finding a girlfriend, much less marrying one. No matter how you sliced it, Tank was pug-ugly, cheeks pock-marked with acne scars, his nose broken too many times. He used Sunny's girls two or three times a week, had dinner sent up to the room, got a quickie before dinner, another one afterwards.

Tank shrugged. "Had a good time, like always. I like the Asian girls. They always treat me good. Dev, I still think you should lie low for a while. See your parole officer and—"

"No. Next week, Renzi's father dies."

19

"Okay," Tank said, expressionless. "And then what?"

Contemplating the next part of his payback plan—the plan he'd thought about every single night, lying awake in his cell at Ray Brook—almost gave him a hard-on.

Offing Renzi's father was just the beginning. The next part was even better.

Devlin smiled. "Then we set up the rest of the payback plan."

CHAPTER 4

SATURDAY October 15 – 10:15 AM – New Orleans

Beneath a cloudless blue sky, Royal Street was jammed with tourists, families with kids licking Popsicle's, parents pushing strollers, others taking pictures of a black trumpet player riffing on a jazz tune, his case open beside him with a sign inviting tips. A perfect day to enjoy the French Quarter, sunny and warm, but not humid.

Frank hoped it stayed that way.

We will not allow Elijah to be a statistic. Elijah Scott is not a number. Not just another victim of black crime in New Orleans. Attorney Rufus King's angry words at the news conference yesterday.

But his anger was misplaced. Frank was angry too, angry at the killers. He could hear the marchers several blocks away, the blare of bullhorns followed by a shouted response from the protesters. He couldn't hear the words, could only imagine them. *Stop the Violence* and *Justice for Elijah.*

Standing beside him, Kelly O'Neil leaned closer and said, "I heard the Mayor won't be marching. He's out of town, allegedly."

"Hiding is more like it. Doesn't want to take sides until he sees which way the wind is blowing."

"The Superintendent put extra uniforms on the street," Kelly said, "but no riot gear."

"Smart. Why stir up trouble? The out-of-town troublemakers aren't here. Not yet anyway."

Two NOPD motorcycle cops roared by them, their white helmets gleaming in the sunlight. Across the street, a dozen blue-shirted patrol officers stood behind metal barriers on the steps of the Louisiana State Courthouse. Soon, the protesters would stop there and give speeches to incite the crowd.

Frank had on his undercover outfit, a Yankees baseball cap, a navy-blue running suit and mirrored sunglasses. Kelly looked trim and fit in white Bermuda shorts and a red halter top that complimented her olive skin and short dark hair. He assumed her Glock-9mm was in the large bag slung over one shoulder. His SIG was hidden in his ankle holster. In case any trouble started.

Together five years and she still captivated him, in and out of bed. Last night he'd stopped by her house. She made him a sandwich and they talked for a while, their usual prelude to lovemaking. But not last night. Too many bigwigs were agitated about the drive-by, so he'd gone back to work.

"You really think the shooters will be here?" Kelly asked.

"Wouldn't surprise me. Blend in with the crowd, see who's marching. Let's hope they don't shoot anyone. Elijah was doing homework when he died. A project about gun laws."

Kelly stared at him, her sea-green eyes wide. "The irony of it is just ... sick."

"The whole thing is sick. A ten-year-old boy dies for no reason?" He fingered the jagged scar on his chin, an unconscious gesture that revealed his emotional state. Emotions he preferred to hide.

"Elijah was their only child. Man, if someone shot Maureen I don't know what I'd do."

"You'd find the motherfucker and kill him."

Shocked, he stared at her. The glint in her eyes told him she wasn't joking. Would he kill the motherfucker? Maybe. He didn't want to think about anything bad happening to Maureen.

"How's she doing?" Kelly asked. "Have you talked to her lately?"

"I called her last weekend. She's a surgical resident now, works crazy hours, goes to the hospital at six to do morning rounds with her supervisor, doesn't get home till eight at night sometimes."

"Baltimore's a tough town, but at least she's in a hospital. I worry about my brother, patrolling the mean streets of Chicago. Last weekend seventy-four people got shot, eleven dead. I'm glad Dad retired last year, after twenty-five years on the job. Your father's still working, right?"

"Yes, but he's in a courtroom. There's beefed up protection inside federal courthouses these days. Let's go see who's leading the parade."

The sounds were louder now, the rat-a-tat of snare drums alternating with the bullhorn and the shouts of the protesters.

What do we want? Justice! When do we want it? Now!

Marching toward them, the parade crossed Bourbon Street led by the VIP protesters, their arms linked together: four black ministers, two black city councilmen and, front and center, Attorney Rufus King, with Alvina Scott on one side, Noah Scott on the other.

Pop. Pop-pop-pop. No mistaking that sound.

"Gun!" Frank yelled, and started running, his first thought and greatest fear: *They're after Elijah's parents.*

Behind him, he heard Kelly shout, "Shots fired! Get down!"

Frank bulled his way through the crowd and saw two husky patrol officers shove Alvina and Noah Scott into a praline shop. He raced to the door and shouted, "NOPD homicide!"

The grim-faced patrol officers recognized him and lowered their weapons. Alvina sat in a chair, sobbing. Standing beside her, clearly shaken, Noah saw him and quickly looked away.

Seconds later, Kelly arrived, breathing hard. Frank went to her and said, "This needs a woman's touch. Tell Mrs. Scott we'll put them in a squad car and drive them home."

"Got it," she said, already approaching the distraught mother.

Confident that Kelly would make sure Alvina and Noah Scott were protected, he left the store and headed north toward Bourbon Street. No more shots, but hordes of wild-eyed people were running his way, screaming, knocking aside metal police barriers as they ran; others took shelter inside any stores that were open.

Sweating profusely, he fought his way through the crowd. As he got closer to Bourbon Street, someone yelled, "Frank!"

He turned and David Lee ran up to him, a recent addition to the District-8 homicide unit in his mid-thirties, and the lone Chinese-American homicide detective. "One down on Bourbon," David said, "gunshot wound in the leg, not life-threatening. The district commander canceled the rest of the march. Are Elijah's parents okay?"

"Shook up, but safe inside a candy store. Kelly's with them. No sign of Rufus King or the councilmen. Any hint of danger, they run and hide. Did you see the shooters?"

Crestfallen, David shook his head. "No. I heard shots and the crowd scattered, left the wounded man lying in the street, so I tended to him first. By then the shooter was long gone. Frank, this gang violence is out of control. How do we stop them?"

"Annihilate them."

Seeing David's shocked expression, Frank smiled thinly. "Okay, we play by the rules, find the bastards and put them in jail."

11:25 AM – Deer Island, Massachusetts

Bridget stood on the grass in the Deer Island cemetery. Off to her left, ominous dark clouds loomed over the ocean, the incoming tide seething with whitecaps, the wind whipping salty spray into her face. Not a soul in sight. Still, she felt uneasy.

She'd be happy to see her brother, but when Brian called last night and told her to meet him here, she knew he wanted something. The site of many family outings during their childhood, this was now Brian's preferred place to meet when they needed to talk privately.

She studied the gray-granite headstone Brian had bought to replace the wooden cross that marked their ancestor's grave.

BRIDGETTE O'HARA

B. 1827, COUNTY KILDAIRE, IRELAND.

D. 1849, DEER ISLAND, MASSACHUSETTS

Dead at twenty-two, her life cut short by whatever pestilence had killed 800 of the 2,400 Irish immigrants who'd landed here. Bridgette had already born two children, a young boy and an infant girl, also named Bridgette, in honor of Saint Brigid, a popular patron saint of Ireland, second only to Saint Patrick.

The origin of the Devlin family curse.

Pa brought them here on the anniversary of their mother's death, not that she was buried here. Bridgette Devlin's resting place was in Boston's North End. But after they placed flowers on her grave—lilies if Pa could afford them, wildflowers if he couldn't—Pa brought them here to remind them of the hardships the Irish had endured, not just in Ireland but also in America.

The distant rumble of thunder interrupted her thoughts. She checked the street, a hundred yards away. Her car was the only one there. No sign of Brian.

Ma had lived to the ripe old age of twenty-three. In 1960, she married Terrance "Terry" Devlin. A year later, their first child was born, a girl. They named her Bridget.

Fifty-one years later, she still hated the name.

Did they think by shortening it, they would avoid the Bridgette curse?

Fourteen months later, Brian arrived, a healthy baby boy, but the next year, Ma's luck ran out. She died giving birth to a nine-pound-three-

-ounce baby girl. Kathleen was blessed with the Devlin family good looks: coal black hair, high cheekbones, gorgeous green eyes and a beautiful smile. Unfortunately, deprived of oxygen during the extended and arduous birth, Kate's brain was damaged, a second curse upon them, one that continued to this day.

Who would take care of Kate if she and Brian died?

In first grade, tests revealed Kate had an IQ of 75. By the age of ten, she had mastered the basic tasks of hygiene, could even dress herself if someone laid out clothes for her, but she was hopeless in school. When the other kids picked on her, Brian beat them up and made them leave her alone.

Give Brian credit. He'd always looked out for Kate.

A seagull cawed as it swooped past her and a gust of wind whipped tendrils of black hair over her face. Brushing them away, she tried to focus on happier days. Pa, carrying on the Irish tradition he'd learned from his father, regaling them with stories when he put them to bed at night, fanciful tales of valiant Irish knights and brave Irish women.

But those days were long gone. Two days out of prison and Brian already wanted something. She dearly loved her brother, but when Brian wanted something he usually got it.

A car horn tooted, one quick honk. She turned and saw Brian get out of a black Toyota. He trotted toward her, sprinted the last few yards and grabbed her in a bear hug. "You look marvelous, Bridget. I'm so happy to see you I can't think straight!"

"That'll be the day, you not thinking straight." She kissed his cheek. "Let me look at you!"

Two weeks ago she had visited him at Ray Brook. Other than the gleeful smile, he looked the same. Clean-shaven, thick black hair flecked with gray, emerald-green eyes regarding her with keen intelligence. A lean five-foot-nine, muscular arms from lifting weights and no flabby gut. Apart from a jailhouse pallor, no one would guess he'd been in prison fifteen years.

"Looking good," she said. "Who drove you home, Tank?"

"Yes, picked me up and drove me straight to Southie."

"No stops at all? Not even for a beer?"

Brian shook his head. "I wanted my first meal to be in Southie. Nothing fancy."

"Yeah?" she said, not believing him. "What about Sunny?"

A sly smile overspread his face. "Well, sure as the priest says Mass on Sunday, I had to see Sunny. A fine reunion, we had. Dinner, fine wine and …" A broad wink. "That's why I'm late."

Bridget forced a smile, waiting for the shoe to drop.

"Thanks for all the things you did for me, Bridget. I couldn't have survived without you."

The first time she visited him at Ray Brook, he had asked her to bring him Oxy pills. He needed them to pay for protection or other inmates would rape him, describing in graphic detail what they would do to him. So twice a month she packed plastic bags of Oxy pills into a large hollowed-out book and drove 320 miles to FCI Ray Brook, terrified that the guard Brian had paid off would bust her for bringing in drugs, enduring the man's disgusting greedy eyes as they roved over her body.

"We're family, Brian. That's what we do. Take care of each other." *Even if we do keep secrets from each other.*

"Family is important, for sure." He gestured at Bridgette's headstone. "Remember how Pa would drag us down here once or twice a year?"

"I do indeed. The first of February we always got our favorite breakfast."

He nodded and smiled. "Pancakes for the feast of Saint Brigid." His smile disappeared. "No pancakes in prison."

"I hated that you were there." That was true at least, never mind what put him there.

Brian pulled out a photograph. "Remember this cocksucker?"

She studied the photo. Dark eyes, dark hair and a hawk-like nose. Mid-to-late-forties, attractive. "Not really, who is he?"

"Frank Renzi. Homicide Detective Frank Renzi. Does *that* ring a bell?"

And everything became clear. "What do you want?" she said.

Brian's face hardened and his eyes grew cold. "Payback."

"What does that have to do with me?"

"I might need your help."

"No killing, Brian. I told you that before."

He barked a curt laugh. "If I want someone dead, I don't need you to make it happen."

"What then? You know I'm teaching. It's the middle of the fall semester."

"Ah yes, the erudite college professor, Bridget White, teaching her students how to survive in this dangerous world, all the while leading a secret life as a gangster."

"I'm not a gangster," she snapped. "Don't lump me in with your mobster pals."

"I'm only teasing. You're smarter than any of them, way smarter than me, top grades in school."

"You were smart enough to go to Yale too, but you never did your homework."

"I did my homework on Renzi," he snapped. "Besides, back then we needed money, four mouths to feed, Pa out of work, Kate needing attention."

Unwilling to argue, she said, "I'm cold, Brian. There's a storm coming. Let's go see Kate. She's only four miles from here." After Pa died, Brian had arranged for Kate to live in a group home for mentally disabled adults in Winthrop.

When it came to Kate, no expense was too great for Brian.

As they walked toward their cars, he said, "How does she like living there?"

"Okay, I guess. You know Kate. She never complains about anything."

"Yeah, well, if she'd complained about that husband of hers a few years earlier, I wouldn't have wound up in jail."

Blaming someone else for his difficulties, as usual.

But truth be told, it was partly her fault. Secrets she'd kept from Brian all these years.

"She's well taken care of?" Brian said. "Healthy food? Good supervision?"

"Yes, they take her to church twice a week so she can sing in the choir." Kate could sing like an angel. Learning the music was easy, the words, not so much. In grammar school, the nuns had taught her the words to all the hymns. "Come on, Brian. She'd love to see you."

"Really?" His eyes revealing a rare hint of insecurity. "Where does she think I've been all these years?"

"I told her you lived far away, across the ocean in Ireland." Seeing his incredulous look, she added, "She's forgotten about the trial, Brian. You should forget about it too."

Brian gave her the savage look he used to warn those who challenged him. "I'm not forgetting about the trial, and I'm not forgetting what Frank Renzi did to Kate."

Making her tell the truth?

Aloud she said, "Do you want to see her or not, Brian?"

"Okay, I'll join you." He took a cell phone out of his pocket. "Take this burner so I can keep in touch with you. Keep it close, Bridget. I might need you in a hurry."

Need her in a hurry for what?

A shudder of dread rippled through her. She didn't want to think about what sort of payback Brian was planning.

CHAPTER 5

SUNDAY October 16 – 10:15 AM – Swampscott, Massachusetts

Judge Salvatore Renzi rose to his feet as the organist began to play a hymn, and glanced around Holy Family Church. Not many families at the ten o'clock Mass these days, mostly older folks like him, widows and widowers, seeking comfort from the Lord. His joints felt creaky when he got out of bed in the morning, but otherwise his health was good.

Not bad for seventy-eight. Lord willing, he'd live a few more years at least.

Five minutes ago Father O'Reilly had given them a moment to remember any ill or deceased parishioners in their prayers. Sal had offered up Patrick's name, not that it would help any. Six months after he retired, Patrick had been diagnosed with pancreatic cancer. Terminal.

As long as he stayed healthy, Sal would never retire. Working five days a week kept his mind sharp. Keeping busy and working at a job you loved were the keys to longevity.

Once a week after work he ate dinner with his friends, judges or federal prosecutors, unwilling to go home to an empty house. Five years ago, he'd begun driving to the fire station twice a week to socialize with the firemen. Provided there were no fire calls, they sat in the break room, chatting or playing cards. That's how he'd met Patrick Flanagan.

They hit if off right away. Patrick had a devilish sense of humor and loved talking about his childhood exploits. The oldest of eight children, Patrick regaled him with elaborate tales about his sisters and brothers. Tales that seemed foreign to Sal. He was an only child. He tuned out the hymn and thought about his son, also an only child. A strapping boy with a mind of his own, Frank took after his side of the family—both his parents were Sicilians—dark hair, dark eyes and a Roman nose.

Sal wanted him to be a lawyer, but Frank wasn't interested. Strong-willed and stubborn, Frank had a mind of his own. After a while, Sal realized it was futile. You can't fit a square peg into a round hole.

In court, lawyers had to be "cool" as his granddaughter was so fond of saying. Frank had too many sharp edges, and an Irish temper like his mother, Mary Sullivan when Sal had met her, a beautiful redhead like Maureen O'Hara. Smart, too, but girls didn't go to college back then.

After attending Boston College for a year, Frank quit and applied for a job with Boston PD. Even as a kid, Frank was a leader, organizing games with neighborhood kids, playing sports and excelling at basketball. In high school, he'd played point guard, leading his team to the State Finals in the Garden. He could still remember how proud he was, watching Frank play his ass off in Boston Garden where the Celtics played, the crowd cheering when Frank drove to the hoop and scored.

Frank wasn't perfect. He had his faults, a quick temper for sure, and a roving eye apparently. Sal had never cared much for Frank's wife, but he adored Maureen, their only child. When Evelyn filed for divorce on grounds of adultery, he was shocked. He couldn't imagine being unfaithful to Mary. He'd fallen in love with her the first time they met. Over the years their love had grown deeper and deeper. Lord, how he missed her.

Even now, recalling how awful she looked in that hospital bed, dying of breast cancer, brought tears to his eyes.

The hymn—*A Mighty Fortress Is Our God*—ended and Sal settled back into his seat. Frank's divorce had caused him considerable pain. When he asked what happened, Frank refused to talk about it. Eventually he had set aside his judgmental feelings. Frank was his son and he was proud of him, a terrific father to Maureen and a fine police officer.

In some respects, they had the same goal. Frank wanted to take the criminals off the street. Sal wanted to put them in jail and—provided they were guilty—keep them there.

Frank had distinguished himself with Boston PD, first as a patrolman, then as a detective. After the tragic incident when the little girl died, Frank had taken a job with the New Orleans police department.

Sal pinched the bridge of his nose. He wished Frank didn't live so far away. Several times a week he got on his computer at home so he could follow the crime-related news in the New Orleans papers.

There had been a bad shooting a couple of days ago. Maybe he'd call Frank later and ask him about it.

After lunch he was going to the hospital to visit Patrick and cheer him up as best he could.

———

3:15 PM – New Orleans

Frank rang the doorbell and waited, an anxious feeling gnawing at his gut. No telling what kind of a reception he'd get. After a moment, Noah Scott opened the door, dressed in a black suit, no tie.

"Sorry to bother you, Mr. Scott. Could we talk for a bit?"

His face impassive, Elijah's father said nothing and took him into the living room. Delicious aromas wafting from the kitchen filled the air. Alvina Scott came to the kitchen doorway, wearing a stark black dress, her face haggard, her eyes still bloodshot from crying. "Hello Detective Renzi. Thank you for asking Detective O'Neil to drive us home yesterday. Don't know what we'd have done without her."

"You're welcome. I was concerned about your safety and so was Kelly. Glad she could help."

"Would you like a bite to eat? Lord-a-Mercy, folks brought us enough food to feed an army."

"Thank you, Alvina. That's very kind, but I've already eaten."

He hadn't, but he hadn't come here to eat. He'd come here to plead his case.

Stone-faced, Noah Scott said, "Have you found Elijah's killers?"

"Actually, I came here to ask you for a favor."

Noah clamped his lips together, his eyes smoldering with anger.

"We need help to find Elijah's killers. I'm asking you ... " He stopped. "No. I'm *pleading* with you. Work *with* us, not against us. Protest marches won't help us find them. They make things worse. These hoodlums show up with guns and shoot more innocent people."

"At least the protest march got us some attention," Noah said, his dark eyes implacable.

"The wrong kind, unfortunately. We want folks to stay focused on Elijah. We want everyone to understand what a fine boy he was." Making it sound like they were a team.

"The best son a mother could ask for," Alvina said, gazing at him, nodding her head.

"Exactly. We need to make them understand that it's not acceptable for an innocent ten-year-old boy to be shot dead inside his own home. We need the mayor and the city council to put more cops in the neighborhoods and more detectives on cases like this."

"All well and good," Noah said. "But the mayor hasn't called us, and I don't plan on calling him. What do you want us to do?"

"Ask your neighbors to help us. Ask anyone in the black community who has information to call us. Because right now, nobody will talk to us. But if you asked them, they might."

"They won't talk to you because they don't trust you," Noah snapped.

"Detective Renzi, you look thirsty." Alvina pointed at the sofa like a traffic cop. "Sit down. You too, Noah. I'll bring us some ice tea, and we'll talk about it."

Grateful for the encouragement, Frank took a seat on one end of the sofa. He hated ice tea, but if it got him some cooperation, he'd drink a gallon of it. Noah sat down at the other end.

Silence in the room. Frank could hear birds chirping outside. Better than gunshots.

Alvina returned carrying a tray with three tall glasses of ice tea, set it on the coffee table and perched on an easy chair beside her husband.

Frank forced down a mouthful of ice tea. After a moment he said to Noah, "I grew up in Swampscott, Massachusetts, a small town near Boston. All my friends were white. I didn't have one black classmate in grammar school. But when I got to high school they started busing black students to my school. Part of the Metco program for ..." He hesitated, searching for an acceptable word. "... disadvantaged black students in the metro-Boston area. You folks follow basketball at all?"

Noah sipped his iced tea. "Not really. This is a football town."

"Well, this black kid from Dorchester got bused to my school, joined the basketball team my junior year. He was a fantastic player, big and strong, a great shooter." Smiling at the memory, Frank said, "BJ was our power forward. I played point guard. Pretty soon we were beating every team in our division, and BJ and I became best friends. He'd sleep over at my house after practice, so he could do his homework and get up for school in the morning. At the end of the season, they hold a statewide basketball tournament. Our senior year, we won our division and went to the Finals."

The next part was ugly. No happy ending to this story.

Girding himself, he drank some ice tea and said to Alvina, "When I saw Elijah in his room, it made me think of BJ."

The room went still and quiet. Alvina nodded, her eyes filling with tears.

"BJ tried out for a bunch of college teams, hoping to get a basketball scholarship, but he didn't. His mom didn't have the money to send him to college." He paused for a moment, considering how to phrase the next part. "I went to college. BJ went into the drug business."

Noah flinched and a sound escaped from his mouth, half groan, half sigh. "Uhhh-mmm."

"Sorry," Frank said. "But I'm not going to lie to you. He joined a gang and made some fast money selling drugs." Seeing Bobby in his mind's eye, laid out in the coffin. A handsome guy and a talented basketball player, with no job prospects and no money. "Next time I saw BJ was at his wake. Twenty years old, shot dead in a drug deal gone bad."

Alvina moaned and dabbed her eyes with a handkerchief. Noah said nothing, just shook his head, looking sorrowful.

Frank's cell phone rang. *Damn, why did it always ring at the worst possible time?* But when he saw the number, he said, "Excuse me, but I need to take this." He went in the kitchen, stood by the sink and answered. "Hi, Dad, what's up? Is something wrong? Are you okay?"

"I'm fine," his father said. "Just thinking about you, thought I'd give you a call."

But he didn't sound fine. He sounded like something was bothering him. "I'm in a meeting right now," Frank said. "Can I call you back in ten minutes?"

"Of course. I'm home for the evening. Call me when you can."

When Frank returned to the living room, Alvina said, "What was your friend's name?"

"Bobby. Bobby Jones, but we called him BJ."

"I'll keep him in my prayers." Giving her husband a pointed look, she said, "Noah will too, won't you, Noah?"

Seemingly lost in thought, Noah stared into space. At last, he turned to Frank and said, "My daddy never trusted white folks, said the slaves were freed after the Civil War, and a hundred years later it's no different. White folks look down on us, think we're shiftless and stupid, don't want us living next door. Only blacks lived in our neighborhood."

Noah sipped his iced tea. "I went to the neighborhood public school, all black students, had to mind the Jim Crow laws even then. But I had a white teacher in seventh grade, a young guy, maybe thirty years old. One day, Mr. Hanson let the other kids go out for recess, kept me after class." He took big swallow of ice tea. "I was scared, you know, figured I was in trouble. But Mr. Hanson said to me, 'Noah, you're very smart. Don't start hanging out with the kids in the gangs. Do your homework, study hard, and you can make something of yourself.'"

"Uh-huh," Alvina said. "That's right."

"Lying in bed that night I thought about what Mr. Hanson said and I decided he believed in me." Noah looked at Frank. "Not that he ever said anything after that, but every now and then, when I got a good grade on a test, Mr. Hanson would look at me, you know, and give a little nod, encouraging me. And I started believing in myself."

"I'm sure he'd be very proud of you," Frank said. "It's a tough job, managing a supermarket. Is he still teaching?"

"No, he left town years ago."

"But he'd still be proud of you," Alvina said, beaming at Noah. "Almost as proud as I am."

Frank finished his iced tea and rose to his feet. "I appreciate your hospitality, but I've taken up enough of your time. I hope you'll think about what I said, Mr. Scott."

"I'll think on it, but I can't promise anything. Best run it by my lawyer first."

Great. Rufus King will nix it in a New York minute.

"Thanks for the ice tea, Alvina. Try and get some rest."

"Thank you," she said, smiling at him. "You too."

Maybe next month, Frank thought as he got in his car. He drove around the corner, parked at the curb, got on his cell phone and called his father, trying to remember when he'd talked to him last. It had been a while. Five or six weeks at least.

"Hi Frank, thanks for getting back to me. I know you're busy."

"Sorry I had to put you off. Seems like we haven't talked in ages. How are you doing?"

"Same as usual, in court five days a week. Not much to watch on TV at night. Everybody got excited about the Red Sox, but they fell apart, didn't even make the playoffs."

Frank laughed. "Hey, I'm a Yankee fan, remember? How do you think the Celtics will do?"

"Drafted a couple of good young players. They might make the playoffs." And after a moment, "I was thinking about you in church this morning. You and your mother." A heavy sigh. "I miss your mother."

Frank said nothing, thinking about his mother, but also about his father, living alone all these years.

"I miss her too," he said at last. "She was the best. And so are you."

34

"Maybe not the best parent. I wasn't home a lot when you were a kid, working all those hours when I was starting my law practice ..."

"What do you mean? You always came to my games." *Unlike BJ, who'd never seen his father, period.*

"You were always there when I needed you." Not mentioning the IAD investigation after the little girl died, but knowing his father would understand what he meant.

"You're a good cop, Frank. I just wish you weren't so far away."

The words took his breath away.

Working five, six, sometimes seven days a week, he seldom had time to think about his father. Or that he might be lonely.

"Why don't you come down for a visit? I've got a two bedroom condo. I'll give you a tour of the French Quarter, maybe show you my office. We'll have fun."

Another heavy sigh. "Not right now. One of my friends is in the hospital. He's not doing too well. Besides, you're in the middle of a drive-by shooting case."

Appalled, Frank said, "You saw it on the news up there?"

"On TV, you mean? No. I read the *Times-Picayune* online after I get home from work."

Keeping track of crime in New Orleans while he ate dinner. By himself.

"What's your friend's name? The one in the hospital?"

"Patrick Flanagan. He's a fireman. Well, used to be. He retired last year and now he's got cancer. But he's got a big family. I met three of his brothers at the hospital this afternoon."

And you don't have a big family. No brothers or sisters, just me and Maureen. And your friend is going to die.

His father sounded depressed and lonely.

"Hey, Dad, why don't I get us some Celtics tickets? Two seats behind the bench, like we used to do when I lived up there."

"Now that would be fun! We can have dinner at one of those burger joints near the Garden." His father sounding animated and happy now that he had something to look forward to.

"I'll go online, see if they've got any home games on a Sunday."

With a smile in his voice, his father said, "Just like old times."

"Just like old times. I'll call you as soon as I get the tickets."

His father chuckled. "My friends at the courthouse will be green-eyed with envy."

"Tell them to eat their hearts out. Talk to you soon, Dad. Love you."

"Love you too, Frank."

CHAPTER 6

SUNDAY October 16 – 5:30 PM – Winthrop, Massachusetts

Kate took him into her room at the group home, beaming at him, her beautiful face wreathed in a smile. "Thank you for taking me out for dinner, Brian."

"Glad you enjoyed it," Devlin said. "I did too. Where did you learn such perfect table manners?"

"Bridget! She takes me out lots of times," Kate said, her emerald-green eyes aglow with happiness. "She taught me how to act proper."

But she didn't teach you to say grace before meals, The nuns did that. At the restaurant Kate wouldn't let him eat his broiled scallops until she crossed herself and said a prayer. But how could he fault the nuns? Now that Kate was an adult, they taught her far more important things. How to behave in social situations, the polite terms to use.

"Do you like my room? I picked up all the clutter. Bridget says I have to keep my room neat and clean. No clutter, Bridget says."

The room was small but bright and cheerful, sunlight pouring through a window opposite the door. Beside it, a bookcase held picture books and stacks of magazines. Kate still didn't read very well, but she liked to look at the pictures. To his right, the headboard of a neatly-made bed sat against the wall, facing the television set on the wide credenza to his left, positioned so Kate could watch TV. "I love your room," he said. "It's beautiful. And very neat."

"Do you like my decorations?" Kate asked. "It's October. Halloween is coming." On the credenza beside the TV set, small white-plastic ghosts and goblins surrounded an orange-painted piece of wood with a black cat and letters that said **Trick-or-Treat**. She went to a large wall calendar and counted the days with her finger. "Fourteen more days. I love Halloween. It's my favorite holiday!"

"Better than Christmas?"

Kate hesitated a moment and said, "I love Christmas. That's when Baby Jesus was born. But I love Halloween best. We get to dress up and hand out candy to the little kids. Remember when I was little and we went out trick-or-treating? I like Candy-corn the best."

"Better than Mars bars?" he asked, teasing her. When he was a kid, he always swapped his other candy for Mars bars.

"Candy-corn is better. It's got my favorite color. Orange!"

Tired of the game, he didn't answer. He'd long ago made the decision not to marry or have children. No wife and kids for rival gangs to target for retaliation. In fact, he already had a child. His sister Kate, whose mental age was ten, and no matter how much Bridget and the nuns taught her, that was never going to change.

"Tomorrow I'm going to Baltimore," he said.

"Baltimore? Where's that?"

He thought about showing her his road map, but why bother? Kate had no concept of the wider world and even less interest in it. Kate's world consisted of her room in the group home, her fellow residents and attending choir practice and Mass at St. Anne's Church. If he told her Baltimore was a country in Africa, she would believe him.

"Will you bring me a silver-neer?"

Puzzled, he looked at her. What the hell was a silver-neer?

"When Bridget goes somewhere, she always brings me a silver-neer."

He laughed and said, "Of course I will. What kind of souvenir would you like?"

"Something orange for Halloween! Something to wear!" She took a *Vogue* magazine with a well-dressed woman on the cover out of the bookcase. "Want to see some pretty outfits?"

"Not right now. I've got errands to do. I'll see you in a few days, Kate. Maybe next week."

"I'll miss you." She put the magazine back in the bookcase and took a small framed photograph off the top. "I miss Pa, too. But he's up in Heaven now."

No, he's not. He's in Hell where he belongs for marrying you off to a man twenty years older than you.

"Come here, Kate. Let's have a hug before I leave."

She rushed over and threw her arms around his neck. "You're the best brother in the world!"

"And you're the best little sister in the world," he said. And meant it.

———

9:30 PM – New Orleans

"Great to have you back, partner," Frank said, and took a swig from his bottle of Becks.

"Glad to get out of the house." Kenyon flashed a mischievous grin. "Tanya wanted me to do laundry. I told her you had to talk to me about a case."

They were seated in a booth in a barroom near Kenyon's house, not their usual hangout, but it was late. Any kind of luck they'd both get some sleep tonight. Tomorrow, anything could happen. Another protest march, another shooting, more heat from the media for sure.

Avoiding troublesome issues for the moment, he said, "How was your vacation?"

"Vacation, hell! Barely had time to breathe. Tina's applying to colleges. We spent a whole day at Emory University in Atlanta, another day at Agnes Scott College in Decatur."

"I hear you. I remember when Maureen was applying to colleges. How old is Tina now?"

"Seventeen. She wants to be an artist. Man, who makes money being an artist? Be better off working at MacDonald's. Jason's fifteen. Two years from now I'll be doing the same thing with him, only it'll be worse. He still wants to be an astronaut."

Frank laughed aloud. "I see big expenses in your future."

"Bad enough with Tina. Both of those colleges cost twenty-five grand a year." Kenyon shook his head. "A hundred grand for four years. I wanted her to go to LSU, cost me next to nothing."

Frank nodded. Kenyon had gone to LSU on a football scholarship. Six-foot-six, 240 pounds, he'd been an all-star linebacker for three years, playing for the LSU Tigers.

Kenyon waved a dismissive hand. "Enough about colleges. I caught a short clip on the news last night, a drive-by shooting and some kid got shot. Gang related?"

"Oh yeah. One banger dead, one wounded. Stray bullets hit a ten-year-old black kid doing homework in his house, over and out. His parents are devastated. I don't blame them, but our favorite black-activist lawyer got his hooks into them. Rufus King."

"Figures," Kenyon said. "I saw the asshole on the news, saying NOPD cops don't care about black victims. Vobitch must be bullshit. Who's lead on the case?"

Frank smiled tightly. "I caught the brass ring and right now I've got nothing. Not only that, King organized a protest march today and somebody started shooting."

"Damn! I didn't hear about that. Any casualties?"

"A wounded spectator, not life-threatening. Kelly and I were there and so was David Lee. Needless to say, the media went crazy. Vobitch called a meeting for tomorrow morning."

"Let the F-bombs begin." Kenyon chugged some beer. "You ID the bangers?"

"Yes." Frank took out his notepad. "Deon West, age 19, died at the scene. You know him?"

"Name's not familiar. Who's the other one?"

"Alonzo Stokes, age 24, gut-shot, currently hospitalized."

"Bada-bing. Alonzo runs with the MSG gang over in Mid-city." Kenyon smiled faintly. "MSG. Not to be confused with mono-sodium glutamate. MSG as in Muthafucka Street Gang. Bangers these days being deficient in cre-a-tivity. You talk to him yet?"

"No. I went to the hospital yesterday afternoon but they wouldn't let me talk to him, said he was still recovering from surgery. Gut-shot, so they probably had to rearrange his innards."

"Let's go see him now." Kenyon took two cellophane-wrapped red-and-white peppermint candies out of a dish and handed one to Frank. "We suck on these, make Alonzo think we just ate a yummy dinner at Antoines."

Frank grinned. "Should I wear a tie? I've got a spare in my car."

Kenyon pulled a face. "Frank. Let's not go crazy over this."

———

10:30 PM – Baltimore, Maryland

Maureen paced around the cramped, one bedroom apartment she shared with Jeremy. The main attraction: it was in a safe neighborhood and didn't cost too much. Both of them were paying off college loans. They'd been living together for four years but they kept separate bank accounts. Now that she was an orthopedic surgery resident, she actually got paid.

But after she paid her share of the rent and put gas in her car there was hardly anything left. She'd even canceled her membership at the riding club. Unlike Jeremy, she couldn't afford it. Jeremy had his own dental practice now and still went riding once or twice a week. To stay in shape, she got up at an ungodly hour and went for a four mile run.

She stopped at the bookcase beside the TV and studied the photographs. Her favorite pictures of Dad. One was taken at her high school graduation, Dad playing proud papa, smiling into the camera as he hugged her. Another at a riding tournament, Dad beaming as she held up the trophy she'd won.

Back then she had no worries. Back then life was simple.

Even in medical school, life wasn't that bad. She'd always been a good student, a perfectionist actually, studying for hours. Then she met Jeremy and skyrockets went off. They both had a passion for horses, they both wanted medical careers, and they got along great in bed.

She glanced at the clock. Almost ten-thirty. Where the hell was Jeremy?

If only she could talk to Dad. But he lived in New Orleans, always busy solving homicides.

Lately, she'd begun to suspect that Jeremy had a girlfriend. Coming home later than usual once or twice a week. Leaving the room when he got a phone call. And damn little interest in sex. Not that she had the energy for it. She was working twelve hours a day and studying for the orthopedic surgery boards at night.

Maybe that's what happened when people lived together a while. Maybe that's what happened to Mom and Dad. Mom was the one who filed for divorce, on grounds of adultery. Back then she was a college freshman, old enough to know what that meant. Dad had a lover.

She wanted to know why, but the one time she dared to ask him about it, he refused to talk about it. "That's between me and your mother," he'd said. "You don't need to know."

The divorce had caused a big rift in their relationship, until Grampa Sal called and told her to stop blaming her father and call him, saying "Your father loves you."

And she loved him, too. Truth be told, she'd always been closer to Dad than to her mother. Maybe it was Mom's uber-Catholic thing. Her earliest memory was being in church with Mom and the priest shaking this clanky metal object and the horrible smell. She started crying so loud Mom had to take her outside. Later, after the divorce, Mom started going to church every single day.

She heard a key in the lock. Her heart pounded. Jeremy was home.

SUSAN FLEET

Now it was after eleven. *Where the hell have you been?* she wanted to shout. But she didn't, waiting for him to speak.

"Hi, Mo, sorry I'm so late." He put his keys on the table beside the door and took off his jacket.

"Did you have dinner?" *Or were you too busy fucking your girlfriend?*

"Yes. Ordered Chinese takeout and ate in the office. You?"

Like he really cared, wandering into the kitchen, opening the refrigerator door. He came back with a bottle of Bud Light and sat on the couch. "Want to watch the news?"

"No. I want you to tell me why the hell you're so late."

"I had a patient with an emergency. She broke off a crown and I told her to come in and I'd fix it. I don't know why you're so upset. I'm a dentist, Maureen. These things happen."

"Four hours to fix a broken crown? A total hip replacement doesn't take that long."

His face softened. "Come sit with me," he said, patting the couch, smiling at her, as handsome as George Clooney was back in the day: dark curly hair, hypnotic brown eyes and a killer smile.

Hating herself for giving in, she sat down beside him. He put his arm around her and nuzzled her neck. "I know you're under the gun, what with the residency and all. I remember how it was, studying all night for the boards."

Full-blown anger rose up inside her. "Don't turn this around on me, Jeremy. Don't make it sound like I'm tired and worrying over nothing. What happened to your phone? If you knew you were going to be late, why didn't you call me?"

"Next time, I will," he said, and started kneading her shoulders with his fingers.

But not answering her question.

Damn, he knew what she liked, knew that a shoulder massage was their prelude to lovemaking.

Her eyes glazed with tears. She felt so alone. Maybe she was imagining things. She liked her colleagues at the hospital, but they were co-workers, not friends, and now that she'd quit the riding club, she had no one to talk to but Jeremy.

He turned her face to his and kissed her lips. Stroked her face and caressed her breasts.

Five minutes later, they were in bed.

CHAPTER 7

MONDAY October 17 – 8:05 AM – New Orleans

Armed with a container of black coffee, Frank straggled into the meeting. Vobitch stood behind his desk, looking out the window. His coffee mug sat on his desk beside an uneaten Danish pastry. A bad sign. Vobitch was probably taking heavy flack from the NOPD top brass.

Stifling a yawn, Frank took a seat beside Kenyon, who raised an eyebrow at him but said nothing. Seated beyond Kenyon, David gave him a nod and a grim smile, also said nothing.

The silence crackled with tension.

None of them expected a pleasant meeting. Three detectives with different styles and personalities.

An experienced homicide detective confident of his abilities, Kenyon had on a polo shirt and scruffy jeans. Always well-dressed, David wore a white Oxford shirt under a sports jacket. Frank had worn his last clean white shirt and a wrinkled pair chinos. Kenyon used humor to defuse tense situations. David rarely spoke at meetings and stuck to the rules.

Frank's motto was FTR. Fuck the Rules.

Except on the basketball court. He and David played on the NOPD District-8 team. As point guard, Frank had a knack for reading the court and creating plays for his teammates. David was shorter, five-seven, a lightning-fast guard who played great defense.

But they wouldn't be playing hoop anytime soon. Not with a hot-potato case topping the news.

Vobitch sank into his chair, his face haggard, his steel-gray eyes bloodshot. Frank hoped the pressure to solve the drive-by didn't land him back in the hospital.

"At this point we got no leads," Vobitch said. "Just the usual crank calls and confessions from assholes looking for attention. The Black Ministers Association put up a twenty-thousand-dollar reward for information leading to the arrest of Elijah's killers."

"Great," Kenyon said sarcastically. "That should up the number of wacko calls. We need to find out who's got a beef with the Hollygrove

43

'bangers. Frank and I went to the hospital last night and asked Alonzo Stokes, but Alonzo gives us attitude, says he's got no idea. Like he's a choir boy."

"Most of these gangs are fighting about who sells drugs on what corner," Frank said. "Probably not Hispanic. Those guys got a beef with someone they slice-n-dice with a machete."

"I agree," Kenyon said. "Could be another black gang, or Asian. David, can you talk to your liaison in the Vietnamese community? See if he's heard any talk about the drive-by?"

"Absolutely," David said. "I'll call him today."

"Good idea," Vobitch said. "In the meantime I want you to re-canvass the neighborhood."

"We did that Thursday night," Frank said. "Knocked on every door on the street and got nothing. I went back Friday to make sure we didn't miss anyone, still got nothing."

"Nobody saw nothin," Vobitch said. "Jesus-fucking-Christ! Expand the canvas. Talk to every resident within six blocks. Compile a list of all the occupants for every address on every street."

A pall of silence fell over the room. Frank sipped his coffee and said nothing.

At last, Kenyon said, "Nobody's gonna talk to cops going door-to-door asking questions. Anybody talks, they could be the next drive-by victim."

"Just do it," Vobitch said. "You know what kind of heat I'm getting from Headquarters? We got a black Superintendent and a black Deputy Super defending themselves against accusations that NOPD doesn't give a shit about black murder victims."

"Blame Rufus King," Frank said. "He organizes a protest march, there's another shooting and it's the lead story on every local newscast."

"And front page in the fucking local rag," Vobitch said. His caustic term for the *Times-Picayune*.

A major tourist attraction, the French Quarter was a money making magnet that drew millions of visitors. Any gunfire there got immediate attention from the mayor, the city council and city business leaders. Saturday's shooting at the protest march was exponentially worse, thanks to all the publicity about Elijah.

"Our homicide clearance rate for the past two years is less than forty percent," Vobitch said.

"Our clearance rate sucks because nobody will talk," Frank said. "They're afraid they'll wind up dead. It's happened before. They watch the news."

"So do the NOPD bigwigs," Vobitch snapped. "The statistics in the mayor's Action on Crime Report don't lie. For the past two years, nine out of ten homicide victims in New Orleans were black. Ninety-five percent of identified suspects were black, mostly male."

"True," Kenyon said, "but most of the victims had long rap sheets, arrested before on drug or gun-related charges. Damn few of them got convicted."

"Slightly over twelve percent, to be exact," Vobitch said.

"That's what Elijah was working on when he got shot," Frank said. "A gun project."

Vobitch frowned. "What kind of gun project?"

"A project on gun laws in countries around the world. His father showed it to me. He said Elijah was worried about all the gunfire in their neighborhood."

"Christ on a crutch! The media gets wind of that we're screwed." Vobitch raked stubby fingers through his mane of silvery hair. "We need an arrest pronto. At the very least a suspect or two."

"Hopefully the bastards who did it," Frank said.

Vobitch iced him with a look. "Yes, Frank, that would be my preference, because the last six cases with black homicide victims that the DA's office took to trial, they got no convictions. Six cases, not one fucking conviction."

Annoyed, Frank said, "We can't just arrest a couple of gangbangers and put out their names to appease the media and politicians. We need evidence, witnesses willing to testify if the DA brings the case to trial."

Stone-faced, Vobitch said, "Kenyon, I want you to take over as lead investigator."

Kenyon stiffened in his chair. "I got plenty of other cases to solve. Why me? Because a black lead investigator looks better?"

"The Superintendent wants me to put you in charge."

"So I can be the fucking media target?" Kenyon said, his deep voice rising in outrage.

"You've got insights Frank doesn't have. You can talk to the family."

"Elijah's parents, but not the 'banger's, right?" Kenyon said. "Did any-body talk to *his* mother? And what do I tell Mr. and Mrs. Scott that Frank hasn't already told them?"

"You're a good detective, Kenyon. Everyone respects you."

"Who? The NOPD bigwigs? They're just looking for a patsy."

"I respect you," Vobitch said, his face mottled with anger, jabbing a thumb at his chest. "Me. Besides, Frank will still be working the case, and I'll have the D-1 detectives help you."

Vobitch supervised the homicide detectives in Districts 1, 5 and 8, but if all hell broke loose, as it had Thursday night, one of them might be called to a homicide outside their primary district, which was how Frank had wound up as lead investigator on a drive-by in District One.

"I got no problem with Kenyon taking the lead," he said, "but I've got a big problem with people who think we don't care about black mur-der victims. That's bullshit."

"True," Vobitch said, "but that doesn't stop a lot of assholes from be-lieving it."

"People believe in the Tooth Fairy, too."

Vobitch smiled grimly. "Yeah, but not as many. The perception down-town is we're not putting the most motivated people on it."

"What a cheap shot!" David exclaimed. "They think Frank and I aren't motivated? We do our jobs. Frank's got twenty years of experience working homicides."

Clearly unhappy, Vobitch massaged his eyes. "I know that. I'm not criticizing you, but perception and reality are two different things. With Kenyon as lead, we might convince some black folks to help us find the bastards who did this."

"You want me on lead?" Kenyon said. "Fine. Tell the damn politicians to stop bitching and make solving homicides a priority. Give us more cops on the street, more homicide detectives."

"You get no argument from me," Vobitch said.

It was no secret that Vobitch kept asking for more help. Five of his homicide detectives covered District-1 and District-5, high crime areas with predominantly black neighborhoods. No shortage of murders there. District-8 had the fewest murders, but three homicide detectives, because it included the French Quarter, where tourists spent big bucks.

"Okay," Kenyon said. "I'll talk to the dead banger's mother, see if she knows anything."

"We better cover Elijah's funeral too," Frank said. "If the shooters go there, could be a bloodbath."

"Do it," Vobitch said. "That's the last thing we need." He pinched the bridge of his nose. "I need you guys to find these motherfuckers ASAP, or somebody's gonna get fed to the wolves. I don't want it to be me."

———

8:10 AM – Castle Island, South Boston

Hunching his shoulders inside his windbreaker, Devlin watched Tank hurry toward him. No need for sunglasses today, the sky leaden with clouds, a stiff wind blowing off the water. Earlier he'd gone for a run. Seriously out of shape, he had to stop after three miles to catch his breath before he kept jogging to Castle Island. Which wasn't really an island. A narrow strip of land connected it to Carson Beach in Southie.

"You got good news?" he said to Tank.

"Better than good. Got a shitload of pictures. I got up early, left at four to avoid the traffic, got to Swampscott in half an hour and found the place, no problem. The house was dark, but ten minutes later the lights came on." Tank grinned. "I brought my own coffee, figured you wouldn't want me to knock on the door and ask the judge for a cup."

"You got that right. Tell me about the house. Does it face the water?"

"No. It's three blocks away, an old-fashioned Cape, might be able to see the water from the second floor. Houses that face the water cost megabucks nowadays."

"Show me the pictures."

Tank took out his smartphone. "I got pictures of the car, too. Wait till you see—"

"Show me the house." The house where Frank Renzi grew up, living a life of privilege in a swanky suburb, doted on by two parents. While he lived with his father and two sisters in a crappy apartment in the North End of Boston. In a public housing project.

Tank handed him the phone. "I didn't take many of the house. Mostly the garage, so Whelan will know how to get to fuck up the brakes."

He studied the house, a two-story Cape with a small front yard. He flipped past it and came to pictures of the garage, one with the door shut, the next one with the door open and a dark green car backing out.

"What's that?" he said. "Looks like an old Ford."

47

"It's a 1981 Mark II Granada. Whelan won't have no trouble with that one. Back then they didn't have computers."

"Yeah, but who drives a thirty-year-old car?"

"Beats me," Tank said. "Maybe he's sentimental. I followed him and found the perfect place for him to have an accident. Check out the next picture."

Devlin studied the photo of an exit ramp. "Where's this, in Lynn?"

"Yeah, right after you go over the bridge that takes you to Revere. You go straight, it might be faster, but the judge took the scenic route along Revere Beach Boulevard. No traffic at that hour." He took out a pen and pointed at the exit ramp photo. "The guardrail ends here. If Whelan gets on his bumper he can force him into this oak tree at the bottom of the ramp."

"You sure that will do the job? He probably wears a seat belt."

"Yeah, being a judge and all. But if Whelan angles it right, he can ram the car into the tree, crush the left side of the car. That should do it."

"If you say so. Did you get any pictures of the judge?"

"Only one and it's a long shot. I followed him into a parking garage near the courthouse, but I didn't wanna park too close. Hold on and I'll zoom in on it."

Devlin studied the photo of Judge Salvatore Renzi, a short man, five-seven tops, wearing a well-tailored suit. The father and son looked a lot alike: a big Roman nose, large dark eyes and black hair. The father's hair was streaked with gray, but the self-righteous expression was the same.

He gave the phone back to Tank and took out his own. "I'll call Whelan, make sure he's set to fix the brakes. I checked the weather forecast. It's supposed to rain like hell tomorrow night."

Tank nodded. "Good. No moon. Nobody out walking a dog."

"Exactly." He dialed the number and waited.

"Hey," Whelan said, "what's up?" Not speaking his name which meant he was with someone.

"You set to fix the brakes on that car we talked about?"

"Good to go, no problem. Got the tools from my mechanic friend."

"Do it tomorrow night. Tank got pictures of the garage, but I want you to go there tomorrow morning and scope things out. Be there by five, so you can follow the target."

"Jesus, that early? I won't get any sleep. I hardly ever hit the sack before two."

"Sean," he said, "I don't like it when you argue with me. You know what happens when I don't like something? I get angry—"

"Okay, okay, I'll go there early. Send me the pictures."

"Tank will show you the pictures. Be at our garage in half an hour," Devlin said, and hung up.

"The guy's a troublemaker," Tank said. "You sure you don't want me to handle this?"

"No. Stick with the plan. Don't show him all the pictures. Just the garage and the car and the target site. Tell him to use different cars tomorrow and Wednesday."

His heart surged with joy, thumping his chest. The payback plan he had obsessed over night after night in prison was going to work. Provided Whelan did what he was told.

"Okay," Tank said. "You're not coming to the garage?"

"No. I'm driving to Baltimore today."

"What's in Baltimore?"

"Not what, who. Maureen Renzi."

Tank's eyes widened. "Renzi's daughter?"

"Correct. I want to get started on the next part of the plan."

"Dev, you can't leave the state. You got jewelry on your ankle. The feds will know—"

"You think a fucking ankle bracelet is going to stop me?"

"No." Tank took hold of his arm. "I'm gonna stop you."

He shook off Tank's hand. "Don't tell me what to do! You forget who's boss here?"

Tank gazed at him silently for a moment. "Dev, you know I'd never forget that. But I'm not letting you drive to Baltimore and have the feds put you back in jail for violating your parole. You need something in Baltimore, tell me what it is and I'll drive there and get it for you."

He fought down his fury. He hated wearing an ankle bracelet, hated the feds for putting it there. But Tank was right. Why take chances and screw up a perfectly good plan?

"Okay. Call me after you talk to Whelan and I'll tell you what I need."

Clearly relieved, Tank said, "You got it, Dev. Call you as soon as I leave the garage."

Devlin clapped him on the shoulder. "You're the best, Tank. Let's keep our eyes on the prize. Tell Whelan to make sure Judge Salvatore Renzi never drives to work again."

49

CHAPTER 8

WEDNESDAY October 18 – 8:30 PM – New Orleans

"Wake up, sleepyhead. I'm hungry."

Frank opened his eyes and grinned at Kelly, naked in bed beside him.

"What," he said. "Only four days since I've seen you and you want to go again?""

"You wish." She got out of bed and slapped him on the ass. "Put some clothes on. I'll see you in the kitchen."

"Why get dressed?" he said, admiring her curves. "You look gorgeous the way you are."

With a seductive smile, she slowly pulled on a red T-shirt and a pair of shorts. "Ah prefer my gentleman callers to dress for dinner," she said in a faux-Southern drawl, and left the room.

He rolled over and got out of bed. He hadn't really been asleep, just enjoying the post-coital bliss. Later he'd go home to his condo and get some real sack time. Sleep five hours, get up and go find the bastards who'd killed Elijah.

When he strolled into the kitchen dressed in a polo shirt and jeans, Kelly nodded her approval. "Pour me another glass of wine, okay? After work, I picked up a honey-barbecued chicken and a container of butter-nut squash at the grocery store."

"Sounds great." And after a beat, "What are you having?"

"Wiseguy. What did Vobitch say at the meeting? Any F-bombs?"

He refilled their glasses from the bottle of Shiraz he'd brought and gave her one. Earlier they had chatted over a glass of wine, but no shop talk. Kelly was working Domestic Violence now, but she had worked Homicide, too. Either way, both of them encountered horrific images: women brutally beaten to death, gunshot wounds, gory crime scenes with multiple victims, some of them children.

Images definitely not conducive to a frolic in the bedroom.

"To tell you the truth, I'm worried about him," Frank said. "He looked old and tired. Two weeks back and he gets a brutal drive-by and an asshole lawyer on TV saying NOPD doesn't care about black murder victims. He's catching serious heat from Headquarters."

"Ironic, considering his wife is black. Don't they know that?"

"Sure, but they're getting outraged calls from politicians and the media. Rumor is, *Sixty Minutes* contacted the Scott boy's parents."

"His lawyer probably called them," Kelly said. She opened the oven and took out the squash and the barbecued chicken. The mouth-watering aromas made his stomach rumble.

"Shall I cut up the chicken?" she asked.

"Nah, just put it on the table. Don't worry, I'll share." He took out plates and silverware, set the table and sat down. Kelly joined him and they helped themselves to the food.

After a moment, Kelly said, "What happened at the meeting?"

He set the bare bones of the drumstick he had devoured on his plate and wiped his fingers on a napkin. "Vobitch put Kenyon in charge of the investigation."

She put down a chicken wing and stared at him. "Wow. There's a kick in the ass."

"Kenyon's not happy about it. I wasn't either, but I let it go. Vobitch is just following orders. He's almost sixty, worried they'll make him retire and give his job to someone younger. But hey, if I was still lead, I'd have spent all day yesterday in Vobitch's office like Kenyon, setting up security for the 'banger's funeral, worrying about starring in a dog-and-pony show at a press conference." And after a beat, "Plus, I'd be too busy to be here enjoying your scintillating company."

Kelly laughed and ran a hand over her dark pixie-styled hair. "Well, there is that."

"After the meeting, I started contacting my CI's. Nothing yet, but maybe I'll get something." Every detective had a stable of Confidential Informants, low-level offenders hoping to bargain for something in exchange for helpful information.

"Any leads on the shooters?" Kelly said. "There's nothing on the news, but I know how it works. Mum's the word until you get something solid."

"Not a whisper. Nobody's talking." He chowed down a bite of chicken and drank some wine. "Yesterday David and I expanded the canvas area and talked to more people. They heard gunshots but saw nothing. Allegedly. I'll go back tomorrow and try again."

On the table beside his plate, his cell phone vibrated. He grabbed it and answered. "Renzi."

He heard nothing and waited. Still nothing. Then, a dial tone.

He checked the call log, didn't recognize the number and put the phone on the table. "Hangup call, unidentified caller."

"Some babe after you," Kelly said, her sea-green eyes mischievous.

"Right. I'll be forty-nine next month, gotta beat 'em off with a stick."

Kelly laughed. "Wait till you hit the big five-o."

"Why? You gonna bake me a cake?"

She gave him a droll smile. "And put fifty candles on it. Make you blow them all out."

His phone vibrated again. Kelly raised an eyebrow, but he recognized the caller. "Yo, Kenyon, what's up?"

Agitated, Kenyon said, "You watching this on TV?"

"Watching TV? No." He motioned to Kelly and she dashed into the living room. Frank followed her as Kenyon said, "Elijah's father is doing an interview."

Eyeing the television screen, Frank said, "I see it. Talk to you later."

In the studio, Noah Scott sat at the anchor desk between Attorney Rufus King and a black anchorman, who said, "Mr. Scott, are you satisfied with the way the investigation is going? It's been four days and no suspects have been identified."

Impeccably dressed in a dark suit and a muted tie, Noah said, "My wife and I will bury our son tomorrow. At yesterday's press conference, the NOPD Superintendent said they were doing everything possible to solve Elijah's murder."

"Putting a black detective in charge of the investigation," King interjected, aiming his perpetually self-righteous puss at the camera. "Which means nothing. That's just for show."

Noah held up a hand to silence him. "On Sunday afternoon, Detective Renzi came to see us at our home. To extend his condolences and offer us a bit of comfort. We chatted with him for a while over a glass of iced tea."

Frank's NOPD badge photo appeared on one side of a split-screen. "Damn!" he muttered.

"Could be worse," Kelly said. "Could be on *Sixty Minutes*."

"It still might. Once your picture's out there, it's like bubblegum on a shoe. It never goes away."

Gazing into the camera, Noah said, "There are those who would like to divide us. But I'm not interested in turning this into a racial issue—"

"Mr. Scott," the anchorman interrupted, "please tell us about the project Elijah was working on."

"A school project on gun laws around the world. Elijah was particularly interested in New Zealand. After a mass shooting there in 1990, they voted to tighten their gun laws."

"That would never work in the United States," Rufus King interjected.

"Maybe not," said Noah, "but I'm not here to talk about gun laws. I want justice for Elijah. A lot of good folks live on our street. Someone must have seen something, but they're not talking. Well, they're talking to their neighbors, but that won't help."

Gazing into the camera, Noah said sternly, "If you saw something or you know who was involved in the shooting, call the NOPD tipline and tell them what you saw. You don't need to identify yourself. Work *with* the police, not against them."

Hearing his own words spoken by Noah Scott, Frank felt a glimmer of hope. Maybe they would catch Elijah's killers after all.

And maybe they wouldn't. People were scared.

Maybe his unidentified caller was one of them.

The caller who'd said nothing and hung up.

———

9:10 PM – South Boston

Devlin sat at the computer in his office, a can of Harp Ale in one hand, a cell phone in the other. Tank had just called from Baltimore, saying he'd left at eight last night to avoid the traffic. "I got here at three AM and found the apartment, no problem. It's the end unit in a one-story building. Did you get the email I sent you? I attached a picture."

Devlin opened the email and studied the photo. "Got it. Did you get pictures of the target?"

"You bet," Tank said. "I parked in the lot opposite her apartment. She came out at four-thirty and went running. I took some pictures. Hold on, I'm sending them now."

He waited impatiently, heard a ping as the email arrived. He opened it and studied the photographs. Maureen Renzi jogging around a small pond, lanky and fit like her father, but shorter. Unlike her father, she had auburn hair, pulled back in a ponytail.

"Two cars were parked outside her apartment," Tank said. "A Honda and a Ford. At 5 AM, I see some guy in a charcoal gray suit come out of the apartment and drive off in the Honda."

Devlin swigged some ale. He knew she wasn't married. Maybe she had a boyfriend. That could be a problem. If Charcoal Gray Suit lived with her, there might be collateral damage.

"Five minutes later she came out and drove off in the Ford," Tank said. "I tailed her into the city. She drove straight to Mercy Medical Center. I didn't bother taking any pictures there."

Devlin nodded. His plan for Maureen didn't involve her workplace. "What about that car we talked about?"

"After I left you yesterday, I met Sean at the garage and we put fresh plates on it."

Telling him they'd put stolen plates on the Land Rover. His heart thrummed his chest. His plan was coming together.

"Great work, Tank. I set up a meet with the cop." The cop they paid to look the other way at corner stores in Southie when their runners collected the betting slips. "He'll meet us at five tomorrow morning, the usual place." To give them a solid-gold alibi if they needed it.

While Sean Whelan made sure Judge Salvatore Renzi died in a violent car accident.

"One last thing, Tank. Before you leave Baltimore, I need you to get me something." Earlier he had surfed the Internet and found a store that sold Baltimore Orioles memorabilia. The team colors were black and orange. On the store website, he'd found the perfect gift for Kate: a bright orange Cal Ripkin jersey.

He gave Tank the address and said, "They sell Baltimore Orioles gear, ballcaps, coffee mugs, sweatshirts, all kinds of stuff. Buy me a Cal Ripkin jersey, the orange one with his name on the back. A ladies' jersey, size medium. It's a gift for Kate."

"You got it," Tank said. "See you tomorrow morning at five."

Pleased, Devlin rose from the desk, went in his kitchen and took a long swallow of Harp Ale.

Everything would be fine, as long as Whelan did his job. But never leave things to chance.

He got on his cellphone and called Whelan.

"Hey Dev, what's up?" Whelan answered.

"Just calling to make sure you're good to go tomorrow morning."

Whelan didn't answer right away. A bad sign. *No more trustworthy than a wolf.*

"I'm good to go, but tomorrow morning I gotta take my sister to the hospital for some tests. She's been feeling sick and her doctor scheduled one of those tests for her, an MRI."

"What does that mean?"

"Means I can't do it tomorrow."

Anger fizzed his brain. Now his head felt like swarm of enraged bees.

"When were you going to tell me, Sean? Oh, wait. I get it. You weren't going to tell me."

"What's the difference, Dev? I'll do it on Thursday. One more day won't make no difference."

Shaking with fury, Devlin drained the rest of the Harp Ale and crushed the can in his hand.

"Here's the difference, Sean. If you don't do it tomorrow, I'll come over there and put a bullet in your head."

Silence on the other end.

"Did you hear what I said?"

"Yeah." A faint whisper.

"I can't hear you, Sean. Speak up. Tell me you'll do it tomorrow like we planned."

"I'll do it tomorrow. Just like you said."

"Good. Call me when the thing is done."

CHAPTER 9

WEDNESDAY October 19 – 5:15 AM – Swampscott, MA

Salvatore Renzi splashed through a puddle in the northbound lane of the Lynnway, sending a geyser of water over the median. Last night it had rained like hell. Today wasn't much better, the sky full of dreary granite-gray clouds. Last night Patrick's brother had called to tell him the end was near. Soon Patrick would be gone, like so many of his friends.

That's what happened when you got old. He felt fortunate that his own health was good. He smiled, recalling what his wife used to say, teasing him. "You know why Italians live longer than Irishmen? They eat that Mediterranean diet and drink wine with their meals. Irishmen drink whiskey and eat too many potatoes."

Now Mary was gone too.

He drove past the parking lot for the ferry. A lot of commuters from Swampscott rode the ferry to their jobs in Boston, but he liked driving to work. In the solitude of his car, he could contemplate upcoming cases or the reports he wrote after hearing testimony in court. Not many cars on the Lynnway at this hour, just a big SUV one block behind him. He stopped at a red light beside a 24-hour gas station and sipped espresso from his insulated travel mug. Two weeks ago, one of the clerks had been shot dead there in a predawn armed robbery. Too many criminals carried guns these days.

The big SUV crept up behind him and swung into the gas station, a dark-brown Land Rover with reinforced bumpers and a dent on one side, looked like it had seen better days. It drove past the pumps and parked beside the store. But the driver didn't get out. He assumed it was a man. What woman would drive a car like that?

When the light blinked green, he set his travel mug in the cup holder and drove off. As he passed Midas Muffler, a tall electronic billboard caught his eye. A flashing Celtics-green Leprechaun dissolved into the words **NEVER MISS A GAME! Get NBA-TV today!**

Watching games on TV was okay, but it was more fun to be there. Especially with Frank. Sit there, smelling the popcorn, hearing the cheers from the crowd, the lights flashing on the JumboTron. Like the fine detective he was, Frank had intuited his bleak mood the other day. Knowing how much he loved the Celtics, Frank had said he'd get them some tickets. He was fortunate to have a son who cared about him and wanted to make him happy. They would have a great time.

But that wouldn't happen for a couple of months.

Patrick would be dead by then.

He drove up an incline onto the drawbridge above the channel that boats used to access their moorings at marinas and yacht clubs. Even here, the sky was dark and forbidding. He usually took the Point of Pines exit and drove along Revere Beach Boulevard. Maybe he'd go straight today and stay on North Shore Road.

Seconds later, he changed his mind. After last night's storm, heavy surf would be pounding the shoreline along the beach. With any kind of luck, he might even catch a glimpse of the sun.

He turned onto the Point of Pines exit and felt something slam his rear bumper. Startled, he glanced at the rearview mirror. Damn! The dark-brown Land Rover was behind him, riding his bumper.

Dire scenarios filled his mind. His heart jolted into a jagged rhythm, pounding his chest.

What was the idiot trying to do? Run him off the road and rob him?

Did he have a gun like the man who'd robbed the gas station?

The bitter taste of fear flooded his mouth. He clenched the wheel with his hands, his fingers ice cold. Maybe he could call for help. He reached inside his suit jacket and took out his cellphone, but the Land Rover slammed into his bumper so hard he dropped it. Forget the phone. The goddamn SUV was propelling his car forward, dangerously close to the exit ramp guardrail.

Fury rose up inside him. Damned if he'd let some punk run him off the road!

He gripped the wheel with both hands and pressed the brake pedal as hard as he could, but his Mark IV Grenada didn't slow down, it swerved to the left, tires screeching. The sound seemed far away, drowned out by the sound of his runaway heart thundering in his ears, pounding, pounding, pounding.

Bam! The Land Rover hit his bumper again and the car swerved into a sickening skid. The idiot was trying to kill him!

Frantic, he looked around, hoping to see another car or a pedestrian who might help him. Better still, a police car.

He saw nothing. No cars, not even a pedestrian walking a dog.

Another vicious thump jolted the car. He gritted his teeth as the SUV inexorably pushed his car down the exit ramp. When they came to the end of the steel guardrail, the big brown Land Rover backed off for a moment, then rammed his right rear bumper. Waves of nausea and dizziness overwhelmed him.

The Grenada shot forward and bounced over the curb.

"Holy Mother of God!" His car was hurtling toward a massive oak tree, it's thick branches devoid of leaves, its gnarled trunk as wide as the door of his garage. He was going to die.

He cried out. "Mary!"

Thinking first of his beloved wife, then of the son he adored.

I hope you find the bastard who did this, Frank.

The Grenada smashed into the tree and ripped off the side of the car with a metallic shriek.

Judge Salvatore Renzi felt a moment of searing pain. Then, nothing.

———

5:15 AM – Castle Island

Devlin watched the patrol cop get into his Boston PD cruiser, an older cop in his fifties with a beer gut. But at least he was punctual. At five o'clock sharp, the cop had greeted him warmly, saying he was glad to see him, happy he was out on parole. Buttering him up. The cop knew who paid him, even if somebody else handed him the envelope with the money.

Standing beside him on the cement walkway, Tank hunched his shoulders inside a navy pea-jacket. Fog welled up around them, a fine mist dampening their faces, the sky full of dull gray clouds.

A desolate sight and a bleak day. But one part of his plan was done. He and Tank had an alibi.

Whelan would do the rest, if he knew what was good for him.

"You think he'll suspect anything?" Tank said.

"The cop? Why should he? If Whelan does the job right, the cops will assume he had a heart attack, lost control of the car and hit the tree. It won't even make the evening news."

58

"Maybe. But he's a federal judge, and his son used to work for Boston PD."

Devlin didn't answer, pacing a tight circle, feeling anxious, waiting for Whelan to call. He hated waiting, especially when it involved something so important to him. He'd been waiting years for this moment.

Where the hell was Whelan? He should have called by now.

He ran his fingers over the bill of his Celtics ball cap, the one with a jolly green Leprechaun on the front.

His cellphone rang and he yanked it out of his pocket. Whelan's number on the caller ID.

When he answered, Whelan said, "It's done."

No it's not. This is just the beginning. "Any witnesses?" he said.

"Nope. I didn't see a soul, no cars, no joggers. I ran his car into the tree trunk, angled it just right, ripped off his side of the car. The guy's DOA."

"You're sure?"

"Positive. You know I always come through for you, Dev."

And always brag about it later. Which could be trouble down the road.

"Where are you now?"

"On my way back to Southie. Should be there in half an hour."

"Good. Put the Land Rover in the garage. We'll decide what to do with it later."

"Whatever you say, Dev. You're the boss."

Devlin smiled faintly, recalling his threat last night. *Do what I say or take a bullet in the head.*

"You got that right," he said, and ended the call.

"It went down okay?" Tank asked.

"According to Sean. I'll believe him when I see nothing on the news."

Tank frowned. "Dev, he's a federal judge. The Boston stations might run it."

"We'll see. In the meantime, we need to figure out how to get rid of the Land Rover."

"Dump it somewhere out of state," Tank said. "Connecticut maybe or New York City. File the VIN off the dashboard and put New York plates on it."

"No. In the prison library I read an article about a college professor who killed a prostitute and put her body in the trunk of her car. He got rid of her, drove her car to New York City, took off the plates and left it in one of those self-service parking garages. You know, take a ticket, park your car, pay when you pick it up."

"Why did he kill the prostitute?" Tank said, frowning at him.

"She was gonna ditch him. He met her at a strip joint in Boston, a married guy with two teenagers, but he was totally obsessed with her, paid her thousands of dollars. But someone found the murder weapon in a dumpster off Route 95 in Mansfield, a bloody hammer, and took it to the State cops. Her pimp told the Staties about the professor, but they couldn't prove he killed her. No body. No car."

"So?" Agitated, Tank waved his hands. "Tell me what happened!"

"A few months later the garage owner had the car towed out of his garage, figured nobody was gonna pay him and parked it on the street in a scuzzy neighborhood. An NYPD patrol cop saw it there two days in a row with no plates, got suspicious and popped the trunk."

Tank gazed at him, his dark eyes sorrowful. "Was she in there?"

"No, but he smelled a bad odor, like a decomposed body had been in there, put out an APB on the car. The Staties up here got wind of it, had it towed back to Massachusetts."

"What about the girl? Did they find her?"

"They never found her body, but the professor went to jail."

"He got off easy," Tank said. "They shoulda strung him up by the balls and shot him."

"Maybe, but here's my point. We don't park the Land Rover. We find an out of state chop-shop and get rid of it permanently."

"Who's gonna drive it there?"

"Not you, and I don't trust Whelan. Have one of your runners do it, make him understand what will happen if he fucks up."

———

10:35 AM – New Orleans

Frank sat in his unmarked two blocks from the drive-by, scribbling in his notepad. Another knock on a door, another dead end, the woman telling him she'd heard the shots, but didn't see anything. Nobody wanted to talk.

Five more names on the list, five more dead ends, probably. Then he had to meet David and stake out the funeral for the dead 'banger. In case, the shooters showed up.

Rain spattered his windshield. Ominous dark clouds loomed ahead of him, promising a deluge of torrential rain that would soak him when he left the car to question the next person on the list.

His cell phone rang and he snatched it off the passenger seat. An hour ago he'd gotten another hangup call, the same "unidentified caller" who'd called him at Kelly's house last night. But then he saw the caller ID and smiled. Rafe, his old friend calling from Boston. "Rafe! Great to hear from you, man. What's up?"

They'd worked several cases together in Boston, Frank in Homicide, Rafe in the Gang Unit. But their friendship had been forged playing hoop on a Boston PD basketball team, Frank playing point guard, lobbing passes to Rafe, a rugged power forward who could score at will and ferociously defended the hoop.

"Got some bad news this morning," Rafe said, his usual mellow voice sounding strained.

"What's wrong? You sound upset. Did something happen to Marcie or one of the kids?"

"No." A heavy sigh. "It's your father, man. Got in a car accident on his way to work."

An invisible fist punched his chest, driving the air from his lungs, his mind conjuring terrible images. He'd covered enough car wrecks to know the terrible injuries they could inflict.

"How bad is it? Where did they take him?"

"Wish I didn't have to tell you this on the phone. Rather be there with you." Another heavy sigh. "He didn't make it, Frank. Your father's dead."

The words, softly spoken, rendered him speechless.

Stunned, he sat there. Devastated. Unable to move. Unable to wrap his mind around it. His father was dead?

He shook his head, a silent denial, as though he didn't understand.

Unfortunately he did understand. Almost thirty years as a cop, he knew how fragile life could be, had seen death first hand, delivered in the most horrible ways imaginable. He knew all too well that a phone call could come at any time, and then an ordinary day dissolved into mind-boggling grief.

"Yo, Frank. You okay?" Rafe's voice jolting him back to reality.

"Just ... thinking." *Thinking how fragile life could be.*

"Talk to me, man. Where are you? In your office?"

61

"No, in my car. I talked to him a couple of days ago on the phone. He seemed depressed. One of his friends is in the hospital. So I tried to cheer him up. Told him I'd get us some Celtics tickets and we'd go to a game—" His throat closed up and his eyes burned with tears.

This was the call he had always known would come, not that he would ever admit it, not even to himself. His father was seventy-eight, had lived a long life full of professional achievements and an equally fulfilling life with the woman he adored.

But the thought of him dying alone crushed him.

"I never met your dad," Rafe said, "but I know he was a big Celtics fan. I'm sure you made him feel better, took his mind off his friend." His voice mellow now, soothing.

But there would be no Celtics game with his father.

Judge Salvatore Renzi was dead.

"Tell me what happened." He had a million questions. Not that the answers would fill the devastating void inside him or ease the terrible ache in his heart.

"He went off the road and hit a tree. They think maybe he had a stroke or a heart attack. I'll tell you more later. Gonna take the day off from work, meet you at the airport."

Work. Airport. Phone calls he needed to make. Maureen in Baltimore. Vobitch. Kelly.

He shoved his anguish into another compartment in his mind, to be dealt with later. "Thanks, Rafe. I better go take care of some things."

"Okay, but take care of yourself first, man. When my daddy died, I couldn't eat for a week. Call me with the flight info, I'll pick you up at the airport."

Frank ended the call and studied his hands. Rock steady, not the slightest tremor. His lungs were working again, too. But tears overflowed his eyes, an unstoppable torrent that ran down his face.

He wiped his face with his shirtsleeve and took a shuddery breath.

Hearing his father's words on the phone after he said he'd get them some Celtics tickets. *We can have dinner at one of those burger joints near the Garden. Just like old times.*

Just like old times. Old times that would never happen again.

Taking comfort in their final parting words.

"Talk to you soon, Dad. Love you."

"Love you too, Frank."

CHAPTER 10

WEDNESDAY October 19 – 10:45 AM – Baltimore, Maryland

Maureen blew her nose, wadded up the tissue and threw it in the toilet. Right after morning rounds, Dad had called. He never called when she was working. At first she thought something had happened to Mom, but Dad told her Grampa Sal had died in a car accident this morning. Already frazzled from lack of sleep, she'd burst into tears. Concerned, her supervisor asked what was wrong. When she said someone in her family had died, he told her to go sit in the break room, but a nurse was in there. She wanted to be alone so she went to the nearest restroom and hid in the handicapped stall.

She leaned against the stall door, hugging herself, trying not to cry. Trying to process the news. *Process.*

What a stupid word. As if you could digest the death of someone you loved dearly like you digested a hot dog.

Grampa Sal was dead. She would never see him again. Never tell him she loved him. No more talks with Grampa Sal.

That's what she'd miss the most, that and his impish smile, his lips curved up at the corners, his dark eyes mischievous. Like the day when she was in high school and Dad took her to Grampa's house for Sunday dinner. Mom had the flu and stayed home. After dinner she asked Grampa Sal if she could talk to him. They sat in his study and she told him her tale of woe. She'd aced her driving test and got her license, but Dad needed his car for work and Mom wouldn't let her drive hers.

"Take her shopping for a new outfit next Saturday," Grampa Sal had said. "When you get home, ask if you can drive the car to your girlfriend's house."

"What a great idea! Mom hates driving on weekends. She says there's too much traffic."

"When she sees how well you drive, she'll have no reason to refuse you."

"Like a bribe," she'd said, which made Grampa Sal smile.

"Not exactly. If you want to persuade someone, do them a small kindness. Then they feel obligated to return the favor."

So she did what he said, and Mom started letting her use the car.

But a year later when she was in college Mom filed for divorce on grounds of adultery. She was shocked at first, then angry. How could he do that to Mom? Dad kept calling her, but she refused to talk to him and wouldn't return his messages. Until she got a call from Grampa Sal. "Your father loves you," he'd said. "Don't shut him out, Maureen. Talk to him. He loves you even more than I do, and I love you a lot."

So she called Dad and they talked. Things were rocky for a while. He wouldn't discuss the divorce, saying that was between him and Mom. Eventually they smoothed things out and now they were as close as ever. Which was great because she loved Dad even more than she loved Grampa Sal. But Dad loved Grampa Sal too.

On the phone, after she managed to stop crying, she'd said, "Grampa Sal was so great to talk to. I'm going to miss him."

Dad didn't say anything. Then he cleared his throat and said in a husky voice, "I'm going to miss him too." He said he'd call her after he made the funeral arrangements and hung up.

Fresh tears glazed her eyes. This was the worst possible time for her to go to Boston, but she wanted to be with Dad. She loved Mom, but she'd always felt closer to Dad. She couldn't wait to feel his arms around her, saying he loved her and everything would be all right.

But she wasn't at all sure everything would be all right.

She went to the sink, ran paper towels under the cold water and held them against her eyes. Her life was in chaos. She was exhausted. Barely eating. Losing weight. The practice test she'd signed up for to prep for the orthopedic surgery boards was two weeks away. Every night after work, she stayed up late, studying for hours. Same thing on the weekends.

She threw the soggy paper towels in the trash and studied herself in the mirror. Bloodshot eyes with dark circles under them. She wasn't getting any sleep. Unwilling to share the bed with Jeremy, she was sleeping on the couch.

She'd suspected he had a girlfriend. Now she had the evidence.

Dad wasn't the only detective in the family. She knew what to look for. She'd done it before when Mom stopped paying the real estate bills for the house. One night after Mom went to bed, she'd found Mom's credit card statements in the file cabinet. Mom was sending money to a Catholic charity instead of paying the bills. When she told Dad, he grew visibly angry. "I'll take care of it, Mo," he'd said. "You shouldn't have to deal with this." That was a relief. She hated arguing with Mom.

But she couldn't tell him she'd broken into Jeremy's file cabinet to get his credit card bill. Dad would assume, rightly, that she didn't trust Jeremy. Picking the lock with a hairpin had taken less than two minutes. And there it was, on Jeremy's latest Visa statement. Sixty-two dollars for dinner at a ritzy Baltimore restaurant. She'd never been there. They couldn't afford it, Jeremy said. But he could, apparently. She'd kept track of the nights when he came home late. The Visa charges coincided with two of those nights. Dinner for one, even with drinks, didn't cost sixty-two dollars.

The clincher: a rental charge at a motel near Jeremy's office, on both dates. Her eyes filled with tears, and she angrily brushed them away.

What the hell was she going to do? She didn't want to keep living with him, but she could barely afford half the rent on the apartment they had now.

She raised her chin and gazed into the mirror. Groomed her auburn hair with her fingers. She had no trouble attracting men. Fuck Jeremy.

She'd had plenty of dates in high school and college. After she passed the orthopedic boards, she'd find a new roommate.

And it wouldn't be a woman.

———

9:45 AM – New Orleans

Frank waited behind several cars outside the parking garage at Armstrong airport. Earlier he'd booked one-way flight to Boston, a tight connection in Philly but he grabbed it. Like a man dying of thirst crawls toward a desert waterhole, he felt a desperate need to be with his father. To touch his face and say goodbye to him. To somehow make it real.

His father had influenced his life in so many ways. Now he was gone.

Vivid memories bubbled up from his subconscious. His father's arms around him after the Swampscott high school basketball team won the State championship in Boston Garden, telling him how proud he was. The aroma of coffee in the kitchen on Saturday mornings as his father sipped an espresso. The sound of his voice as he bantered with Mom, who gave it right back to him.His father taking him outside after breakfast to watch him practice jump shots on the hoop attached to the garage, laughing when Frank drove around him and scored.

The line for the garage crept forward, only one car ahead of him now.

Always do your best, Frank, on the court and on the job. Judge Salvatore Renzi's oft-spoken credo.

So much of his life had revolved around basketball. Watching Celtics games with his father on TV or at the Garden. Meeting BJ, the high school friend he'd made and lost. Playing hoop on the Boston PD team with Rafe, who'd become his closest friend. His friends in New Orleans, David Lee and Kenyon Miller, who'd played football at LSU but was also a big NBA fan.

He flashed his NOPD badge at the security guard outside the garage, who waved him up the ramp. He found a parking spot on the fourth level, grabbed his suitcase and headed for the terminal.

Earlier he'd called Vobitch to tell him what had happened.

"I'm really sorry to hear that, Frank. Do whatever you gotta do."

"I know you're under the gun for the drive-by—"

"Don't worry about it, Vobitch had said gruffly. "Take care of your father."

He entered the concourse, got in the security line and checked the time. 9:55. His flight was boarding in twenty minutes.

His most difficult phone call had been to Maureen. When he gave her the news, she burst into tears. Then, her heartbreaking words. *"Grampa Sal was so great to talk to. I'm going to miss him."* It was all he could do not to start bawling. He managed to hold it together, said he'd call her after he made the arrangements, and hung up.

Then he'd called Kelly. She told him how sorry she was, saying she knew how close he was to his father, and offered to drive him to the airport, but he had declined. He wasn't ready to talk to Kelly up close and personal. Far more than bed partners, they were emotionally tuned into each other. If he talked to her now, he might break down completely.

He got through security and stopped at a kiosk for a bottle of Starbucks Frappuccino, hoping it would settle his acid stomach. Then he stopped beside an empty gate and called Rafe.

"Yo, Frank, where are you?"

"At the airport, about to board my flight. It gets into Logan at 3:45."

"Got it. Meet you at Departures, you know the drill."

Frank smiled faintly. Indeed he did. The State troopers at Logan Airport relentlessly policed the Arrivals area. No parking to wait for arriving passengers, keep moving or you'll get a ticket.

"Text me when you land," Rafe said. "Look for my beat-up black Ford Explorer."

"What, I don't get a limo?" Trying to act cool when his heart was broken.

"Don't get any naked babes either. See you soon, partner."

"Thanks for everything, Rafe. You're the best."

"We'll argue about that later. Order up a double cognac on the plane and enjoy the flight."

His throat thickened. Lost in thought, he towed his suitcase toward the gate. What would he do without friends like Rafe? And Kenyon and David and Vobitch and Kelly.

Friends and lovers in New Orleans, old friends and lovers in Boston.

Did Gina know about his father, he wondered. She worked for the *Boston Herald* and she had a police scanner.

————

12: 30 PM - Winthrop, Massachusetts

Devlin stepped into Kate's room, relieved to escape the rank smell in the hallway. The nuns did a great job keeping the place neat and clean, but at meal times disgusting cooking odors permeated the air: Brussels Sprouts, boiled cabbage and hard-boiled eggs. "I brought you a souvenir," he said, and put two plastic bags on Kate's bed.

Beaming with delight, she said, "Can I open them now?"

"Sure. Open the big one first."

She pulled the Cal Ripkin jersey out of the bag. "An orange shirt! I love it!" She threw her arms around his neck and said, "You're the best brother in the whole world!"

Pleased, he kissed her cheek. "Try it on, see if it fits."

When she started to unbutton her blouse, he said, "No, don't do that. Put it on over your blouse." Sister or not, the last thing he needed was for someone to come in the room and see him with her half-naked.

"What's this?" she said, pointing to the letters RIPKIN and the big number 8.

"That's Cal Ripkin's jersey. He's a famous baseball player."

Kate laughed and danced around the room, chanting *Rip-kin, Rip-kin, Rip-kin.*

Smiling, he said, "Let me help you put it on." He pulled the jersey over her head and helped her smooth it over her blouse.

"Excellent," he said. "It fits fine."

"I can wear it on Halloween, when I hand out candy to the kids!"

Damn! He hadn't thought about that. What if someone asked how she got it? But seeing the sparkle of excitement in her eyes, he didn't have the heart to forbid it. "Okay. Open the other bag."

She pulled out the bag of candy. "Candy Corn! My favorite! Can I have some now?"

"Yes, but only four," he said, holding up four fingers. "Don't spoil your lunch."

"And four for you," Kate said. "The nuns always tell us to share our goodies."

He tore a corner off the bag and poured Candy Corn into her hand. Kate counted out four pieces, gave them to him, took four for herself and put the rest back in the bag. With a contented smile, she sat on the bed to eat her candy. He slipped his four into his pocket and watched her, pleased that she was happy, heartbroken that her happiness was so limited.

"Enjoy your day, Kate. I have to do some errands."

"So soon?" she said, pouting. "Stay and have lunch with me."

"I'd love to, but I have to go meet someone." He bent down and kissed her cheek. "I'll come back next week and take you out for lunch." No way was he eating here.

"Okay," she said, smiling now. "Thank you for the candy and the new shirt. I *love* my Rip-kin shirt! I can't wait to show Bridget!"

"I'm sure she'll love it," he said. *And equally sure she'll ask how you got it.*

He left the group home and got in his car, his mind already focused on the tasks that lay ahead. Meet Tank and talk about getting rid of the Land Rover. And Sean Whelan. Then he would set up a meeting with Bridget and get started on the rest of his payback plan.

Did Renzi know about his father yet? Probably. After the cops pried what was left of Judge Salvatore Renzi out of the car, they would have found his license. Then it was only a matter of time until they notified his next of kin. Homicide Detective Frank Renzi. Too bad he couldn't be there when Renzi got the news.

Devlin smiled, imagining Renzi's pain and grief when he found out his father was dead. A world of heartbreak and sadness.

Soon his world would be rocked again.

Emotional distress to the max. Exactly what the bastard deserved.

CHAPTER 11

WEDNESDAY October 19 – 2:35 PM – South Boston

Devlin finished his fried clam roll and wiped his lips with a Celtics-green paper napkin. Seated beside him, Tank was eating a cheeseburger. Seven days a week the Leprechaun Pub opened at 11:00 AM, began serving lunch at noon and stayed open until the wee hours. He loved the place, loved owning it, not that his name appeared on the deed. Years ago, he'd bought it from the previous owner, who refused to pay for protection. Made him an offer he couldn't refuse.

Back then it was The Irish Pub. He renamed it, pasted a Celtics Leprechaun on the door and hung photographs of Celtics players on the long wall opposite the bar: Larry Bird, Kevin McHale, Bob Cousy and legendary coach Red Auerbach, lighting a cigar after the Celtics won a championship. No photos of JoJo White and K.C. Jones, black players who'd never dare step foot in Southie.

Ahead of him, several regulars sat at the ten-stool bar, drinking beer as they watched ESPN on TV. Opposite the bar, groups of men were eating lunch at square tables. Beyond the bar and the tables, a narrow horizontal window high on the wall near the ceiling let in a bit of light. That was the only window.

No one walking past the Leprechaun Pub, including any nosy cops, could see inside.

Tank set aside his plate and drank from his mug of Budweiser. "I'm using my top runner to get rid of the Land Rover. He's a good kid. Does what he's told, don't ask no questions. We put a set of stolen plates on it an hour ago."

"Was Whelan there?"

"No." Tank gave him a pointed look. "Keep him in the dark, he can't tell nobody about it. The chop-shop is in Rhode Island. The kid will drive the Land Rover. I'll follow him to make sure he don't get stopped for speeding."

70

A stocky red-headed man approached their table in the back corner. No one else was allowed to sit here. Devlin always sat with his back to the wall, a practice he'd adopted in prison to survive.

Stay alert and maintain situational awareness at all times.

"Great to have you back, Mr. Devlin," the red-haired man said, giving him a broad smile. "We missed you around here. How's Kate?"

Devlin flashed his charming smile. "Happy to be here, Red. Thanks for asking about Kate. She's doing fine. I just saw her this morning."

"May the wind be always at your back," Red said, still smiling as he moved away from the table.

"And yours as well," Devlin replied, his usual response to the traditional Irish saying.

After Red left the Pub, Tank said, jiving him, "You got fans, Dev."

He waved a hand. "Always good to keep the locals happy. We might have a problem with the other thing. I heard some chatter on my police scanner."

Tank frowned. "What kind of chatter?"

"The exit is still closed. The State cops are doing an accident reconstruction."

"I told you this was dangerous, Dev. This ain't no ordinary guy. He's a federal judge. After the cops got him out of the car, they'd check his identification, see who he was."

"And notify his next of kin," Devlin said, unable to suppress a smile.

"Who happens to be a cop." Tank leaned closer and lowered his voice. "When I was at the garage I took a good look at the Land Rover. The left front fender's got a dent in it and scratched paint. What if the cops find paint fragments on the other car?"

"Jesus, Mary and Joseph," Devlin said, uttering his father's habitual curse. "Whelan said it went off without a hitch. The bastard fucked up. That's it, Tank. I want him gone."

Expressionless, Tank said, "You want me to take him for a ride?"

"No. You and I can't be involved. The cops know we're connected to Whelan."

"I can take care of it, set up an alibi with a guy we trust, do the thing while you go see your parole officer and pee in a cup."

"No. Too obvious."

Tank pursed his lips. "Maybe Sunny could do it. She hates the guy."

Devlin sipped his Harp Ale, considering. Would Sunny do it? She was tough, that's for sure.

Years ago, he'd overheard the lecture she gave her girls every week. "Your customers come here for a good time. Your job is to make them happy. But no S&M, no bondage. I make that clear before I give them the appointment. Some will be businessmen or tourists with fat wallets, looking for a quick thrill. Your best customers are the damaged ones, men who are too ugly or too fat or grieving for a dead spouse. They're not just looking for sex. They want someone to listen to them, make them feel wanted. Treat them right and they'll be back every week." Then Sunny had said, her blue eyes cold and hard, "But never see them outside this hotel. If you do, you're gone."

"That might work," he said. "I'll talk to her tomorrow. But first we need to get rid of the Land Rover, the sooner the better."

Tank took out his cell phone. "I'll tell the kid we're leaving now."

———

2:45 PM – Boston

"Why are we stopping here?" Frank said as Rafe pulled into Waffles and Wings, a soul food diner on Massachusetts Avenue near Boston Medical Center. "I want to go to the hospital."

Rafe looked at him, his dark eyes full of concern. "Frank, you got a lot of decisions to make and right now you're hurting. When my daddy died, I was a basket case, bawled like a baby until Marcie took over, made me eat a bowl of cereal while she made a list of what I had to do." Rafe shrugged. "You know Marcie, the fashionista businesswoman goes into crisis mode, gotta take charge."

"I want to see my father."

Rafe shook his head. "You don't want to see him in a body bag. We go inside, eat some steak and eggs, I'll tell you what happened this morning. Every single detail, I promise."

Frank massaged his throbbing temples. At Logan, Rafe had wrapped him in a bear hug and told him to get in the car, he'd take him wherever he wanted to go. But when Frank asked him what happened, Rafe had said, "Wait till we get situated, I'll tell you everything."

"I can't eat anything," he said. "My stomach's too jumpy."

"Order up a glass of milk. That be the answer, fix a jumpy stomach like nobody's bidness." Rafe giving him street jive now.

Reluctantly, he followed Rafe into Waffles and Wings, their former hangout when they wanted to talk. The spicy aroma of barbecued chicken permeated the air. The place wasn't busy, the lunch rush over, too early for the dinner crowd. All the waitresses and kitchen staff were black. Most of the customers were too, other than a few white and Asian workers from Boston City Hospital, dressed in scrubs.

Their waitress, a wiry older woman, came to their table with a pot of coffee and said to Frank, "Good to see you. Where you been? Haven't seen you for ages."

He forced a smile. "Hiding out in New Orleans."

"Been meaning to go there sometime," she said, smiling as she filled Rafe's coffee mug.

"No coffee for me," Frank said. "I'll have a vanilla milkshake."

"The man going soft in his dotage," Rafe said. "Next up, be eating baby food."

The woman laughed and set two menus on the table. "Watch out, Rafe, you're no kid, either."

Eager to talk to Rafe, Frank said, "Let's order now. I'll have some scrambled eggs."

"Want bacon or sausage with it?"

"No thanks, just wheat toast."

"Same for me," Rafe said, "with a side order of sausage."

After she left, Frank said, "Tell me what happened. Tell me everything."

Rafe puffed his cheeks. "Someone in a nearby house heard the crash and called 9-11. A Revere patrol cop got there first, called for an ambulance right away. The car was wrapped around a tree, the driver's side ripped off." Rafe rolled his lips together, frowning. "Your father was in bad shape, Frank. Serious injuries. The cop checked for a pulse, didn't find one."

Frank breathed deep, down to his diaphragm, the technique he'd used in high school to calm himself before taking a trumpet solo with the jazz band. Using it now to control his anguish. Murder scenes were bad, but car accidents were often worse. Vomit-worthy blood and gore. A truck crossing the divider. A high-speed head-on collision. A tree shearing the car in half, bumper to backseat.

"How soon did the ambulance get there?" For crash victims with severe injuries, there was only a small window. No pulse, no CPR for more than ten minutes, the brain is dead.

"Four minutes, the cop said. I know what you're thinking, Frank, but I'm not sure it mattered. By then, a State trooper was there, caught it on the scanner. A friend of mine, worked a gang-related case with me. He located your father's DL, recognized the name and called me right away. He knew you used to work for Boston PD. I told him not to call you, said I wanted to call you myself. Also told him to wait for me, said I'd be there ASAP."

Moved by Rafe's thoughtfulness, he said, "Thanks. That means a lot."

The waitress set his milkshake on the table, said their order would be out soon an left. Frank unwrapped a straw, stuck it in the milkshake and took a sip. The cold liquid soothed his throat, but didn't quiet his mind.

"No other cars involved? No witnesses?"

"No. I beat the rush hour traffic, got there in ten minutes. My friend figured your father had a stroke maybe, or a heart attack. Seventy-eight years old, it could happen."

"I guess. It's just hard to imagine." He shook his head. "Whenever I see him, he always seems so energetic and happy ... " And realized he had just done what so many grief-stricken survivors did, refer to the dead person in the present tense.

"Happy because he was with you," Rafe said.

His throat closed up and he sat there, unable to speak. He was saved by the waitress who delivered their food. His platter of scrambled eggs gave off a delicious aroma that made his stomach rumble. He forked up some eggs, chewed and swallowed. Rafe was right. He needed food to give him strength for the tasks that lay ahead. Call the funeral home and make the arrangements, post an obituary in the Swampscott and Boston papers, contact some of his father's friends.

"I had your father's car towed to the BPD evidence garage." Rafe ate some scrambled eggs and sliced his sausage into bite-sized segments.

"Man, he loved that Mark IV Granada. Twenty years old but he refused get rid of it." He set down his fork. "He took good care of it but ... you think the brakes could have failed?"

"We'll see what they say." Rafe paused a moment and said, "You know anyone who might have a grudge against your father?"

Surprised, he said, "Why? You think it wasn't an accident?"

"He sent a lot of people to jail."

"That's what judges do. Put criminals in jail. Tell me what happened at the scene."

"The tow guy winched the car onto a flatbed wrecker and left. I went to the hospital."

"Did you see him?" Unwilling to say *Did you see my father's corpse?*

Rafe heaved a sigh. "Yes. The ME had already signed the death certificate. It's in my glove compartment, told him I'd give it to you. An orderly had already taken your father to the morgue."

"How bad was it?"

"Frank, you don't need to know. You've seen accident victims."

"Just tell me." Clenching his fists, prepared for the worst.

"Crushing chest injuries, head lacerations, multiple broken bones. If it's any consolation, he must have died fast, ten seconds tops."

But he died alone. Frank pushed his plate aside. "I should make some calls."

"Call a funeral home," Rafe said. "Have them transport his body there, go see him after they clean him up."

He didn't answer right away. Was that what he wanted? Maybe he should go to the morgue.

"Frank, think about the last time you saw your father. Remember how he looked then. That's the important thing. Remember how happy he was when you said you'd get Celtics tickets so you could go to a game together." Rafe squeezed his hand and said softly, "In the end, that's all we got left, amigo, memories of the good times we had with them."

"Okay," he said. "I'll use the funeral home in Swampscott, the one we used for my mother."

Rafe wiped his fingers on a napkin and stood. "I'll get the check. Go call the funeral home. I'll drive you to the house in Swampscott. You're staying there, right?"

He nodded and took out his wallet. "Here, take some money for the food."

"No chance, partner. I got it. Take my car keys and make your calls."

He went out to Rafe's car, sat in the passenger seat, got on his cell phone and located the number for the funeral home. The owner remembered him, offered his condolences and said he would send a hearse to the hospital to transport the remains to the funeral parlor. "I'd like to see him before you … get him ready for the viewing."

"Certainly, Mr. Renzi. If you'd like to come here at five o'clock, we can discuss when the wake and the funeral will be. Would that be convenient?"

He said it would and ended the call. Rafe was right. Too many decisions to make. When's the wake? When's the funeral? He would have to call the church and talk to the priest. And rent a car so Rafe didn't have to keep driving him around.

His phone rang, startling him. He answered right away, "Renzi."

"Hi Franco. I just heard about your father. Are you okay?"

Franco. Gina was the only one who ever called him that. His longtime lover, friend and soulmate.

"Hey," he said, his voice husky, "thanks for calling me."

"Where are you? Can you talk?" A familiar phrase, checking to see if he was alone.

"I'm in Boston. Rafe picked me up at the airport. He's about to drive me to Swampscott so I can make the arrangements."

"I wish I could give you a hug. I know how much you loved your father." And after a beat, "Can we have a drink later?"

"I'd love to, but I'm not sure what time I'll finish tonight. How about tomorrow? Want to meet at that place in Nahant? Seven o'clock?"

"Perfect. See you there. Take care of yourself, Franco. Love you."

"Love you too," he said, and ended the call.

Rafe opened the door and got behind the wheel. "Didn't want to interrupt while you were on the phone. Everything okay?"

"Yeah. I talked to the funeral director. I'm going there to see my father at five o'clock. But that wasn't the funeral director. It was Gina."

Rafe smiled at him, his eyes crinkling at the corners. "Excellent. When you gonna see her?"

"Tomorrow night." Rafe didn't know Gina well, but he knew about her. Rafe had helped him get through the ugly divorce after his wife found out about his affair with Gina.

"Always good to hear from old love partners," Rafe said. "Help get you through a crisis."

He said nothing, his mind churning. Would a hug from Gina be enough to get him through this?

Or would a hug lead to a kiss, followed by passionate lovemaking in his bedroom in Swampscott?

CHAPTER 12

THURSDAY October 20 – 7:15 AM – South Boston

"Got time for breakfast?" Sunny asked, smiling at him as she ran her hand over his chest.

Devlin glanced at the clock on her bedside table. He didn't want breakfast, he wanted Sean Whelan dead. He caressed her cheek. "You're spoiling me, Sunny, but I like it."

"I enjoy spoiling you. Always did, remember?"

"I do." He kissed her lips and swung his legs over the side of the bed. "Breakfast with you is tempting, but I have to get to work. Do the techs sweep your apartment?"

"Of course." She got out of bed and slipped into her red silk robe. "I don't want some Vice cop taping my private activities. Why?"

He put on his pants and buttoned his shirt. "I need to talk to you about a problem. Tank knows about it, nobody else."

"What's the problem?" she asked, giving him her full attention now.

"Sean Whelan, I don't trust him."

Sunny grimaced, her blue eyes glinting with anger. "I don't either. That's why my Rottweilers won't let him step foot inside the hotel without my say-so." The Rottweilers were strong-armed thugs posing as doormen. They made sure no Vice Squad cops came inside unannounced and shooed away drunks or unruly clients who might harm the girls.

"Why don't you trust him?"

She silently clenched her jaw, a muscle working in her cheek.

"Tank says you hate him."

"Hate him? I despise him!"

He'd never seen her like this. Even if she was angry or hurt, she never let it show. He circled the bed and gripped her shoulders. "Why? What did he do to you?"

A flash of pain showed in her eyes, quickly replaced by anger. "He raped me."

"Jesus, Mary and Joseph!" He cupped her face in his hands and gazed into her eyes. "No wonder you hate him. When was this?"

"While you were in prison. He came to the hotel one night and said he needed to talk to me. Otherwise I would never have let him in here. We sat in the living room and I offered him a drink. I never liked him, but he was running the business for you, so I tried to be ... hospitable."

"Sunny," he said sternly. "Tell me what happened."

"He downed a scotch on the rocks and made himself another without asking me. Then he sat down beside me on the sofa and squeezed my breasts. I pushed him away and told him to get out and he slapped me."

"He *hit* you?" Anger stirred inside him like a hungry beast.

She nodded, her eyes blazing. "Then he ripped off my dress and pulled off my bra. I scratched his face and he punched me in the jaw. It pissed me off so bad I spit in his face. He swore at me and yanked my earring out of my ear." She touched her earlobe. "See the scar? It hurt like hell, not to mention bleeding all over me."

The hungry beast turned savage. It had been many years since he'd been this angry.

"Then he shoved me down on the floor and raped me. It was awful, Dev. I couldn't get him off me, couldn't stand the smell of him. When he was done he zipped up and warned me not to tell you or he'd come back and do it again."

"The bastard! I'll kill the motherfucker!"

"No. You'll get in trouble."

Enraged, he clenched his fists. That Whelan had hurt Sunny was bad enough. But that wasn't why he'd raped her. He'd done it deliberately, knowing Sunny wasn't just his business partner, she was his woman. He'd warned her not to tell him, knowing he'd be a dead man if she did. Also knowing that raping Sunny gave him a psychological advantage. He had screwed the boss's woman, and the boss didn't know it.

"Why didn't you tell me?"

Sunny licked her lips and let out a sigh. "I told Tank—"

"You told Tank?" he said, incredulous. "Why didn't he tell me?"

"Please don't be mad at Tank. I made him promise not to tell you. I didn't want you lying awake at night in a jail cell, thinking about it. After I told Tank, he hired the Rottweilers and told them never to let Sean Whelan into the hotel."

He put his arms around her, stroking her long blonde hair, then released her. "If I'd known, I would have had him killed. I hate that he did that to you. No man should treat a woman like that."

"Exactly," she said, her eyes hard and cold. "That's why I protect my girls. And myself. After that night, no man has touched my body unless I wanted him to."

"Whelan is scum, but you're right, Sunny. I can't kill him. The feds are watching me. Tank can't either. If Whelan winds up dead, we're the first ones the Boston cops would question."

She nodded. "They'd throw you in jail, hunt for the evidence later."

"What if I asked you to do it?"

Her eyes widened for an instant. Then she smiled, a cold feral smile. "How about tonight?"

He burst out laughing. "Sunny, you are too much! Not tonight, but soon."

"The sooner the better," she said grimly.

"How about Monday? Tank and I need an alibi. Monday is Irish night at the Leprechaun Pub. Plenty of people will see us there."

"Monday night is fine."

Sunny was his soulmate alright. Tough, smart, pragmatic and ruthless. "How will you do it?"

Another feral smile, showing her even white teeth, her blue eyes mischievous now. "I want him to suffer. How about the old choked-on-a-chicken-bone trick? I'll invite him over for dinner."

"In your apartment?" he said, aghast. "Sunny, you don't want the cops coming here."

"Of course not. I'll reserve the executive suite on the second floor, light some candles to set the mood for an intimate dinner, have the kitchen send up two plates of gourmet chicken."

"But how will you get him here? He knows you hate him."

She smiled at him, amused. "Dev, I didn't survive in this business all these years without understanding how to manipulate men. Rape isn't about sex, it's about power and control. I'll call him tell him I need him to do something for me. He'll think I'm going to have sex with him, to get him to do what I want."

The feral smile reappeared, deadly and dangerous.

"Don't worry, Dev. I'll take care of it. I'll make sure Sean Whelan never rapes another woman."

———

7:15 PM – Nahant, Massachusetts

Frank backed his rental car into a space facing the Clam Shack, a local restaurant overlooking the ocean with affordable seafood dinners and a well-stocked bar in the lounge. The main attraction: neither he nor Gina were likely to run into anyone they knew.

He gazed at the sunset, recalling the nine years they'd spent together, not married but intimate partners in every sense of the word. In sickness and health, in good times and bad.

Lord knows they'd weathered some difficult times. Gina consoling him after his mother died, being supportive during the devastating IAD investigation after the little girl died when he and his partner served the murder warrant on a drug dealer. But then Evelyn filed for divorce on grounds of adultery and named Gina as the "other party."

Gina's borderline-abusive husband heard about it, leading to dire consequences. Frank's lawyer advised him to file a counter-suit, claiming denial of conjugal benefits. True enough, but he declined, unwilling to air their dirty linen in public, knowing it would upset Maureen.

So he got a job with NOPD, kissed Gina goodbye and moved to New Orleans. Gina got a divorce and remarried, only to get hit with Stage III breast cancer. Fighter that she was, Gina had survived, but the treatments had been brutal.

Now she was waiting for him in the Clam Shack lounge. Her red Mazda was parked three spaces away, a newer model, but it still sported a *Boston Herald* bumper sticker.

On a flagpole beside the restaurant an American flag undulated in a gentle sea breeze. A rustic boat wheel with wooden spokes was mounted on the door. The nautical theme continued inside, fish net with starfish draped on the walls, a marlin mounted on a wooden plaque.

The luscious aroma of seafood filled the air as he passed the door to the dining room. He paused at the door to the lounge to the right.

Perched on a tall captain's chair at the bar, Gina was chatting with the bartender. The sight of her took his breath away. Short dark hair, a curvy five-foot-four, looking sexy as hell in a formfitting burgundy dress.

Perhaps sensing he was there, she turned and saw him. She hopped off her chair and held out her arms for a hug.

He wrapped his arms around her, savoring her familiar spicy scent.

"Franco," she said in a low husky voice. "I'm so sorry about your father."

"Thanks," he murmured. "Great to see you, especially now. You didn't know my father, but—"

"But you told me so much about him it seemed like I did." She took her purse off the chair beside hers and flashed a grin. "Look, I saved you a seat."

"I'm surprised some guy didn't make a move on you. You look gorgeous, as usual."

"You know how to make a girl feel great, Franco. I'm having Merlot. Want some?"

"Yes. Need a refill?" He sat on the chair beside hers and signaled the bartender.

"Not yet. How are you doing? I know it was a car accident. What happened?"

He gave the bartender his order and said, "We're not sure. No other car involved, no witnesses. The cops at the scene think it might have been some kind of medical event."

"What do *you* think?" she asked, gazing at him, her liquid brown eyes puddles of concern.

"He had no history of heart trouble. But heart attacks can happen anytime, I guess."

The bartender delivered his glass of wine and left them alone. He drank some Merlot and recapped what Rafe had told him, intermittently interrupted by Gina, asking for more details. "Rafe's been great," he said. "Picked me up at the airport. Took me to Waffles and Wings."

"How's he doing? Every now and then I see him at a crime scene."

Gina covered the crime beat for the *Boston Herald*. That's how they'd met, Gina doing her intrepid female reporter act at a murder scene, looking for a scoop, Frank trying to get rid of her, then relenting and having a cup of coffee with her. One thing led to another and …

"Earth to Franco," she said, nudging him. "How's Rafe doing?"

"No complaints. Marcie's fashion design business is thriving, the kids are good, and Rafe's still moonlighting, managing their three-decker rentals in Dorchester." He traced a finger down her cheek. "How are *you* doing? Health-wise, I mean. You okay?"

"Yes. My mammograms are fine and the blood tests are good. No sign of any recurrence."

Not mentioning the dreaded C-word. "Excellent," he said. "I'm glad to hear it."

His cell phone vibrated in his pocket. He took it out and said, "Sorry, I gotta take this."

When he answered, Kenyon said, "Yo Frank, I'm really sorry to hear about your father. How you doing, man?"

"Thanks, Kenyon. I'm doing okay. Better now that I'm in Boston."

Now that he'd said goodbye to his father. Yesterday the funeral director had taken him to the preparation room. His father's body was on a table, draped with a sheet. The director said they had washed him, but he'd look better after they prepared him for the wake, and left the room.

Frank pulled the sheet away from his father's face. His eyes were closed. Other than a deep gash on his face, he almost looked peaceful. Unwilling to look at the other injuries, he touched his father's cheek. "I'm sorry we won't get to go to the Celtics game, Dad. You were always there for me. I'm sorry I wasn't there for you when this happened."

Cutting into his somber recollection, Kenyon said, "Tell me about the arrangements."

"The wake is tomorrow, two to four. The funeral is Saturday afternoon at two."

"Okay. Vobitch and I will fly up for the funeral. Tanya and Juliana are coming with us."

"Great, but what about the drive-by?" Frank said, gazing at Gina, knowing she was listening.

"Vobitch says not to worry about it. Take care of yourself, Frank. We're thinking of you."

"Thanks, partner. Look forward to seeing you. " He ended the call and put his cell phone on the bar.

"I'm glad your friends are coming up from New Orleans," Gina said. "What's the drive-by?"

"Last Thursday I caught a gang-related shooting. A ten-year-old boy died in the crossfire. His parents are devastated. Needless to say all hell broke loose, protest marches, the works."

"Sounds familiar." Gina twirled a lock of dark hair around her finger. "Gang-related cases are tough to solve. Nobody will talk. I see that in Boston all the time. The little boy was black?"

"Yes. So were the drive-by victims, one dead, the other, a known drug dealer, in the hospital."

"Retaliation?"

"Probably. Territorial, no doubt." Thinking *Just like old times.* He and Gina had spent many a night here discussing homicide cases.

His phone rang again. Unidentified caller, but he recognized the number, had added it to his contact list after the first hangup. He punched on and said, "Renzi."

Silence on the line. Faint breathing. Then a click.

Creepy-crawlies prickled his neck. Someone wanted to talk to him. Was it a tip on the drive-by?

"Another hangup call," he said to Gina. "I got one last night when I was at Kelly's house." Damn! He'd said it without thinking. His subconscious mind, reminding him of Kelly while he enjoyed a reunion with his former lover.

Sometimes he lied on the job, telling parents of a missing child not to give up hope, knowing in his heart the child was dead. Other times he lied to suspects, saying he had more information than he actually did, trying to shake them up so they would confess.

But lying to deceive someone you cared about was a different matter. Even when he was married and left the house to see Gina, he didn't lie to his wife. Evelyn didn't ask where he was going, and he didn't tell.

For nine years he had never cheated on Gina. Why screw up a good thing? They were happy together.

Gina touched his arm. "It's okay, Franco. I'm glad you and Kelly are still together. You deserve to be with someone who makes you happy."

He said nothing, lost in thought. Kelly made him happy. More than happy. Did he love Gina? No doubt. He'd give anything to spend the night with her. But then he would have to lie to Kelly, and he couldn't imagine doing that. Even if he didn't tell her, he'd feel guilty, knowing in his heart that he was betraying her trust.

"She reminds me of you," he said. "Smart, sexy and feisty as hell."

Gina gave him a wistful smile. "I haven't forgotten the wonderful times we had, but that was then and this is now. I'll be thinking about you this weekend. You've always been there for me, Franco. Call me if you're feeling down and want to talk."

He put his arm around her and pulled her close to give her a hug. "Thanks, Gina. You're the best."

CHAPTER 13

FRIDAY October 21 – 4:05 PM – Swampscott

Maureen freshened her lipstick, left the ladies lounge and stood in the doorway of the viewing room. In the far right corner, a dozen gorgeous bouquets surrounded the casket. Even from here she could smell the sweet fragrance of lilies and orchids.

The casket was closed. Dad had given the funeral director a large color photograph to put on a wooden easel beside it: Grampa Sal looking distinguished in his black judicial robe, smiling faintly.

The smile she would never see again. Seeing the photograph brought fresh tears to her eyes.

More than two hundred people had come to the wake. For two hours she'd stood beside Dad, the line moving slowly as people murmured condolences, some of them grasping her hands, telling her how sorry they were. Most of them were Grampa Sal's friends and colleagues, but others looked vaguely familiar, Dad's friends and colleagues when he worked for Boston PD.

Mom wasn't here. This morning she'd begged off, claiming she had a headache. Maureen didn't believe it. Mom got nervous in crowds and hated talking to people she didn't know. She probably didn't want to talk to Dad, either, but she'd be at the funeral tomorrow. Mom never passed up an opportunity to pray.

She was staying with her at the house in Milton, a major annoyance. She'd rather rent a motel room and a car, but she needed to save money. Mom wanted her to drive her home right after the Mass, but she wanted to stay with Dad. After the interment at the cemetery, people would gather at Grampa Sal's house to reminisce and tell stories about him.

She didn't want to miss that.

Earlier, when she'd mentioned this to Dad, he immediately took out his wallet, handed her fifty dollars and said, "Give this to the limo driver and have him drive your mother home. Don't tell her until you leave the church or she'll give you an argument." Dad was great that way. Mention a problem, he solved it right away. No let-me-think-about-it, no indecision, he just fixed the problem.

Too bad he couldn't fix the Jeremy problem.

Before she left, they had a big fight when she confronted him with the VISA bill. Furious, Jeremy had yelled at her. "You went into my file cabinet? How can I trust you?"

Trust *her*? He was the one who was cheating. But she didn't say that. Miraculously, given her anger, she calmly pointed out the restaurant charges and asked him who he'd taken to dinner.

"Beverly," he said, "my receptionist. She's been good about not asking for a raise, so I took her out to dinner. Big deal."

"Twice in one month?" she said, her cheeks flaming with anger as she pointed out the other incriminating items on the bill. "Before you took her to a motel and fucked her brains out?"

Jeremy didn't have an answer for that one. He stomped into the bedroom and slammed the door. She slept on the couch. Or tried to, staring at the ceiling, fuming. At daybreak she got up and went in the bedroom and packed her suitcase, slamming drawers shut, not caring if it woke Jeremy, the conniving creep who was cheating on her.

When he came out of the bedroom dressed for work, she delivered her ultimatum. "Pack your things and find another place to live, Jeremy."

"Why should I move?" he said. "*You're* the one who's unhappy."

Her rage boiled over. "I'm unhappy because you're a cheat and a liar!" she screamed. "I thought we were partners, but you decided to have a girlfriend on the side. Well, that's fine with me. I don't know what I ever saw in you."

"Calm down, Maureen. You're acting like a child."

"Bullshit! You're a fucking asshole. A manipulative son-of-a-bitch! Pack your things and get out. Don't you dare bring your floozy here while I'm gone and screw her in *the bed that I paid for!* When I get back Sunday, your stuff better be gone."

Whereupon Jeremy had grabbed his car keys and left the apartment.

But what if he was still there when she got home? Anxiety verging on panic rippled through her, followed by a hollow feeling of dread. What if she had to hire a lawyer to get him out? She didn't have the money to pay a lawyer.

"Hey gorgeous, you holding up okay?" Rafe said, putting his arm around her shoulder.

Mustering a smile, she said, "I'm doing okay. Thanks for helping Dad with everything."

"That's what friends are for. See you later. I gotta talk to your Dad."

She watched him stride to the front of the viewing room and start talking to Dad. Rafe was the handsomest black man she'd ever seen outside of a movie theater: coal-black skin, chiseled features, sensuous lips and enormous dark eyes.

She'd known him for years, ever since she was a little girl. But now she was an adult, viewing him with fresh eyes.

Rafe probably met plenty of women on the job. Did he cheat on his wife, she wondered.

Marcie was beautiful, six feet tall and impeccably dressed, looked like she'd stepped out of the pages of *Elle* magazine. She was a fashion designer and owned her own business. Marcie had hired some caterers for the get-together at Grampa Sal's after the funeral.

Some of Dad's NOPD colleagues were flying up for the funeral. She hoped Kelly O'Neil would be there. She'd never met her. Kelly was an NOPD detective like Dad. They'd been together for a while, but when she asked Dad if they were going to get married, he said, "No, once was enough." Then, seeing her stricken look, he had put his arms around her and said, "You're the best thing that ever happened to me, Maureen. Never forget that."

Tears misted her eyes. What a great Dad. What would she do without him? She knew he was hurting, his face pale, somber eyes, his posture stiff and rigid like he was struggling to hold himself together. Grief-stricken because his father had died. She couldn't bother him about Jeremy now. And she couldn't talk to Mom about it.

Maybe she'd get blitzed tonight, sit in an upscale bar, flirt with a decent-looking guy and hit the sack with him. When you got used to regular sex, going without it was hard. She wouldn't do that, of course. Too dangerous. Go to bed with some guy you didn't know, you might catch a venereal disease or find out he got off on beating up woman.

Her stomach clenched, the hard knot inside that refused to go away. She massaged her forehead, fighting the incipient headache that lurked behind her eyes. Two days from now she'd be back in Baltimore.

What if Jeremy refused to move out?

The practice test for her board exam was two weeks from tomorrow. She hadn't studied for two days, no time to study tomorrow or Sunday either. Not only that, on Monday she'd have to catch up on the work she'd missed at Mercy Medical Center.

Damn it to hell! How did her life get so complicated?

———

2:35 PM – Carson Beach – South Boston

Devlin leaned against the metal railing, watching people in shirtsleeves stroll along gravel paths. Others dressed in shorts were jogging on the hard-packed sand near the water. It was unseasonably warm for October, the temperature in the mid-sixties. The tide was out and he could smell the pungent odor of seaweed. A seagull cawed as it swooped low over a clump of sea grass, flapped its wings and flew off with a tasty morsel in its orange beak.

It was a gorgeous day, sunny and warm. A perfect day for Judge Salvatore Renzi's wake. Renzi had posted a notice in the *Boston Globe*, giving the hours of the wake. The funeral was tomorrow.

He took off his jacket to soak up some sun. Sunny said he looked pale and told him to work on his tan. But he kept his Ray Bans on and his Red Sox baseball cap. He didn't want some Southie resident to notice him and strike up a conversation. He had business to conduct.

A car door slammed. He turned and saw Tank flick the locks on a black SUV, then hurry toward him. "Sorry I'm late, Dev. Got hung up in traffic. Big funeral in Southie."

And another one tomorrow in Swampscott. "How'd it go yesterday?"

"Excellent," Tank said, smiling broadly. "You wouldn't believe what they do at this place."

Enjoying his enthusiasm, he smiled. When Tank decided to solve a problem, he put his heart and soul into it. "Where is it?"

"Foster, Rhode Island, a rinky-dink little town out in the boonies near the Connecticut border. The guy that runs it hadda tell me how to get there. It's at the end of a dirt road that ain't on the map."

Tank tapped his head. "The guy's smart, don't want no cops to find it and start asking questions."

"No trouble on the highway? No speed traps?"

"No. The kid drove the Land Rover. I followed him in one of our disposables, a Toyota Camry, to make sure he didn't speed. After we got to Foster, I got in front, so he could follow me."

"You sure the guy who runs it won't talk?"

"Positive. Paid him in cash, said I might have more business for him, and we might. He's got a slick operation. He wanted nine hundred, but I knocked him down to seven. Worth every penny."

They fell silent as a young woman pushing a baby stroller approached them. Devlin smiled at her. "Beautiful day, isn't it?"

"Yes. I can't believe it's October. Feels more like April," she said, and kept walking.

"So," Tank said, taking up where he left off, "the kid drives the Land Rover through a big gate in an eight-foot chain link fence. I park the Camry inside the fence and the guy—his name is Ralph—chains the gate shut. He gives the Land Rover keys to one of his guys, has him drive it past some trees to this enormous crusher, plenty big enough to hold the Land Rover. A bale crusher, Ralph called it."

"You watched him do it?"

Tank's eyes lit up like a kid at a circus. "Are you kidding? I wanted to see how it works. They got it down to a science, Dev. First they pull out the battery and drain the the A/C unit. Then this yellow forklift with a big claw picks up the Land Rover like it's a Tinker Toy, puts it in the crusher."

"Did you take pictures?"

"Nah. Ralph wouldn't let me, said he don't want them showing up on the Internet. Anyways, then another guy starts the crusher." Tank made his eyes go wide and motioned with his hands. "This huge hydraulic press crushes the car, top down and from all sides. Two minutes later the Land Rover looks like a bale of hay, only metal, you know? A solid cube, three feet high, two feet wide, and five feet long."

"Wow!" Devlin said. "Imagine what could happen if someone was in the trunk."

Tank laughed. "That's how I got the idea. You ever see that movie *Goldfinger*? That's how he got rid of one guy. Anyways, after it's crushed into a metal cube, they load it onto a big flatbed truck with a bunch of other cubes. I called Ralph this morning. He said his crew loaded them onto a ship in Providence bound for China. The Land Rover is history."

Devlin clapped him on the shoulder. "Great work, Tank. You never cease to amaze me."

"What did you expect?" Tank said, grinning at him. "We're family."

"We need to set up a special Irish night at the Leprechaun Pub on Monday."

"What's happening on Monday?"

"That's when Sunny takes care of our other problem. Sean Whelan."

Tank frowned, his eyes serious now. "I don't know, Dev. That could be dangerous. I don't want him to hurt her."

"You're the one who suggested it. When I asked her, she wanted to do it right away. I told her to wait till we set up our alibi. I'll add a few extras for Monday's Irish night, order in extra food, maybe have some Irish music, and set up a dart contest in the game room so we'll have plenty of witnesses. You and I stay in the game room all night and bingo. There's our alibi."

"Okay," Tank said, still looking dubious. "How's Sunny gonna do it?"

"Invite him up for dinner, drug his drink and stick a chicken bone down his throat."

Tank burst out laughing. "Far out! We play darts while Whelan chokes on a chicken bone."

"Exactly. Once that's done, we get to work on the next part of my payback plan."

"What's the next part?" Tank said.

"We kidnap Maureen Renzi.

CHAPTER 14

Frank sat in the front pew of Holy Family Church, thinking about the last time he was here with his father. Christmas morning last year. They had spent the whole day together. After church they visited his mother's grave and left some flowers, went home and watched a Celtics game on TV, then went out for dinner.

A fantastic day, one that would never happen again.

Maureen was sitting beside him, with Evelyn on her other side. His NOPD friends filled the rest of the pew: Vobitch and Juliana, Kenyon and Tanya. Last night they wanted to treat him to dinner so he'd taken them to a local seafood restaurant overlooking Swampscott beach. Vobitch had prohibited any talk about the drive-by.

"Tell us about Swampscott," he'd said. "Tell us about your father." So they had a few drinks and ate seafood, and he talked about growing up in a small town by the ocean, population thirty-five thousand. Quaint and historic, until it went touristy with upscale bars and restaurants. A good place to grow up, and a good place to grow old. Until death came calling.

He'd said nothing about Judge Salvatore Renzi. His emotions were still too raw and he didn't trust himself not to break down.

But now he had to talk about his father.

He rose from his seat, paused at the center aisle to touch his father's casket and walked past the front pew where Rafe and Marcie were seated facing the pulpit. Rafe caught his eye and gave a nod of encouragement. Seated beside Rafe were five of his father's colleagues, three DA's and two federal judges.

Last night he hadn't slept much, lying awake in the house where he grew up, worrying about what to say at the funeral. But when he got up this morning and made himself a shot of espresso, the words had come to him, almost as if his father had sent him a message.

91

He adjusted the microphone and looked out at the congregation, the men dressed in somber black, some of the women wearing white, others wearing pastel-colored outfits like Marcie. All of them looked at him expectantly, wondering what he would say. Oddly, now that it was time for him to speak, he felt calm, almost peaceful.

"Thank you for coming. It makes me proud that so many people wanted to honor my father. To be honest, I couldn't decide what to say about him. I don't need to tell you what a great guy he was. A judge with integrity. A loyal friend. A loving husband and a wonderful father."

He gestured at the casket. "My father laid down the law in his courtroom and he laid it down at home, too. We didn't argue much. Until I got to high school and discovered girls and wanted to stay out late on the weekend." He saw a few nods and knowing smiles. "But my father never raised his voice. The only time I ever heard Dad raise his voice—"

He glanced at Rafe in the pew in front of him and smiled. "The only time I ever heard him raise his voice was at Boston Garden when one of the refs blew a call."

Laughter rippled through the church.

"Dad loved the Celtics." He paused a moment to steady himself. Now came the hard part.

"The last time I spoke to him—hard to believe it was less than a week ago—we talked on the phone. We gabbed about the Celtics for a while. Then Dad said he missed my mother." Recalling his father's words, he felt a rush of sadness. "They had an amazing relationship, a lifelong love affair. When she died ten years ago, he was devastated." He gripped the podium and uttered the fateful words, the words that tore at his heart.

"Then Dad said he wished I didn't live so far away."

Dead silence in the church.

He swallowed hard, fighting the lump that clogged his throat, knowing every eye in the church was focused on him. "And I thought about him, living by himself all those years after my mother died, his only child fifteen hundred miles away. He sounded … lonely. So I told him I'd get us some Celtics tickets, two seats behind the Celtics bench and we'd go to the game and have a great time."

Frank paused, hearing his father's voice in his mind.

"Just like old times, my father said." He touched the scar on his chin, willing away the tears that sprang to his eyes.

"He sounded happy like he always did when I saw him." He breathed deep to control his emotions.

"I never had time to get the tickets. But when I get home, I'm going to buy two tickets, two seats behind the Celtics bench where we always used to sit. Then I'll fly to Boston and go to the Garden and sit there and watch the game."

He paused a moment. "My father's seat will be empty."

He heard several gasps and audible sobs from some of the women.

Looking down at his father's casket, he raised his hand in a final farewell. "I'll be thinking about you, Dad, every second of the game, wishing you could be there with me. You're the best, Dad, the best father anyone could ever have. Love you."

Blinking back tears, he left the podium. As he passed the front pew Rafe got up and gave him a bear hug. "Beautiful, Frank. Your daddy'd be proud of you today."

"Thanks," he whispered, and kept walking. Blinded by tears, he sat down beside Maureen, who had tears running down her cheeks, her body shaking with sobs.

He put his arms around her and hugged her close. After a moment, she whispered, "What a beautiful thing to say, Dad. Grampa Sal was the best and so are you."

———

3:15 PM – South Boston

Bridget dabbed tartar sauce on a fried scallop and popped it in her mouth. Savoring the sweet juicy morsel, she looked around the Leprechaun Pub. Other than an older woman sitting with her husband at the bar, she was the only woman here. The Leprechaun Pub wasn't overtly macho—no fighting and no swearing allowed—but it was definitely male oriented, photographs of triumphant Celtics players mounted on the wall, celebrating their victory.

Chosen by Brian, no doubt. He only liked winners. Losers be damned.

Seated around the corner from her, he set aside his plate. A waitress hurried to their table and said, "How's everything, Mr. Devlin?"

"Excellent, Mary. Couldn't be better." Smiling at her, basking in the deferential attention.

"Can I get you anything else? Another beer? Some dessert?"

Brian turned to her and said, "Want something else, Bridget?"

"No thanks. I'm fine. The scallops were delicious."

After the waitress took their plates and left, Brian winked at her and said, "How's Bob?"

"Same as always, his usual crabby self." Her usual response to their in-side joke. Brian laughed, but she was in no mood to join him.

Yesterday he'd called and asked her to meet him here, an 80-mile round trip from her cottage in Plymouth. He didn't care if she had work to do, student papers to correct, midterm grades due at the registrar's of-fice. Impatient to leave and go home, she said, "You said Tank would be here. What's keeping him?"

"He'll be here soon. I wanted to eat lunch with you first. What's new? Anything exciting?"

"Did you see the news last night?"

He looked at her sharply, his eyes narrowed. "What news?"

"John Hinckley's lawyer is trying to get him extended visits with his mother, three weeks at a time. How can they do that? The guy is crazy! Thirty years ago, he shot President Reagan and wounded three other men. Reagan's press secretary, James Brady, almost died."

"Thirty years is a long time to spend in jail."

"He's not in jail, he's in a mental hospital for the criminally insane. Next thing you know they'll want to let him out for good so he can live with his mother!"

"So? He's an old man now, must be close to sixty."

"It doesn't matter how old he is. He's a creep. I saw him at Yale once when he was stalking Jody Foster. At the time I didn't know who he was. Jody had her circle of friends and I wasn't one of them. But after he shot Reagan, his picture was all over TV and I remembered seeing him."

Even now, recalling the dead look in his eyes gave her chills. Back then it had shaken her so badly she had Tank run background checks on her boyfriends to make sure they weren't nutcases. She could always de-pend on Tank.

He was like another brother. The one who wasn't in jail.

Brian glowered at her. "Thirty years is an eternity when you're locked up. Twice as long as I was, and that was bad enough."

"But you're not crazy like Hinckley. He convinced the psychiatrists that he was over his obsession with Jody Foster, but he wasn't. The first time they let him out, he bought a magazine with her picture on the cov-er. Another time when they let him visit his mother, he went to a book-store, sat in a corner reading books about presidential assassins."

Brian looked at her, his eyes cold as ice. "Sometimes we do what we have to do."

"John Hinckley is totally manipulative. He'll do anything to get what he wants." *And so will you.*

Unnerved by Brian's words and her reaction to them, she left the table, went in the ladies room, locked the door and stood at the sink. *Sometimes we do what we have to do.*

Brian wasn't crazy like Hinckley, but he would do whatever it took to get what he wanted. He might not lie to her. He just didn't tell her everything. That's what the Devlin family had always done. Present a normal facade to others and hide their secrets. There were certain things she didn't tell Brian, either, especially where Kate was concerned.

Sins of omission.

She took a bottle out of her purse and swallowed two extra-strength Tylenols, hoping to quiet the headache building behind her eyes. And the guilt feelings that plagued her.

The past is never dead. Her fate was sealed when Mom died giving birth to Kate, a cruel fate exacerbated by the dark dramas of childhood. She and Brian had made certain decisions in the distant and not-so-distant past. Irrevocable choices that had forever altered their future.

Back in 1995, Brian was twenty-four, busy running his Shamrock Gang. She was twenty-five, a college professor. Kate was twenty-three, still living with Pa in Southie. Pa wanted to entertain his girlfriend in private, so he introduced Kate to his drinking buddy, Jimmy O'Malley. Recently divorced, Jimmy was fifty-two and looking for a wife.

He fell for Kate in a big way. Why not? Kate was beautiful, and Jimmy wasn't looking for highbrow conversation. Kate was deliriously happy to have a boyfriend. A month later Jimmy proposed to Kate and gave her a diamond ring. Kate was thrilled and so was Pa. Even Brian was pleased, saying marriage would be good for Kate.

But they didn't have to worry about what would happen if Kate got pregnant and had a baby she was ill-equipped to care for. They assumed Bridget would take care of it. Like hell she would!

A motherless child thrust into adulthood far too soon, she had taken care of Kate for many years. Carefree games and childhood frivolity were for other girls, not her.

Years ago she had made sure she would never get pregnant. She had no intention of assuming responsibility for an infant.

She made an appointment with a sympathetic female gynecologist and explained the problem. Two days later, the doctor performed Kate's tubal ligation in her office. Kate thought the procedure was something all women did before they got married. "No need to tell Pa and Brian and Jimmy about it," Bridget had told her.

But there were unintended consequences. Impulse control had never been Brian's strong suit. He tended to shoot first and ask questions later.

She massaged her temples, recalling Kate's desolate expression at Jimmy's funeral, hauntingly beautiful in a black dress, copious tears flowing from her gorgeous green eyes.

Brian didn't attend the funeral. Jimmy's killer was in jail.

She still felt guilty. But not guilty enough to reveal her secret.

She closed her purse and left the restroom. Brian hadn't asked her to come here so they could have lunch together. He wanted something.

When she returned to their table, he said, "You know what's happening right now?"

"No. What?"

"A funeral for Judge Salvatore Renzi. Frank Renzi's father."

Shocked speechless, she stared at him.

"I told you it was payback time. I need your help for the next part."

"If you think I'm going to help you kill someone, you're crazy!"

"Bridget, I told you before. If I want someone dead, I don't need you to make it happen. How's your schedule next week? Got time for a quick trip to Baltimore?"

Baltimore. She gnawed her lip, recalling the shirt Kate had showed her when she stopped by this morning, the orange one she was wild about. A Baltimore Orioles jersey.

"What's in Baltimore? Is that where you got that jersey for Kate?"

Brian laughed, his eyes sparkling with delight. "She loved it. I got it for Halloween."

"What's in Baltimore, Brian?"

"Let's wait for Tank in the game room," he said and gave her his snake-charmer smile. "After he gets here, I'll tell you about Baltimore."

CHAPTER 15

SATURDAY October 22 – 3:00 PM – Swampscott

Maureen refilled her wineglass from a bottle of Merlot on the kitchen counter. Christ Almighty, her hands were shaking! Her nerves were shot, stressed to the breaking point from all the emotional turmoil.

Distraught about Grampa Sal, worried about Dad, worried most of all about the Jeremy problem.

Moments ago she'd met Dad's NOPD colleagues. Kelly O'Neil wasn't here, but Kenyon Miller was, teasing her. "Frank told me his daughter was beautiful, but sometimes Frank lies. Good to know he was telling the truth." Kenyon was even taller than Rafe, and his wife was tall, too.

Morgan Vobitch was the only one who didn't tower over her. Dad said his boss often dropped F-bombs, but not today. Maybe because his wife was with him. A beautiful black woman, tall like Marcie and Tanya. Morgan had put her at ease right away, asking how she liked being a doctor. She told him about her work at the hospital, saying she wasn't ready to do any hip replacements yet, but if he ever needed one to keep her in mind. That got a laugh.

But then he said, his slate-gray eyes full of concern, "Where's the hospital? Baltimore's a tough town. High crime rate, a lot of homicides."

"I know, but we live in a safe area." Saying *we* automatically. Appalled, she'd made an excuse and fled to the kitchen.

Forget *we*. No more plural pronouns. But the incident had reignited her fears.

When she got home tonight would Jeremy still be there?

She gulped some wine and went to the kitchen door. A white-paneled van stood in the driveway, the rear doors wide open, facing the steps to the door. Bold black letters along the side said: **3 GUYS CATERING.** Marcie's caterers had done a fabulous job. The kitchen table was almost as colorful as the foliage in Grampa Sal's backyard. Two kinds of dip for the red, yellow and orange pepper slices, assorted crackers, and slabs of brie, cheddar and Roquefort cheese. A huge platter held sandwich rolls: turkey, roast beef and tuna salad. Another held brownies and cookies.

Similar assortments were on tables in the living room, but she hadn't eaten anything. Her stomach was too jumpy.

But it was a gorgeous day, bright and sunny, warm enough for the men to take off their jackets. This almost felt like an open house, dozens of people coming and going, Grampa Sal's friends and colleagues, Dad's friends, some of the neighbors along the street.

The bathroom door down the hall opened and Marcie entered the kitchen, svelte and gorgeous in a slim black skirt and a hip-length mauve-and-gold tunic. "How you doing, girl? You look great in that dress, very stylish. Where'd you get it?"

"Thanks. I got it in Baltimore. Saks had a big sale two years ago. I figured I could always use a little black dress. I love your outfit. Did you design it?"

"Yes. It's one of my more popular ones." Marcie smiled. "Some folks don't like wearing black to a funeral. They prefer to send off their loved ones in something more … celebratory."

Maureen gestured at the table. "Your caterers did a marvelous job."

"If you want good food nicely presented, hire gay guys. Speaking of which, I better go see if they need anything." Marcie opened the kitchen door and went outside. Two seconds later she was back. "Your dad wants to see you in the sun porch."

Fearing something bad had happened, Maureen hurried down the hall past the bathroom and hooked a right to the sun room. Glassed in on three sides, it faced the backyard. The foliage was in full bloom, dozens of maple trees dotted with yellow, orange and red leaves.

To her relief, Dad was smiling, talking to an older man with freckles and red hair streaked with gray. Dad waved her over and said, "Say hello to Mike Flanagan. He was just talking about you. His brother was one of Grampa Sal's best friends."

"Hi Mike Flanagan," she said, smiling as she shook his hand. "Happy to meet you."

"Sure and it's a pleasure to meet you," Mike said, in a lilting Irish brogue. "I was just telling your dad what Patrick said about you. He's in the hospital, so I didn't tell him about your Grampa. Didn't want to distress him. Sal often came to visit him in the hospital, never missed a day on the weekend. They were great pals." With a broad grin, Mike said,

"They used to trade stories about their families. Sal was mighty fond of your Dad, and over the moon about you!"

"I felt the same about him," she said. "We're going to miss him, right Dad?"

Dad nodded, somber-eyed. "We're going to miss him a lot."

"I'm sure a fine man like Sal will be looking down upon you from Heaven," Mike said. "He was Patrick's friend, but I feel privileged to have met him."

"You're quite a guy yourself, " Dad said. He hesitated, then added, "Tell Patrick he'll see Sal in Heaven."

"That I will," Mike said. "I'd best be off to visit Patrick."

But as soon as Mike left, Rafe strode through the sun porch door, his face a dark thundercloud, his eyes angry.

He didn't even say hello to her.

"Frank," he said, " we need to talk. Outside."

———

4:05 PM – South Boston

Devlin flung a metal-tipped dart at one of the two dart boards mounted on the dark-paneled wall. Damn! Nowhere near the bulls-eye. He'd have to do better than that for the contest he'd set up for Monday night. While Sunny worked her magic on Sean Whelan.

The game room had no windows so he'd turned up the ceiling lights. A regulation pool table stood in the center of the room with a rack of balls on the green felt. At the far end, to the right of the emergency exit was a small bathroom with a toilet and sink. Monday night there would be music, but now the room was silent.

Bridget was sulking, pissed as hell because he wouldn't tell her about Baltimore until Tank got here. Seated at the poker table to the left of the exit door, she sipped from a bottled water, not looking at him, drumming her fingers on the edge of the table, silently fuming.

Bridget had an Irish temper only slightly less volatile than his own. Dangerous. He needed her help for his plan to work.

He heard the lock on the game room door click and heaved a sigh of relief. Other than Tank, he and the security tech were the only ones who had the code to unlock the door.

Tank burst inside, his shirt damp with sweat, and shut the door behind him. "Sorry I'm late, Dev." Then he spotted Bridget. "Hey Bridget, great to see you!"

Smiling, Bridget rose from her chair and embraced him.

"Want a beer, Tank? I'm having one," Devlin said.

"That'd be great," Tank said, taking a seat beside Bridget.

"One for you, Bridget?"

"No." Pointedly looking at her watch. "It's getting late and I have to drive back to Plymouth."

Ignoring her veiled complaint, he went to the bar beside the game room door, a three-foot-wide enclosure, no stools. Behind it, glasses and liquor bottles stood on a shelf. He bent down, took two bottles of Harp Ale out of a half-sized refrigerator and carried them to the poker table.

He took the chair beside Tank, popped the cap off his Harp Ale and took a swig.

"How was your day, Tank? Bridget and I had a fine lunch in the Pub."

"Brian, I have work to do, papers to correct," Bridget said. "Can we get on with it?"

Expressionless, Tank said nothing. He knew all about Bridget's Irish temper.

Devlin fought down his annoyance. He hated it when someone challenged him, but Bridget was family, and family was what this meeting was about. On the surface, at least.

"I know it's a hardship to drive here from Plymouth," he said, "but I've got a lot on my mind right now. Some of it has to do with Kate."

Bridget frowned. "What about Kate? She's fine. I stopped by to see her this morning."

"Right now she is, but that's not what I'm worried about. That's why I need you and Tank to go to Baltimore next week."

"And do what?" Bridget said. "You're not making sense."

"I need you to kidnap Maureen Renzi."

"Jesus-fucking-Christ! Are you out of your mind?" Bridget's cheeks flamed bright red. "I'm not killing anyone for you, Brian. How many times do I have to tell you that?"

Tank said nothing, silently staring at the poker table as if a winning hand lay before him.

100

"I don't want you to kill her. I want you and Tank to *kidnap* her. Wear masks so she can't see your faces, put her in a van and drive her to your cottage in Plymouth."

Bridget stared at him, her green eyes glinting with anger. "And then what, Brian? What am I supposed to do with her?"

"Take good care of her. Feed her, keep her comfortable."

"Keep her comfortable? Where? Not in my bedroom! Not in my office. Where the hell do I put her?"

"Wrong question. After we kidnap her, we send Renzi a ransom note."

Bridget started to speak but he silenced her with his hand.

"Do you ever worry about what will happen to Kate after we die? We're both getting older, Bridget. Something could happen to either of us. Terminal cancer, a heart attack or a stroke. Kate's well taken care of right now. But what happens when we die and the money runs out?"

Bridget said nothing, looking anxious now, fingering the pearl necklace around her neck.

"Renzi used Kate to put me in jail," he said. "I think it's only fitting to make him pay for her care, as long as she lives."

"How much ransom?" Bridget said.

"A million dollars." Again she started to speak, again he cut her off. "Don't tell me he hasn't got it. His father's house is worth plenty. He can use it as collateral for a loan. Bottom line, I don't give a damn how Renzi gets the money. If he cares about his daughter, he'll get it."

"Yeah, but how do *we* get it?" Tank asked, gazing at him now, his eyes somber.

"He packs it in a big suitcase, brings it to me, and we give him his daughter."

"He's a cop!" Bridget said, raking fingers through her long black hair. "With cop-friends. He might even ask the FBI to help him. Think, Brian! Kidnapping a person and transporting them across state lines is a federal crime."

"You worry too much, Bridget. I'll take care of it."

Take the money and kill the bastard.

———

Frank followed Rafe outside, hurrying to keep up with him. "What's wrong, Rafe?"

"Gotta show you something." Rafe took him behind the garage and pointed at the window.

He looked at the window, unlocked and open a half inch. "What about it?"

"That's how the bastard got in to fuck up the brakes on your father's car."

Stunned, he stared at Rafe. "Are you sure? How do you know?"

"Just got a call from my buddy at the BPD evidence garage where they towed your father's car. He told me someone fucked up the brakes." Rafe clenched his jaw, clearly angry. "Not only that, they found a three--inch dent in the back fender with paint flakes lodged in it. That was no accident, Frank. Your father was murdered."

"Sonofabitch," he muttered, his heart thundering in his chest, a sick feeling in his gut, chaotic thoughts whirling through his mind. Not an accident. Murder.

Rafe squeezed his shoulder, his dark eyes full of concern. "I know it's hard to believe, Frank. Could hardly believe it myself when he told me. But the evidence is there. If we send the paint flakes to the lab, we might ID the car that ran him off the road."

Overwhelmed, Frank tried to gather his thoughts. Bad enough that his father was alone when he died. A heart attack was one thing. Someone forcing him off the road into a tree was different.

A red haze of anger clouded his vision. "We need to find the fucker who did it. I'm flying back to New Orleans tomorrow, but I'll be back next Friday."

Rafe nodded. "I hear you, man. I'll get to work on it tonight, keep in touch by phone. You know anybody who had a grudge against your father?"

"No, but he put a lot of criminals in jail."

"So did you, Frank. We best check that angle, too."

Lost in thought, he didn't answer, the rage building inside him. His father, murdered.

No. His *Sicilian* father. Assassinated.

A scene from *The Godfather* spun into his mind, the restaurant scene when Al Pacino leaves the table and goes to the men's room to retrieve a gun taped to the tank of a toilet. A rival gang had tried to assassinate his father, leaving him comatose in the hospital. Back at the table, a member of the rival gang sits with the crooked cop who helped them do it.

Frank clenched his jaw, reliving the scene as if he were there, the stillness in the room as Pacino returns to the table, his face blank, the gun he will use to avenge his father hidden inside his jacket. The dirty cop's astonished expression when Pacino takes out the gun and puts a bullet in his forehead and another in the mobster's head.

"We'll get them, Frank," Rafe said, jolting him out of the movie.

But not completely.

He'd seen *The Godfather* many times, had even watched it with his father once. After the restaurant scene, Judge Salvatore Renzi had said, referring to Pacino's character: "The death of innocence that will lead to his ultimate downfall." At the time Frank had kept silent, thinking: *I would have done the same thing.*

Now, he said in a quiet voice, "Correct, Rafe. We will get them and we will make them pay."

CHAPTER 16

SUNDAY October 23 5:45 PM – Plymouth

Relieved that her midterm grades were done, Bridget left her office and went down the hall to the kitchen. She opened a cabinet, took out a bottle of Glenfiddich and set it on the counter. Tomorrow she would hand in her grades at the Registrar's office. But then she had to talk to her department chair.

I won't be in for the rest of the week. I have to go to Baltimore with my gangster friend and kidnap someone.

Yeah, right. She filled a rocks-glass with ice cubes, poured two fingers of scotch over them and took a sip, savoring the smoky taste. The fiery liquid soothed her scratchy throat but not her fears.

After she got home yesterday, she had used her laptop to find the obituary in the *Boston Globe*. Last Wednesday Salvatore Renzi, age 78, had died from injuries suffered in a car accident. Preceded in death by his beloved wife, Mary Sullivan Renzi. Survivors included a son in New Orleans, Franklin Sullivan Renzi—no mention of a wife, but maybe he was divorced—and a granddaughter, Maureen Renzi.

But it didn't say where Maureen lived.

How did Brian find out she lived in Baltimore? One of his hi-tech henchmen, probably. Brains or brawn, there were plenty of men ready, willing and able to do Brian's bidding.

Even as a kid Brian had swagger, and a furious intensity that frightened her. He didn't look like a gangster, no flashy suits, no pinky rings, but like all gangsters, he demanded respect and obedience.

Brian's emotional dependency needs demanding to be fed.

She sipped some scotch, recalling Kate's excitement when she showed her the orange jersey. "Brian got it for me," Kate had said. "He's the best brother in the whole world!"

A brother willing to kill anyone who got in his way, including Frank Renzi's father. She didn't believe the bit about a car accident. Accidents could be made to happen. If she asked Tank about it, he might not tell her. His fealty was to Brian, not to her. At yesterday's meeting, he hadn't said much. Tank seldom voiced any opposition to Brian.

Brian was hellbent on kidnapping Maureen Renzi and wanted her to hide the woman here.

But where would she put her? Her cottage was small—two bedrooms, a kitchen and a living room—the last house at the end of a cul de sac. Towering fir trees surrounded the cottage on three sides, hiding it from any prying eyes. Her closest neighbor lived beyond the garage.

Damned if she'd put the woman in her bedroom. The other bedroom served as her office. Forget the unfinished attic. The only access to it was a pull-down ladder. That left the basement.

Reluctantly, she went to the basement door in the hall and descended the stairs. It was chilly down here. No heat in the basement. An open doorway to the left led to the utility room. To her right, an arched door-way led to her workout room.

She flicked a light switch in the utility room, and two bare bulbs in the ceiling lit up a gray cement floor. The room smelled of heating oil. A 500-gallon oil tank and a furnace filled one wall. Opposite them, a deep cast-iron sink served as a drain for her washer. Beside the washer, a large dryer was vented through a small window. There was no room for a bed.

She shut off the lights. Opposite the basement stairs, a solid-steel door secured by a bolt lock opened onto walk-out stairs. When they drove Renzi's daughter here, they could back the van down the driveway and bring her in through the basement. And keep her there.

That way, Renzi's daughter would never see the inside of her house. Never be able to describe it after they let her go. Provided things went according to plan and they let her go.

But what if they didn't?

She hugged herself to ward off a sudden chill.

She turned on the lights in the exercise room. After she moved in, she got up early every day to jog on the beach three blocks away. But the winters were horrible: frigid temperatures, howling winds and mounds of snow.

After the first winter, she paid a local contractor to build her an exercise room, nothing fancy, knotty-pine paneling and two ceiling light fixtures. But she'd splurged on exercise equipment: a Nordic Track treadmill with a digital display, and an elliptical machine, easy on the joints and a great cardio workout.

Plenty of room for a folding bed here, and a portable toilet. Bridget wrinkled her nose. Damn! She'd have to come down here and empty the stinking pot in the toilet upstairs. And feed the woman, not that Brian would care. He made the plans and expected others to implement them.

Unwilling to think about it, she shut off the lights and went upstairs to the kitchen. She put fresh ice in the rocks-glass, added a healthy splash of Glenfiddich and sat down at the kitchen table. Was she really going to do this?

What if something went wrong in Baltimore?

What if they got the woman here and Renzi wouldn't pay the ransom?

What if the cops found the house?

Her overactive imagination supplied the sound track: the *whup-whup* of helicopters above her house, FBI agents on bullhorns yelling: *Come out of the house with your hands on your head!*

Jesus-fucking-Christ, she'd go to jail! A shudder wracked her. She knew exactly how bad life in prison could be, had seen this countless times when she'd visited Brian.

Maybe she wouldn't do it.

But if she refused, Brian would hate her.

Well, he might not hate her. They'd been through too much together as kids, dealing with an alcoholic father who drowned his sorrows in booze and a mentally handicapped sister. Even when Brian killed Kate's husband, she didn't hate him for it. In fact, she was relieved. Good riddance to the bastard. Kate was better off without him.

But she still felt guilty. Kate's tubal ligation had led to unintended consequences. An angry husband who wanted a son. Brian locked up in prison fifteen years for killing him.

In the end, it always came back to Kate. And family.

She drained the last of the scotch, ruminating over what Brian had said yesterday. "Kate's fine right now, but who will take care of her after we're dead and the money runs out?"

He was right. Last year, another professor in her department had been diagnosed with Stage IV breast cancer. Despite a double mastectomy, chemotherapy and radiation treatments, the woman had lasted only three months.

What if that happened to her?

A million dollars would insure that Kate was taken care of for the rest of her life, no matter what happened to her and Brian. Besides, how could the cops find out she was involved? Even if they suspected Brian, they wouldn't connect him to her. Like a puff of smoke, Bridget Devlin had disappeared after that bogus ceremony years ago when she'd married Bob White.

Everyone at the college and around town knew her as Bridget White, the name that appeared on the deed to the cottage.

Not only that, if she refused to help Tank kidnap Renzi's daughter, Brian would get Sunny to do it. She'd met Sunny once at her cat-house in Southie, a Nordic blonde with a hard face and bright blue eyes, smiling when Brian introduced them. But her eyes remained cold.

A fitting partner for Brian, both of them posing as upstanding citizens, even as they broke the law with impunity.

No doubt about it. If she didn't help Tank kidnap Renzi's daughter, Sunny would. Not only that, Brian would have a psychological club to hold over her. Kate was family, and she had refused to help him look out for Kate's future welfare.

Tomorrow night he and Tank were holding some sort of shindig at the Leprechaun Pub. On Tuesday morning, she and Tank would drive to Baltimore. She would use one of Brian's disposable cars.

Tank would drive a van with dark tinted windows and a roomy rear compartment.

Where they would hide Maureen Renzi and drive her to Plymouth.

———

6:05 PM – Boston – Logan Airport

When Rafe took the turn for Terminal C Departures, Frank pocketed his phone. No weather delays. His plane would land in New Orleans before midnight. He wanted to stay here and find the bastard who'd murdered his father, but yesterday he had told Vobitch he'd be back on Monday to work the drive-by case. That was before Rafe dropped the bombshell last night.

Hip to his dark mood, Rafe hadn't said much during the drive to the airport. When Frank thanked him for his help and asked how much the caterers cost, Rafe had said, "Don't worry about it, Marcie gets the bill, she'll send you a copy, and we'll split it."

Now Rafe pulled his unmarked SUV to the curb, turned to face him and said, "Did you tell Maureen the accident wasn't an accident?"

"No. She's flat out right now, working twelve hours a day, five days a week, studying for the board exams on weekends. I wasn't even sure she'd be able to come up for the funeral. She doesn't need to be worrying about this right now."

"I think you should tell her, Frank. Warn her to be careful."

Frank was about to speak when his phone rang. He took it out and checked the Caller ID. Unknown caller. The same number as before. "Sorry, Rafe. I gotta take this."

He punched on and said, "Renzi."

Silence on the other end. Faint breathing. His neck prickled.

"Talk to me," he said softly.

A faint quavery voice said, "It's Angela. I need to talk to you, but not on the phone."

She sounded scared. "Are you safe?"

"No." A whisper. "I can't talk now. Can you meet me?"

"Yes, but not tonight. I'm in Boston, be back in New Orleans tomorrow. Can you meet me tomorrow night? Our usual spot?"

"Yes." And the line went dead.

"Damn." To Rafe, he said, "That was one of my old CI's, might have a tip about that drive-by I told you about. She already called me twice, didn't say anything and hung up. She sounded scared. I haven't seen her in five years. She might have gotten mixed up with the wrong people."

"Mmm-mmm," Rafe said, shaking his head. "Gang-type people?"

"Yes, unfortunately. I'll meet her tomorrow night, see what she's got to say."

"Good luck with that," Rafe said. "You'll be back next weekend?"

"Yes. Get in late Friday night, fly back Sunday night, same flight as this one. I talked to the couple who live next door to my father's house. They said they'd keep an eye on it. I gave them a key so they can take the mail inside."

"Good. I'll ask my trooper pal to swing by the house twice a day, make sure things are okay."

"Thanks. But the most important thing is the investigation."

"Already at the top of my list," Rafe said. "My gang-unit guys will help me get a list of the men your father put in jail, see if any of 'em got out on parole. I'll check the Boston PD files, find out who you sent to jail when you were working homicide."

"Why? Someone killed my father, not me. If they wanted to kill me, they'd have done it already. Check the paint flakes, see if you can ID the car that forced him off the road."

Rafe frowned at him, clearly unhappy. "Partner, I'm gonna lay it on the line. Whoever killed your father was no amateur. No telling what they might do next. Maybe your ex-wife and daughter aren't even a blip on their radar screen. But maybe they are. Tell them to be careful."

"I can't tell Evelyn. She'd flip out. You know how she is, calls me at two in the morning sometimes when she has one of her panic attacks."

"I'll contact the Milton cops," Rafe said, "have them keep an eye on the house. But talk to Maureen and tell her to be careful. Call her tonight when you get home."

"Okay," he said, knowing he wouldn't. By the time he got home, Maureen would already be in bed, sleeping.

He'd call her tomorrow after she got home from work.

———

7:15 PM – Baltimore

"Jeremy, why are you still here?" Maureen said, furious but trying to stay calm. "I told you to move your stuff out of the apartment before I got back."

"Why should I get out while you're in Boston? I need time to—"

"Bullshit!" she screamed. Forget calm. She was too tired to be calm, too exhausted to listen to his excuses. "I just got home from a funeral, Jeremy. My *grandfather's* funeral. The grandfather I adored ever since I was a kid. The man who loved me a hell of a lot more than you do!"

"No need to scream at me, Maureen. I need to pack a lot of stuff—"

"Take tomorrow off, pack your belongings and hire a U-Haul to put them in. Do I have to explain how to do that or could you figure that out all by yourself?"

Silence in the room.

Glowering at her, Jeremy stood by the kitchen counter. She wanted to slap him. Fearing she would, she clenched her hands behind her back.

"I can't take tomorrow off," he said. "My schedule is packed solid until seven PM."

Shaking with anger, she fired her last-resort salvo, the one she'd spent three hours thinking about on the plane. "If you're not out of here by seven o'clock Tuesday morning, I will file a breach of promise suit against you. I already talked to a lawyer." She hadn't, but so what? Jeremy had lied to her plenty of times.

"I thought you'd calm down after we spent three days apart, but I guess you haven't. Why should I get out by Tuesday? I already paid my share of the rent."

"Fuck your share of the rent! If your stuff isn't gone by seven AM on Tuesday, I'll go see my lawyer. I've got evidence, remember? Credit card statements with restaurant and motel bills. Think about what *that* will do to your dental practice when it comes out in court."

Dead silence in the room. A venomous glare from Jeremy.

At last he said, "Okay, if that's the way you want to play this, I'll get someone to help me move out Tuesday morning. But I want my share of the rent money back."

"You'll get it after your stuff is gone. I'm tired and I have to work tomorrow. Tonight I'm sleeping in *my own bed*." She jerked her thumb at the door. "Use your damn credit card and sleep in a motel tonight."

CHAPTER 17

On Irish Night the Leprechaun Pub was always jumping. Tonight even the game room was jammed. Leaning against the bar, Devlin smiled. If he needed an alibi, it didn't get much better than this.

Packed with boisterous revelers, the room was so noisy he could barely hear the music in the Pub dining room. He'd hired an Irish folk duo, a girl fiddler who sang traditional Irish songs and her boyfriend who played the concertina.

Off to his right, Tank had cracked open the emergency exit door to let out the smoke from his cigar. No smoking allowed in the Pub, but no one would dare question Tank. He caught Tank's eye and gestured around the room. Tank gave him a thumbs-up, but no smile, worrying about Sunny, Devlin presumed. Whelan was supposed to meet her in the executive suite at her hotel at six and it was already ten past.

Cheers and catcalls erupted at the opposite end of the room where men were pitching darts at two dart boards. Yesterday he'd posted fliers along the street about the contest. A dozen men had signed up on the scroll of paper he'd taped to the wall beside the targets. The winner of each game advanced to the next round.

Eventually, it would come down to two men. The winner of that game got to play Brian Devlin for the big prize.

He would lose, of course, and give the happy winner five crisp one-hundred dollar bills. Should questions later arise, everyone would remember that Brian Devlin had been playing darts here, while Sean Whelan choked to death on a chicken bone.

The spicy aroma of barbecued chicken filled the air as two waitresses entered the game room, beautiful Irish girls with auburn hair, Irish blue eyes and flawless complexions. One carried a large pan of barbecued chicken legs and wings, the other a platter of sandwiches.

Raising her voice to be heard, the prettiest one said, "Hi Mr. Devlin, how's it going in here?"

"Everything's perfect, Maggie. Thanks for putting out a great spread."

"You're welcome, Mr. Devlin. Irish Night is always fun! Everyone heard about the dart contest, so we've got an overflow crowd tonight."

The women carried the containers of food to the poker table in the corner. Now a wide board topped with a green-and-white tablecloth covered the table. They set down fresh food, collected the empty platters and returned to the dining room. A few men ogled them as they passed, but didn't bother them.

The Leprechaun Pub had strict rules. No fighting, no cursing and no hassling the waitresses. Anyone who broke the rules was immediately escorted outside. Most never returned.

A sharply-hit ball striking freshly-racked balls on the pool table drew his attention. Two men stood beside the table. Devlin went to the pool table and put his arm around one man's shoulder. "How's it going, Red? You feeling the luck of the Irish tonight?"

Red beamed him a smile, his blue eyes sparkling with delight. "Indeed I am, Mr. Devlin, thanks to you. Sure and it's a fine thing that you do, maintaining our Irish heritage."

"It's the least I can do. We all know the obstacles our ancestors had to overcome and we must never forget them."

He raised his bottle of Harp Ale. "Let us celebrate their successes."

"Hear, hear," said the man beside Red, raising his beer bottle.

Other men nearby joined in the chorus. "Hear hear!"

"Enjoy the game," he said, as Tank caught his eye and jerked his thumb at the exit door.

Devlin went to the door and stepped outside into the cool night air.

Anxiously puffing his cigar, Tank said, "I'm worried about Sunny. One of the Rottweilers just called. Whelan's there, didn't look happy when he found out he wasn't meeting Sunny in her apartment."

"Don't worry. Sunny can take care of herself."

Tank frowned. "Jesus, Dev. He's got a hundred pounds on her. Fuck this chicken bone shit. What if he beats her up and—"

Devlin iced him with a look. "That's the plan, Tank. Sunny will be fine."

She'd better be. If Whelan hurt her, he'd kill the bastard himself.

———

With a delicious sense of anticipation, Sunny smoothed the sleeve of her carefully chosen dress and waited, her heart thrumming her chest. Soon Sean Whelan would knock on the door, never dreaming she was about to inflict her long-awaited revenge upon him.

He expected to have sex with her. Like hell! He would choke to death on a bone instead.

Two Rottweilers would stand outside the door, ready to protect her.

All well and good, but she had her own weapons. The sleeves of her knee-length teal dress were fitted to the elbow, then flared out to her wrists. Beneath the flared sleeve, a five-inch knife was Velcroed to her left forearm. A small derringer was Velcroed to her thigh.

A sharp rap sounded on the door, then another.

She put on a welcoming smile and opened the door. "Hello, Sean. Thanks for meeting me."

Wearing black slacks, a white shirt and an ugly frown, he stepped into the room. "How come we're meeting here? I thought we were meeting in your apartment."

"They're renovating it. The place is a mess, so I booked us the executive suite." She gestured around the room. "It's lovely, isn't it?"

The lights were on a dimmer, lowered slightly for a hint of intimacy. A three-cushion black leather couch stood against one wall. In front of the couch, a low rectangular table was decorated with two red roses in a crystal vase and elegant place settings for two: fine china, silverware and linen napkins.

Leering at her, he said, "I wanted to meet in your apartment. I got great memories of the last time we were there."

The night when you raped me. With a business-like smile, she said, "Let's have a cocktail. I had the chef prepare a special dinner for us. Sauteed asparagus, potatoes Almondine and Irish game hens."

Cornish game hens, actually, but Whelan was too stupid to know the difference.

"You still look great, Sunny. Big tits and a great ass. How about a kiss?"

He took a step closer, but she held up her hand. "Not now, Sean. Let's have a cocktail."

She went to the sideboard on the wall opposite the couch. An ice bucket stood beside cut crystal glasses and several liquor bottles.

"What would you like?"

He came closer, his predatory eyes devouring her body. "I'd like to rip off that dress and see you naked."

A gusher of fear rose inside her, but she fought it down.

"Bad idea, Sean. That would force me to tell Brian about it. Let's have a cocktail." She opened the ice bucket, used metal tongs to put ice cubes in a rocks glass and poured a generous amount of Dubliner Irish Whiskey over the ice.

He took the glass and set it on the sideboard. "You're a tease, you know that, Sunny? Put on a sexy low-cut dress and expect me to settle for a drink."

"When I invite a man to have dinner with me, I expect him to act like a gentleman."

Without warning, he grabbed her and pulled her against him, slobbering over her, his lips seeking her mouth, his muscular arms pressing her arms against her torso.

Damn, he was strong! Scarcely able to breathe, she turned her face away to escape his disgusting lips.

He raised one hand to grasp her head, still slobbering at her, but she managed to free her right arm. She reached inside her sleeve, pulled out the knife and pressed the blade against his throat. "Let go of me or you're a dead man. This knife will slice through your carotid artery like butter. You'll bleed out in thirty seconds."

His eyes widened and he released her. "Jesus Christ, Sunny! Calm down, okay? I didn't mean nothing."

"You meant to force yourself on me and I don't like it. Take your drink and sit on the couch."

Pouting, he did as he was told.

Shaken by the encounter, she put the knife beside the ice bucket and fixed herself a watered-down cocktail, calming herself to prepare for the next move. Deliberately taking a seat on the opposite end of the couch, she raised her glass. "Here's to a pleasant evening, Sean. How's your drink?"

He gulped half of it down, set the glass on the table and swiveled his brawny hard-body toward her, his eyes brimming with anger. "You said you needed a favor. What's the favor?"

"How's life treating you, Sean? Things must be different now that Brian's out of prison."

"Yeah, well, he ain't no pushover to work for, that's for sure." Whelan picked up his glass and gulped some whiskey. "Someday he's gonna make some dumb-ass mistake and go to jail forever. Whaddaya gonna do then, Sunny?"

"Brian doesn't make mistakes, Sean." She rose to her feet. "Let me freshen your drink."

She took his glass and went to the sideboard. Now came the tricky part.

"This room has a magnificent view at night. Go look out the window and see all the lights." *So you won't see me doctor your drink.*

Whelan rose from the couch and turned toward the window.

A knock sounded on the door.

Damn, dinner is here and I'm not ready.

Whelan turned, his expression sullen.

She gave him her happy face and said, "Room service, Sean. Our dinner has arrived. Could you let them in?"

Whelan crossed the room and opened the door. One of the Rottweilers pushed a cart into the room. He was six inches taller than Whelan and considerably wider, his tuxedo barely contained his broad shoulders. Giving her a pointed look, he said, "Everything okay, Sunny?"

"Everything is fine, thank you. Leave the cart beside the sideboard. We're going to have another cocktail before we eat dinner."

The Rottweiler nodded and went to the door. "Call me if you need anything."

"Thank you, I will." What she needed was something to make Whelan stop watching her so she could drug his drink.

Then, like a bolt sent from Heaven, fate intervened.

"Where's the bathroom?" Whelan said. "I gotta take a leak."

"Right through there," she said, pointing at the door to the bedroom beside the couch.

As soon as he disappeared she refreshed his drink, opened the drawer of the sideboard and took out the vial of GHB. She squirted it into Whelan's glass and smiled. Now *that* was a cocktail.

She heard the toilet flush. Her heart sped up, thumping her chest. Hurrying now, she added ice cubes to her own glass, took both glasses to the coffee table and sat on the couch.

Whelan came out of the bedroom, went to the room service cart and took the metal lid off one of the dinners. Delicious aromas filled the air.

"Smells great," he said. He replaced the lid, sat down on the couch and gulped his drink. "How come you need me to do you a favor? Why didn't you ask Brian to do it?"

"It's complicated." She held up her cocktail. "This Dubliner Irish Whiskey is excellent, isn't it?"

Eyeing her steadily, Whelan said, "What's the favor?"

"One of the doormen has been bothering my girls. I warned him about it, but he didn't get the message."

She raised her glass and took a pretend-sip. *Keep drinking you idiot.*

Whelan silently drank from his glass and set it on the coffee table.

"I need someone to teach him a lesson, Sean."

She raised her cocktail to her lips, willing him to drink more of his.

He didn't, gazing at her, expressionless.

"You're good at that, Sean. Rough him up a bit, so he'll stop bothering my girls."

Whelan smiled, preening at the praise, downed the rest of his whiskey and nodded. "I could do that."

"That would be such a big help to me."

"Why don't you have Devlin handle it?"

She put down her glass and smiled into his eyes. "I'm afraid Dev would kill him."

He looked at her, bleary-eyed, his eyelids drooping. "Yeah?"

That was the last word Sean Whelan spoke. Like a giant Sequoia cut down in a forest, his thick muscular body slowly tilted to one side and toppled sideways onto the couch.

Sunny rose to her feet and heaved both of his legs onto the couch.

Okay, the first part was done. She dashed to the sideboard, took a pair of latex gloves out of the drawer and put them on. She sidestepped to the room service cart and took the lid off the game hens. Ignoring the zesty aroma, she grasped one game hen and ripped off part of the ribs.

Holding them in her gloved hand, she approached the couch.

Whelan lay on his back, eyes shut, his mouth partly open. Perfect.

CHAPTER 18

MONDAY – October 24 – 6:15 PM – New Orleans

Frank drove past Popeye's, turned right at the next corner and parked beside a huge live oak tree. No sign of Angela's car. A high-school dropout, she'd been busted for hooking, got off with probation and got out of the life. Eight years ago in 2003, he'd recruited her to be his CI.

By then she was twenty-four, with no husband and two-year-old twin boys. She and the boys lived with her mother. He never paid her for information, but he usually bought her a big bucket of Popeye's chicken.

Now Angela was twenty-nine. What cards had life dealt her since then? Given her obvious fear when she talked to him on the phone, nothing good.

A flash of motion caught his eye, and then Angela was tapping on the passenger side window.

"It's open," he said, waving her into the car.

She got in and slumped in the passenger seat, not looking at him. His dome light was rigged to stay off when the door opened, so he couldn't see much of her face, but he could see her outfit. A short black skirt that ended mid-thigh, a low-cut red blouse and high-heeled red shoes. A hooker outfit if ever he saw one.

"Good to see you, Angela. I didn't see your car so I was worried you wouldn't show up."

Still not looking at him, she said, "Don't have a car no more."

"Talk to me, Angela. You know something about the drive-by?"

"Know what car they used." She rolled her lips together and heaved a sigh. "Heard about that little boy that died, made me want to cry."

"Your boys must be getting big now. How are they doing?"

Her hands clenched in her lap and a muscle jumped in her jaw.

After a moment, she said, "That car they used? They torched it and dumped it over in Hollygrove."

117

His heart sped up, thrumming his chest. "What kind of car?"

"Big black BMW, don't know what year. A couple years old maybe."

"Great. Can you show me where they dumped it?"

"No! They find out I tol' you, they'll kill me!" Gazing at him, her large dark eyes wide, pin-prick pupils. Coked-up, he realized, and she knew he'd seen it, ducking her head now.

He reached over and took hold of her arm, so thin he could almost feel her bones. Doing drugs and not eating.

"You don't have to show me," he said quietly. "What's going on? They pimping you out?"

A tiny nod. "Got me hooked on the shit, you know, and now I got nothin'." She stifled a sob and whispered, "They took my boys."

Fearing the worst, he clenched his jaw. "Who did?"

"Social services. They be cryin' and carryin' on one day at school, tol' the teacher I didn't get up for two days, so she reports me and social services came to the house and took them."

His heart ached for her. The twins had always been her pride and joy, bragging about them: *Jamal's talking up a storm. Rasheed, he's into everything. Got a mind of his own.* And when Frank warned her not to do drugs: *No drugs for me. Got my boys to think of.* Smiling at him back then, her white teeth gleaming, looked like a model in a magazine ad.

Now she was strung out on dope, smoking crack probably, and hooking again.

"Angela, you did a brave thing, calling me, telling me about the car. But you need to get away from these guys. I've got a friend in Boston who can get you into rehab—"

"Boston? My kids are here! I can't leave them here." Frantically scratching her scalp, like a strung-out addict.

"You're not thinking straight, Angela. You need to get clean, get yourself together and come back here. Then you'll get your kids back."

She hiccoughed a sob and brushed tears from her cheeks. "You always been good to me, Frank. But I got no money. How do I get to Boston?"

"Don't worry about that. I'll take care of it. Can you get away from them tonight?"

"Not tonight," she said quickly. "Might be able to do it tomorrow."

"Good. Tell me where they dumped the car."

"Dead end dirt road off Fig Street." Gesturing vaguely with her hand.

"Thanks. I'll find it." He took out his wallet. "You need money?"

Another heavy sigh. Not looking at him, she mumbled, "Tol' him I be meetin' a john."

Sickened by the thought, he took out two twenties and gave them to her. "Take a bus to the Lakeside Mall tomorrow. Be there by six o'clock. Wait in the parking garage outside the second floor entrance to Dillard's and I'll pick you up."

"Thank you," she whispered, and opened the car door.

He grabbed her arm and made her look at him. "Make sure you meet me tomorrow. You can do this, Angela. Don't do it for me, do it for your boys."

She nodded, her eyes gleaming with tears. And then she was gone.

———

7:15 PM – South Boston

Sunny stood between the coffee table and the couch, her heart pounding a fierce rat-a-tat-tat inside her chest. Ten minutes had passed since Whelan collapsed on the couch. He hadn't moved since, but soon he would come out of his drug-induced stupor. She had already crammed the ribs from one game hen into his mouth and partway down his throat.

Now came the hard part.

An ampule of succinylcholine—a 40 mg dose—lay on the table. Brian had friends in convenient places, in this instance a veterinarian, a heavy gambler deeply in debt who owed Brian money. He used a succinylcholine to put sick and severely disabled animals out of their misery. He had readily agreed to give her the drug and hadn't asked why she needed it.

But the timing was crucial.

If she injected the drug too soon, it would paralyze Whelan within seconds, his extremities first, then his arms and legs, then his torso. Swallowing and breathing would become increasingly difficult. Unable to breathe, he would die within sixty seconds.

She didn't want him to die right away. She wanted to talk to him.

But if he awoke from his stupor before the drug took effect, he would gag on the bones in his throat and try to remove them. She had considered binding his wrists with zip-ties, but if he struggled to free his hands, as he surely would, the zip-ties would leave marks on his wrists.

The cops would notice them and suspect foul play.

She couldn't have that.

Sunny glanced at the clock. Twelve minutes since he'd fallen into a stupor. Whelan was tremendously strong. Even with zip-ties on his wrists, he might lash out and hurt her. Worse, desperate to get the bones out of his throat, he might lunge to his feet and charge around the room, knocking things over. She couldn't have that, either.

She couldn't ask the Rottweilers to protect her. When she delivered her speech to Whelan, she didn't want any witnesses. She pulled up her skirt, released the Velcro strip that held the derringer against her thigh and set the gun on the coffee table.

Worst case scenario, she'd shoot him.

Best case scenario, the bastard would die a slow terrifying death.

With her gloved-hand, she picked up the ampule of succinylcholine, twisted off the cap and set the cap on the table. The least noticeable place to inject the drug was his scalp. A single needle prick, hidden by his hair. Hit him with the drug and slap his face to wake him up.

She set the needle against his scalp behind his ear and pushed the plunger.

Whelan moved slightly and his hands twitched.

She slapped his face. "Wake up, Sean. Time for us to have a little talk."

His eyes opened and fixed on her face. Then he frowned.

He raised his arms. Opened his mouth. Made a guttural sound. "Er-rrg."

His arms dropped to his chest.

She smiled. "What's the matter, Sean? Are the bones in your throat bothering you?"

His pale blue eyes widened, the frown lines them deepened and his face got red.

His mouth opened and emitted a choking sound. "Awwwwk."

In a matter-of-fact voice, she said, "This is how it feels to be power-less, Sean."

His right leg moved an inch or so and flopped on the couch. His face got redder, making the freckles on his cheeks stand out, his lungs desperately seeking a life-saving breath of air.

"How do you like being powerless, Sean? Not much fun, is it?"

"Auuwwwk." Another choking sound.

And the moment she had been waiting for arrived. Fear entered his eyes, then full-blown terror.

She picked up his limp right hand. Smiling at him, she said, "This hand will never squeeze another tit."

She waggled his forefinger. "And this finger will never invade another woman's pussy."

His face turned crimson, and veins stood out on his forehead.

But not a muscle in his body moved, not even his nostrils.

She gave him her feral smile. "No more sex for you, Sean. No more forcing women to do what you want."

Now his eyes were bugging out of his head, the veins in his forehead throbbing wildly.

"No point in struggling, Sean. In a few seconds you'll be dead."

Ten seconds later he was, his pupils fixed, his mouth open.

She placed a gloved finger against the artery in his throat. No pulse. She pumped her fist in the air. "May you rot in Hell!"

But she had no time to savor her triumph. Moving quickly, she took a large trash bag out of the sideboard drawer and returned to the coffee table. She put the cap on the ampule and dropped it into the trash bag.

Leaving remnants of the game hen on Sean's plate, she scraped the potatoes and asparagus into the bag to make it appear that he had eaten most of his dinner. She did the same with her own plate, not that she had eaten anything. It was all about appearances. Leave no evidence.

Fearing Sean's glass might have traces of GHB in it, she took it in the bathroom, flushed the contents down the toilet, put the glass in the trash bag and returned to the sideboard. Took the empty vial of GHB out of the drawer and put it in the trash bag. She fixed another cocktail for Sean, mostly water, a bit of ice, a dollop of Dubliner.

Her glass was fine. But her weapons had to go.

She took out a smaller trash bag, put the knife and the derringer into it and took a final look around the room.

Her carefully-crafted plan had gone off without a hitch.

An orgasmic sensation rippled through her, warming her cheeks and dampening her crotch. The ultimate satisfaction that comes when you defeat your most hated enemy.

But she still had things to do. Have one Rottweiler take the trash bag with the weapons to her apartment; have the other one put the large trash bag in the hotel dumpster. Then call hotel security.

No hurry on that score. Whelan wasn't going anywhere.

Suitably frantic, she would tell them her dinner companion had fallen ill. Let them call 911. While they waited for the ambulance, she would mentally rehearse what she would tell the EMT's.

No worries there. She had her story down pat.

She took out her burner phone and dialed a number.

———

Devlin stood outside the emergency exit with Tank, sweating in the cool night air, anxiously awaiting Sunny's call.

Clearly worried, Tank said, "It's after seven, Dev. Want me to call the Rottweilers?"

"Not yet. Let's wait for Sunny to call." But he was worried, too.

Then, as if the mere mention of her name conjured her call, his phone rang. Sunny.

He nodded to Tank, punched on and said, "How's it going?"

"Mission accomplished!"

"Excellent," he said. "Are the accessories taken care of?"

"Yes, but I'll explain later. Right now I have to work myself into a believable state of semi-hysteria and call security."

"Don't get into what happened with them," he warned. "Loose lips."

"Don't worry, I won't. Rest easy, Dev. It's done," she said, and ended the call.

"No worries," he said to Tank. "Sunny's got everything under control."

"Great!" Tank said. "She's something, ain't she?"

"Indeed she is. Now that Whelan's out of the way, are you set to drive to Baltimore?"

"First thing tomorrow. I'm meeting Bridget at her place in Plymouth at seven."

"Good," Devlin said. "But she's not happy about this. She gives you any problems, call me and I'll talk to her." He smiled grimly. "I'll make her understand that this is one job she can't refuse."

CHAPTER 19

TUESDAY October 25 – 6:30 AM – New Orleans

Ten hours after they located the burned out BMW, Frank and Kenyon went to see the 'banger who had survived the drive-by. Alonzo Stokes wasn't happy to see them, lying in a hospital bed hooked up to a multitude of machines, a feeding tube threaded down his nose.

"Why you messing with me?" Alonzo said. "I got enough problems, never take a normal shit again as long as I live."

Frank offered him no sympathy. "Word on the street says you popped one of the MSM boys a while back,"

"That's bullshit, man. Don't know what you're talking about."

"Talking about the MSM gunslingers that ambushed you," Kenyon said.

"Give us names," Frank said. "You know who they were."

Alonzo glowered at them. "Fuck that, man."

They pushed him for twenty minutes but he wouldn't budge, didn't know nothing, didn't see nothing, didn't hear nothing.

Frank took Kenyon out in the hall and said, "Why won't he talk?"

Kenyon shrugged. "No mystery there. If he talks and they hear about it, he'll be dead by sundown."

"Those MSM gunslingers didn't just happen to be there. They set it up. Probably sent him a text. That's how these thugs communicate these days. Let's get a warrant for his cellphone."

"Okay," Kenyon said, "but how? It's personal property, locked in his locker."

Frank smiled. "I know how to do it."

Two hours later, exhausted but energized, they walked into Vobitch's office. Eagerly awaiting them, Vobitch said. "You got good news for me? Please tell me you got names."

"We got a name," Kenyon said. "Stayed up all night to get it."

"Excellent," Vobitch said, smiling at them. "I knew you two would solve this fucking case."

"Got a tip from one of my old CI's," Frank said. "She wasn't involved in the drive-by, but she told me where the shooters ditched the car. I called Kenyon right away."

"The car was a burned out hulk," Kenyon said. "No plates, but we got the VIN off one of the engine parts and called it in. A black BMW stolen two months ago. We had it towed to the evidence garage, got a warrant to search the car. We'll see what they find."

"We did a sweep of the ground all around the car," Frank said. "We found two shell casings and a couple of blue latex gloves, used."

"Great," Vobitch said. "Might get DNA off the gloves if we're lucky."

"Not anytime soon," Frank said, "but the lab techs worked overtime, processing the casings."

"That's what got us the name," Kenyon said. "They lifted a print off one casing, ran it through the computer and guess who we found?"

"Jesus Christ!" Vobitch exclaimed. "Tell me before I wet my pants!"

Kenyon laughed, a low-pitched rumble. "Okay. Wouldn't want you to embarrass yourself. A Hollygrove banger, name of Jamal "Tiny" Jackson. But here's the best part. Frank and I took another look at the surveillance videos we collected from businesses near the drive-by. Two AM we're bleary-eyed, spot a black BMW driving past a convenience store two streets over."

"We zoomed in on it," Frank said. "One guy's driving, another riding shotgun, both of them wearing latex gloves and hoodies. Kenyon saw enough of the driver's face to ID Jamal Jackson."

"What about the second guy?" Vobitch asked.

"No ID," Frank said, "but if we nail Jamal Jackson and squeeze him, he might talk."

"We got nothing off the dead banger's phone," Kenyon said, "but we figured all along that Alonzo Stokes was target. And Alonzo got lucky, lived to shoot another day."

"We've still got guards posted at the hospital, right?" Vobitch said.

Kenyon glanced at Frank and said, "I'll let Frank tell you that part."

"When we talked to him, Alonzo wasn't very cooperative, didn't want to give us any names. So I asked him if he'd seen any of those crime shows on TV where someone sneaks into a hospital room while the patient is asleep and snuffs him."

A heavy-duty frown appeared on Vobitch's face.

"I told him we were short of funds," Frank said. "Might have to eliminate the guard outside his door, but if he gave up his cell phone, we might find enough bucks to keep a guard on his door. So Alonzo signed a permission form to let us take it."

"Christ on a crutch!" Vobitch exploded, his cheeks mottled with anger. "You know what will happen if the media vultures get wind of it? They'll raise holy hell, a shitstorm like you've never seen."

"But they won't," Kenyon said. "We were the only ones in the room, and Alonzo thinks we're his buddies now. We told him we might, you know, cut him a break on any future charges."

"And protect him when he gets out of the hospital," Frank added.

Slightly mollified, Vobitch said grudgingly, "You get a warrant to access his phone?"

"You bet," Kenyon said. "And hit paydirt. It was a premeditated hit, no doubt. The day of the drive-by, Alonzo gets a text at five PM from an unidentified number—probably a burner—telling him to come to Lincoln Avenue at eight o'clock that night so they can negotiate a truce."

"A truce." Vobitch shook his head. "More like, come meet us so we can kill you."

"Exactly," Frank said. "Like a ping-pong game with guns and ammo. You shoot one of ours. We shoot one of yours."

"Ain't that the truth. Now that we got probable cause to arrest Jamal Jackson, let's figure out how to bust the motherfucker. He's probably holed up somewhere with his cronies."

"But we can't do it today," Frank said.

Vobitch frowned. "Why the hell not? This is the break we've been waiting for!"

"My CI might be with him. These MSM 'bangers got her hooked on drugs. I want to get her out of New Orleans and get her into rehab. Rafe might be able to get her a spot, but I need money for plane fare to get her to Boston."

"I dunno about that," Vobitch said dubiously. "The department budget is spread thin as it is."

"Hey, what's a couple hundred bucks?" Frank countered. "She gave us the car and the evidence to grab them."

"No doubt," Kenyon said. "Without that fingerprint we wouldn't be able to bust Jackson."

Vobitch sat there, not saying anything, tapping a pen on his desk.

At last he said, "Okay. I'll call the Super, give him the good news on the drive-by investigation, see if I can squeeze him for a one-way plane fare to Boston. I'll tell him it's a reward for the tipster."

"Thanks," Frank said. "That would help a lot."

Provided Angela met him at the Lakeside Mall tonight at six o'clock, which was by no means guaranteed. A callback from Maureen wasn't either. Last night he'd called, got no answer and sent her a text, telling her to call him ASAP. But she hadn't.

Another worry, festering in his mind like a sore tooth.

—————

6:05 PM – South Boston

Devlin tapped on the door of Sunny's apartment, not knowing what to expect. As far as he knew, Sunny had never killed anyone before, and killing someone could be traumatic, even if you hated the person.

Many years had passed since he'd killed Kate's abusive husband, a man he totally despised, but he still remembered how he felt afterward. Gratified, yes, but sickened by the result. The stench when Jimmy's bowels let go, the horrible look on his face, his eyes bugged out, his tongue protruding from his mouth. The first man he'd ever killed with his own hands. And the last.

If he wanted someone dead, he had someone else do it.

Sunny opened the door and smiled at him. "Great to see you, Dev. Let's have a drink and celebrate."

He stepped into her living room and kissed her deeply. "How are you feeling, Sunny? Are you okay?"

Her smile broadened, a joyful smile. "Better than okay. Whelan is dead and good riddance to him!" She went to her built-in bar and took a bottle of champagne out of an ice bucket.

"I raided the wine cellar, got us a 2007 Perrier-Jouet Belle Epoque. Open it up and we'll celebrate!"

He popped the cork and poured champagne into the glasses she gave him. The liquid foamed over the top of one glass and dripped onto the carpet. Sunny laughed, her bright-blue eyes sparkling like diamonds.

"That's how I feel, Dev. Bubbling over with happiness."

They clinked glasses and sat on her couch. "What happened after you called me?" he asked.

"First things first. Any incriminating evidence is gone. I put it in a trash bag and had one of the Rottweilers put it in the hotel dumpster. The trash company collected it this morning."

"Good." He sipped his champagne. "What about the body?"

"I called hotel security, acting distraught, saying it was an emergency. By then, Whelan was dead on the couch. Two security guards came up right away. I told them I went in the bathroom to use the toilet. When I came back, Whelan seemed to be choking. They called 911. Ten minutes later two EMTs arrived with a gurney. They checked for a pulse, loaded Whelan onto the gurney and took him out to the ambulance."

"Where did they take him?"

"Boston City Hospital." Sunny gave him one of her feral smiles, her eyes cold as winter. "Not that it would do him any good. By then the succinylcholine had worn off, so his range of motion would appear normal. I injected it into his scalp under his hair. I doubt they'll spot it. They might not even look for it when they find the bones in his throat.."

"Let's hope so. What did the cops say?" *That's the most important thing.*

"Two Boston detectives showed up a half hour later, an older white guy, early fifties, and a younger black woman. By then I didn't have to fake being nervous. I was worried. They asked me what happened and I repeated the same story I gave to the hotel security guards."

"You think they believed you?"

Sunny tilted her head to one side, considering his question. "The woman seemed to, but the male cop asked me why Whelan was here."

"Of course," Devlin said. "He knows who Whelan is, and knows he works for me."

"I told him Whelan called, asking to meet me for dinner, but I turned him down because he'd groped me in a restaurant once and it was very embarrassing. That got the female cop's attention. I said Whelan insisted he needed to talk to me in private, so I agreed to meet him in the executive suite and kept my cell phone handy so I could call for help if he tried anything."

"You think they bought it?"

"The woman did, I don't know about the guy. I didn't want to answer any more questions, so I faked a nervous breakdown."

Devlin laughed aloud. "Damn! Too bad I wasn't here to see it."

"I squeezed out some tears and started crying." Feigning hysteria, dabbing at her eyes, she said in a quavery voice, "Officer, this has been terribly upsetting and I'm exhausted." Sunny smiled. "So they left."

He leaned over and kissed her. "Thanks for helping me, Sunny."

"Happy to do it. Thanks to you I got my revenge on Whelan." Sunny sipped her champagne. "You know what the best part was? Having him lie there, paralyzed, while I asked him how it felt to be helpless, seeing the terror in his eyes."

Devlin nodded. "Payback can be very rewarding. Whelan deserved it, no question. I've got a payback scheme of my own going."

"Really? Who's the target, anybody I know?"

"The cop who put me in jail. Tank is already in Baltimore, preparing the next step."

Sunny snuggled closer. "Interesting. Tell me about it."

————

6:10 PM – New Orleans

Frank sat in his unmarked Dodge outside Dillard's. Plenty of women hurrying into Dillard's, but no sign of Angela. No call from Maureen, either. After the meeting with Vobitch, he'd sent her a text. *Call me, Mo, I need to talk to you.* Then he took a three hour power-nap, but kept his phone beside the bed. No callback.

Eight hours later, still no phone call. Why didn't she call him? Had something bad happened to her?

The idea terrified him. Fear rose inside him like a river overflowing its banks. His nerves were shot, sleep deprivation to the max, obsessing over his father's murder, hunting for Elijah's killers.

Waiting for leads. Waiting for Mo to call. Enough waiting to make him scream.

Get a grip. Focus on the here and now. Where was Angela?

Would she show up tonight? Or was she out doing tricks for her pimp-boyfriend. Who may or may not have killed Elijah.

He hadn't called Rafe yet to ask if he could get Angela into a rehab facility in Boston. That would involve phone calls and paper work, a waste of Rafe's time if Angela didn't show. Rafe had enough on his plate already, working his own cases in the Gang Unit, working overtime to help figure out who killed Judge Salvatore Renzi.

A tap sounded on the passenger side window and Angela slipped into the car. "Sorry I'm late, Frank. Had to change my clothes." Gesturing at the worn pair of jeans and a long-sleeved sweatshirt, she said, "Borrowed them from a girlfriend."

Relieved to get her in the car, he said, "I'm glad to see you, Angela. NOPD will pay for your plane fare. After my friend in Boston gets you a spot in a rehab facility, I'll put you on a flight to Boston." Making it sound like a sure thing so she wouldn't change her mind.

He cranked the engine, pulled out of the space and realized she was crying, mascara-laced tears staining her cheeks.

Damn, he hated it when women cried. He never knew what to say.

In the heavy silence he concentrated on leaving the parking garage. Angela wouldn't be happy about where he was taking her, but it was better than the lockup. A temporary stay at the District-8 station, plenty of female cops around to ride herd on her. And her drug addiction.

"This is really hard," she said, sniffling. "Hate being so far away from my boys."

"I know, but focus on the good part, Angela. You get clean, come back here and we'll get you an appointment with social services. Tell them you helped us solve a homicide, got into rehab, got off drugs and you want them to live with you."

"But where am I gonna live?" she asked, gazing at him, her eyes solemn. No pinprick pupils today.

"What about your mother? You and the boys used to live with her."

More tears leaked from her eyes. "My mom died two years ago. Heart failure, they said. Ain't going back to my boyfriend. He might kill me for leaving him."

"We'll worry about that when the time comes. You're going to be fine," he said, unsure if he was trying to convince Angela or himself.

"If you say so," she said listlessly. "I 'preciate what you done for me, Frank."

"I didn't just do it for you, Angela. I did it for your boys, too. I know how much you love them."

Because that's how it was when you were a parent. He loved Maureen more than he could ever say, more than any words could express, and he wanted to talk to her. Why hadn't she called him?

If someone hurt her, he didn't know what he would do.

CHAPTER 20

Most people sleep most deeply between three and five AM, even hardened criminals. But not cops.

At 4:25 AM Frank and Kenyon had watched a ten-man SWAT team enter a run-down duplex with a blue door on the right, a pink door on the other. Jamal "Tiny" Jackson lived behind the blue door. Vobitch had nixed their participation, saying he didn't want his best detectives to get shot by some asshole 'banger.

Now the sun was breaking through a thin layer of clouds and they were leaning against Frank's unmarked Dodge. NOPD cruisers blocked off the street, a predominantly black neighborhood, but several nearby residents stood outside on porches or sat on their front stoop.

Showtime in New Orleans. Thankfully, no shots had been fired.

Behind the blue door, the SWAT team had found Tiny Jackson, his younger brother, Marcus "Kid" Jackson, two young women stoned on crack, and a serious amount of drugs and cash, enough probable cause to arrest all of them. After the SWAT team brought them out of the house, he and Kenyon would go inside and inventory the evidence.

"Good thing you got Angela away from this guy," Kenyon said. "Hate to see her go in the slammer with these asswipes."

"You know it," Frank said. Angela was currently in a holding cell at the D-8 station. He didn't dare book a flight to Boston until he talked to Rafe.

Kenyon nudged him. "Get a load of this. Tiny ain't so tiny."

Frank watched members of the SWAT team bring a large black man out the blue door, his hands cuffed behind his back. Tiny Jackson was six-foot-four, had to weigh at least 300 pounds, tossing his head to fling dyed-gold dreadlocks out of his face. His brother was a normal-sized six-one, 190 pounds, no dreads.

Two minutes later two black girls came through the door, skinny as pencils, their eyes fixed on the ground. Frank figured the Jackson brothers were pimping them out, the sad consequence of drug addiction. Driven by a desperate craving, they'd do anything for a hit.

His cell phone vibrated inside his jacket. He took it out and said to Kenyon, "It's Rafe. I better take this."

He got in his car and answered. "Yo Rafe, what's up?"

"Got some info for you," Rafe said. "Slept at the station three night running after you left. Marcie's pissed, thinks I got a girlfriend. I told her I was sleeping with a computer, compiling a list of the homicide cases you solved."

"Good, but my father sent a lot more guys to prison than I did."

"Got that covered, too. Told the Suffolk County DA what we needed, he put three State Troopers on it. But you didn't do so bad yourself, put a dozen stone-cold killers away. Two died in the slammer, seven are still locked up, but three of them are out on parole, living near Boston."

Three suspects living near Boston. Now they were getting somewhere. His heart accelerated. The thrill of the hunt.

"First up," Rafe said, "Edward Mills, age 33, convicted of first degree murder in 1995 when he was seventeen, but tried as an adult, remember him?"

"Oh yeah." He'd never forget the blood-drenched room where Eddie stabbed his female neighbor ninety-two times, or the dead look in Eddie's blue eyes, like he was watching his own private movie from hell, when Frank interviewed him. "How did he get out? The kid was a nutcase then. I doubt that he's changed."

"Parents got big bucks, you know, hired a high-priced lawyer and a bleeding-heart shrink. She said Eddie shouldn't have been tried as an adult, claimed a seventeen-year-old's brain is still developing and he's not responsible. The usual psycho-babble bullshit. Two months ago they released Eddie into the custody of his parents."

"Wonderful. The same parents who couldn't figure out how fucked up he was. Who else?"

"Jesús Alejandro Gabriel DeCastro, got a name longer than his dick probably. Currently age 32, nineteen when you put him away for killing his father."

"Another beauty. His father wouldn't let him use his car, so Jesús went out to the garage, got a claw hammer and beat his father's head to a pulp. He's out on parole?"

131

"For the past six weeks," Rafe said. "His surviving parent, Maria De-Castro, told the parole board Jesús had found God and repented his evil ways. His PO claims Jesús is a model client, never misses an appointment. Man, you'd think he was a saint."

"Jesús is no saint. At the time we thought he was involved with an MS-13 gang, but we couldn't prove it."

"I hear you on that. MS-13 gangs were just getting started back then. Got one in Dorchester right now giving us fits. They'd as soon slice you to ribbons with a machete as look at you."

"Who's the third guy?"

"Brian Devlin, age 50, got out of FCI Ray Brook in upstate New York twelve days ago. Kingpin of a South Boston gang, allegedly. He killed his sister's husband in 1995. Remember him?"

"Yes, but I never interviewed him. He lawyered up right away. Sad case. His sister was beautiful, but brain damaged at birth. Devlin's lawyer claimed Kathleen had an IQ of 75, didn't want her to testify in court, but I interviewed her before the trial."

He paused, dredging up the memory. "She said Brian went in the kitchen to talk to her husband, came back ten minutes later, said he had to go out and told her to wait in the bedroom until he got back. We figured he left to get one of his pals to help get rid of the body. But Kathleen got curious, went in the kitchen and found her husband dead on the floor, strangled. She freaked out and called 911. Devlin's lawyer claimed the husband was abusing her."

"Yeah, well, dead men tell no tales," Rafe said. "The jury bought the story, found Devlin guilty of manslaughter, extenuating circumstances. Also found him guilty of federal RICO charges: loansharking, protection shakedowns, drug dealing. Bottom line, he got 25-to-life."

Frank yawned and massaged his eyes. His memory of Kathleen was vivid: long black hair, gorgeous green eyes, flawless white skin. When he took the stand to testify about what she'd told him, the prosecutor had asked him to point her out. Kathleen was sitting behind Brian. His hair was shorter, but otherwise he looked remarkably like Kathleen.

"Twenty-five to life, how'd he get out so soon?"

"The usual model prisoner bullshit. Now he's home in Southie, sees his PO twice a week. Frank, all three of these guys have reason to hold a grudge against you. Devlin and DeCastro might not have driven the car that forced your father off the road, but they could have had someone else do it. And parental supervision being what it is, no telling what Eddie Mills has been up to."

Frank rubbed the scar on his chin, his anger building like slow-boiling water in a kettle.

"Thanks for all the hard work, Rafe. Can you email me the details and their mugshots?"

"Consider it done," Rafe said, "You need me to pick you up at the airport on Friday?"

"Thanks, but I'll get a rental car. I don't know how long I'll be there."

However long it took to find the bastard responsible for murdering his father.

"Okay," Rafe said. "Let's meet on Saturday, figure out what to do with suspects we got so far. Did you talk to Maureen?"

"Not yet," he said. "To tell the truth, I'm worried. I've called her twice and left messages asking her to call me, but she hasn't. Last night I texted her. Maybe she'll call me this morning."

"Make sure you warn her, Frank. These guys are douche-bags. If they've got a hard-on for you, no telling what they might do."

"I will, definitely. Listen, I need a favor. My CI gave me the tip on the drive-by case, but she's mixed up with a gang, got hooked on drugs. Any chance you could get her into rehab up there? I'm afraid she won't live to testify if I don't get her out of town."

"I hear you on that, man. Lemme make some calls and call you back."

"Thanks for everything, Rafe. I owe you big time. See you Saturday."

"Talk to your daughter," Rafe said, and ended the call.

———

7:05 AM – Baltimore

Slouched low behind the wheel, Bridget eyed the sideview mirror. Last night when she and Tank had cased the Renzi woman's apartment, a fifteen-foot U-HAUL truck stood in the driveway. An hour ago when she'd parked the white Ford Focus in the lot opposite the apartment, the U-HAUL was still there.

Her radio handset crackled and she raised it to her ear.

"Any sign of our target?" Tank asked, sitting in a white cargo van, parked around the corner.

"No. Two guys brought out some boxes, loaded them in the U-HAUL and went back inside. Maybe Target is moving somewhere else. What do we do then?"

"Hell if I know."

"Hold on," she said, eyeing the mirror. "They just came out again. The blond guy got into the U-HAUL. The dark-haired guy is walking toward the Toyota parked on the street."

"No sign of Target?"

"No. Wait! Target just came out, dressed in hospital scrubs, might be going to work. Whoa! She just yelled at the dark-haired guy and gave him the finger!"

Tank laughed. "Maybe Target's not moving out, but the boyfriend is."

"Let me make a call on my burner," Bridget said, "see what he says." She didn't have to say who. Tank would know.

She called Brian's burner. He answered right away. "Talk to me. What's happening?"

"Two guys loaded boxes and some furniture into the U-HAUL. One got in the truck. The other guy went to get in the Toyota, but then Target came out dressed for work, yelled at him and gave him the finger."

Brian laughed. "Maybe they had a fight and she made him move out. That will make things easier for you and Tank."

Maybe, Bridget thought. And maybe not.

"Target just got in the Honda. Do you want us to follow the U-HAUL or Target?"

"Have Tank follow the U-HAUL. You follow Target to make sure she goes to work. You know where, right? I gave you the address."

"Yes. But what if the boyfriend is there tomorrow?"

"Tank will take care of it."

"What does that mean? No killing. I told you that before."

"Bridget, listen to me. You're the driver. Let Tank handle it."

A click sounded in her ear. Damn Brian and his payback scheme to hell.

Using the radio handset, she said, "He wants you to tail the U-HAUL. I'll follow Target to work and call you from there."

"Okay," Tank said. "I could use some breakfast, you?"

"Yes. Once you nail down the U-HAUL truck location and I make sure Target went to work, let's meet for breakfast and make a plan for tomorrow."

9:10 AM – New Orleans

Alvina Scott opened the door. "Detective Frank, how nice to see you." Smiling at him, but her eyes were still bloodshot from crying. "Come in and sit down. Would you like some ice tea?"

He didn't want ice tea. He wanted Maureen to call him.

"No thanks," he said, and took a seat on the couch. "Is Noah here?"

"He's at work. Did you need to talk to him? I can call—"

"No, that's okay. I can't stay. We arrested the men who killed Elijah."

Alvina clasped her hands together and exclaimed, "Lord be praised! How did you find them?"

"It's a long story." He had no time to explain. He had too many other urgent matters to worry about. If Rafe got Angela into rehab, he would have to buy her a plane ticket, call Rafe and give him the flight info so Rafe could meet Angela when she got off the plane.

But his biggest worry was Maureen. He had to tell her his father's accident was no accident and warn her to be careful. But she still hadn't called him. That wasn't like her. Something must be wrong.

But he didn't know what it was, and with uncertainty came dread, like battery acid eating at the lining of his gut.

"You seem upset," Alvina said. "What's wrong?"

"Nothing you need to worry about. It's been a tough week. I didn't get much sleep."

Alvina took his hand. "I know what that's like. Hard to sleep when you've got a lot on your mind. What's troubling you, Frank?"

"It's complicated."

"Tell me about it. I can handle complicated." Stroking his hand, her dark eyes warm with concern.

"My father died last week." Blurting the words, unable to stop them.

"How terrible!" Alvina said. "What happened? Was it sudden?"

"It was a car accident."

No it wasn't, it was premeditated murder. He wanted to find the bastard who did it, wrap his hands around his neck and strangle him.

Alvina squeezed his hand, her eyes on his face. "Seems like you've got something else on your mind, Frank. What is it?"

"I'm worried about my daughter." Worried? He was frantic. But he couldn't get into that with Alvina.

"She loved her grandfather very much."

135

"And you loved him, too," Alvina said. Quiet words to convey her sympathy. "I know how that is. Boys are extra close to their father."

Overwhelmed, he couldn't speak, struggling to suppress his emotions. The anguish of losing his father. The revelation that his father had been murdered. Assassinated.

Knowing the bastard who'd done it was free as a bird. While his father lay in his grave. Awaiting justice.

But he couldn't tell Alvina his personal life was a train-wreck. She had sorrows enough of her own.

Better to wrap this up and leave. "NOPD will hold a news conference tomorrow," he said. "They'll explain everything."

They had arrested Elijah's killers, but he knew what would happen. The DA would file charges, the shooters would get lawyers and many months would pass before the case went to trial.

He couldn't tell her about that, either.

"I'll call Noah and tell him," Alvina said. "Go tend to your daughter, Frank. But take care of yourself, too. Losing a beloved member of your family is a terrible thing. No matter if he's ten years old like Elijah or a grandpa like your daddy."

Frank squeezed her hands. "Thank you for understanding, Alvina."

Relieved, he left the house and got in his car. Now he could focus on getting justice for his father.

Watch out motherfucker, your days are numbered.

CHAPTER 21

Eager to go to work, Maureen filled her travel mug with coffee and set it on the kitchen counter beside her car keys. Now that Jeremy was gone she could get on with her life. Take the prep test for the surgical boards on Saturday, see how that went, and find a new roommate.

Yesterday at lunch, she had bumped into another resident. Literally. When she left the register in the staff cafeteria, her tray bumped his arm. But he was really nice about it, smiling at her, saying, "No spills, no worries."

She was too flustered to check his name tag. He wasn't a surgical resident, but he seemed friendly and he had gorgeous eyes, dark and mysterious. Sexy.

If she went to the cafeteria at the same time today, maybe she'd see him, strike up a conversation and ask what his specialty was. After that, anything could happen, hopefully something good.

Dad had texted her yesterday, asking her to call him, but she hadn't.

What could she say? *Jeremy's cheating on me and I threw him out.*

It would be a relief to tell him, but Dad was still upset about Grampa Sal. She was too, but now that she was back in Baltimore, her usual frenzied schedule had taken over. She'd call him tonight after work.

So much to do, so little time.

The doorbell rang.

Her first thought: Jeremy had forgotten something.

At work yesterday, she'd called a locksmith and asked him meet her here last night when she got home from work to change the locks. Expensive, but worth it. She didn't want Jeremy coming in here when she wasn't home. Didn't want him in here when she was home, either.

She went to the window and parted the curtain. Why was a white van in the driveway backed up to her door?

She went to the door and looked out the peephole. No one was there.

Was Jeremy playing games with her? Wanting to take more furniture? Fat chance. She'd tell him to take a hike.

She opened the door, but no one was there.

Leaving the door ajar, she stepped outside. Strange. She didn't see anyone.

All of a sudden, someone grabbed her from behind and clamped a hand over her mouth.

Stunned, she couldn't move. Then she remembered her self-defense training. Feigning helplessness, she sagged against him. She knew it was a man. His clothes reeked of cigar smoke.

She kicked him in the shin, jerked away and turned to get a look at him.

Whoa! He was enormous and a black ski-mask covered his face.

Thoughts raced though her mind. Who the hell was he? Not Jeremy or any of his friends, that's for sure.

What did he want? Did he intend to rob her? Grab her purse off the kitchen counter and steal her wallet?

She didn't have much cash and both her credit cards were maxed out.

With a muttered oath, he grabbed her again and wrapped his arms around her.

Damn! Her cell phone and car keys were on the counter. Maybe he wanted to steal her car. Not if she could help it.

She elbowed him in the ribs. He swore at her and backed away.

She took a step toward the door, but he grabbed her arm and wrenched it behind her back.

Grappling with him, fighting to escape, she kicked him again, harder than before. But that didn't stop him. He just spread his legs so she couldn't kick him again.

Terrified, she struggled hard, wrenching her body this way and that with all her might. But he was so strong, his arms wrapped around her in a fierce grip, imprisoning her arms against her torso.

Panting now, she threw back her head, trying to head-butt him, but he ducked to one side and put her in a headlock his forearm. She opened her mouth to scream, but he slapped a wet cloth over her nose and mouth.

Damn! She couldn't breathe! She had to get the cloth off her face!

But she couldn't. Her arms were pinned to her torso.

Desperate for air, she inhaled through her nose and a pungent chemical odor filled her nostrils.

She heard a distant sound, her cell phone chiming inside the kitchen, the special ringtone she'd set up so she'd know it was Dad. If she could get to it, Dad would send help!

But the chemical smell was making her woozy. She felt like a rag doll with no strength.

Drugs? she thought, trying to make sense of it.

The man picked her up and walked toward the van.

And the world faded to black.

———

5:35 AM – New Orleans

Frank took a shower, got dressed and wandered into his kitchen. Last night he'd slept for ten hours straight, the most rest he'd had in weeks. He got a shot of espresso going in the espresso machine and perched on a stool at the dining counter.

After the press conference at noon, he would tell Vobitch he needed to take some time off. What he needed most was to talk to Maureen. She still hadn't called him.

Recalling the urgency in Rafe's voice—*Warn her to be careful*—he got on his cell phone and dialed her number.

It rang once and went to voice mail. He didn't leave a message.

Where the hell was she? Already at work?

When he got to the office, he'd call her again, and keep calling until she answered.

He put a cup under the coffee machine spout and waited for it to fill. The rich aroma of espresso reminded him of his father. Assassinated by unknown killers.

At this very moment they were walking around free, somewhere near Boston probably.

Rafe seemed convinced they were after him, not his father.

As a cop, he'd been shot at several times, had been hit twice, most recently three years ago. He could still remember the excruciating pain, the clammy sweat on his face, the thought that he might die. These close encounters with death had made him view life differently.

At this point, he figured he was living on borrowed time.

SUSAN FLEET

In life or death situations, cops had to make choices. He'd shot a few killers along the way. If the bastards who murdered his father were after him, so be it. When he found them, he would shoot to kill and not give it a second thought.

Sipping espresso, he went in the living room and stood at the window, looking at the street below. It was a dreary day, the sky overcast, a few pedestrians hurrying to work. That's where he'd be in half an hour, at his desk in the D-8 homicide office.

Yesterday after he left Alvina Scott, he'd called Kelly and left a message: *Got back late Sunday night. Work has been crazy, call you as soon as I can.* But the rest of the day passed in a blur, so he'd gone home and fallen into bed, exhausted.

Maybe he could catch her before she went to work. He dialed her number and she answered right away.

"Hey Frank. I got your message so I didn't call you. Judging by the lead story on the news, you've been busy."

"Remember that hangup call I got at your house? It was one of my old CI's. She called again and I got her to meet me. Long story short, she's mixed up with the 'bangers involved in the drive-by. She told me where they dumped the car. Kenyon and I found it and got the evidence that led to yesterday's arrest."

"I'm sure Vobitch is happy," she said, "but how are you? How did it go in Boston?"

Two questions he didn't want to answer. They would only lead to more questions, questions that had no answers. Yet.

"Vobitch is thrilled, got the NOPD brass off his back, for the moment anyway." He sipped some espresso. "Boston was ... difficult. But I got through it, thanks to my friends. Vobitch and Kenyon brought their wives to the funeral."

"Frank, you don't sound too good. Do you really have to go back to work so soon after the funeral? Now that the drive-by is solved, why not take a few days off? Chill out and relax."

"It wasn't an accident."

"What wasn't an accident?"

"Someone forced my father's car off the road into a big oak tree and killed him."

Kelly gasped. "Frank, that's ... monstrous."

"Yes it is. And I'm gonna find the fucker who did it and make him pay."

"How did you figure out it wasn't an accident?"

"My friend Rafe had the car towed to the BPD evidence garage. Someone fucked with the brakes, and a dent in the rear fender had paint chips in it. Rafe didn't find out about it until after the funeral. He's working the case now. I'm flying up there Friday after work, not sure when I'll be back. I haven't told Vobitch yet, so don't say anything. I'll tell him after the press conference."

"I can take a few days off, come up there and help you."

"Thanks, Kelly, but I'm not sure what will happen when I get there. Rafe got some names of possible suspects, guys I put in jail when I worked homicide up there."

"Why would they kill your father if they're after you?"

"Some sort of payback, Rafe thinks. He's checking the men my father put in prison, too."

"Bad enough that your father's dead, Frank, but murder? That's devastating. Come to my house after work and we'll talk about it."

His throat closed up. Kelly tuned into his mood so well it frightened him sometimes, knowing when he needed to talk, backing off when he needed space.

"Sounds good," he said, his voice husky. "I missed you. How about seven o'clock?"

"Perfect. I've got plenty of wine and food. Just bring yourself."

He smiled. "Okay. Make sure you've got your birthday suit on when I get there."

Kelly laughed. "We'll see about that."

———

6:48 AM – Baltimore

Bridget's heart slammed her chest as she slowly drove out of the apartment complex. She had dressed in dark clothes, nothing unusual: black jeans and a long-sleeved navy sweatshirt.

Tank was in the rear compartment with the hostage, and a gun.

He was wearing a ski-mask, but she wasn't. Too conspicuous. Attract no attention.

At three o'clock this morning, Tank had followed her to the airport so they could ditch the Ford Focus. After he put a stolen Maryland plate on the Ford, she had left it in long-term parking.

Fortunately, her fears that the boyfriend might be there were groundless. Tank said the woman put up a fight, but the chloroform had knocked her out long enough for him to get her into the van.

Next stop, Plymouth. Just another innocuous white van driving north on the interstate. Unless an overzealous patrol cop decided to stop her and search the van. She didn't want to think about what might happen then.

Or what Tank might do with his gun.

She got on her radio handset. "How's it going back there?"

"Okay," Tank said. "Let's stop at a drive-thru for coffee and pastry. And a bottled water for you know who. She's out like a light, but she pissed her pants."

"Damn! We better get her some new ones, stop at a Walmart maybe."

"Okay, but not until we put some distance between us and the apartment. She don't show up for work, they might call her. Or send somebody over there."

"You took her cell phone, right?" Brian had been adamant about that.

"Yes. It's in her purse with the car keys. Made it look like she went to work."

"But her car is still there."

Tank chuckled. "Yeah, with a flat tire. I let the air out before I got in the van."

Bridget smiled. "Brilliant, Tank. I'll get off the highway at the first exit with food signs. We'll have breakfast and make a call, let the man know how things went."

———

Drifting in and out of consciousness, Maureen gradually became aware of her predicament. A hard floor underneath her.

Blindfolded. Her wrists and ankles bound together. Her mouth taped shut.

She still felt woozy but at least she could breathe.

She tried to remember what happened, but her head felt fuzzy.

The doorbell. A man in a black ski-mask. A wet cloth over her mouth. Then nothing.

Wait. He'd put her into a van. A white van.

But it didn't feel like it was moving, and it was quiet. She couldn't hear anything. Her heart thumped her chest.

Where was the man? Where was he taking her?

She tried to roll over, felt wetness between her thighs. Eww. She'd wet her pants. Disgusting!

Tears filled her eyes. Dad didn't know what had happened. He'd tried to call her while she was trying to fight off the masked man. She should have called him last night, but she was tired, exhausted from getting Jeremy out of the apartment.

Jeremy didn't know what had happened either. Not that he gave a shit. But the hospital did. When she didn't show up for work, they would call her.

But so what? She didn't have her cell phone. She pictured it on the counter beside her purse and car keys.

If she didn't answer maybe they'd send someone to the apartment to look for her.

She heard a door slam, then another, the driver's side first, then the passenger side door.

There were two of them!

She heard faint voices, too faint for her to hear what they were saying. What did they want?

Not her car, obviously, and she didn't have much cash. They could use her credit cards until they maxed out, which wouldn't take long.

What would happen then? Would they kill her and dump her body somewhere?

A shudder rippled through her. She had to stop thinking like that.

She had to stay positive and figure out a way to escape.

She lay very still and got control of her breathing.

Think, Maureen. Think.

CHAPTER 22

THURSDAY October 27 – 4:15 PM – Plymouth

Bridget stood in the doorway, her face hidden by a ski mask.

Maureen Renzi sat on the folding bed, blindfolded, her mouth taped shut, her wrists bound with zip-ties, her hands in her lap. One ankle was shackled to the base of the elliptical machine with a cord long enough to allow her to use the portable toilet beside the bed.

"Sit up straight so I can take your picture," she said. Using the camera on Maureen's cell phone, she lined up the shot.

Maureen covered her face with her hands. "Mmmm! Aaarrh! Mmmm-yahh."

Cursing her probably, the words muffled by the tape. Annoyed, she stepped closer and said, "Want to go home? Cooperation is the key. Sit still so I can take your picture."

Maureen kept her hands over her face. "Mmm-yaa! Aaaaaarrh!"

Bridget slapped the side of her head, then slapped it again harder.

And recoiled in horror.

How could she strike a defenseless woman, a woman who had never done anything to her? Or anyone else, probably. Her only fault was being fathered by the wrong man. Frank Renzi.

Emphasizing each word, she said in a firm voice, "Sit. Still. Now."

The woman did as she was told, silent and still, hands in her lap, shoulders slumped.

Bridget stepped back, snapped two pictures, checked to be sure they were okay and strode across the room.

"Hold still while I take the tape off your mouth." Knowing it would hurt, she ripped the tape off quickly to minimize the pain.

"Oww!" Maureen said, touching her cheeks with her fingertips.

"I brought you a sandwich and a bottled water. Don't try to take off the blindfold. You're a smart woman. Think about what might happen if you see me. Nothing good, I promise."

144

"What do you want?" Maureen said, tilting her head back, but unable to see her.

Bridget set the bottled water and a paper plate on the bed beside her.

"Eat your sandwich. I'll be back in a little while to make sure you're behaving yourself." Make her anxious, wondering when her captor would return. *Control, control, control.*

Disgusted with herself, she went upstairs, shut the basement door and went in the kitchen. She leaned against the counter, massaging her temples. She had the mother of all headaches. Awake since 3:00 AM, so she and Tank could dump the Ford in a parking garage. Stressed out by the kidnapping. On the road for ten hours, worrying about patrol cops.

And angry, not just at Brian, but also at herself for agreeing to take part in this dirty business. That's what it was. Gangster business.

Brian wanted to punish Frank Renzi for helping to send him to prison. He wanted revenge and didn't care who he hurt to get it.

She opened the photos on Maureen's cell phone, sent them to Brian and went in her living room. The shades were drawn but a table lamp spotlit the reproduction of a painting on the wall above it. The Scream by Edvard Munch, a lurid red sky, a murky landscape and a terrified figure, wild-eyed, its hands clutching his head, its mouth open.

Like her prisoner. Alone and scared and innocent.

She used her burner to call Brian, who answered immediately.

"Fantastic pictures," he said. "Exactly what I need."

"Good, but crop them, so it only shows her face."

"Of course. How's the hostage?"

"Frightened. And angry. I don't know how long I'll be able to keep her quiet. She's not a teenager, Brian. She's a grown woman. How soon will you send the ransom request?"

"Is his phone number on her smartphone?"

"Hold on." She found three numbers for "Dad" in the contact list. "I've got home and cell phone numbers, and a work number. You want all of them?"

"Yes, but I won't use the work number. The New Orleans police department might have trap-and-trace on their switchboard."

She read the numbers to him and said, "Where's Tank? I can't ride herd on her all by myself."

"What's the problem? She's tied up, isn't she?"

145

"Yes," she snapped. "But you're not the one who has to wipe her ass with toilet paper and empty the piss pot! I've been up sixteen hours straight. Where's Tank?"

"In Rhode Island getting rid of the van."

"Why? We'll need it when we let her go."

Silence on Brian's end. Then, "I'll send Sunny down there tomorrow to help you."

"Fine," she said, and ended the call. But it wasn't fine. Having the Bitch from Hell come to her cottage, her only sanctuary, was the last thing she wanted. Minding the hostage was bad enough.

Dealing with Sunny would be worse.

Damn it to hell! Another thing to worry about.

———

Seated in his office chair, Devlin slammed down the phone. Bridget was already freaking out and this deal wouldn't be over in a day or two. It would take time for Renzi to raise a million bucks, and setting up a secure location to get it would also take time. Bridget was bitching about toilet paper and keeping the hostage quiet, asking where Tank was.

Tank was getting rid of the van. If they needed another van, he would have Tank steal one.

Sunny would drive to Plymouth and help Bridget mind the hostage. No problem there.

Bridget was the problem. She seemed to think he sat around doing nothing, but this part of his plan had taken hours of thought and careful preparation. From now on he had to be even more careful.

Leave no clues that might reveal where the hostage was. He didn't need Bridget to tell him to crop the photos she'd sent him. He'd use an untraceable burner to send it to Renzi.

He left his office, went in the kitchen and opened a bottle of Harp Ale. Years ago he'd bought the one-story three bedroom house for the Devlin family. Pa slept in one bedroom, Bridget and Kate slept in another. He had his own room, which he now used as his office.

While he was in prison, he'd paid a handyman to maintain the property: mow the lawn, tend the gutters, paint the trim when necessary. But nothing ostentatious. No one would guess that a gang kingpin lived here.

Except for the fucking feds, who were monitoring the electronic bracelet permanently attached to his right ankle twenty-four/seven.

He had devoted considerable time on the text that would accompany the photo. *We've got your daughter. Don't contact the cops or the FBI. If you do, she's dead. We'll be in touch soon. Have a nice day.*

Too bad he couldn't be a fly on the wall when the bastard read it. Would Renzi follow orders? He'd better.

He chugged some Harp Ale and looked out the kitchen window. From here, he could see the exit door at the rear of the Leprechaun Pub. He smiled, recalling the Irish night party Monday night, his alibi while Sunny killed Whelan.

But now he needed a new enforcer.

He thought about his two replacement candidates. Joey was forty-two, experienced but set in his ways, reluctant to adapt to new methods.

Mike was thirty-six, less experienced but eager to learn. The biggest plus: Mike's wife worked at a hospital.

That might be helpful if Renzi refused to pay the ransom.

———

Maureen sat on the lumpy cot, shivering. Damn it was cold in here! She touched the side of her head. The woman who'd hit her had gone upstairs and shut the door. Hopefully she wouldn't be back for a while.

Groping with her hands, she found the bottled water. Damn, she hated this! Unable to see, her wrists bound together. Her ankle shackled to something so she couldn't get up and move around.

She managed to open the bottle and gulped half of the contents.

Who the hell were these people? What did they want?

She should have called Dad. Now that she thought about it, his text had seemed urgent. But she hadn't called him, and now she couldn't. She had no idea where her phone was. Maybe it was still in Baltimore. Maybe the woman had it, or the man who smelled of cigar smoke.

But what difference did it make? Bottom line she had no way to call for help.

She was all alone, utterly dependent on her captors.

Her stomach rumbled. She found the sandwich and took a bite. Turkey, with mayonnaise and lettuce. She devoured half of it, set the rest aside, drank some water and went over what she knew.

After she heard voices in the van, it had driven off, but after a while it stopped. The woman took her outside, made her squat down and pee. Her bowels rebelled, a violent explosion of diarrhea. Humiliating. The woman gave her a wad of toilet paper and told her to wipe herself. It took a while, because her wrists were bound together. The woman took off her shoes, pulled off her urine-soaked pants and gave her a clean pair to put on. Then the woman had put her back in the van.

She had no idea how long she was in there. It seemed like forever. She didn't know where she was, didn't even know if it was day or night. She plucked at the blindfold with her fingers.

Think about what might happen if you see me. Nothing good, I promise.

Tears flooded her eyes. She was a prisoner. Kidnapped by two people.

The man hadn't been around since they sat her down on the bed. Maybe he was upstairs. No telling what he might do if she took off the blindfold, and the memory of woman's cold voice sent chills down her spine.

Well, fuck that! She was a prisoner, but she was no wimp.

Dad would want her to be strong. Sooner or later he would find out she was missing and hunt for her.

Most kidnappers wanted money. She'd seen a movie once about a kidnapping and they asked for proof of life. If they asked Dad for money, he would probably do that, too. Maybe if they let her talk to him, she could give him a clue. She didn't know much about the bitch woman. The man was big and strong, a cigar smoker.

She sat still and listened, hoping to hear a passing car or sounds of nearby traffic. Nothing.

Where the hell was she? She sniffed the air and smelled heating oil. It seemed like she was in the basement of a house, someplace where it was cold. She listened again. At first she heard nothing. Then a far-away sound, one she'd often heard when she was at Grampa Sal's house.

Seagulls, cawing. She was near the ocean!

Now all she had to do was figure out how to give the clue to Dad.

But this wasn't a movie. What if they wouldn't let her talk to him?

Her stomach heaved and bile rose in her throat.

Groping with her hands, she touched the arm of the portable toilet. Struggled to her feet. Bent over the toilet and vomited.

On the brink of despair, she sank onto the bed.

She was all alone. Kidnapped by two monsters.

———

4:30 PM – New Orleans

Frank left the station and got in his car. It had been a long day. After the presser about the drive-by arrests, he'd told Vobitch what really happened to his father. Vobitch told him to go up there and find the motherfuckers who killed him. That was exactly what he intended to do.

His cell phone pinged. Thinking Maureen had texted him he dug out his phone. He accessed the text and gasped.

A photograph. Maureen's face, blindfolded, her mouth covered with tape. Jesus Christ! What had they done to her?

Seeing the vile image sent stabbing pains into his gut. The text was worse.

We've got your daughter. Don't contact the cops or the FBI. If you do, she's dead. We'll be in touch soon. Have a nice day.

The bottom dropped out of his world, an out-of-control free-fall that left him panic-stricken, barely able to breathe. He stared at the photo of his daughter, blindfolded, her mouth taped shut.

Have a nice day. The motherfuckers taunting him. Rage mushroomed inside him.

He wanted to rip them apart with his bare hands. But first he had to find Maureen. Set aside his anguish and act like a cop. He'd dealt with kidnappers before. Don't contact the cops? Fuck that! He called Rafe.

"They took Maureen. Texted me her picture and a message."

"Fuck all!" Rafe exclaimed.

"I texted her last night and told her to call me ASAP, but she didn't. I called her this morning and got no answer so I'm not sure how long they've had her."

"What's the message?"

After he read it aloud, Rafe said, "Call Evelyn and tell her she needs to get out of the house. I'm in my car, heading there now."

"Thanks. I'm going to Mo's apartment in Baltimore to see if they grabbed her there."

"What about the hospital where she works?"

"I don't want to call them yet. If I tell them she's missing, they might call the police."

"Right. Keep it quiet for now," Rafe said. "Call me after you get to Baltimore."

"It might be late."

"Whatever. Call me, and we'll figure out what to do. Tell Evelyn I'm on my way."

Frank ended the call and punched in Evelyn's number. Even under normal circumstances conversations with his ex-wife tended to be complicated. This would be far worse. He didn't want to scare her, but he had to make her understand the danger.

"Hello, Frank. You hardly ever call me. Is something wrong?"

Yes, something is very wrong.

"You need to leave the house for a few days. Someone's ... angry with me, and they know where you live."

"Leave the house? Where will I go? How will I get there?"

Focused on problems as usual, not solutions. "Rafe will pick you up soon. Pack some clothes."

"But what about—"

"Just do it, Evelyn. My father didn't die in an accident. Someone forced him off the road."

Silence on the line. Then, "How do you know they did?"

Exasperated, he said, "I know! Pack some clothes and wait for Rafe."

"Maybe I'll go to Baltimore and stay with Maureen."

"No. She's busy right now."

Busy trying to stay alive, and my heart is breaking and I don't have time to argue with you.

"Call your cousin in Hartford. She'll let you stay there for a while."

"But I haven't seen her for a long time. Two years at least."

He clenched the wheel, willing himself not to scream. "Evelyn, call your cousin. *Now.* Tell her you need to stay with her for a while. Then pack some clothes. Rafe will be there soon."

"What about Maureen? They wouldn't hurt Maureen, would they?"

Yes, Evelyn, they would, and I have to stop them.

"Bring your cell phone. I'll call you tomorrow."

He ended the call, wiped sweaty hands on his pants and mentally sent Maureen a message. *Stay strong, Mo. I don't know where you are, but I'm going to find you. I promise.*

Then he would make the motherfuckers who'd taken her wish they'd never been born.

CHAPTER 23

FRIDAY October 28 – 1:15 AM – Baltimore

Piloting an economy-sized rental car, Frank entered an apartment complex and drove around a small pond lined with shade trees, wooden benches and a gravel jogging path. A peaceful scene that didn't jibe with his black mood.

He didn't expect to find the kidnappers in Maureen's apartment, but his SIG was tucked in the small of his back under his windbreaker. Better to have a gun and not need it than to need a gun and not have it.

Where they had taken her was a mystery, one he was desperate to solve.

He turned right onto a street lined with brick buildings. Most of them were dark, other than lights behind a few curtained windows, night-owls watching TV probably. A minute later he arrived at Building 226. Mo lived in the end unit: 226-F.

His pulse quickened. The Honda she'd bought when she moved to Baltimore was parked out front, right wheels to the curb, not in the driveway.

He'd visited her in Baltimore twice, quick trips while he was working cases. They had a great time, but when he asked about the apartment, Mo said there were lots more interesting things to see in Baltimore. Including Jeremy, apparently. He'd never met him, but Mo had sent him a snapshot, Jeremy gazing into the camera. A good-looking man with an earnest expression and a wide toothy smile, like a car salesman eager to make a sale.

But Mo seemed happy. She'd been living with him for four years.

No lights in the apartment. Her car was the only one parked outside the apartment. Was Jeremy out partying?

Didn't he know Maureen was missing?

He parked behind Mo's car and killed the headlights. He put the pen-light and the Swiss Army knife he'd bought at the airport in his pocket, set the dome light to the off-position, got out and quietly shut the door.

An eight-foot stockade fence to the left of the driveway was good for privacy, also good concealment for burglars. Or kidnappers. Thick clouds obscured the moon, but a halogen streetlamp cast light over the building. He went to Maureen's Honda, flashed the penlight over the interior. Nothing unusual inside the car, but the right front tire was flat.

Bad news. The neighbors might see it and think Mo was out with Jeremy, using his car. But he knew different.

He walked up the driveway and went to the door. A filmy white curtain covered a window in the upper half. To the right, a similar curtain covered a smaller window. He'd never been inside, but he figured the kitchen and living room were in front, bedroom and bath in back.

Close to the building, he crept to the rear of the apartment. A small window set high on the wall was probably in the bathroom. Ten feet beyond it, dark curtains were drawn behind a tall sash window with a large pane of glass on the bottom, six small panes in the upper half. A screen covered the lower half. He took latex gloves out of his pocket, put them on, used the Swiss Army knife to pry off the screen and leaned it against the foundation.

The lock in the center of the frame didn't appear to be in the locked position. He put his ear to the glass and heard nothing. Using the fingers of both hands, he eased the window open.

Listened again. Dead silence.

Was Jeremy asleep in bed? Only one way to find out. Propelling himself with his elbows, he went in fast, landed on his hands and knees and pulled out his SIG. "Police! Show me your hands!"

Loud, but not loud enough to wake the neighbors.

Silence, apart from his own ragged breathing. He rose to his feet. Moving quietly in the darkness, the SIG up and ready, he approached the bed. Off to his right, dim light filtered through an open door. As his eyes adjusted to the darkness, he saw that the bed was empty. Beyond the bed was another door, a closet perhaps.

He silently crept to the door. Flipped the light switch beside it and whipped open the door. No one hiding inside. Not many clothes either, just Maureen's outfits. No men's clothes. Odd, but he'd think about that later. He shut off the light.

The apartment remained silent and still. He left the bedroom, the SIG extended in front of him. Unloaded, but sometimes optics were more important than reality. He checked the bathroom. Empty.

Easing into the living room, he flicked a light switch. No one in the living room or the galley kitchen beyond it.

He holstered the SIG and studied the room. No couch, just an empty space near the wall with dust balls on the floor. No TV on the media stand on opposite wall, just a small sound system with built-in speakers. Mo's laptop sat on a small table in the corner beside her old bureau.

Three framed photographs of him with Maureen stood on top, a photo-montage of her life from middle school to high school to college. Pictures that tore at his heart. His sweet little school girl. His beautiful teenager. And his smart, career-minded daughter.

Visualizing another photo in his mind. Maureen, blindfolded, with tape across her mouth. Kidnapped.

His throat closed up and his eyes glazed with tears.

"Damn it to hell!"

But curses wouldn't help him find Maureen. *Get a grip and focus.*

He went into the kitchen. The first thing he noticed: Mo's insulated travel mug stood on the counter, the one she filled with coffee whenever she went somewhere in the morning.

No car keys or house keys. No handbag. No cell phone.

He returned to the bedroom, searched for her handbag, didn't find it, returned to the kitchen and checked the entry door.

It was locked. No doubt by the person who'd taken her keys.

He picked up the travel mug. Almost full. He opened the lid and sniffed. Dripped liquid on his finger and tasted it. Lukewarm coffee.

Due at the hospital at seven, Maureen usually left by six-thirty.

But yesterday someone had grabbed her before she went to work. Now it was 2:00 AM. Almost twenty hours later.

Fear rippled through him, and the hairs on his forearms stood up. Mo had a temper. He doubted that she'd gone quietly, and these were dangerous people. The same fuckers who'd murdered his father.

He got on his cell phone and called Rafe.

After two rings, Rafe answered. "Yo, Frank, where are you?

"Did I wake you ?"

"No. Talk to me."

"I'm in Maureen's apartment in Baltimore. The bed is made, coffee in her travel mug on the kitchen counter. Looks like the fuckers grabbed her before she went to work yesterday morning. I figure twenty hours ago, give or take."

"What about the boyfriend? He's not there?"

"No. That's another weird thing. Looks like he might have moved out. None of his clothes are here, no car, nothing."

"Huh," Rafe said. "You think he's involved?"

"I don't know, but he's a dentist, must have an office somewhere near here. I intend to be there when it opens to see what he says."

"Good move. Call me after you talk to him. I've got a couple more scumbag suspects. You got a place to stay?"

"Yes, but I haven't checked in yet. I'm headed there now, grab a few winks, then talk to Jeremy."

"Sounds like a plan," Rafe said. "Call me after you squeeze Jeremy."

———

3:00 AM – Plymouth

Bridget jolted upright in bed, her heart pounding in the darkness. What was that horrible sound?

Jesus! The woman in the basement was screaming.

Furious, she got out of bed, put on a bathrobe, went to the basement door and opened it.

"Let me out of here, goddammit! You're a fucking bitch!"

Maureen Renzi cursing at her.

She went back in the kitchen, pulled on the ski-mask and and stomped downstairs. The yelling stopped.

She stepped into the room, put on the lights and approached the bed.

"Don't curse at me! Shut your mouth and be quiet. I give you something to eat, take the tape off your mouth and you wake me up at three o'clock in the morning?"

Seated on the bed, her legs dangling over the side, Maureen raised her chin and said, "You're a monster."

"Wrong. I'm the only friend you've got. There's no point in screaming. No one can hear you."

"My father's looking for me. He'll find me and when he does, you'll go to jail."

"In your dreams."

154

"He's a police detective!" Maureen screamed. "He'll find me and—"

Bridget slapped her. "Shut up! He's not going to find you."

"You don't scare me! You can't even fight fair. I'm tied up and you hit me! You're a bitch!"

Bridget ripped off two lengths of duct tape and fastened them over the woman's mouth.

"Mmmmmmaaaaagh!" Raging at her, flailing her arms, trying to hit her.

She shut off the lights, went upstairs and slammed the door. In the kitchen, she yanked off the ski-mask and put it in a drawer. Her hands were shaking. Her mind filled with self-loathing.

The woman was right. She was a monster. Striking a defenseless hostage. And what Maureen said was true.

If Renzi found his daughter in her cottage, she would go to jail. Renzi was a cop, with plenty of cop friends.

Brian would tell him not to contact them, of course. But how would Brian know if he did or not?

Headlight beams swept over the kitchen window as a car pulled into her driveway. Startled, Bridget shrank back and knelt beside the counter, her heart pounding.

Holy Mother of God! They were already here.

Wait. Now the car was backing out of the driveway and leaving, the headlights sweeping over the wall of the kitchen. She stood up, her hands clammy with sweat, parted the window curtain and watched the car drive away, its noisy muffler rumbling.

Probably some drunk from a nearby tavern, looking for a shortcut to the highway, not realizing this was a dead-end street.

But next time it might be different.

Next time, it might be Frank Renzi and his cop friends.

———

Maureen held her breath and listened. A car had pulled into the driveway, she was certain of it. The muffler must have a big hole in it, rumbling like a biker revving his motorcycle. But now it was going away, the sound growing fainter and fainter.

Tears flooded her eyes. The car was gone.

Full of despair, she hunched her shoulders and clasped her hands together in her lap.

No one was going to find her, not even Dad.

The woman was a bitch. Hitting her while her hands were tied and she couldn't fight back.

Fuck you bitch! Silently screaming the words in her mind.

She sniffled and wiped her nose on her sleeve. She had to stop crying. Her nose was so full of mucus she could barely breathe.

Maybe the woman wasn't so confident after all. Maybe it was just an act to scare her. Make her submissive.

When she said she'd go to jail if Dad found her here, the bitch had slapped her.

But at least she knew what time it was. Three in the morning, not three in the afternoon. If she kept goading her, maybe the bitch would let something else slip.

Another thought struck her. If they had her cell phone and turned it on, Dad could track it. She didn't know exactly how they did it, but he'd told her about it once.

She hugged herself, wrapping her arms around her chest. Damn, it was cold down here. Maybe she'd ask for a blanket and figure out how to use it. She smiled, contemplating what she'd like to do.

Tear it into strips, braid them together and strangle the bitch.

But for now, all she could do was send Dad an ESP message.

I know you're looking for me, Dad. Please hurry. I don't know how much longer I can take this.

CHAPTER 24

FRIDAY October 28 – 7:15 AM – Carson Beach, South Boston

"Bridget's already bitching about minding the hostage," Devlin said. "What's the setup? Is there a problem?"

"Not really," Tank said. "Her cottage is at the end of a dead-end street, surrounded by woods. Renzi's the problem. Ten to one he's already in Baltimore, nosing around her apartment. We need to get the loot and let the girl go."

Get the loot for sure. Let the girl go? Maybe.

"Where did you put her?" he said, hunching his shoulders inside his windbreaker to ward off the icy wind gusting across the water. "

"Downstairs in the basement on a folding bed beside a portable toilet. Blindfolded, so she can't see nothing, but me and Bridget wore ski-masks just in case."

"Nobody saw you take her in there?"

"No. The closest neighbor lives on the other side of Bridget's garage. But the girl's feisty, Dev. Kicked me twice, tried to headbutt me before I knocked her out with the chloroform. We can't keep her too long."

"We'll keep her until Renzi gets the dough." *What happened after that was up to Renzi.*

"I'll send him a message tonight, tell him to get the money."

"What if he talks to his cop friends or the FBI? We got no way of knowing if he does."

"Tank, you worry too much. I've got it covered."

"But she works for a hospital. She don't show up for work, they might ask the Baltimore cops to check her apartment."

"They won't find anything, right?"

"No. I wore gloves when I grabbed her so they won't find no prints. Took her purse, car keys and cell phone, like you said. But if a doctor goes missing, a pretty girl like that, they might put it on TV, have people looking for her."

Hearing the distant rumble of thunder, Devlin studied the line of ominous dark clouds headed their way, certain to bring a deluge of rain. "I asked Sunny to go down and help Bridget."

Tank frowned. "I don't know, Dev. Them two don't get along too good, might get into a cat fight."

Devlin smiled, recalling Sunny's triumphant tale after she killed Whelan, rejoicing in her victory.

"Don't worry, Tank. Sunny won't take any shit from Bridget. Or the hostage."

———

8:05 AM – Baltimore

When the receptionist unlocked the door, Frank strode into the office. The woman, an attractive blonde with a curvy figure, seemed surprised. Beverly according to the name plate on her desk, smiling at him as she sat down. "Good morning, sir. Did you want to make an appointment?"

"I need to speak to Jeremy," he said, grimly. "*Now.*"

"I'm sorry, sir, but Doctor Lyons is getting ready for his first patient. Could you tell me what the problem is?"

Frank put the palms of his hands on the desk and leaned forward, looming over her. "The problem will get a lot worse if you don't take me to his office." He took out his badge. "Frank Renzi, New Orleans Police Department. Go tell Jeremy I need to talk to him."

Beverly's cheeks flushed crimson. "Yes, sir. Right away." She rose from her chair, but a bell dinged as an older woman entered the office. Flustered, Beverly froze, but recovered quickly. "Good morning, Mrs. Adams. The doctor will be with you shortly." No smile. Beverly opened a door to the left of the desk and disappeared.

"It's cold out this morning, isn't it?" said Mrs. Adams. "Before you know it, we'll have snow."

In no mood for chitchat, Frank didn't reply, pacing back and forth near the desk. Jeremy's diplomas were mounted on the wall. Beside them, a framed photo showed him guiding a horse toward a jump. No photos of Maureen, though.

Beverly came back and said, "Come with me, sir."

He followed her past three treatment rooms to an open door and strode into the office. Seated at his desk, Jeremy flashed his car-salesman smile. "Detective Renzi, I'm so happy to meet you. Maureen has told me so much about you."

He rose from his chair, circled the desk and offered his hand. Frank ignored it. If Jeremy was involved in the kidnapping, the best way to find out was to blindside him and see how he reacted.

"Where's Maureen?"

The salesman-smile disappeared. Clearly taken aback, Jeremy said, "At work, I assume. Why?"

"When did you see her last?"

Frowning, Jeremy said, "Wednesday morning."

Frank shut the office door and walked over to Jeremy, crowding him, invading his personal space. "What time Wednesday morning? Where?"

Jeremy didn't answer, his dark eyes wary. Frank could see the wheels turning in his mind. "What's this about? Why are you questioning me?"

"Answer the question."

"Wednesday morning at our apartment before I left for work."

"You didn't see her yesterday?"

"No." Jeremy licked his lips, avoiding Frank's eyes. "We, uh, we had an argument and Maureen asked me to move out."

Now they were getting somewhere. "What did you argue about?"

Jeremy shrugged. "Nothing, really, just a silly argument. You know how it is."

"No, Jeremy, I don't know how it is. Tell me about it."

"Maureen was tired, you know? Working long hours, studying for the boards."

Frank shoved him against wall and put him in a choke-hold, his forearm across Jeremy's throat. "Don't put the blame on Maureen. What did you argue about?"

Jeremy tried to push him away, struggling, his eyes bugging out.

"Tell me what the argument was about or I'll break your neck." He upped the pressure on Jeremy's throat and saw panic in his eyes.

"Okay," Jeremy croaked. "Let me go and I'll tell you."

He stepped back and flexed his fingers. "Start talking."

Massaging his throat, Jeremy said, "She found out that I've been, uh, seeing another woman."

"For how long?"

"A couple of months. Maybe three. It's hard to explain. I knew you'd be mad if I told you."

Good guess, asshole. "And she told you to move out?"

"Yes. Wednesday morning, a buddy of mine helped me load my stuff into a UHAUL."

"You haven't seen or talked to her since?"

"No." Jeremy glared at him. "You've got a helluva nerve, coming here and treating me like this. You're a police officer. You're not allowed to use violence when you question me. I could file a complaint."

Anger rose up inside him and boiled over. "Listen carefully, Jeremy, because I'm not going to say this twice. Keep your mouth shut. Tell no one I was here. If you do, I will find out and I will come back here and fuck you up so bad you won't be screwing your new girlfriend or anyone else for a very long time."

———

9:30 AM – Plymouth

Bridget heard a car door slam, went to the kitchen door and saw Sunny flick a key fob, the lights flashing on a silver Audi in the driveway. Just what she needed. Dealing with Brian's partner in crime.

She opened the door and called, "My car's in the garage, Sunny. Park your car on the street."

Sunny didn't look happy about it, but she got back in the Audi and backed it down the driveway.

Bridget leaned against the kitchen counter and massaged her aching temples. After Maureen woke her, she'd gone back to bed, lying there, wide awake, feeling guilty that she'd slapped Maureen. Eventually she fell asleep, but she kept jolting awake, worrying about cops.

Sunny entered the kitchen, jingling her car keys, and said, "Nice setup you've got here. Last house on a dead-end street, no close neighbors. Dev said the hostage was giving you problems."

"He needs to get things moving so we can let her go."

Sunny's bright blue eyes grew cold. "He's doing his best to make that happen. He's got plenty of other things to worry about."

"He doesn't have to feed the hostage three times a day and empty the piss pot." *Or worry about Renzi and the cops showing up here.*

Ignoring her, Sunny went in the living room and called, "I love the Munch print. The Scream is one of my favorites."

Silently fuming, Bridget clenched her teeth and followed the bitch-from-hell into the living room, her annoyance escalating.

"The print would look much better over there." Sunny pointed at the wall above the couch. "So it catches the light through the window."

"This isn't a real estate showing, Sunny. Let's talk about what you can do to help with the hostage. That's the only reason you're here."

If I had my way, I'd never lay eyes on you again.

Sunny's mouth quirked in annoyance. "Fine. What do you want me to do? Dev told me you're keeping her in the basement."

What else did he tell you? "I need to buy groceries, easy food for her to eat. She's blindfolded and her wrists are bound together with zip-ties."

"I assume she's already had breakfast," Sunny said.

"Yes," she said, lying to her, beaming her a big smile. "But I didn't empty the stinky piss pot. You can do that."

Stone-faced, Sunny said, "How do I get to the basement?"

Bridget took her in the hall and showed the light switch for the stairs. "Turn right at the bottom. Tank set up a folding bed in my workout room. The portable toilet is beside it. Shut off the light when you leave and make sure you keep this door closed."

"Okay. Can you make some coffee? I could use a cup. Then I'll empty the potty and figure out what to feed her for lunch." Adding with a sarcastic smile, "While you do your *errands*."

"I already made coffee." Bridget went in the kitchen, took out a mug and set it beside the coffeemaker. "Slim pickings for lunch, but I'm sure you'll make do." Aiming a faux-smile at Sunny. "That's why I need to buy groceries. Be careful when you feed her. She's no pushover."

Sunny poured coffee into the mug. "Don't worry. I can handle her."

"Cover your face so she can't see you."

"I thought she was blindfolded."

"She is, but I always wear my ski-mask, just in case."

"Okay, I'll use yours."

"No. I don't want your germs on it. Cover your face with a scarf or something." *Take that, bitch.*

"Fine," Sunny said in a cold voice. "Go buy the groceries."

Relishing the angry glint in her eyes, Bridget suppressed a smile.

Make things unpleasant enough, Sunny would never come here again.

Next time she needed help, she'd ask Tank to help her.

CHAPTER 25

FRIDAY October 28 – 12:15 PM – Baltimore

Frank stood at a window in the airport gate area overlooking the tarmac, fighting the despair growing inside him, an unbearable pain pressing against his heart. He opened his phone and studied the photograph of Maureen.

His only child held captive by the same evil men who'd murdered his father, while he waited to board a plane in an airport.

But ninety minutes from now he'd be in Boston, figuring out a plan to find Maureen. He dialed Rafe's number.

"Yo, Frank, how's it going? You get anything from the boyfriend?"

"They had a fight and Mo made him move out. Jeremy said he loaded his stuff into a UHAUL Wednesday morning before work, hasn't seen her since. Bottom line, I don't think he's involved."

"Uh-huh. Why'd she make him move out?"

"Tell you when I see you. I'm about to board a flight to Boston. I talked to Mo's next door neighbor, an old guy in his bathrobe, said he hardly ever sees her, probably watches TV all day. No sense asking the other neighbors. Mo's not here. By now she could be anywhere."

Or she could be dead.

"Somewhere near Boston be my guess," Rafe said. "I got more info for you. Nothing urgent, but useful."

"Speaking of useful, I need ammo for my SIG 9mm and the usual helpful accessories, including a Kevlar vest. My plane lands at Logan at two o'clock. I'll rent a car and meet you in town."

"Good," Rafe said. "I'll round up what you need. Meet me at Wings, I'll have it for you."

"Thanks, Rafe. Gotta go." He clicked off and glanced at his own gate across the concourse. Two people in wheelchairs were already boarding, but he had time for another call. He punched in a number and waited.

"Boston Herald, news desk," Gina said, letting him know she was at work.

"Got a minute to talk?"

"Just a moment, sir. I'll take care of that."

He waited, watching other passengers slowly pass the gate agent to board his flight.

"Franco! Good to hear from you. What's up?"

"Nothing good. They kidnapped Maureen."

"What??? That's terrible! When? What happened?"

"I'm about to board a flight to Boston. Can you meet me for dinner? I might need your help."

"Absolutely. Our usual spot? Seven o'clock?"

"Great. Tell you all about it when I see you."

"I'm so sorry to hear this, Franco. Take care of yourself. Love you."

"Love you too." He ended the call, fighting the lump in throat. He didn't need Gina to help him solve the case. He needed to feel her arms around him, needed to tell her his worst fear.

Maureen was dead.

————

12:45 PM – Plymouth

After the bank officer left the viewing room, Bridget opened her safe deposit box. Three inches high, ten inches wide, eighteen inches deep, big enough to hold a hundred grand in cash, bundles of fifty-dollar bills from Brian, money she used on her vacations. A few years ago she'd begun buying gold coins. They were probably worth another sixty grand.

But that wasn't why she'd come here.

My father's a cop, and he's going to find me and put you in jail.

If Renzi found his daughter in her cottage, she'd go to jail. Even if he didn't, she had to consider another problem. The manila envelope on top of the cash held certain items that could put her in prison. Everyone in Plymouth knew her as Bridget White, the name on the deed to her cottage. That's why Brian wanted her to hold Renzi's daughter there.

But what if Renzi found out Bridget White was really Bridget Devlin?

Sister of Brian Devlin. A gangster out on parole. The man Renzi had helped send to prison.

A violent shudder ripped through her body, so powerful it threatened to morph into a panic. If a kidnapping was involved, Renzi's cop pals would have no trouble accessing her safe deposit box.

If they did, she was screwed. Her birth certificate was in the envelope, plus the bogus certificate of marriage between Robert White and Bridget White, the name on the deed to the cottage.

Enough evidence to send her to prison for a long time.

She opened the envelope and took out a New Hampshire drivers license. Her photograph, Irene Gillan's name, Brian's married cousin, allegedly. When she refused to use her Bridget White license to visit Brian in prison, Tank had paid one of Brian's associates, a shifty-eyed old man who owned a house in Nashua, New Hampshire, to list Irene Gillan as a resident and put the electric bill in her name. The bills went to his house every month, but she paid them online. Whenever she had to renew her New Hampshire DL, she drove to Nashua, collected the most recent bill, went to the RMV with the electric bill and her current license, took the eye exam and forked over the money.

The license was good for another two years.

Maybe Irene Gillan should go somewhere far away and stay there for a month. Let Brian handle the rest of his payback scheme.

But she couldn't leave Maureen in the basement. She'd starve to death or die of thirst. Bad enough that she'd hit her again. Unwilling to face her this morning, she'd lied to Sunny, saying Maureen had already eaten breakfast.

And what about Kate? Other than singing in the church choir, Kate lived for her visits. Lunch twice a month, plus shopping expeditions for clothes. Bridget could go on vacation, have flings with interesting men and come home refreshed, ready to go back to work. Something Kate could never do.

Kate's life was as drab and colorless as a rainy day, monotony to the max. Living in a group home with others like herself. Attending the same activities, week after week.

No. Any thought of escape was wishful thinking. She had to tough it out. But she intended to protect herself. She closed the envelope and tucked it under her arm. She'd hide it in the trunk of her car.

She glanced at her watch. It was late. She still had to buy groceries, take them home and deal with Sunny. And the hostage. The woman she'd slapped because she was exhausted and frightened and couldn't control her Irish temper.

Maureen was right. She was a monster.

PAYBACK

———

1:25 PM – Plymouth

Maureen heard the basement door open. She was dying of thirst. Maybe the Bitch was bringing her some water. She sat up and swung her legs over the side of the cot.

Footsteps on the stairs. *Thunk-thunk-thunk.* Not the Bitch.

These footsteps were heavier, marching across the floor. Maybe it was Cigarman.

No. Not Cigarman. She could smell perfume. Who was it?

"Hold still while I take the tape off off your mouth."

A woman's voice. Definitely not the Bitch. This voice was different, lower pitched and forceful. Damn! There were three of them! Cigarman, the Bitch and another woman. Ripping duct tape off her mouth now, sending searing pain over her cheeks and lips.

"Ow! That hurts! I'm thirsty! I need some water."

"Be polite and you'll get some. Say please."

She gritted her teeth and said, "Please." Thinking, *Fuck you bitch!*

Thunk-thunk-thunk across the floor. Thunk-thunk-thunk on the way back.

"Here's your water." The woman put a room-temperature bottle of water into her hand, the bottle cap into the other.

She gulped some water and said, "Can I have some chap stick? My lips hurt from the tape."

"Tough. This isn't a hotel and I'm not a maid."

"I'm hungry! I haven't had anything to eat for hours!"

"You had breakfast a couple of hours ago."

Her heart beat an angry tattoo inside her chest. "I did not! I'm hungry!'

"Stop yelling at me," the woman said in a cold voice.

Thunk-thunk-thunk across the room. Thunk-thunk-thunk back. The woman set a tray on her lap and put a plastic spoon in her hand.

"I made you some mashed potatoes. If you behave yourself, we might give you something good for dinner."

Like what? A surf-n-turf with steak, shrimp and french fries?

But she'd better not mess with this woman. If she did, she might not get anything.

165

No food and no water, just nasty comments from Dragon-Lady. Holding a spoon in one hand, the paper dish in the other, she spooned mashed potatoes into her mouth. Yuk. Lukewarm and it tasted awful.

She spit it out on the floor. Silence. Her heart pounded. She waited, not daring to speak.

Suddenly, Dragon-Lady smooshed mashed potatoes over her face, mashing it against her nose and mouth.

"I hate you!" Maureen yelled. "You're a fucking asshole! And a bully!"

Icy fingers grabbed her chin in a vise-like grip. "Shut up. I'm taking your food upstairs. One word out of your mouth, I'll come down and put a bullet in your head."

Her heart jolted into a frenzied gallop, beating her chest like a jackhammer. *Thunk-thunk-thunk.* Footsteps going up the stairs.

But Dragon-Lady didn't shut the door.

One word out of your mouth, I'll come down and put a bullet in your head.

Dragon-Lady was worse than the Bitch. Did she really have a gun? Would they really kill her?

Why would they go to all this trouble and then kill her?

Tears filled her eyes. This had been the worst two weeks of her life. Jeremy cheating on her. Grampa Sal dying in a car accident. Getting kidnapped. She sniffled, sucked snot down her throat and swallowed.

She had to stay strong. Had to think positive. Dad would find her, she was certain of it.

Maybe Rafe could help him. He worked for Boston PD.

She didn't know where they'd taken her, but she'd heard seagulls so it had to be near the ocean like Grampa Sal's house in Swampscott. And someplace cold, a house with a basement and a furnace that ran on heating oil. She could smell it, and every so often she heard the furnace start up.

Please find me soon, Dad. Not daring to speak the words aloud. If she did, Dragon-Lady might shoot her.

Damn it to hell! Now they were minding her in shifts. Feeding her mashed potatoes. She hated mashed potatoes.

Hated feeling helpless. Unable to see. Unable to move around the room, her ankle chained to something, her hands tied together.

If they weren't, she'd scratch Dragon-Lady's eyes out.

CHAPTER 26

FRIDAY October 28 – 2:35 PM – Boston

Frank forked up some mashed potatoes, then a bite of chicken. Seated beside him at a table in Wings, Rafe was chowing down barbecued chicken, mashed potatoes and collard greens.

"Glad to see you got your appetite back," Rafe said, eyeing his plate.

"First thing I've eaten all day, except for a bag of chips on the plane. You said you had more info for me."

"Indeed I do," Rafe said. "Dropped in to see Eddie Mills yesterday, big swanky house on Beacon Hill. Daddy Warbucks wasn't home, out making the big bucks. Mom said Eddie was sleeping. I told her to get him up. He lumbered into the living room in his pajamas, gotta weigh at least three-hundred pounds, could barely put two words together. Bottom line, Eddie's too fat, too doped up and too stupid to pull something like this."

"Okay, cross him off the list. That leaves Jesús DeCastro and Brian Devlin."

Rafe guzzled some ice tea. "Jesús works at a car wash in Mattapan. He found God and repented his sins, remember? Mom takes him to church every morning before work, twice on Sunday. My money's on the gangster in Southie. Got on the BPD computer and found out Brian Devlin grew up in public housing. Here's the interesting part. Kathleen's not his only sister. He's got another one, a year older, named Bridget. I ran her name through wants and warrants, got nothing."

"A housing project in Southie?"

"No, East Boston, near St. Mary's Church. The kids went to the parochial school next door."

Frank pushed his plate aside, took out his notepad and jotted down the information. "Thanks. I'll go there tomorrow, see what I can dig up."

"Talk to the nuns be your best bet." Rafe grinned at him. "Use your Renzi charm."

Frank fingered the scar on his chin, picturing Maureen, blindfolded, her mouth taped shut. He was in no mood to be charming.

"Also got two more suspects," Rafe said, "courtesy of the Staties at the DA's office. Thomaso Ippolito, a Worcester mobster, beat a club owner to death fifteen years ago for not paying the vig, convicted of Murder Two. Your father denied his appeal, so he served sixteen years in Club Fed. Got paroled six weeks ago, currently living in Worcester."

"And mob connected," Frank said.

"Correct. I haven't talked to his PO yet, but I will. The other guy, Adrian Hall, shot three black guys in Springfield, chopped them up with a chainsaw to hide the bodies." Rafe pulled a face. "A white supremacist skinhead, you know, got all those the lightning-bolt tats, symbols of the Aryan Brotherhood. Not to mention Hitler. Convicted of Murder One, got life without parole."

Rafe drank some ice tea and set the glass on the table. "Your father denied his appeal, but you know how it is these days, overcrowded jails and such. He got out on parole last month. These skinheads are hooked up with the Hells Angels. Not to be messed with."

Frank pushed his plate aside, suddenly queasy. "No signs of a struggle in the apartment. They grabbed her outside, might even have drugged her. Mo wouldn't go down without a fight."

Rafe said, his eyes full of concern, "Let's hope she doesn't give them too much grief. These fuckers won't stand for it."

"That's what I'm worried about." Worried? Hell, he was frantic.

"Still no word from them?" Rafe said.

"No. What do they want? Money?"

"Probably," Rafe said. "In addition to making you sweat."

"They took Mo's cell phone. If they fire it up, maybe we can get the location from the phone company."

"I'll get on that right away, got a buddy who gets me that kind of info. The items you wanted are in the trunk of my car. Plenty of ammo for the SIG and a few other goodies."

"Excellent." He grabbed the check. "Lunch is on me. Let's go get it." Go get the ammo and load up his SIG so he could settle the score with these motherfuckers like Al Pacino in *The Godfather*.

———

168

3:35 PM – Plymouth

Bridget parked the car and carried two bags of groceries into the cottage. At the kitchen table, Sunny didn't look up, thumbing through a fashion magazine. Beyond her, the basement door was wide open.

She set the groceries on the counter, went in the hall to shut the door, and returned to the kitchen. "I told you to keep the basement door shut, Sunny."

"The girl gave me a hard time. I found a box of instant mashed potatoes and made her some for lunch, but she spit it on the floor." Sunny gave her a faux smile. "I left it there so you could see it. Then I spread mashed potatoes over the spoiled brat's face and threw the rest in the garbage."

Bridget gritted her teeth, fighting a slow-simmering anger. "Why is the door open?"

"She mouthed off at me, called me a fucking bitch. I told her if I heard another word out of her mouth I'd come down there and put a bullet in her head. *That's* why the door is open."

Speechless, Bridget stared at her.

"You need to toughen up, Bridget. Show her who's boss."

Fearing she'd punch the woman, she clenched her fists behind her back. In a quiet voice, she said, "Get out of my house."

Glaring at her, Sunny rose from the table. "Brian wants me to help you mind the hostage. My suitcase is in the car. I'd like to get settled. Where do I sleep tonight?"

"Not here. Go back to your cat-house hotel in Southie."

"Don't tell me what to do! Brian gives the orders, not you."

The slow-simmering anger boiled over. Bridget opened a drawer beside the sink and took out a corkscrew, gripping the wooden handle in the palm of her hand, the metal corkscrew protruding between her knuckles. She stepped closer and jabbed the corkscrew at Sunny's face.

"If you're not out of my house in thirty seconds, I'll put your pretty blue eyes out."

Sunny jerked her head away and stepped back toward the door, her eyes ablaze with anger. "Fine. I'll tell Brian you don't want anyone to help you mind the hostage."

"Mind your own fucking business, Sunny. I don't ask Brian to fight my battles. And I don't beat up on blindfolded hostages when their hands are tied."

Sunny shot her a murderous look, opened the door and left.

Shaking with fury, Bridget sank against the kitchen counter. Good riddance to the Bitch from Hell, but this would cause trouble. Sunny and Brian were lovers, thick as thieves and twice as devious.

And she was just as bad, her parting shot the ultimate hypocrisy.

I don't beat up on blindfolded hostages when their hands are tied.

Bullshit. That's exactly what she had done. Twice she had lost her temper and slapped Maureen.

Chimes erupted from her purse. She took out her cell phone and answered, hoping Sunny hadn't already talked to Brian.

"Hi Bridget, how are you doing today?" Kate said.

Terrible. Gathering herself, she pasted on a smile and said, "I'm fine, Kate, how are you?"

"Great!" Kate exclaimed. "I'm getting ready for Halloween. There's a parade in Winthrop on Sunday. Can you take me? It's in the afternoon. First we go to Mass, then we eat lunch."

Halloween, Kate's favorite holiday. She'd forgotten all about it. She always spent Halloween with Kate.

But how could she? She couldn't leave the hostage.

Unwilling to upset Kate, she said, "I hope so, but I'm not sure."

"Pleeeze," Kate said. "I'm going to wear my new orange shirt. The one Brian gave me."

Bridget clenched her jaw. The Baltimore Orioles shirt that Brian saw when he was planning the kidnapping in Baltimore. Fully intending to have her hold Maureen in her cottage.

"I've got an appointment, but I'll try to get out of it. Right now I've got company. I'll call you tomorrow." Lies, lies and more lies.

"No appointments on Halloween, Bridget. Pleeeze?"

"Talk to you tomorrow."

She ended the call and massaged her aching temples. She couldn't take much more of this. Dealing with Sunny. Minding the hostage. Buying special groceries because Brian said to keep her healthy.

How could she spend her customary time with Kate while Maureen was in her basement? Impossible. She opened the drawer, put away the corkscrew and slammed the drawer shut.

Now she had to go deal with Maureen.

———

4:10 PM – South Boston

Devlin rose from his desk, stretched his arms over his head, went in the kitchen and took a bottle of Harp Ale out of the refrigerator. He'd just spent an hour tinkering with the ransom demand, tweaking it here and there. Not finished yet, but close.

He swigged some Harp Ale and ran the important points through his mind. One million dollars, cash. The deadline: Monday. And the all important threat. No cops. No feds. Or she dies.

Concise and to the point. No details about the swap.

Renzi would shit a brick when he got it.

His cell phone rang. He took it out of his pocket, punched on and said, "Hey, Sunny, how's it going down there?"

"I'm not down there, I'm home in my apartment."

"Why? What happened?"

"Cutie-pie in the basement got nasty with me, so I told her to shut up or I'd put a bullet in her head. Then your sweetheart of a sister came home with the groceries and told me to get lost."

He said nothing, recalling Tank's warning that Sunny and Bridget didn't get along. At the time, he hadn't taken it seriously. Maybe he should have. The problem with the hostage concerned him.

"What did cutie-pie do?"

"Mouthed off at me, spit food on the floor. Nothing I couldn't handle, but I think Bridget might be a problem. Seems like she's too tight with cutie-pie, very protective of her. Sort of like Stockholm syndrome in reverse."

"Why? What did she say?"

"She yelled at me for threatening her."

"Yeah, well, Bridget's got a temper, you know?"

Silence on the other end. Then, Sunny said, "What if she decides to let cutie-pie go?"

"She'd never do that."

"She's your sister, Dev. You can't see her the way I do. Push come to shove, she'll betray you."

He frowned. Would Bridget betray him? Doubtful. They were family, bonded by blood and bound by their miserable childhood. But he'd keep the thought in mind.

To placate Sunny, he said, "I'm composing a love note to send to cutie-pie's father."

Sunny chuckled low in her throat. "Great. When will you send it?"

"Later tonight. Tank and I figure he went to Baltimore to scope out what happened there. We don't know where he is now, but I've got his cell phone number. I'll text him with my disposable burner."

"You think he'll talk to his cop friends?"

"He better not. My note tells him exactly what will happen if he does."

"Goodness, I can't imagine what that would be." Sunny uttered a low throaty laugh, the one that always gave him a hard-on. "Want to come over and celebrate with a drink after you send it?"

Devlin smiled, picturing her gorgeous body, naked beside him.

"Definitely. Celebrate with a drink and a magnificent orgy in bed."

CHAPTER 27

FRIDAY October 28 – 4:45 PM – Plymouth

Maureen heard the basement door open. Her heart jolted into a ragged rhythm.

Was Dragon-Lady going to shoot her?

She'd been sitting here for hours, quiet as a mouse, feeling sick to her stomach, any thought of food forgotten.

One word out of your mouth, I'll come down there and put a bullet in your head.

She clamped her lips together so she wouldn't scream. Damned if she'd let the woman know how terrified she was.

Footsteps on the stairs, not thunk-thunk-thunk, quieter footsteps, coming toward her.

"Are you going to shoot me?" Loathing the tremor in her voice that revealed her fear.

"No one's going to shoot you. Hold still while I wash your face."

The Bitch's voice. She heard water drip and felt a warm wet cloth dab-dab-dab at her face, scrubbing at the mashed potatoes crusted on her cheeks and nose. "This shouldn't have happened. And I shouldn't have slapped you."

No you shouldn't. But at least it wasn't Dragon-Lady with a gun.

"I'm heating up some chicken nuggets for you. I'll bring them down in a minute."

"Thank you. My lips really hurt from the tape. Can I have some Chapstick?"

"Yes. If you promise to be quiet, I won't put any more tape over your mouth."

"I'll be quiet," she said quickly. "I promise."

"Good. No one can hear you anyway. Except me."

What did that mean? Was Dragon-Lady gone?

Relieved, she said, "Where am I?"

"Never mind. Here's a bottle of water. I'll be back in a minute."

Maureen drank some water. *No one's going to shoot you.* Fine, but no one could hear her scream. Just the Bitch.

Cigarman must be somewhere else. Maybe he was negotiating with Dad, asking for ransom money.

Dragon-Lady was someplace else, too, far away, she hoped.

Footsteps descended the stairs and approached her. She smelled a spicy aroma, barbecued chicken. Her stomach rumbled with hunger now that she wasn't terrified.

"Here's a plate of chicken nuggets and some apple slices. I put a napkin beside the plate."

"Thank you." Groping with her fingers, she found a chicken nugget and took a bite. Delicious. Her stomach gurgled as she chewed and swallowed. She finished that one and groped for another.

"I put a tube of Chapstick beside you on the bed."

"Thank you so much." Butter her up, maybe she could get more information.

"Eat your food. I'll be back in a while with a toothbrush so you can brush your teeth."

Why was the Bitch being so nice to her? Feeding her decent food, giving her Chapstick, saying she'd bring her a toothbrush. Was she feeling guilty? Another avenue to pursue.

"Dad is probably worried sick about me. How would your dad feel if someone kidnapped you? I bet he'd be frantic."

"My father's dead and so is my mother."

"Oh. That's too bad. I'm very sorry to hear that. My dad is great."

"Mine wasn't."

"What about your mother?"

Silence in the room.

"Why am I here?" she said. "What do you want?"

"Money, what else?"

"Money for what?"

"To take care of my disabled sister."

Sudden rapid footsteps retreated toward the stairs.

Seconds later Maureen heard the door slam. She picked up an apple slice and took a bite, savoring the juicy morsel, reviewing what she'd learned. The woman was an orphan. Both parents were dead, but she had a disabled sister.

She devoured another chicken nugget.

Maybe the orphan woman wasn't so bad after all.

If she kept being polite and acted sympathetic, maybe the Orphan would let her go.

———

7:10 PM – Nahant

Frank took a swallow of wine, set his glass on the bar and stared out the window, conscious of the minutes ticking by. Thirty-six hours since Maureen had been taken and no word from the kidnappers. Not good. The rule of thumb with homicides: Solve the case within forty-eight hours or it might never be solved.

Was Maureen still alive? What if she wasn't?

He banished the thought, unwilling to contemplate what that would mean. A lifetime of grief and second-guessing himself. Woulda-coulda-shoulda.

The Clam Shack was always busy on Friday night, the dining room packed, couples sitting in the lounge, awaiting a table. He'd put his jacket on the seat beside him to save it for Gina.

After he left Rafe at three-thirty, he'd driven to the house in Swampscott, got caught in the usual Friday night exodus from Boston, didn't get there until four-thirty. After he unpacked his suitcase he'd sat in the kitchen, organizing his notes. Thinking about Maureen. Wondering where she was. Wondering if she was alive.

A flash of motion caught his eye as Gina entered lounge, dressed in her work outfit, a charcoal-gray pantsuit and an aqua blouse. Eager to greet her, he got off his bar stool.

She hugged him and whispered, "Sorry I'm late, Franco. Traffic was a bear."

Unwilling to let her go, he held her close, inhaling her familiar scent, his jangled nerves soothed by the human contact. At last, he released her and said, "Let's get you some wine."

She kissed his cheek and slipped onto her chair. "Work was crazy today, shots fired during a bank holdup in Cambridge, but I couldn't stop thinking about you. Tell me about Maureen."

He waggled two fingers at the bartender, pointed at his glass of Merlot and took out his cell phone. "First, I got this."

He showed her the photograph of Maureen.

Gina gasped and looked at him, her dark eyes somber. "You must be out of your mind! When did you get this?"

"Thursday afternoon after I left work."

The barkeep arrived with their wine. Frank waited until he left to tell her about his trip to Baltimore. He told her what he'd found at Mo's apartment and recapped his talk with Jeremy the next day. "He moved out Wednesday morning, hasn't seen or talked to her since. They took her thirty-six hours ago. Since they sent the photo and the text, I've heard nothing."

Gina drank some wine, then said, "They took her cell phone?"

"Yes. I figure they got my cell phone number from her contact list."

"What's the story with Jeremy?"

"Maureen found out he was having an affair and threw him out."

"There's a kick in the ass. She didn't tell you about it when she was here for the funeral?"

"No. She probably didn't want to bother me." He gulped some wine. "Rafe's the only one who knows about this. Beside you."

Gina fished a cashew out of a dish on the bar and ate it. "No one in New Orleans?"

Meaning Kelly, he assumed. "No. The fewer people who know about this the better. You saw the text. No cops, no feds or she dies."

"If she didn't go to work, wouldn't that set off alarm bells at the hospital where she works?"

"No doubt. Another thing to worry about. If they send a Baltimore cop to her apartment for a wellness check and she's not there, they'll probably call me."

"What will you tell them?"

"I don't know."

"Better think up a story, Franco. Is Evelyn's number on Maureen's emergency contact list?"

"No. Maureen knows her mother's useless in an emergency. Even if they called the Milton number, Evelyn's not there. Rafe and I made her go stay at her cousin's house in Connecticut."

"What does Rafe say?"

"Sit tight and wait for them to contact me. Ever since my father's funeral, he's been working overtime, rounding up suspects. We've already eliminated some of them."

"Who's left? Anyone I know?"

"Doubtful. A gangster in Worcester and a white-supremacist in Springfield. My father denied their appeals. Plus two men I helped put away for murder. Jesús DeCastro and Brian Devlin, an Irish gangster from Southie. All currently out on parole."

Gina combed her fingers through her short dark hair. "I don't know DeCastro, but I've heard rumors about Devlin. Handsome and charming, but he'd as soon kill you as look at you. Come to think of it, one of his top lieutenants died in a South Boston hotel on Monday. I'm surprised Rafe didn't tell you about it."

"Not Rafe's territory. He works Dorchester and Roxbury. Who died? How did it happen?"

"Sean Whelan, reputed to be Devlin's enforcer, choked to death on a chicken bone." She grinned at him. "Don't laugh. It happens. But maybe not in this case. He died at the Seaview Hotel, managed by Sunny Jensen. It's no secret that she and Devlin have been lovers for years."

Frank took out his notepad and jotted notes. "What do you know about her?"

"Not much. I've never met her but I've seen pictures. She's gorgeous, a blonde blue-eyed Nordic type. Rumor has it the Seaview Hotel is a high-class brothel that Devlin set up for her years ago. Not that she's ever been busted for it."

"Did the Boston cops investigate Whelan's death?"

"Yes. The Herald reporter who covered the story showed me a copy of the police report. After Whelan ate dinner with Sunny, she called security. The security guards found Whelan unresponsive and called an ambulance. They took him to City Hospital. Two detectives questioned Sunny. The report said she acted distraught, but her answers seemed rehearsed. The medical examiner found bones in Whelan's throat. A toxicology screen showed no drugs, but he'd been drinking. The ME report listed the COD as undetermined."

"Interesting. Maybe Rafe and I should have a talk with Sunny."

His cell phone pinged and he grabbed it off the bar. Dreading what he would find, he opened the text.

No photo this time, just a text.

How much is your daughter worth? One million dollars cash. All hundreds, shrink-wrapped. Have it ready by Monday. No cops, no feds or she dies.

He read the last part again. *No cops, no feds or she dies.*

Devastating words. He clenched his jaw and showed the text to Gina.

"What bastards!" she said. "Asking you what your daughter is worth. Where the hell are you supposed to get a million dollars?"

That was the least of his worries. No picture this time, but he knew they had Maureen. Just thinking about it made him want to puke. He had to find her and get her away from the bastards. And make them wish they'd never been born.

"I don't know. Lemme call Rafe, see what he says."

When Rafe answered, Frank said, "I just got a ransom demand. A million dollars, cash."

"Fuck all!" Rafe said. "Where are you?"

Gazing into Gina's eyes, he said, "At the Clam Shack in Nahant, with Gina."

"She knows about Maureen, right?"

"Yes. I just showed her the text."

"Don't answer it," Rafe said. "Meet me at the house in Swampscott and we'll figure out a plan. I'm in Dorchester, be there in half an hour. Bring Gina. Always good to have a woman's input."

"See you there," he said, and ended the call. "Rafe wants us to meet him at the house in Swampscott so we can plan what to do." Not mentioning the questions raging in his mind.

After they decided on a plan, Rafe would go home. Would Gina?

Or, driven by his current emotional turmoil, would their fiery sexual attraction ignite as usual, leading to its inevitable conclusion?

CHAPTER 28

FRIDAY October 28 – 8:30 PM – Swampscott

The Clam Shack takeout seafood platter on the table filled the kitchen with luscious aromas. Rafe and Gina were noshing on fried scallops, fried clams and french fries. Frank wasn't.

How could he eat when his nerves were shot and his daughter was missing and time was running out?

How much is your daughter worth? The bastards taunting him. Knowing he'd be desperate to get her back.

"Where the hell do I get a million dollars?" he said.

Rafe set his bottle of Becks on the table and said, "Hold on a minute. We need proof of life. Not a picture. Tell them you want to talk to Maureen on the phone."

Gina nodded, gazing at him across the table. "That's what any parent would want."

Fuck proof of life. He wanted to kill the bastards. He wanted to hold Maureen in his arms and never let her out of his sight again. Ridiculous, of course. She was a grown woman. Not only that, he was thinking like a father, not a cop, like Rafe.

"Okay, but how do I get the money?"

"You don't," Rafe said. "Once they get the money, you got no leverage. Frank, you know what can happen. The motherfuckers want to make sure no feds are watching, send you here and there, have you drop the money in one place, but Maureen is somewhere else and they make you jump through hoops to find her."

Gina touched his hand. "You know he's right, Franco."

Fighting the urge to scream, he gulped some Merlot. It wasn't their kid sitting in a room blindfolded with her mouth taped shut. And Rafe had left out the worst scenario.

The fuckers take the money and he finds Maureen somewhere, dead.

But if he kept thinking like that, he'd never get through this. He had to stay focused.

Find Maureen and bring her home. Period.

"Show me the phone number that sent the text," Rafe said. "Ten to one it's a burner, but I'll check it. You never know."

"Read me the note," Gina said.

He opened his phone, showed Rafe the number and read the text aloud. "How much is your daughter worth? A million cash, all hundreds, shrink-wrapped. Have it by Monday. No cops. No feds. Or she dies".

"Tell 'em you can't get that much cash by Monday," Rafe said. "But make 'em *think* you're getting it. These fuckers are pros, might be watching you. They know where this house is. Go to the bank tomorrow and talk to somebody. Make it look like you're applying for a loan."

Gina took out her note pad and started writing.

Unable to sit still, Frank went in the living room, his stomach queasy, his mind full of dread. He went to a window and parted the curtain. The sky was dark, the moon hidden by clouds. Was one of the bastards out there now, watching the house? No suspicious cars parked on the street.

But if someone drove by the house they would see three cars in the driveway. His rental, Rafe's black van, no telltale signs to indicate it was a police vehicle, and Gina's red Mazda. With a *Boston Herald* bumper sticker.

He went back to the kitchen and sat at the table. Gina showed him the note she'd written. *I want proof of life. Not a picture, a phone call. I'll have the cash by Tuesday. When do I talk to my daughter?*

He showed it to Rafe, who nodded and said, "Good, but set a time for the phone call."

"No. I want to talk to Maureen. I don't care when they call."

"Okay," Rafe said. "Send it and see what they say."

He typed the text message and hit Send. Feeling heartsick. Nine o'-clock on a Friday night, he was with his friends.

But Maureen was in a room somewhere. All alone.

"We're gonna find her," Rafe said. "And arrest these motherfuckers."

Or kill them. Aloud, he said, "Thanks for all your help, Rafe. Thanks for keeping me on track."

"That's what friends are for. They'll think on it, so you might not get a response right away. Call me when you do. Time for me to hit the road." Rafe rose from his chair and gave Gina a sly look. "Take care of my partner, Gina. He's hurting, needs some TLC."

Gina smiled. "I can do that."

———

9:15 PM – South Boston

Lying in bed beside Sunny, Devlin read the text message and smiled. Renzi would have the cash by Tuesday. A day later than he'd hoped, but for a million bucks he could wait an extra day.

"What did Daddy Dearest say?" Sunny asked, tracing her fingers over his chest.

When he showed her the text, she said, "Progress, of a sort. He's worried about her. Are you going to let him talk to her?"

"Maybe. We'll see how it goes. He said he'd get the cash."

"But not until Tuesday."

"Right." Devlin sat up, took his wineglass off the bedside table and took a big gulp, planning his moves. First, make sure Renzi got the loot. Saying he'd get it was one thing. Actually getting it was something else.

Too bad he couldn't plant a bug in Renzi's house and listen in when he talked to people on the phone. That didn't seem feasible, but he'd have Tank watch the house, keep an eye on Renzi to see where he went.

Sunny stroked his thigh, smiling at him. "A penny for your thoughts, Lover-man."

"Thinking about the text I'm going to send him."

"Good, but don't send it now."

"Why not?"

"You want him to worry, don't you? Make him wait. Make him lie awake in bed worrying about his daughter." Smiling her feral smile. "Like *Sleepless in Seattle* without the happy ending."

He burst out laughing. "Brilliant, Sunny. Why didn't I think of that?"

She responded with her sexy come-hither smile. "Your payback plan is brilliant, Dev. It just needs a woman's touch here and there."

He pulled her on top of him and kissed her. "Have I told you lately how wonderful you are?"

———

9:45 PM – Swampscott

Frank snuggled against Gina, savoring the warmth of her body and inhaling the scent of her hair. Intoxicating. Just like old times.

But guilty thoughts crept into his mind. What about Kelly?

Raising herself on one elbow, Gina caressed his cheek. "I smell wood burning, Franco. Having guilt pangs, thinking about Kelly?"

Reading his mind. "Thinking about a lot of things. Divided loyalties, mostly. Aren't you?"

"I love my husband, Franco, but I never stopped loving you. Nine years together, we've got a history. We had some great times, but some bad ones, too. The IAD investigation after the little girl died. Evelyn filing for divorce, naming me as the other woman, my former husband finds out about it and flips out."

Gazing into his eyes, she said, "You're a tough cop, but you're human like everyone else. Your father died, then you find out he was murdered, and someone kidnaps your daughter. Your life is in turmoil right now. You need someone to comfort you. Why feel guilty?"

He thought about it. Truthfully, wasn't this what he wanted? He loved Kelly, no question about that. In the five years they'd been together, cheating on her had never entered his mind. But Kelly was New Orleans. Gina was in Boston, and what she said was true. They'd never stopped loving each other.

"When I asked you to meet me tonight, I was hoping we'd wind up in bed. I wanted to make love to you and hold you in my arms afterwards and talk, like we always did."

Gina nodded, gazing at him. "That's what I wanted, too. Why complicate things? You have a life in New Orleans with Kelly. I live here with my husband." She kissed his lips, a long, lingering kiss. "Want an excuse? If you hadn't stopped that weirdo killer, I'd be dead. You saved my life so I'm repaying you."

Amused by her twisted logic, he said, "The Jackpot Killer. Back then I had a lot on my mind. Hunting a serial killer. Dealing with Evelyn and the divorce, Maureen angry at me, refusing my phone calls." He smiled and shook his head. "I even started smoking again. When life goes in the toilet, don't give up your favorite crutch."

"Making love beats smoking any day," Gina said, with a mischievous grin. "I'm thirsty. Want some water?"

"Yes. There's bottled water in the refrigerator. Hold on, I'll get it."

"Relax. I gotta pee so I have to get up anyway."

He watched her leave the room, thinking how lucky he was. Gina was a wonderful lover, not a cop like Kelly, but she was feisty and smart, a savvy news reporter plugged into the Boston crime scene, comfortable talking shop with him.

But losing himself in sexual oblivion didn't change anything.

The kidnappers still had Maureen.

He lay on his back and stared at the ceiling, seeing the picture of Maureen in his mind, blindfolded, her mouth taped shut. An evil act by an evil man. The same man who'd murdered his father.

Right now he had five suspects, but Rafe said to forget Eddie Mills. He trusted Rafe's judgment so that left four. Jesús DeCastro and Brian Devlin, two killers he'd sent to prison. His father had denied appeals from mobster Thomaso Ippolito and skinhead Adrian Hall, which kept them in prison for a long time.

Plenty of time for their hatred of Judge Salvatore Renzi to fester and grow. But if the Worcester mobster or the Springfield skinhead hated his father enough to kill him, why would they kidnap Maureen? It didn't make sense.

That left Jesús DeCastro and Brian Devlin.

At the parole hearing, DeCastro's mother claimed he'd repented and found God, but Jesús ran with an MS-13 gang, men who would as soon kill you as look at you. If Jesús wanted to kill Judge Salvatore Renzi, he wouldn't run him off the road, he'd jump him somewhere and hack him to death with a machete.

Which left Brian Devlin.

He reviewed what Gina had told him. Sean Whelan, reputed to be Devlin's enforcer, had died under suspicious circumstances, and Sunny Jensen, Devlin's lover, was there when it happened.

A eureka moment jolted him upright in bed. Sometimes, thanks to many years of detective work and his intuitive feel for criminals, all the puzzle pieces fell into place. The mobster in Worcester didn't murder his father and kidnap Maureen, and the skinhead in Springfield didn't, either. Cross Jesús DeCastro off the list, too.

Brian Devlin was his man.

He opened his phone and studied the mugshot Rafe had sent him, taken fifteen years ago after Devlin murdered his sister's husband. A handsome man with cold eyes and a hard expression.

A mob kingpin out on parole, living in South Boston, fifteen miles from Swampscott. Devlin had told Whelan to force his father's car off the road, he was certain of it. Then, fearing Whelan might talk, Devlin had him killed.

Not that he could prove it. But he knew it in his gut.

He was going to get the son-of-a-bitch, and Gina might be able to help him.

She entered the room with two tall glasses, handed him one and said, "I hate drinking out of plastic bottles. What's up, Franco? You look like you're excited about something. Other than me, I mean."

He pulled her close and kissed her. "I'm always excited to see you, but you're right. I know who's got Maureen."

Gina gasped. "Who?"

"You helped me figure it out. Brian Devlin." He showed her Devlin's mugshot.

"Scary-looking guy. You're sure it's him?"

"Positive. I'm gonna get the bastard, and you're going to help me. What else you know about him?"

Gina drank some water. "I hear he hangs out at the Leprechaun Pub in Southie. Rumor is he owns it, but it's probably not in his name. What about Sunny? You think she's holding Maureen in the hotel?"

"No. Too close to home. Same with Devlin's house in Southie. But I think she's somewhere nearby. I need to find out where. Rafe told me Devlin grew up in public housing in East Boston. His parents are dead, but he's got two sisters, Kathleen and Bridget. Kathleen lives in a group home in Winthrop for disabled adults, but I need more info on Bridget. Can you search the *Boston Herald* morgue and dig up every story you can find about Bridget and Brian Devlin?"

"Of course. I'll go into the office tomorrow and get to work on it."

"Great. They went to a parochial school in East Boston. I'm going there tomorrow and talk to the nuns."

Gina frowned. "Be careful, Franco. Rafe says these guys are pros. They might be watching you."

"Forget careful. They've got Maureen and I need to find her."

CHAPTER 29

Maureen held the breakfast sausage in one hand, took a bite and chewed, savoring the smoky taste. She washed it down with a swallow of milk, determined to stick to her plan. Be polite to Orphan, say please and thank you, act sympathetic, and maybe she'd let her talk to Dad.

"Thank you for the sausage. It's delicious. Tell me about your sister.. What sort of disability does she have?"

"Eat your breakfast. I'll be back in a few minutes."

"Wait, don't go yet," Maureen said. "Can't we talk for a minute? I get lonely down here all by myself."

"I can't talk to you now. I have things to do." Speaking curtly.

"After you finish your errands, can I take a shower? I'll behave, I promise." She touched her straggly hair. "My hair is really scuzzy."

Silence. Then, "We'll see. Finish your breakfast."

She heard footsteps on the stairs, then a door close. Orphan seemed out of sorts this morning.

But at least she hadn't hit her. Maybe her plan was working. The sausages and buttered toast really did taste good, and a carton of milk was better than bottled water.

If Orphan let her take a shower and wash her hair, maybe she could pick up more clues about where she was. What was wrong with the sister? Orphan said they wanted money to take care of her.

She drank some milk and ate a bite of toast.

In medical school, she'd learned about all sorts of disabilities. Some of them were awful, requiring round-the-clock care.

She scratched her cheek with her fingers. Damn! The itchy blindfold was driving her crazy. So what if Orphan had a disabled sister!

That didn't give them the right to kidnap her and expect Dad to pay for someone to take care of her.

———

Bridget sat down at the computer desk in her office and took out the burner phone.

Tell me about your sister. What sort of disability does she have?

What was she thinking? She should never have told Maureen they wanted money to take care of her sister.

She punched in the number for Brian's burner and waited.

"Hi Bridget, what's up?"

"I need Tank to mind the hostage tomorrow. Kate asked me to take her to a Halloween parade. She wants to wear that Baltimore Orioles shirt you got her. Why did you give it to her? I don't want to be seen standing beside someone wearing anything connected to Baltimore."

"Christ Almighty! Get her another one! It's Halloween. The stores are full of orange shirts."

Bridget gnawed her bottom lip. He sounded angry, swearing at her. Never rock the boat when Brian's angry.

"Renzi says he'll get the money, but he wants to talk to his daughter."

Smart. He wants proof that she's alive. "How does that work?"

"Use a new burner. Tell her what to say before you make the call. Hi Dad, I'm fine. Pay the money so I can go home, something like that. Tell her something bad will happen if she doesn't stick to the script."

Something bad will happen. Spoken in his stone-cold killer voice.

A shudder of dread rippled through her. "Like what?"

"Tank will come down there tomorrow so you can take Kate to the parade, but he can't stay. I need him to do something on Monday."

"But I have to work on Monday."

"Tell them you've got the flu or something."

She clenched her teeth to keep from screaming. "Brian, I teach classes Monday, Wednesday and Friday, and hold office hours on Tuesday."

"Want me to send Sunny down there?"

Fury rose up inside her. Brian threatening her. He knew damn well she didn't want Sunny here.

"No. How soon can we make the swap? Maureen wants to take a shower and wash her hair."

Silence. Then, "Tank will be there tomorrow at nine. Tell Kate I said Happy Halloween."

A click sounded in her ear.

Bridget put down the phone and massaged her aching temples. Another migraine, a daily occurrence lately.

What the hell was she going to tell her department chair?

I won't be in Monday because I can't leave the hostage alone in my basement.

Like hell. Maybe she'd tell him she had the flu. She really did feel sick.

Trapped in a situation not of her own making.

Lord-a-mercy, would this ever end?

———

Devlin set the burner on his desk, the one he only used to talk with Bridget. Sunny was right. Bridget was getting too cozy with the hostage, using her name, saying Maureen wanted to take a shower. Asking how soon they'd make the swap. Eager to let the hostage go. Fretting about not being able to go to work.

Bridget was a wimp. Unlike Sunny, who feared no one. He smiled, recalling their delightful orgy last night and the discussion that followed, especially Sunny's brilliant suggestion.

Don't answer him right away. Make him wait. Make him worry.

But Bridget was right about one thing. The sooner they got the money the better. Sooner or later, if Renzi's daughter didn't show up for work, someone at the hospital would call her landline and cell phone. If they didn't hear from her, they might contact the media. That's how it worked these days. A pretty young white woman goes missing, the reporters went crazy and put her picture on TV. Local news first, but if the national media got hold of it, that could cause all sorts of trouble.

He dropped to the floor and did fifty push-ups, his usual response to stress, a practice he'd begun in prison. Do fifty push-ups, then fifty more, whatever it took to calm himself.

After one hundred push-ups he sprang to his feet. Pleased that he wasn't winded, he went in the kitchen and poured himself a cup of coffee, ruminating over potential problems that might arise.

They had snatched Renzi's daughter on Thursday, three days ago. Most employers collected emergency contact information from their workers, family members usually. Who had Maureen Renzi listed? Her father? Probably.

Jesus-Mary-and-Joseph! What if they called her mother? He had no hold over the mother, didn't even know where she lived. Then again, she might not know her daughter had been kidnapped.

187

Unless Renzi told her.

The crucial question: If the cops called Renzi, would he tell them his daughter had been kidnapped?

The text he'd sent had made it very clear what would happen if he did. *No cops. No feds. Or she dies.*

But Renzi wanted proof of life. *When do I talk to my daughter?*

Devlin sipped his coffee. Not before Monday. No way could Renzi get a million bucks before then. Tank was in Swampscott watching the house right now to see if Renzi went to the bank to get things rolling with the ransom money.

Renzi wanted proof of life? Fine. He'd send Renzi the text he and Sunny had cooked up last night.

Want to talk to your daughter? Show me the money.

But not right away. Make the bastard wait.

He set his coffee mug in the sink, returned to the office, got on his computer and checked the weather report.

A storm was brewing in the mid-Atlantic. Excellent. He'd already decided where to make the swap.

Get the loot and shoot the self-important son-of-a-bitch.

———

8:45 AM – East Boston – St. Mary's Parochial School

When Frank entered the principal's office, Sister Mary Ignatius was seated at her desk. An older woman of indeterminate age dressed in black, a silver cross dangling from her scrawny neck, her pink scalp visible beneath strands of wispy white hair.

Regarding him warily with sharp blue eyes, she said, "My assistant said you had questions about one of our students, but I can't give out that sort of information. Privacy laws won't allow it."

Rafe had told him to use his charm. Sister Mary Ignatius didn't appear all that susceptible to charm, but he did his best. He gave her his most persuasive smile and said, "Not about a current student. About a family that lived near here a long time ago. The Devlin family."

Her blue eyes remained wary. No smile. "What about them?"

"I understand the children went to school here. Bridget and Brian and Kate."

Sister Mary Ignatius heaved a sigh. "Poor Kate. She was retarded, had a terrible time with schoolwork. Some of the other children used to tease her about it." The nun's lips tightened. "Her brother beat them up and made them stop. Up to no good, as usual."

Feigning surprise, Frank said, "Brian was a troublemaker?"

"Oh, Brian could be charming. A fine-looking boy he was, always had a smile for his teachers. When he was here. Half the time he played hooky and fell in with evil companions. A gangs of kids who robbed delivery trucks when they parked outside of stores."

Frank nodded. Back then tailgating was a lucrative scam for younger boys. Wait for the driver to take a load of merchandise into the store, one kid goes in the store and distracts the driver while his pals steal cartons from the truck. Plenty of buyers in poor neighborhoods like East Boston.

"What about Bridget?" Frank said. "Was she a troublemaker?"

But like a bulldog on a bone, the nun went on about Brian. "Brian was smart, but he didn't study, never did his homework. When he was sixteen, he quit. He had no time for school. He was too busy being a gangster. Making a lot of money."

"That's what gangsters do, right?"

An indignant nod. "Exactly. Stealing from stores, illegal gambling, intimidating people. Brian made enough money to buy a house in Southie. Moved his father and his sisters into it."

"So Bridget didn't graduate, either?"

"Oh, she graduated. By then, she was a senior, so we let her finish her studies here." The nun flashed her first smile, exposing yellowed dentures. "Bridget was very smart, a beautiful girl and a hard worker. She graduated at the top of her class and got a merit scholarship to Yale."

"Wow, that's very impressive." Now he was getting somewhere. Bridget went to Yale.

"You don't know the half of it. Bridget had a very difficult life. Her mother died giving birth to Kate, and the father got in an accident working on the docks. Injured his arm so badly he couldn't work there anymore. No heaving lifting. That's how the family got into public housing."

"What did Bridget study at Yale?"

"I'm not sure. Psychology, I think. She was very smart."

Smart enough to mastermind a plot to kidnap Maureen?

"What happened after she graduated from Yale?"

"I don't know. I assume she got a good job. No reason she wouldn't."

"Do you know where she is now?" Forget the phony charm, tell me where she lives. "I need to contact her about a legal matter."

Alarmed, the nun fingered her silver cross. "A legal matter? Is Bridget in trouble?"

Yes, if she helped kidnap my daughter. A world of trouble.

"No, nothing like that. Someone willed her some money and we need to find her." Lying through his teeth to a Catholic nun, probably go straight to Hell.

"Oh. Well, I hope you find her. I never heard from Bridget after she left St. Mary's."

Disheartened that he hadn't gotten Bridget's address, Frank left the school and got in his car. Maybe Rafe could contact the Yale Alumni office and get her current address.

He checked his cell phone. Damn. No text from the kidnappers.

As he held it in his hand, the phone rang. A Baltimore area code. Double-damn. He answered, "Frank Renzi."

A female voice said, "Mr. Renzi, this is Officer Lea Birch, Baltimore police department. Your daughter's employers are concerned because she didn't come to work on Thursday or Friday and they can't reach her. Have you spoken with her recently?"

Avoiding the question, he said, "Maureen's had a tough time lately. She broke up with her boyfriend and her grandfather died last week."

"Do you know where she is?"

"I think she's staying with a friend." Lies, lies and more lies.

"She's all right then?"

"As far as I know. I'd hate to see the media get hold of this. Maureen would be embarrassed."

"That's not up to me, sir. That's up to the hospital administrators. But I'll tell them what you said."

Frank ended the call. Bad news on all fronts. No information about where Bridget Devlin was living, and now he had to call Vobitch in case Baltimore PD tried to contact him at the station.

Which meant he could no longer avoid calling Kelly.

CHAPTER 30

SATURDAY October 29 – 9:20 AM – Plymouth

Bridget sat at her makeup table, languidly brushing her hair, a luxury she could only indulge on weekends. At work she wore her hair in a French twist. None of her students or colleagues had ever seen her with long black hair draped over her shoulders.

Prim-and-proper Professor White also wore spectacles with thin metal rims, and a plain gold wedding band to discourage any budding Lotharios from hitting on her. Her faux-husband never attended faculty social events. Robert White was away on business or tied up in meetings.

She put down the brush and arranged glossy black hair around her face. Admiring her flawless complexion and emerald green eyes in the mirror, she put on a seductive smile the way she did on vacation, flirting with a handsome businessman at the bar in her ritzy hotel. After the usual preliminaries, she'd take him up to her room and have a delightful romp in the sack, no strings attached.

But she wasn't on vacation. She was in her cottage, minding Renzi's daughter. Feeding her, cleaning up after her, emptying the piss-pot from the portable toilet. Making excuses for why she couldn't go to work.

An hour ago, she'd called the department secretary. Barking a faux cough, she apologized for calling her at home, saying she'd come down with the flu and couldn't teach on Monday. The woman had been sympathetic, commiserating with her, telling her to get well soon.

That took care of Monday. She'd worry about her Wednesday classes later.

She pulled her hair into a ponytail and secured it with an elastic band so she could hide it under the ski-mask. Maureen was behaving herself lately, but why take chances when the end was in sight?

She left the bedroom and went into her office. She'd been checking the Baltimore news every morning to make sure there was no news about a kidnapped doctor.

Nothing so far. She got on her laptop and googled "Baltimore news." A list of headlines appeared, most of them crime-related: murders, domestic incidents, armed robberies. Nothing about a missing doctor. To make sure, she scrolled down to the bottom and clicked on the next page of results.

Her heart jolted. Mother of God! A headline about a missing doctor. She clicked on it which took her to a local newspaper article with a photograph of Maureen. Hospital officials were worried because one of their doctors hadn't come to work for two days. Anyone knowing Maureen Renzi's whereabouts should call Mercy Medical Center.

She scrolled through two more pages of results. No more headlines about a missing doctor, but if CNN or Fox News got wind of the story and ran it, they'd be in deep shit.

She opened a desk drawer and took out the burner to call Brian. Her hands were sweaty and her temples were throbbing like a bomb had gone off in her head. Brian was already angry, swearing at her this morning, threatening to send Sunny down here to mind the hostage.

Brian had always been impulsive. Shoot first, think later, metaphorically speaking.

Tell her something bad will happen if she doesn't stick to the script.

Unwilling to contemplate what that might be, she massaged her aching temples, a futile attempt to calm her nerves.

Maybe she wouldn't tell him.

Brian said Renzi had agreed to get the money. If he got it by Tuesday, they could do the swap on Wednesday, Thursday at the latest, and poof. No more hostage. Brian gets the money, Renzi gets his daughter, Bridget White goes back to work and things would get back to normal.

She put the burner in the desk drawer and went in the kitchen. No way could she let Maureen take a shower. Taking the zip-ties off her wrists and ankles was too risky. Tank said when he grabbed her, she had kicked him, elbowed him in the ribs and tried to headbutt him.

She put on the ski-mask and went in the bathroom to check herself in the mirror to make sure all her hair was tucked underneath. Damn! She'd promised to let Maureen brush her teeth.

She found an extra toothbrush, ran cold water into a plastic bowl and took it downstairs.

Maureen sat on the bed with the breakfast tray balanced on her knees.

"I brought you a toothbrush and a bowl of water." She set the bowl on the tray, took the wrapper off the toothbrush, put it into Maureen's hand and placed her other hand on the bowl of water.

"Be careful. Don't spill the water."

"I'll be careful. No spills, I promise."

She watched Maureen brush her teeth, brushing and spitting, swooshing water around her mouth and spitting into the bowl.

Two minutes later Maureen held up the toothbrush and said, "Thank you. My mouth feels so much better. Can I take a shower now?"

Bridget picked up the plastic bowl. "No. But we might let you talk to your Dad."

"Great!" Maureen said, her face wreathed in a smile. "Today?"

"No, but soon. Maybe tomorrow." *Tomorrow when Tank is here. Let him take care of it.*

"That would be great. I'm sure Dad's worried about me."

Worried enough to get the money, Bridget hoped. "Someone else will be here tomorrow."

Maureen's smile disappeared. "The woman with the gun?"

"No." Tank had a gun, but he wouldn't shoot her. "He'll be here right after breakfast so I can take my sister to a Halloween parade."

Maureen tilted her head back and smiled up at her. "Can I come?"

Amused, Bridget smiled. The girl had a foul mouth, swearing at her, using the F-word, but she also had a sense of humor apparently. "I don't think so."

"Too bad. I bet you'll have fun with your sister. If I can't take a shower, can I have some clean underwear? I've had these on forever."

Not forever, three days.

"Okay, I'll bring you a clean pair."

"And a sweater?" Maureen said. "It's cold down here."

"One thing at a time. Underwear first. I'll bring you a sweater later."

Later, when she didn't have so much to worry about.

What if the Baltimore cops contacted the FBI?

Vicious pain hammered her temples. The feds could access records in every state, dating back years.

Incriminating things like old drivers licenses and marriage certificates, with Bridget Devlin's name on them.

———

9:20 AM – East Boston

After he left Sister Mary Ignatius, Frank stopped at the nearest Dunkin Donuts. He bought a pumpkin muffin and a black coffee and sat at a table by the window. He sipped his coffee and ate half of the muffin, reviewing what the nun had told him, planning his day.

Tell Rafe what the nun said and ask him to work on the Yale angle. Then make the call he'd been dreading: tell Vobitch about Maureen and the call from the Baltimore cop. Maybe he'd ask Vobitch to tell Kelly.

A cop-out, but he couldn't get distracted by guilt feelings. He had to find Maureen.

After he talked to Vobitch, he'd go to a bank in Swampscott and futz around to make it look like he was getting a loan, in case the bastards were watching him. After lunch he'd hit the Leprechaun Pub and try to get more information about Bridget.

Topping his wish list: where does she live?

His cell phone shimmied on the table, followed by a ping. His heart sped up. A text message.

Get the cash in hundreds and send us a picture of it. After we get the picture, your daughter will call you. Then we can set up the swap.

He puffed his cheeks. He was relieved to get the text, but how was he going to get a picture of a million bucks in hundred-dollar bills. No call from Maureen until he sent them one.

He tossed the rest of the muffin in the trash, took the coffee out to his car and called Rafe.

"Yo, Frank, what's up?"

"I just got a text from the kidnappers," he said, and read it aloud.

"Okay," Rafe said, "here's what you do. Text him *Okay*, just the one word."

"But how do I get a photograph of the money?"

"I can maybe get you one tomorrow, by Sunday for sure. Plenty of Benjamins confiscated from drug dealers in the evidence lockers. I'll have the cop that minds the evidence room help me take a picture and send it to your phone. You send it to them and wait for a call from Maureen."

"But not until Monday. I'm about to go to the bank, but that's the preliminary visit. The bank is closed on Sunday. That means I have to go back with a suitcase on Monday to make it look like I got the money. That's two days from now."

"True, but it gives us more time to find Maureen. After you talk to her, get the time and place of the swap, that's the most important thing."

Frank added up the days. No swap until Tuesday at the earliest. Maybe not until Wednesday. Four days from now. Four days while Maureen sat in a room somewhere, alone and defenseless.

"I got my buddy to hack into Mo's phone records," Rafe said. "Last incoming call was yours Thursday morning, nothing since. By then they already had her, probably took out the SIM card, shut off the phone and dumped it somewhere."

"No. They kept it. That's how they got my cell phone number. We might get lucky if they turn it on, but I'm not counting on it. I just talked to the principal at St. Mary's School, an older nun who knew the Devlins. She had nothing good to say about Brian, but she liked Bridget, said she was smart, got a scholarship to Yale in 1979. Can you call the Alumni Office and get her current address?"

"I'll get on it right away. Do a nationwide search for a DL from that year forward. But if she got married, she might have a different last name. Worth a shot, though."

"I'll take whatever I can get. Last night Gina told me Sean Whelan, Devlin's enforcer, died under suspicious circumstances in a Southie hotel last Monday. Sunny Jensen, Devlin's lover, was with him when he died."

"Interesting," Rafe said. And after a beat, "You have a good time with Gina last night?"

Better than good. Aloud he said, "So good I had one of my eureka moments. Forget the mobster in Worcester, the skinhead in Springfield and Jesús DeCastro. Brian Devlin had Whelan kill my father and whacked him to keep him quiet. His lover helped do it."

"You think she's holding Maureen in the hotel?"

"Possible, but I doubt it. Devlin wouldn't risk holding her there. Too close to home. He only lives a few blocks away, and too many people know he's involved with Sunny."

"Okay," Rafe said. "After I read the police report on Whelan, I'll go to the hotel and grill Sunny."

"No. She'd tell Devlin and he'd know we're onto him. According to Gina, Devlin hangs out at the Leprechaun Pub in Southie. I'm going there this afternoon, see what I can dig up on Bridget."

"Good, but not while Devlin's there. He's wearing an ankle bracelet. I'll keep track of it and call you if he leaves his house. Keep your eyes on the prize, Frank. We got fresh leads and the bastard's gonna let you talk to Maureen. Text him *okay* right now. I'll get to work on finding Bridget and getting a photograph of the cash."

"Thanks, Rafe. After I finish at the bank, I'll go home and work up a cover story for the Pub and wait for your call."

"Okay, partner. Told you a woman's touch would do you good."

Frank smiled and ended the call. He couldn't argue with that.

————

10:30 AM – Plymouth

Maureen flexed the muscles in her body one by one, naming each one in her mind like it was an anatomy class, first her feet, then her legs and her torso, then her arms, hands and fingers. No shower but at least she had clean underwear.

Orphan seemed nervous today. First she undid the zip-ties on her ankles and took off the slipper-socks. Then she made her stand up and helped her take off the running pants and the smelly underpants. "These go in the trash," Orphan said—the only words she'd spoken the whole time—and handed her a soapy washcloth so she could wash herself.

Which took a while with her wrists bound together. Then Orphan helped her put on the clean underpants, running pants and slipper-socks. When she thanked her, Orphan hadn't said anything, just went upstairs and shut the door.

But she didn't care. Tomorrow, she would talk to Dad!

Now she had to figure out how to slip in a clue. Seagull. To let Dad know she was near the ocean.

Damn it was cold in here. She eased off the bed and stood on the floor. Maybe if she did some exercises, it would warm her up. Warm up her brain cells, too. It wasn't easy with her ankles bound together.

She spread her feet as far apart as she could, six inches or so, squatted and straightened up. Extending her arms in front of her for balance, she squatted again and got into a rhythm. Up and down, up and down. Fifty times.

Damn! Fifty squats and she was winded.

She was used to jogging every day before breakfast, but other than fighting with Cigarman when he grabbed her, she hadn't been able to do any exercise since. Hours and hours. Counting the days in her mind.

Wait! Was this Saturday?

Damn it to hell! She should be taking the practice test for the surgical board exam right now. These dickhead dirtbags were fucking up her life.

She did fifty more squats and rested again, thinking about tomorrow's phone call and the clues she would try to give Dad.

What else beside seagulls?

She heard the furnace rumble, sniffed the air and smelled heating oil. Seagulls, furnace and heating oil.

She didn't dare mention the gun. Dad would freak out.

But how would she slip seagulls and furnace into a sentence?

She did fifty more squats, but nothing came to her. She leaned against the bed and drank from the bottled water Orphan had given her.

Sometimes if she thought about a problem before she went to sleep, the solution would come to her when she woke up.

She smiled and thought about Dad. Maybe he would send her an ESP message while she was sleeping.

She lay back on the bed, wishing this was all a bad dream and she'd wake up tomorrow and everything would be normal.

But it wasn't a bad dream. She couldn't see, couldn't move around, couldn't even tell what time it was. And she was cold.

When Orphan brought her the sweater, she'd punch her in the face.

Well, maybe not. For all she knew, Orphan had a gun, too.

She wanted to scream, but didn't. "Dad's gonna make you pay for this," she whispered.

CHAPTER 31

SATURDAY October 29 – 12:10 PM – Swampscott

Frank made himself a double shot of espresso, living on caffeine these days. Bad for his stomach, but it kept him going. For an hour the woman at the bank had told him all about mortgage loans: thirty year loans, fifteen year loans, adjustable rate loans. He had to force himself to look interested, his mind focused on one thing. Finding Maureen.

He drank some espresso and took out his cell phone. This time on a Saturday—11:15 in New Orleans—Vobitch was probably home doing chores around the house. Not a call he wanted to make, but it had to be done. He dialed Vobitch's cell phone and waited.

"Frank," Vobitch said, "how you doing? Any leads on who killed your father?"

"They kidnapped Maureen." Just speaking the words aloud sickened him.

"The motherfuckers! When? Gimme the details."

"After I left the office Thursday afternoon, they texted me her picture, blindfolded, her mouth taped shut. I flew to Baltimore and went through her apartment, looking for clues. I'm convinced they grabbed her there before she went to work Thursday morning."

"Any idea where they're keeping her?"

"Somewhere near Boston probably. I'm staying at the house in Swampscott. Last night I got a ransom demand. One million dollars."

"Jesus Christ! What makes them think you got that kind of dough?"

"Doesn't matter," he said, pacing the kitchen. "Rafe says make them think I'm getting it. I sent them a text saying I'd have it by Tuesday. The ransom note said no cops and no feds or—"

He took a breath and spoke the fateful words. "Or she dies."

Silence for a moment, then a muttered curse. "What can I do to help?" Vobitch said.

"Are you at home?"

"No, in my office. Came in to do some paperwork. Tell me what you need."

"Here's the problem. When Maureen didn't go to work on Thursday or Friday, the hospital called Baltimore PD and had them do a wellness check. Obviously, she wasn't home. Two hours ago, a Baltimore police-woman called my cell, probably got my number from Maureen's emergency contact info. She asked if I knew where Maureen was. I told her Maureen was upset about her grandfather's death, might be staying with a friend. But if she doesn't show up on Monday, the hospital might contact the local TV stations. If the cable news outfits get wind of it—"

"Hold on. Lemme get on my computer, see what's shaking in Baltimore."

Frank sipped his espresso. If CNN got wind of the story, the kidnappers might see it. Damn! What if Evelyn saw it? She never watched the news at home, too much crime, she said. But she was at her cousin's. For all he knew, her cousin might be a CNN fan. He'd better call Evelyn, maybe talk to the cousin. Another unpleasant task.

Vobitch spoke into his ear. "I found a blurb in a local rag with Maureen's picture and a phone number for the hospital. Her bosses are asking for information. If the national media vultures get hold of this, it could mushroom out of control. Want me to call Baltimore PD and ask them to keep a lid on it?"

"No. I asked the policewoman to keep it quiet, but she said that's up to the hospital. Here's the problem. The hospital's got my work number, too. Can you have the desk officers route my calls to you? Then you can tell them I took personal leave to settle my father's affairs."

"I can do that, no problem. What else is Rafe doing?"

"We're working some leads, killers I helped put in jail, currently out on parole." *Like Brian Devlin, the prick who assassinated my father.* "Rafe said to ask for proof of life. I sent them a text saying I wanted to talk to Maureen by phone, so I know she's—" He stopped, unable to speak.

"Frank," Vobitch said quietly. "I know you're upset and I don't blame you, but you gotta stay positive. You're gonna find Maureen and put these motherfuckers in jail. I'll monitor the Baltimore news, let you know if anything breaks. Call me right away if you need anything."

Moved by the offer, Frank said, "Thanks, Morgan. Kelly doesn't know about Maureen yet. Can you tell her and ask her to keep it quiet? Tell her I'll call her as soon as I can."

As soon as he felt able to talk without sounding like a guilty lover.

―――――

12:35 PM – Boston

Devlin cruised down Newbury Street in the Back Bay. Along the tree-shaded street, brick-front buildings once owned by 19th century business tycoons had been converted to condos, snapped up by wealthy professionals. Two blocks down, ritzy boutiques sold overpriced merchandise to women leaving stores with outfits that cost more than a monthly car payment.

Years ago when he was a kid, Pa had told him any fool could get rich, but only a clever man could be interesting. Pa's sorry excuse for his inability to provide for his family. He was the one who'd taken care of the Devlin family.

He'd convinced Bridget to help with the kidnapping, saying they needed the money to insure Kate's future.

But what about his future?

The feds were watching him, monitoring the electronic ankle bracelet, looking for any excuse to send him back to prison. When Pa died, they wouldn't even let him attend the funeral. He had other targets on his back, too, gang leaders who had gripes with him and his gang. He wasn't in prison, but he was always looking over his shoulder.

Maybe he'd just kill Renzi and split. A passport with his photo and a different name was inside the safe in his bedroom. He had more cash in safe deposit boxes in Texas. Take Sunny with him, collect the cash and drive to Mexico. Buy a hacienda and live happily ever after.

Years ago he had taken other lovers, until he grew tired of them. But Sunny was different. But he never tired of being with Sunny. He wanted her Till Death Do Us Part. Not that he would ever tell her this. Then she would own him. Unacceptable.

He entered the Hotel Colonnade garage and parked on the second level. His lawyer was meeting him in Brasserie Jo's, a swanky French restaurant on the first floor. If he went to Sasso's office, the feds would track him and wonder why he was there. But it didn't matter if they met in Sasso's office or in a public restaurant. Attorney-client privilege was in force.

When he entered the restaurant, the asshole at the reservation desk regarded him with thinly disguised contempt, clocking his green polo shirt and chinos. Didn't like the long-billed Red Sox cap he'd worn to defeat any security cameras, either.

But when he said Peter Sasso was expecting him, the man gave him an unctuous smile and showed him to a table in the far corner, conveniently distant from any nearby diners.

Sasso wasn't flashy like some mob lawyers, but his appearance conveyed power and importance: his face clean-shaven, flecks of gray in his black hair, a tailored suit, a white shirt with gold cuff links, a Rolex on his wrist. Sasso was topnotch: a formidable opponent in the courtroom, supremely confident, and obnoxious when he had to be. Barely fifty, Sasso had amassed a small fortune by representing Italian mobsters, getting large retainers up front. Win or lose, Sasso got his money, even if his clients went to jail, like Brian. "But not on death row," Sasso had said as they took him away in manacles.

Now, regarding him warmly, Sasso smiled and said, "Nice to see you out and about, Brian."

"Glad to be out," he said, sinking into the padded Ox-blood leather chair opposite Sasso. "I could do without the ankle bracelet though."

Sasso sipped some ice water, gazing at him with his dark-brown, almost-black eyes. "Not a problem as long as you don't leave the state. Or start packing a gun."

"I don't like feds knowing where I am and what I'm doing every minute. That's why I asked to meet you here."

"Shall we order lunch, or would you prefer something to drink?"

"No lunch. But I'll take a bottle of Harp Ale."

"I'll join you." Sasso raised his hand and a waiter instantly appeared at his elbow. "Two bottles of Harp Ale and a bowl of mixed nuts."

"Certainly, sir." The waiter scurried away.

Getting down to business, Sasso leaned forward and put on his professional smile. "What can I help you with today?"

"I want to make sure Kate will be taken care of, if something happens to me."

Sasso raised an eyebrow. "I send payments from your bank account every month to pay for the group home in Winthrop. What do you mean, if something happens to you? Are you ill?"

"No." Devlin smiled. "But some of your *friends* might like me to go away permanently. As in *dead*. If that happens, I want you to sell my house in Southie. Sell the Leprechaun Pub, too. It's not in my name, but you can make it happen. Use the money to see that Kate is well cared for."

"In perpetuity," Sasso said, giving him legal lingo as the waiter delivered their Harp Ale, two frosted glasses and a bowl of mixed nuts. After the waiter left, Sasso said, "I can do that. What about the hotel?"

"Sunny keeps it." If he went to Mexico with Sunny, he didn't want Sasso or anyone else to know.

Sasso nodded. He never wrote anything down. Devlin figured Peter Sasso had enough incriminating information in his head to put a lot of wiseguys in jail for a very long time.

"I need some of the cash that you keep in your safe deposit box," he said. "Two grand."

Sasso studied him, his eyes wary. "Why? Are you going somewhere?"

"Yeah, a quick trip to the Riviera." Devlin smiled and spread his hands. "Peter, I'm not going anywhere. I just like having a few bucks in my pocket. You know, have some fun, maybe buy a few lottery tickets."

Expressionless, Sasso said, "When do you want it?"

"Be nice to have it by Monday,"

————

1:30 PM – South Boston

Frank parked five blocks from the Leprechaun Pub and walked there to get a feel for the neighborhood. Not his territory when he worked for Boston PD, but he'd been here a few times.

An hour ago Rafe had called, saying Devlin had driven into Boston, but didn't offer to join him at the Pub. A predominantly blue-collar Irish neighborhood, Southie wasn't hospitable to blacks, or cops.

Most of the streets had names with numbers or letters. The L-Street Brownies were famous for their New Years Day tradition, plunging into the frigid waters off Carson Beach for a swim.

He threaded his way through a maze of narrow streets lined with three-deckers built early in the twentieth century, with porches on each floor. Music wafted from open windows, drifting over cheap Fords and GMC trucks parked at the curb. Enjoying the bright sunny day, residents sat on their porches, chatting with friends.

Ten minutes later he reached the Leprechaun Pub, which sported a Celtics Leprechaun on the door. He stepped inside, inhaling the smell of stale beer and deep-fried fish, surveying the room. Fifteen tables ahead of him, ten bar stools along the bar to his right. On the back wall, a sign on a door said Game Room.

Men in casual clothes occupied most of the tables. Anticipating this, he'd worn a tan polo shirt and chinos. He took a seat at the bar beside an older man with red hair and ordered a draft beer. The bartender's nose had been broken at some point, and his hair had a dyed-green streak in it. Maybe he was celebrating St. Patrick's Day early.

After the bartender delivered his beer, the redhead turned to him and said, with a hint of an Irish brogue, "Ya must be new to the neighborhood. Haven't seen yee here before."

"I'm in Boston on business," he said. "Wanted to visit an Irish pub to check out my family heritage."

"Sure and you must have a bit of Eye-talian in yee."

"On my mother's side." He extended his hand. "David Sullivan. My friends call me Sully."

"Pleased ta meecha." The man shook his hand. "Nolan's my name, but everyone calls me Red."

Frank chugged some beer and gestured at the wall opposite the bar. "I love the Celtics pictures. Those guys were great. I grew up in Chicago, but I always rooted for the Celtics."

Red raised an eyebrow. "And Red Auerbach, I hope?"

"Definitely. He was great. So was Kevin McHale, the man with the seven-foot arms."

"And a fine Irishman," Red said, smiling at him. "That's the important thing."

After they chatted about the Celtics for a while, Frank said, "Seen Brian Devlin lately?"

"Saw him last Monday. That's Irish night here. Mr. Devlin keeps the Irish traditions alive."

"Glad to hear it. How's his sister?"

"Kate? She's doing fine, I hear."

"What about Bridget?"

Red drank some beer, appeared to be thinking about something. At last he said, "I don't see her much. She doesn't live around here."

Where *does* she live? Frank wanted to scream, but didn't. He checked his watch. He'd been here forty minutes. When working undercover, don't hang around in one spot for too long.

"Nice chatting with you, Red. I'd stay and talk, but I've got an appointment. The beers are on me." He put a twenty on the bar and left.

CHAPTER 32

SUNDAY October 30 – 12:10 PM – Plymouth

Maureen lay on the cot doing isometric exercises, too excited to keep still. This morning after she woke up, she'd figured out how to slip in a hint to Dad about seagulls.

Damn! Heavy footsteps descending the stairs. Was it Dragon-Lady with a gun?

She sat up and swung her legs over the side of the cot, unable to see who it was, feeling vulnerable and exposed.

Footsteps approached her and stopped, close enough for her to smell the faint odor of cigar smoke. Cigarman, the asshole she'd fought with outside her apartment.

He set a tray down on her lap and said in a gruff voice, "I brought you a turkey sandwich and a container of milk."

She stuck to her plan. Act grateful and be polite. "Thank you," she said. "I love turkey sandwiches, don't you?"

"Eat your lunch while I empty the pot." A minute later footsteps sounded on the stairs.

She picked up the sandwich and took a bite. She was hungry and it tasted good, but she wanted to talk to Dad, desperate to hear the sound of his voice, even if it was only on the phone. She devoured the sandwich, finished her milk and waited.

After a while, she heard footsteps on the stairs. She heard Cigarman slide the pot under the portable toilet. Then a swoosh-swoosh hiss. She inhaled a fresh lavender scent. An air deodorizer, she realized.

"That's better," he said. "Now the room don't stink so bad."

Stink? She'd been smelling it for so long she hadn't noticed. The room wouldn't smell so bad if they'd let her take a shower and use a normal toilet. But no complaining. Be nice.

"You done with your lunch?" he asked.

"Yes. Thank you, it was delicious. When can I talk to Dad?"

"I don't know nothing about that."

"The woman said I could talk to him today. She promised!"

"Not today."

He took the tray off her lap, went upstairs and shut the door.

Overcome with despair, she hugged herself, rocking back and forth. Tears filled her eyes. She was all alone. Cooped up in a smelly room, unable to move around, unable to bathe properly.

All she could do was sit here and think.

She conjured up the pictures of Dad on her bookcase. Weeks might pass when she didn't look at them. Just knowing they were there was comforting, remembering how Dad put his arms around her when she was little, making her feel safe, saying he loved her with all his heart. Dad would keep looking until he found her and put these miserable rotten kidnappers in jail.

She got off the cot and did some squats, her mind filled with evil thoughts. When everything turned to shit, hate was what kept you going.

Dragon Lady had smeared mashed potatoes on her face and threatened to shoot her. She did more squats and imagined herself smearing potatoes on Dragon Lady's face and putting her in a cage with rats like the man in the movie, *1984*.

Orphan was just as bad, slapping her, lying to her, promising she could talk to Dad. She did five more squats. Maybe she'd put a cockroach in Orphan's ear. Let it scuttle past her ear drum and run around the cochlea until it drove her crazy.

She did more squats and tried to think of a suitable punishment for Cigarman.

———

12:25 PM – Swampscott

Frank sat at the kitchen table eating lasagna. Earlier when he went next door to thank Peggy for collecting the mail, she'd said he looked drawn and pale, and gave him a pan of homemade lasagna and some apple strudel. He'd sorted the mail into three piles: bills, junk and a stack of envelopes addressed to the Renzi Family, condolence cards probably.

He couldn't bear to read them.

The lasagna sat in his stomach like a rock. He drank some ice water. This time on a Sunday, Kelly was probably reading the newspaper, and, assuming Vobitch had called her, worrying about Maureen.

He wished he was there so he could talk to her.

She'd calm him down, tell him he'd find Maureen and punish the fuckers who'd kidnapped her. Then he'd take her in the bedroom and make love to her. As if everything was normal.

But if he didn't find Maureen, his life would never be normal again.

He'd searched the social media sites for Bridget Devlin, had even Googled her name, but the women he found were either too young or too old. He was stymied. He couldn't even access the federal data bases on the BPD computers, could only wait for Rafe to do it.

His phone rang and he grabbed it. "Hey, Gina, whaddya know?"

"Hi Franco, got a few tidbits for you. What's doing on your end?"

"I got a text from the kidnappers. After I send them a photograph of the money, they'll let me talk to Maureen. Then they'll set up the meet for the swap."

"Excellent. The sooner the better."

He recapped what the nun had told him. "Rafe and I figure Devlin wouldn't dare keep Maureen in Southie, but Bridget might be helping him. Rafe's trying to find out where she lives."

"Good," Gina said. "I didn't find anything in the *Herald* morgue about Bridget, but I found an article about Devlin's lover, Sunny Jensen. Born in Warwick, Rhode Island, in 1964, which makes her three years younger than Devlin. Her parents weren't well-off, but Sunny was smart, got a partial scholarship to Brown University, double-majored in accounting and business management."

"Convenient. Learned how to cook the books and run a brothel."

"Exactly. After she graduated, she moved to Southie. That was before Devlin went to prison. The story ran when she took over the Seaview Hotel." Gina chuckled. "No mention of the cat-house. The owner of record is Seaview Trust LLC, managed by Attorney Peter Sasso.

"Devlin's probably got a piece of it. Sasso is his attorney."

"Sunny lives on the top floor. I dug up a copy of the building plans. There's a fancy restaurant and a lounge on the first floor, three floors of rooms above that, two rooms on the top floor. I'm in my office, just got back from the hotel."

Incredulous, he said, "You went there?"

Gina laughed. "You think you're the only detective in town? I put on my fancy interview outfit, waltzed past the big bruiser doorman like I belonged there and got on the elevator, thinking I'd check out the top floor. But you need a key to access it. I got off on the fourth floor and wandered around, didn't see any half-naked hookers, went downstairs and sat at the bar."

Man, he loved this woman. "You are something else, Gina."

"I sat beside a businessman-type in a suit and ordered a Bloody Mary. We got talking and I asked him if there was anything interesting to do around here. He smiled and said, if you've got the right phone number. But when I asked him for it, he got off his stool and left. I think he thought I was a cop."

"Gina, that's dangerous. Rafe said these fuckers don't mess around."

"I don't care. I want to help you find Maureen. I think you should talk to Sunny."

He thought about it. Have Rafe squeeze her, ostensibly about the Whelan death. But not until he talked to Maureen. "Rafe will call the Yale Alumni office tomorrow. Any kind of luck, he'll get Bridget's current address from them. Thanks for the new info, Gina."

"No problem, Franco. Love you."

"Love you too," he said, and ended the call.

People said you couldn't love two women at the same time. But he loved Gina as much as he loved Kelly and that wasn't going to change.

———

1:35 PM – Winthrop

Bridget stood beside Kate on the crowded sidewalk, the aroma of buttered popcorn and roasted chestnuts filling the air. Kate had on the new shirt she'd bought her, an orange T-shirt with a big black cat on the front. It was beautiful day, sunny and warm for October, temperatures in the low-sixties. Huge crowds lined the street awaiting the parade, parents with toddlers in Halloween costumes, other kids clutching helium balloons decorated with Halloween witches or big white ghosts.

Kate grabbed her arm. "Here they come! I can hear the drums."

Bridget smiled at her, enjoying Kate's enthusiasm. "I can, too."

A high school band in purple-and-gold uniforms appeared, playing a snappy march. Six gymnasts in skimpy gold skirts followed them, smiling at the crowd as they turned cartwheels. Next came open convertibles bearing elderly veterans, their uniforms festooned with medals and ribbons, smiling and waving to the cheering crowd.

Bridget watched them, thinking everyone's happy but me.

She couldn't stop worrying about the article in the Baltimore paper. It reminded her of Ray Liotta in *Goodfellas,* fretting in his kitchen, the cops after him for dealing drugs, a helicopter hovering over his house. Imagining a helicopter hovering over her cottage and flinty-eyed FBI agents with guns standing in her kitchen.

Damn it to hell! She wanted to forget helicopters and cops and FBI agents, wanted to get on a plane and fly to California for a relaxing hassle-free vacation. But if she did, Brian might send Sunny to the cottage to mind Maureen. Or worse. A chilling thought.

Maybe she should just let Maureen go. Put her in the car, drop her off somewhere, keep driving and disappear.

But she couldn't. Her stomach clenched in a spasm of fear. Brian would hunt her down and kill her. He wouldn't do it himself, of course. He'd send someone else to kill her.

Besides, she couldn't leave Kate, tugging on her arm now, her gorgeous green eyes sparkling with delight.

"This is so much fun, Bridget. I love Halloween parades, don't you?"

She forced a smile. "Yes. Halloween parades are awesome!"

"I love my new shirt," Kate said. "I'm going to wear it tomorrow when I hand out candy to the kids that come trick-or-treating."

Good, Bridget thought. Put the Baltimore Orioles shirt in the closet where no one will see it.

————

1:35 PM – South Boston

Devlin strolled along the sidewalk, reveling in the festivities. His first Halloween in Southie in fifteen years. He felt great, enjoying his freedom on a bright sunny day, watching toddlers dive for Halloween candy, pimple-faced teens in outlandish costumes wandering around in packs.

Salem had haunted houses and witches. Concord had Revolutionary War reenactors in period costumes, brown woolen trousers, white cotton shirts with billowing sleeves, muskets slung over their shoulders as they fought pretend battles in fields. In Southie the Halloween parade was a warm-up for St. Patrick's Day. Across the street, a bare-chested man halfway up a telephone pole drank from a can of Budweiser. Others walked around swigging beer from bottles inside paper bags.

The cops were out in force, but they paid the beer-drinkers no mind. Most of the cops in were Irish. They knew the drill.

Native Americans in brilliant colored feather-lined costumes passed him, chanting and beating drums. Then vintage cars: ancient black Fords with running boards, pastel-colored fifties Buicks with knife-like fins, trailed by a glamorous white Cadillac fit for Elvis.

His neck prickled, the feeling he got when someone was watching him. He scanned the crowd. He didn't see any grim-faced feds in suits and dark glasses, but that didn't mean they weren't there.

He ducked between a pair of three-deckers and waited in the backyard to see if anyone followed. No one did, but his upbeat mood had turned dark as a thundercloud.

Five minutes later he walked into the Leprechaun Pub.

Seated at the bar, Red waved him over and said, "Have a beer on me, Mr. Devlin. I got something to tell ya."

He smiled and clapped Red on the shoulder. "Thanks, Red. I'll have a Harp Ale."

The bartender immediately opened a bottle, set it in front of him and said, "How's it going, boss? Good to see ya."

"Thanks. I was enjoying the Halloween parade, thought I'd stop in for a beer."

"Sure and I'm glad ya did," Red said. "Some guy was here yesterday asking about ya."

Expressionless, he sipped his beer. "Really? Who was he?"

"Said his name was Sullivan, but he looked like a wop. Dark hair, a big Roman nose. Slinging blarney at me about his Irish ancestors. He asked me about your sisters. Kate and Bridget."

Renzi, he thought. "What did you tell him?"

"Told him nothing. I said Kate was fine and Bridget didn't live around here so I didn't see her much." Frowning now. "Was that okay, Mr. Devlin?"

"Perfect, Red. Thanks for letting me know." He finished his beer and left.

Five minutes later he was home in his office, furiously doing pushups, a single thought running through his mind.

Get the loot, kill Renzi and hit the road.

CHAPTER 33

MONDAY October 31 – Halloween – 5:30 AM – Swampscott

Frank got up at five-thirty, woken by a vague notion he couldn't quite grasp plinking his mind. He put on his running suit and left the house. Following his usual route, he jogged through side-streets to Lynn Shore Drive, a curving road that bordered the ocean. It was cool at this hour, a stiff wind blowing salt sea air over him, the rosy glow of the sun peeping over the horizon.

Focused on Maureen, he ran faster, his feet pounding the sidewalk. He refused to consider the possibility that she might be dead. She was alive and he was going to find her.

He passed a seafood restaurant and cawing seagulls circling a huge dumpster. Across the street, ocean-front mansions were decorated with Halloween witches, goblins and pumpkins carved into Jack-O-Lanterns.

Two miles later, he sprinted around the circle at the end of Lynn Shore Drive and jogged back to the house, thinking about Maureen, wondering how he'd find her.

After a quick shower and shave, he sat in the kitchen, sipping espresso, waiting to hear from Rafe. He hated waiting. Hated the terrifying uncertainty of it all. Where the hell was Maureen? Would Rafe find out where Bridget Devlin lived? What if Bridget was holding Maureen at her place and he couldn't find her?

The homemade apple strudel his neighbor had given him sat on the counter, but he couldn't eat anything. It felt like battery acid was burning a hole in his stomach.

He took out his notepad and studied his notes. No answers there, only questions, first and foremost: where was Maureen?

At ten past eight his cell phone rang, Rafe saying, "I got bad news and good news."

"What's the bad news?"

PAYBACK

"I just called the Yale Alumni Office and asked for Bridget's contact info, but they won't give it to me without a warrant. Gave me the usual bullshit about privacy laws, blah-blah-blah. At this point, I don't think we've got probable cause to get a warrant."

Disappointed, Frank said, "What's the good news?"

"I'll get to that in a minute. Been in my office since seven, did a computer search on Connecticut RMV. Bridget Devlin got a DL in 1979, but it expired in 1983. After she graduated, probably. Also found a 1975 Mustang convertible registered in her name, also expired in 1983. I ran the plate. No wants, no warrants. I searched the VIN, no record it was ever sold. I'm thinking she doesn't live in Connecticut anymore."

"I'm thinking she got married and has a different last name."

"I'll check RMV for every state in New England in case she didn't."

Frank sipped his espresso. "What's the good news?"

"Just talked to my man in the evidence locker and told him what I needed. He said to come down after lunch and he'll help me take a picture, said he's got plenty of shrink-wrapped Benjamins. Head over to your bank with a suitcase, make it look like you got the bucks."

"I will, as soon as they open. Tomorrow I'm going to the group home in Winthrop where Kate lives, see if I can dig up some information about Bridget. I'd go today, but it's Halloween. They might have holiday activities planned for the residents, and I don't want to run into Kate. It's been a while, but she might recognize me."

"Good thinking," Rafe said. "If Bridget visits her on a regular basis, it will narrow the search. She's probably not driving there from Maine or Vermont. Soon as I get the photo I'll text it to you. When you send it to Devlin, tell the fucker you want to talk to Maureen."

"Don't worry, I will. Thanks, Rafe. Keep me posted."

———

12:30 PM – Plymouth

"This sandwich is delicious," Maureen said. "Sort of like a Reuben."

Standing beside her, Orphan said, "I figured you might be sick of turkey, got some pastrami and Swiss cheese at the deli."

Maureen smiled at her, not that she could see her, because of the damn blindfold, but it seemed like her battle plan was working. This morning she had decided to think of this as a war. Her and Dad versus the evil kidnappers.

211

"Did you have fun with your sister yesterday at the parade?"

A brief silence, then, "Yes. We had a good time. The parade was great."

Where was it? she wanted to scream. *Give me a hint about where I am.*

She sucked up some milk with the straw. "How old is your sister?"

A longer silence. "Old enough to enjoy the parade. I've got work to do. I'll leave the door open. Call me when you finish your lunch."

"Can I talk to Dad then? Yesterday, I asked the man who was here and he said he didn't know anything about it."

"Did he treat you okay?"

"Yes. But when do I talk to Dad?"

"Soon. Things are moving along."

"What does that mean?"

Orphan didn't answer. Then she heard footsteps on the stairs.

Damn it to hell! If things were moving along, why couldn't she talk to Dad? Maybe he was getting the money so they'd let her go.

She couldn't wait to feel his arms around her. Like when she was a kid and he took her to the beach in Swampscott. After they got done swimming and building sand castles, they'd sit on a blanket and watch the sunset, the waves gleaming in the fading light. Then they'd go back to Grampa Sal's house and cook hot dogs on the grill. For dessert, they ate toasted marshmallows, burnt on the outside, gooey on the inside.

Thinking about it made her mouth water. She ate the rest of her sandwich, sucked up the last of the milk. Orphan was treating her better, no more tape on her mouth, no more slaps in the head.

But so what? The woman was still a bitch.

She pictured a cockroach, scampering round and round Orphan's cochlear, slowly driving her mad.

———

1:30 PM – Swampscott

Seated at the kitchen table, Frank set aside the condolence card from Patrick Flanagan's brother, wishing him well, saying Patrick was still hanging in there. After the funeral, Mike had told him Patrick would meet up with his father in Heaven someday.

Frank didn't believe in Heaven. Whatever sort of life you lived, good or bad, happened right here on Earth. He had a million fond memories of his father, a man who'd lived an exemplary life, personally and professionally. But someone had brutally ended that life, and he intended to punish the man who'd done it. Brian Devlin.

His cell phone pinged and he snatched it up. A text from Rafe.

Here's two pix. Send the best one to the fucker. Tell him to have Mo call you.

He opened the photos. Stacks of shrink-wrapped hundred-dollar bills on a table, nothing visible in the background but a blank wall. Amazed at what a million dollars looked like, he chose one photo and hit the Plus button to create a new text.

Here's the photograph. Have Maureen call me.

He attached the photo and hit Send. Now the ball was in Devlin's court. He couldn't wait to hear Maureen's voice. Maybe he could slip in a word of encouragement. Tell her to stay strong, he'd see her soon.

Unable to sit still, he got up and paced the kitchen. After he talked to Mo, Devlin had said he would tell him the place and time for the swap. Soon, he hoped. Maybe tomorrow.

He clenched his fists. If Devlin didn't bring Maureen to the swap, he'd kill the motherfucker.

But he had to be careful.

Do it wrong and he'd go to jail. Then he'd never find Maureen.

———

1:35 PM – South Boston

Devlin studied the photograph, stacks and stacks of shrink-wrapped hundred-dollar bills. This morning, Tank had called and said he'd seen Renzi go into the bank in Swampscott with a suitcase at ten o'clock and come out an hour later.

Renzi was desperate to get his daughter back, had gotten the money in record time. Maybe his father had connections at the bank.

He read the text again: *Here's the photograph. Have Maureen call me.*

The arrogant prick giving him orders.

On Saturday Renzi had gone to the Leprechaun Pub, questioning Red about Bridget, nosing around Southie.

Southie was *his* territory. Which meant Renzi suspected him.

But he'd never be able to prove it. Whenever he texted the bastard, he used a fresh burner. Time to get rid of this one. He had a carton of fresh burners in his basement.

He went downstairs to his cellar where he took care of certain unpleasant aspects of his business. Threatening gamblers who were behind on the vig or business owners who refused to pay for protection.

His workbench held the proper tools to persuade them.

The bench also came in handy when he loaded dum-dum bullets into weapons. And destroyed burners so no one could trace them. He removed the SIM card from the burner, dropped in a trash barrel, and set the phone on a small granite slab.

Picturing the self-righteous look on Renzi's face when he testified at the murder trial, Devlin picked up a claw hammer and slammed it down on the phone. Pretending it was Renzi's head, he pounded the burner to bits.

Soon he would meet the bastard face-to-face.

And packing a gun, not a hammer.

Have Maureen call me.

Renzi wanted to talk to his daughter right away.

To hell with that. Let him wait. Let him suffer like he'd suffered, locked in a jail cell for fifteen years, unable to escape the incessant noise, the disgusting stench of other inmates, eating slop unfit for pigs. While Renzi walked around, free as a bird.

Now it was payback time.

Have Renzi meet him for the swap and blow him away.

————

3:35 PM – Swampscott

Frank sat at the kitchen table. The house was silent and still, so quiet, he could hear his breathing, the minutes creeping by slower than death, despair growing in his chest. Two hours had passed since he'd sent the text.

No call from Maureen. No text from Devlin.

He looked at the clock on the wall beside the stove. His mother had bought it years ago because she loved the Irish saying on the face. **May the wind always be at your back.**

His mother claimed it brought good luck. But it wasn't helping him. Far from it. With every tick of the clock, his chances of finding Maureen got slimmer and slimmer.

Devlin was mind-fucking him again. Making him wait, while Maureen sat in a room. Alone and frightened.

Fury rose inside him like a savage beast.

"God damn it to hell!" His words reverberated around the kitchen, bouncing off the cabinets and the tile floor.

He got on his phone and called Rafe.

"What's up, Frank? Did Mo call you?"

"No. I sent the photo and text over two hours ago. Nothing."

"Maybe he's not with her. Maybe he needs time to set up the call."

Frank clenched his jaw, fighting for control. He wanted to punch his fist through the wall. Better still, through Devlin's face.

"Rafe, we know he's not with her. He's home in Southie, and he's not holding Maureen in his basement. She's somewhere else. He's dicking me around. I think it's time for you to squeeze Sunny."

"Don't have to ask me twice," Rafe said. "I'm in my office. Put on my spiffy suit, should be at her place of business in half an hour."

CHAPTER 34

MONDAY October 31 – 4:15 PM – South Boston

Sunny massaged the tense knots in her shoulders, trying to calm her frazzled nerves. Thirty minutes ago, the desk clerk had called. A Boston police detective was here and wanted to ask her a few questions about the unfortunate event that happened last Monday. She told him to have the cop wait, she'd call back when she was ready.

At the time, she'd been relaxing in her apartment, about to pour herself a glass of wine. She changed into a business suit: a white silk blouse under a black jacket, black trousers and shiny black pumps. She combed her hair, freshened her makeup and rode the elevator down to the second floor. Only then had she called the desk and told the clerk to send the cop up to the executive suite.

The scene of the crime. A crime she had put behind her, thinking it was over. But maybe it wasn't.

Sweat dampened her palms. What did the detective want?

A tap sounded on the door. Her heart thudded inside her chest. She wiped her palms on her trousers and opened the door. To her surprise, a large black man in a well-tailored suit smiled at her and said, "Thanks for seeing me on such short notice, Ms. Jensen." He flashed his badge and extended his hand. "Detective Rafe Hawkins. Got a few questions about last Monday night."

She smiled and shook his hand. "Of course. Come in and sit down." She didn't offer him a beverage. Finish this fast and get him out of here.

She went to the black leather sofa and perched on one end. The BPD detective sat on the matching easy chair around the corner and set his leather briefcase on the floor. She said nothing, studying him. A handsome man with clean-shaven ebony skin and a rugged build, silently regarding her with penetrating dark eyes.

"You said you had questions," she said.

"I read the other detective's report. He asked you why Sean Whelan was here, but you didn't answer him. Why not?"

"I was too distraught. It was very upsetting. Having him die like that."

"I'm sure it was. But that was a week ago. Why was Whelan here?"

"I don't know." She couldn't very well say, *he wanted to fuck me.*

The detective spread his hands, enormous hands with long fingers. "I find that hard to believe, Sunny." Smiling at her. "Is it okay if I call you Sunny? You can call me Rafe."

"Since we're being so *friendly,* why don't you tell me why you're here?"

He gazed at her, no smile. "Sean Whelan is a known associate of Brian Devlin, who just got paroled from a federal prison. Sent there on a murder rap. Was Devlin here last Monday?"

"No. He was at the Leprechaun Pub. The other detectives already verified that."

"How convenient. Why was Whelan here?"

"I never liked the man," she said, and stopped abruptly. That sounded like a motive for murder. "He sexually assaulted me once in a restaurant. I explained all that to the other detectives."

"Did you file a complaint?"

"No, but last week he called and said he needed to talk to me about an urgent business matter. I don't know what it was because the creep took a big bite of game hen and choked to death."

Detective Rafe Hawkins opened his briefcase, removed a stack of papers bound together with a wide black clip and flipped through the pages. "According to the report, Whelan got here around six. You didn't call security until after eight-thirty."

"We had cocktails before dinner. Sean likes his booze." *Almost as much as he liked raping women.*

"What did you talk about?"

"The beautiful sunset," she snapped, gesturing at the window.

"How romantic. What about your boyfriend, Brian Devlin?"

"He's not my *boy*friend."

"Okay, your lover for twenty-five years. When he's not in prison."

She ostentatiously looked at her watch. "This is getting tedious. I have work to do."

"So do I." He thumbed through more pages. "Devlin claimed he was at the Leprechaun Pub when it happened. Was his sister there?"

"Kate? Of course not. She's ... mentally handicapped."

"How about Bridget? Was she there?" Gazing at her, expressionless.

217

Her mouth went dry as a cotton ball. Why was he asking about Bridget?

"I don't know Bridget. I've never met her."

"I think you do. Where's the girl?"

She reeled back as if he'd hit her with a sledgehammer. How did he know? And what else did he know?

"I'm thirsty. Would you like a bottled water?" She went to the sideboard, bent down and took two bottles out of the mini-fridge. Steeling herself, she returned to the couch, set one in front of the cop, opened hers and took a long swallow.

"You're lying, Sunny. Where's the girl?"

"I don't know what you're talking about. What girl?"

Rafe smiled but the smile didn't reach his eyes. "This could go either way, Sunny. Cooperate and we'll play nice. Otherwise, bad things could happen."

Glaring at him, she rose to her feet. "You have no right to threaten me. Get out of here."

He stood up, looming over her, put his enormous hands on her shoulders and forced her to sit down on the sofa. "Don't lie to me, Sunny. You know what girl. Where is she?"

Her heart pounded her chest in a frenzy.

Locking eyes with her, his eyes full of fury, he said, "Whelan's sister already claimed his body and buried him. But if we exhume the body you could be in a heap of trouble. We run more tests, who knows what we might find? Some new killer drug, maybe."

She gulped some water and sat there, still as a statue, unable to speak, barely able to breathe.

"His sister might even file a wrongful death suit because you didn't call 9-11 in a timely manner." He leaned forward, his eyes fixed on hers. "Why take the heat for Devlin? Call him and ask him where the girl is."

Her hard-won survival skills kicked in. If a cop threatens you, attack.

"The only person I'm calling is my lawyer. I asked you to leave and you laid hands on me. If you do it again, I'll scream bloody murder and say you tried to rape me."

She rose from the couch and walked toward the door. She wanted to run, but she couldn't afford to show fear. If she did, it was over.

After what seemed like an eternity, she reached the door, her hands shaking, her legs weak as jelly. She opened the door.

One of the Rottweilers stood outside. "Everything okay, Sunny?"

"Please escort this policeman downstairs," she said.

But the cop didn't go quietly.

"Think about what I said. Why should you take the heat?" Detective Rafe Hawkins handed her a business card. "Call me."

The instant he stepped into the hall, she closed the door and sagged against it, her mind churning with horrible scenarios.

Exhume the body.

Suspicious death.

Wrongful death suit.

Damn it to hell! Whelan's cold dead body was in the ground and he was still haunting her.

———

5:15 PM – South Boston

Agitated, Devlin paced his office, his phone to his ear, listening to Sunny ramble on about what had just happened. He knew exactly what happened. Renzi had sent one of his Boston PD pals to threaten her about Whelan, and he was going to pay for it. But the cop's questions were really directed at him. Asking about Bridget and the girl.

The one weak link in his plan: Renzi might discover the connection between Brian Devlin and Bridget White, owner of the cottage in Plymouth. Maybe the Boston cop was bluffing, trying to rattle her.

Sunny, bless her murderous heart, had denied knowing Bridget. And the girl. But if Renzi found out Bridget Devlin was Bridget White, his plan might fall apart. Not only that, it could happen at any time, a day from now, or an hour from now.

"Don't worry, Sunny. I'll take care of it."

"The bastard put his hands on me, Dev. I tried to get up off the couch and he wouldn't let me. What if they exhume Whelan's body? What if there's some kind of test—"

"Sunny. Listen to me. It's all going to work out. Daddy got the loot and sent me a picture of it."

And told me to have his daughter call him. Like hell. Renzi was going to get something and it wasn't going to be a call from his daughter.

"All well and good, Dev, but what if the cop comes back with an arrest warrant?"

219

"Relax. You'll never see him again. Get your business dealings in order and pack a suitcase. After the swap, we're going on a trip." Devlin smiled. "Think tropical, Sunny. Bring your bikini."

"I like the sound of that. How soon?"

"Wednesday maybe, Thursday at the latest. I've got calls to make. Go fix yourself a stiff drink and relax, Sunny. I'll come see you tonight and explain everything."

———

5:25 PM – Swampscott

Frank stared at the text. *No call from your daughter. You called the cops.*

Enraged, he stalked around his bedroom, consumed with fury.

You called the cops. That could mean only one thing. After Rafe leaned on Sunny, she called Devlin, who assumed, rightly, that Rafe had gone there at his behest.

But why let Devlin have the upper hand? Time to go on the offensive.

He composed a reply: *No phone call, no $$.*

He hit Send. Hoping he'd done the right thing, he went to his bedroom closet, took a small pouch off the top shelf, brought it downstairs and spread his cleaning supplies over the kitchen table: lubricant, cotton patches, a copper bore-brush and cleaning rod, and a soft cotton cloth.

When the time came to confront Devlin, he wanted his weapon in perfect working order.

He took the SIG out of the holster in the small of his back and unloaded it. At this point he could take it apart and reassemble it blindfolded, didn't even have to think about it. Which left his mind free to contemplate Brian Devlin. The man who had ordered his father's assassination and kidnapped his daughter.

He conjured an image of Devlin's face and imagined the light disappearing from his cold hard eyes. Fade to black.

Inhaling the scent of Hoppe's No.9, he wet several cotton patches with the solvent, ran each of them through the barrel, followed by a dry patch. Then he lubricated a dry patch and ran it over the frame, the slide, recoil assembly and breech face. Confident that his weapon was in good working order, he reassembled the SIG, reloaded, racked a round into the chamber and set the SIG on the table.

His phone rang. When he answered, Rafe exclaimed, "Frank! I'm positive Sunny knows where Maureen is. Just about wet her pants when I asked where the girl was."

"Maybe so, but she called Devlin. He just sent me a text: No phone call. You called the cops."

"Damn!" Rafe said. "I'm sorry. Maybe I shouldn't have—"

"No, you did the right thing. It's time to go on the offensive. I already texted him back. No phone call, no money. But we need to find Maureen fast, as fast as possible."

If they didn't, he'd go to Devlin's house and break his fingers one by one until the bastard told him where Maureen was.

————

5:30 PM – South Boston

Seething with fury, Devlin studied the text. *No phone call, no $$.*

Renzi wanted to play hardball? Fine. He got on his burner, punched in a number and waited.

Mike, his new enforcer, answered right away. "Hey, boss, what's up?"

"Does your wife still work at that hospital?"

"You bet. In fact she's there right now, works the late shift in the morgue. It's kinda creepy. She cleans up dead bodies before the funeral homes pick them up. Why?"

Devlin smiled. "I need her to do me a favor."

CHAPTER 35

TUESDAY November 1 – 9:35 AM – Plymouth

Dreading what she might find, Bridget opened her laptop. Every morning she checked the Baltimore news to see if there were any updates about a missing doctor. But first she had to check her email to see if there were any messages from the college. To the professor who claimed to have the flu.

Excellent. No messages from the college, just an email from the Yale Alumni Office. Brian's computer tech had set up a remote drop box for Bridget Devlin that forwarded email to her Bridget White account. Twice a year the Alumni Office sent out a newsletter about Yale graduates. She made sure her name wasn't mentioned and deleted them.

But it wasn't a newsletter, it was a courtesy notice from the Alumni Office. Yesterday someone had contacted them requesting her current address and phone number. Her heart catapulted into her throat. Jesus! Was it a cop?

The last line of the email said, "Per your request, we did not give out that information."

She closed the email and deleted it. But that didn't change anything.

For a moment she feared she would vomit. The nausea passed, but the feeling of dread didn't. The cops were after Brian and now they were after his sister. If they found out Bridget Devlin was now Bridget White, they would come here and find her. And Renzi's daughter.

She went in the kitchen, opened a bottled water and chugged half the contents, her mind churning with horrible scenarios. To calm herself, she fixed a sandwich for Maureen, the task giving her a surreal sense of purpose. *Keep her healthy so Brian can collect the big bucks.*

Unbidden, her favorite Beatles tune back in the day, *Eleanor Rigby*, started playing in her head. Old songs and old memories stuck in her mind like sticky burrs on a sweater, lost time she'd never get back.

And a future that might include a jail cell.

Ohhh, look at all the lonely people.

Back then she had been one of them. No mother to confide in, an alcoholic father glued to the TV set. In school, the girls hated her for being smart and pretty. The boys figured she'd put out because she lived in the projects and hated her for rejecting them. Not that it mattered. She had no time for friends. She'd been too busy taking care of Kate.

And it was no different now. She felt utterly alone.

Kate might hug her and kiss her, but she couldn't talk to Kate about her hopes and dreams. Or her fears.

She couldn't talk to Brian either, thanks to his monstrous payback scheme. Brian thought he could outwit the police, but the fifteen years he'd spent in prison proved he couldn't.

An icy chill wracked her, followed by a mushroom cloud of dread.

To hell with Brian. He only cared about punishing Frank Renzi.

She had to get out of here. Leave town and never come back. Stop being the prim-and-proper professor, let her hair down and enjoy life the way she did on vacation.

But this vacation would be permanent.

She sipped some water, planning her moves. She couldn't leave Maureen here by herself. The girl might starve to death before anyone found her. Not that Brian would care. She went in her office, opened a desk drawer and took out a burner. She'd call Tank, tell him she had to work tomorrow and ask him to mind the hostage.

———

10:05 AM – Winthrop

On his way to the group home, Frank took evasive action to make sure no one followed him, zipping off highway exits at the last second, looping around through side streets, then getting back on the highway.

No cars behind him when he parked around the corner from the group home, but the crushing fear that he might never see Maureen again was worse than ever.

No text from Devlin. No phone call from Maureen.

He left the car and took a package out of the trunk. The sky was overcast, a portent of things to come. Hyped by the Weather Channel, a nor-easter was headed this way. Fearing high winds and power outages, people were rushing to supermarkets and liquor stores to stock up on food and booze.

223

The grounds of group home, a four-story red-brick structure, were immaculate, but when he stepped inside, the place smelled like a school cafeteria, boiled eggs and burnt toast.

A young woman behind the reception desk greeted him with a smile. Sister Mary Margaret, according to her name tag. Even white teeth, beautiful blue eyes, light brown hair. What a waste. An attractive woman in her twenties destined to live life without male companionship.

"Good morning," he said, smiling as he set a pastry box on the desk. "I brought some Halloween cupcakes for Kate Devlin. A day late, but my plane was delayed in Chicago."

"How nice of you," she said. "Kate will be happy to see you."

"Unfortunately, I can't stay. I've got a business meeting. Could you give them to her?"

"Of course! I'm sure she'll be thrilled."

"Thanks. I'm an old friend of the family. Has Bridget been here to see Kate lately?"

"Bridget? Yes. She was just here on Sunday. She stopped by and took Kate to the Halloween parade."

Frank's heart thrummed his chest. "She comes here often then?"

"Two or three times a month, weekends mostly. The woman's a saint, utterly devoted to Kate." The nun smiled. "Beautiful, too, what with all that long black hair."

"I'd love to see her before I fly home. Can you give me her address and phone number?"

The nun's smile disappeared. "I'm sorry, sir, but I can't do that. We're very strict about privacy laws here." Gazing at him with her innocent blue eyes. A woman who always obeyed the Ten Commandments, and every law on the books.

Concealing his disappointment, he said, "But she lives near here?"

"Not right around the corner, but not too far, a half hour or so." She covered her mouth with her hand. "I shouldn't be telling you that."

"No worries," he said. "I won't tell anyone. Give my best to Kate."

Fearing she would ask for his name, he turned and left. A misty drizzle dampened his face as he hurried to his car. He hadn't gotten Bridget's address, but the nun said she lived a half hour or so from here. That meant she lived in Massachusetts, which narrowed things down.

Was Bridget holding Maureen captive? Sickened by the thought, he muttered, "Hang in there, Mo. I'm coming for you."

PAYBACK

———

11:35 AM – South Boston

Devlin stood in the game room with a dart in his hand, wishing it was a gun. *No phone call, no $$.* Renzi's latest text, a power play if ever there was one. He threw the dart at the target. Not a bulls-eye but close.

But close didn't cut it. His goal was within reach, but a Boston cop had threatened Sunny, which meant Renzi was onto him. If they found out Bridget White was his sister, things would fall apart in a hurry.

He thought about the Chinese proverb he had stumbled upon one day in the prison library. *A journey of a thousand miles begins with a single step.*

Or a single screw-up.

Even as a kid, he had been a risk-taker, living life at the edge, joining a gang, biding his time until he took over as leader. Making life-and-death decisions, like bungee jumpers and sky divers.

They didn't back away from crucial decisions, and he didn't either. He embraced them as a challenge. The problem was, you might get away with a bad decision, but not a major screw-up.

Maybe he shouldn't have had Bridget keep the hostage at her house.

His cell phone rang. He answered immediately. "What's up, Tank?"

"Bridget just called and said she's gotta work tomorrow. She wants me to mind the hostage. What do you want me to do?"

His immediate thought: *Why did she call Tank instead of me?*

Answer: Bridget was no risk-taker, she was weak and fearful. Paranoid and jittery, certain his plan would fail.

"I need to think about it, Tank. Call you back in a few."

He left the game room and strode through the backyard to his house. From long experience, he was certain of one thing. When the shit is about to hit the fan, only one person gave the orders. Brian Devlin.

Tank understood this. Bridget did not. She had tried to go around him. A major betrayal, but one that might work to his advantage.

He went in his office and called Tank. "Okay, here's what you do. Go to the cottage tomorrow morning, early enough so she can go to work. Take a fresh burner with you. Daddy wants proof of life. I'll call you after Bridget goes to work and tell you when to make the call. Hold a gun to the girl's head to make sure she follows the script."

"What script?" Tank said.

"A short message that she's okay and he should pay the money. I'll explain when I call you. "

"Okay. Want me to call Bridget and tell her I'll be there?"

"Yes. Call her now so she doesn't get worried." *And do something stupid.*

He put down the phone and went to his closet. A metal safe was embedded in the wall near the baseboard, a six-inch cube with a combination lock. He spun the knob, opened the safe and took out an envelope with his false papers: Kevin Halloran's U.S. passport, current drivers license and two credit cards. Under the envelope were bundles of cash, the two grand Peter Sasso had sent him.

Collect the loot from Renzi, kill him and hit the road with Sunny. Peter Sasso would make sure Kate was taken care of.

He hated to leave Tank holding the bag, but he had to look out for himself. If he didn't, no one else would.

———

2:10 PM – Swampscott

Downstairs in the laundry room, Frank took his clothes out of the dryer and sorted them into piles: T-shirts, briefs, polo shirts and running togs. He began folding them, his mind on other matters.

Earlier, he'd called Rafe to tell him what he'd learned at the group home. Rafe said he would check the RMV records in Massachusetts for Bridget Devlin. No news yet.

The doorbell rang. Odd. He wasn't expecting anyone, but maybe it was his neighbor.

He ran upstairs and opened the door. A small package the size of a paperback book sat on the welcome mat, wrapped in plain brown paper, addressed to him. Strange. No return address, no postage.

How did it get here? Off to his left, he caught a glimpse of a dark colored sedan turning a corner before it disappeared.

Alarm bells went off in his mind. Could be a gift from a friend. Could be a bomb.

He squatted and studied the package. No grease on the paper, no wires protruding from it. He put his fingers on opposite sides of the package and cautiously lifted it an inch or so. It wasn't heavy, seven or eight ounces maybe.

Somewhat reassured, he took the box in the kitchen, set it on the table and put his ear to the package.

No ticking sounds. He bent down and sniffed. Semtex, an explosive commonly used by bomb-makers, has a distinctive odor, but he didn't smell anything.

Using scissors, he carefully cut away the brown paper wrapping, exposing a plain white box, similar to those gift shops used. He eased off the cover. Saw something wrapped in tissue paper.

He parted the folds of paper and let out a scream. "Aaaaagh."

Packed in dry ice was a neatly severed finger.

Saliva flooded his mouth and bile rose in his throat. He ran to the bathroom and vomited into the toilet. Panting, he knelt on the floor, his head over the toilet. Another spasm rocked his body. He braced himself, gripped the toilet and spewed more vomit.

Eventually, the waves of nausea passed, but his body was soaked with sweat, and spittle dripped from his chin. He struggled to his feet, wet a hand towel and wiped his face.

He returned to the box on the kitchen table. Bile rose in his throat but he fought it down.

Inside the box was a message, printed in large block letters.

NO MORE COPS OR NEXT TIME IT'S HER HAND.

A flood of anguish overwhelmed him. Maureen, his only child, the light of his life, her hand butchered. The pain she must have suffered. Not only that, her career as an orthopedic surgeon, the career she had worked so hard to attain, might be over.

Ended by a vile scumbag. The personification of evil.

Devlin was a butcher, a man without conscience.

A haze of blind fury consumed him. With it, came certainty.

He would hunt the butcher down and make him pay. It wouldn't be like a movie where the villain gets blown away at the end with a shot to the head. Not like Pacino in the *Godfather*.

Crowd pleasing, but too easy.

Forget cop rules. Time for Renzi rules. Show no mercy.

He would make sure Devlin got exactly what was coming to him.

227

CHAPTER 36

WEDNESDAY November 2 – 8:10 AM – Plymouth

Bridget tucked an errant strand of hair into her French twist and checked herself in the wall mirror. The chestnut-brown pantsuit clashed with her black hair, but it would look fine when she put on the wig. The roll-on suitcase locked in the trunk of her car held toiletries, a change of clothes, the envelope with her getaway documents and a few other necessities.

She left the bedroom, stopped in her office to get her laptop and continued down the hall to the kitchen. Tank was sitting at the table, sipping coffee as he read the *Boston Herald*.

He set aside the paper and looked at her. "Geez, you look different with your hair like that."

"My prim and proper look for my students. I'm actually looking forward to seeing them. Teaching Psychology 101 is way less stressful than what we did last week."

Acting like they were co-conspirators. Reminding him they were a team. Convincing him she was going to work.

"Be careful driving," Tank said. "All this rain, there's a lotta wet leaves on the roads."

"I will," she said. "No speeding today." The last thing she wanted was a cop stopping her. "How's Brian? Have you talked to him lately?"

Tank picked up the newspaper and said, not looking at her, "He's hot to get the money."

She got the feeling that wasn't all Brian had said. Tank seemed edgy today. *When will he do the swap?* she wanted to scream. She waited, hoping he would tell her. He didn't.

"Aren't we all," she said. "Thanks for helping me, Tank. I made two sandwiches, one for you and one for the hostage. I'll be home by five to cook dinner." Lies, lies and more lies.

She went out the kitchen door and dashed to her car. Wind-whipped rain slashed her face as she slung her laptop and shoulder bag inside.

228

Her hooded winter jacket and snow boots were in the passenger seat foot-well. She backed her car down the driveway. Tank's van was parked on the street, but he'd move it to the driveway after she left.

Despite the rain and the slick roads, twenty minutes later she stood in the viewing room at her bank. Her safe deposit box sat on the table beside her suitcase. She methodically counted bundles of fifty-dollar bills as she put them into a trash bag. If she was frugal, a hundred grand would last for a while. The gold coins in the drawstring bag were likely worth another seventy-five grand. Portable and anonymous, no serial numbers. Sometimes she put one in her wallet when she went on vacation and cashed it in for small bills.

But if she tried to board a plane with the bag of coins, they would show up on the security scanner, a TSA agent would search her bag and find a hundred grand in cash. A big no-no. The agent would march her into a room and hard-eyed federal agents would question her. Some airports even used sniffer dogs trained to find drugs and large amounts of cash inside luggage. Visions of TSA agents and snarling dogs filled her mind.

She took a sample-sized bottle of cologne out of her shoulder bag and spritzed the cash inside the trash bag. Would that confuse the dogs? Maybe she wouldn't take a plane.

She jammed the trash bag into her suitcase and zipped it shut. Before she slid the box into its slot, she took out a five-dollar gold piece and dropped it in her shoulder bag for luck.

Today she needed all the luck she could get.

She returned to the safe deposit desk and signed out in the ledger book. The cops would find her safe deposit box eventually, but by then she would be somewhere else. But where? And how would she get there? If Brian did the swap today, she didn't have much time.

By midnight she wanted to be as far away as possible, preferably on the west coast. A bus would be safest, just buy a ticket and board, but slow. A train would be faster, but not fast enough to suit her.

A plane would be the fastest, but also the most dangerous, requiring a succession of ID and security checks.

Too bad she couldn't ask Scottie to beam her up like *Star Trek*.

But this wasn't a TV show. If the cops caught her, life as she knew it would be over.

———

9:15 AM – Boston

Inhaling the familiar odor of gunpowder and sweat, Frank stepped into an empty cubicle. When he worked for Boston PD, he and Rafe had used this shooting range so he knew his way around. Today, he'd signed in with Rafe's guest pass. Rafe was at the BPD lab.

So was the box with the finger.

Last night, Rafe had driven to Swampscott, hoping to find evidence near the front door. He didn't. When Frank mentioned the car he'd seen, Rafe said it might have been a courier service. Before he left, Rafe had asked him for Maureen's blood type. He would have a BPD lab tech run tests to see if her blood type matched the blood on the finger.

A barrage of gun shots penetrated his ear-protectors, another shooter three cubicles to his right. Time to get to work.

Frank put on a set of goggles, opened his box of ammo and loaded hollow point rounds into his SIG 9mm. Fifteen in the magazine, one in the chamber. He clipped a full-size human target to the pulley, hit a switch and watched the target shimmy to the far wall.

Years ago when he was a rookie patrolman in Boston, a saying was posted on the squad room wall. Fate said to the warrior, *"You cannot survive the coming storm."* And the warrior said, *"I AM the storm."*

Now he was the warrior. He didn't know when or where he would do battle with Devlin, what the situation would be or if others would be with him. What he did know: Devlin was a dead man.

Rage boiled into his throat but he fought it down. When the time came, he needed to be calm and dispassionate. Merciless.

He faced the target, aimed for the kill-zone and fired until the SIG was empty. He pressed the switch and the target shimmied toward him. Not bad, every shot but one inside the kill-zone.

He re-loaded and set up a fresh target. He raised the SIG, took a breath, aimed at the kill-zone and emptied the weapon.

This time when he checked the target, every shot had penetrated the kill-zone.

The shrinks on TV liked to talk about choices. Make the right choice and you'll be healthy, wealthy and, if not wise, content. But unlike civilians, police officers had to make decisions with far more serious consequences. Make the wrong decision, you could wind up dead. And he didn't intend to die.

Devlin no doubt had an arsenal of weapons at his disposal. He might also have a Kevlar vest. At the police academy, weapons instructors advised: If your target is wearing body armor, aim for the knees or the head.

Frank set up a standard match target, a large black circle with ever-smaller concentric circles inside, the smallest the size of a pencil eraser. Visualizing Devlin's kneecap, he aimed and fired.

The first few rounds were accurate enough, but he had to work on speed. He got into a rhythm, slow at first, feeling the recoil, then a little quicker, then quicker still. Ten minutes later, he could get off four shots per second and put each one into the innermost circle.

He set up another human target and visualized Devlin's forehead with a bullet hole in it. Took aim and fired. Bulls-eye.

Put up a fresh target. Another bulls eye.

A fresh target, another kill.

When he finished, his shirt was soaked with sweat and his box of ammo was empty. He returned the ear-protectors and goggles to the desk and went out to his car.

Rafe was waiting for him, his hands jammed in the pockets of his leather jacket, his breath steaming in the cold air.

"It's not Maureen's finger," Rafe said. "Wrong blood type."

A wave of relief swept over him, then a spasm of anger. Devlin was mind-fucking him.

"Good," he said. "But still no phone call from Maureen."

Rafe nodded, his eyes somber. "Stalemate. You got any ideas?"

He did, but none he wanted to share.

"I'm going home and wait for a phone call. Can you monitor Devlin's ankle bracelet and tell me where he is?"

"Sure, no problem." And after a beat, "What if Mo doesn't call?"

Frank smiled tightly. "I'll go to Devlin's house in Southie and cut off his balls."

———

10:30 AM – Plymouth

Seated in the reference room at the Plymouth Public Library, Bridget opened her laptop, accessed the free WiFi and got on the Internet. Rain slashed the windows facing her table, and gusty wind whipped the branches of several fir trees.

What was Maureen doing, she wondered. In this kind of weather, her basement was cold and damp. She should have given her a sweater.

What would Tank do when she didn't come home at five o'clock? He'd said Brian was hot to get the money. Did that mean they'd do the swap today? Not knowing made her nervous.

She surfed to the Green Airport website. Logan Airport was closer, but that's the first place the cops would look for her. Green was in Warwick, Rhode Island. She clicked Book a Flight, put in today's date and searched for flights departing 3:00 PM and after.

No direct flights to the West coast, but Delta had a flight to Detroit departing at 4:55 PM. A connecting flight left Detroit at 8:15 PM and landed at Seattle-Tacoma International Airport at 10:20 PM local time. That would work.

But would a seat be available when she got to Green Airport? She didn't want to buy the ticket online with Irene Gillan credit card. Leave no paper trails. Tacoma would put her near the Canadian border, in case she had to make a run for it.

Brian wouldn't be after her, but the cops might.

She checked the time. Almost eleven. She closed her laptop and left the library. Hunching her shoulders inside the winter jacket, she sprinted to her car. No one gave her a second glance. People were wet and miserable, eager to get home, delayed by the traffic congestion. The storm was worse now, sheets of rain blown sideways by the wind.

She jumped in the car and reviewed her check list. Convince Tank she was going to work. Check. Collect the cash from her safe deposit box. Check. Find a flight to the West coast. Check.

But she had to hurry.

She had a lot to do before she got to the airport.

———

11:15 AM – Swampscott

Frank toweled his hair dry and went in his bedroom. The weather was getting worse and so was the traffic. It had taken him an hour to drive home from Boston. He put on a black T-shirt and a pair of dry jeans, and tried not to think about Maureen. Impossible.

He got his gun-cleaning pouch out of the closet and took it downstairs to the kitchen. When facing the enemy, use a weapon that works every time. All the shooting practice in the world was irrelevant if your gun misfired.

After he finished cleaning his SIG, he went in the living room and sat down, waiting for the phone to ring. Damn! He hated waiting. Maureen was waiting too, waiting for him to find her. He believed she was at Bridget Devlin's house, somewhere in Massachusetts. But he had no idea where it was and no way to find it.

Devlin was playing mind games. Sending him a dead finger. Not letting Mo call him.

A black tide of anger rose inside him. Unable to sit still, he went to the window. Horizontal rain battered the glass. The sky was iron gray and thick with clouds. A depressing sight that matched his mood.

He went to the stereo and sorted through the CDs he'd left here when he moved to New Orleans.

How about some Blood, Sweat and Tears? He put on their *Greatest Hits Album* and paced the room, digging the brass section, especially the trumpet riffs.

The second cut was "Go Down Gamblin," one of his favorites.

Go down gamblin. Say it when you're running low.

He was beyond running low. He was running on empty.

Cards are bound to break me, but I ain't busted yet. Go down gamblin.

And he thought, why not? Why let Devlin call the shots? Why give him the upper hand?

He opened his phone and typed a text message. *If I don't get a call from Maureen by 1 PM, I'll go to Winthrop and ask Kate where Bridget lives.*

Devlin would know he was onto him, but what difference did that make now? Maureen was a prisoner and time was running out.

He hit Send and waited, saw the text go through. *Go down gamblin.*

He went upstairs to his bedroom and packed his suitcase. No clothes, just boxes of ammo, a Kevlar vest, a flashing light for his rental car, gloves, a small flashlight and the Swiss Army knife.

Then he took the suitcase down to the kitchen and made himself a thick sandwich of ham, pastrami and Swiss cheese. Stoke up on energy and wait for Maureen to call.

If she didn't, he'd drive to Devlin's house and make the bastard tell him where Maureen was. He knew how to do it.

A cop for twenty-plus years, he'd seen a few torture victims.

CHAPTER 37

WEDNESDAY November 2 – 11:10 AM – South Boston

Devlin stood at the window in Sunny's apartment, gazing down at the rooftops of his beloved Southie. Not born and raised here, but years ago when he moved his family into the house he'd bought, he felt like he had come home.

An Irish stronghold and home of the Shamrock Gang.

Rain slashed the window pane. The storm was a raging tyrant now, whipping up whitecaps along Carson Beach, causing traffic jams on the streets below, rivers of rainwater filling the gutters.

"Want me to call down and order some lunch?" Sunny asked.

He turned and looked at her. "I'm not in the mood for lunch."

Seated on the sofa, Sunny formed her lips in a pout and patted the cushion beside her. "Come sit with me and we'll figure out what to do."

Devlin clenched his jaw. He didn't need any help figuring out what had to be done. But his payback plan had hit a snag, melting like a snowman in a spring thaw. Renzi was onto him.

If I don't get a call from Maureen by 1PM, I'll go to Winthrop and ask Kate where Bridget lives.

Threatening to browbeat Kate, like he did after her abusive husband got what he deserved.

As leader of the Shamrocks, he had adopted certain rules. Before ordering a hit that involved another gang, he considered what he knew about them. How many shooters did they have and would they retaliate? The hardest part was trying to guess what could go wrong.

When he devised his payback plan, he had been focused on one goal: inflict as much pain as possible on Renzi, then kill him. That might have to change. A good leader adapts and adjusts his strategy.

Forget the money. Kill Renzi and get out of Dodge.

"Renzi's desperate to talk to his daughter," Sunny said.

Her complacent attitude grated on his nerves.

"He knows where Kate lives," Devlin said. "He wants to know where Bridget lives. Why do you suppose that is?"

Sunny waved a hand. "He's bluffing."

"Like hell he is!" Devlin shouted, and gave her his don't-fuck-with-me look.

Sunny flinched, her Nordic blue eyes wide with fear.

"Kate's not your sister, Sunny. She's my sister. We're family. We look out for each other. I don't want Renzi anywhere near Kate, understand?"

"Of course," Sunny said quickly. "You know what's best, Dev."

"Damn right I do. Renzi knows I'm the one that's fucking with him. You freaked out when the cop grilled you about Whelan. Got worried he might come back with an arrest warrant. Here's what I'm worried about. The feds are hellbent on sending me back to prison."

He raised one pant leg and pointed at the electronic bracelet on his ankle. "This fucking charm bracelet tells them where I am every minute of every day. Christ, they probably know when I'm in bed with you."

Silence in the room. After a moment, Sunny said, expressionless, "What do you want me to do?"

Was her composure fake, or did she not care what happened to him? With Sunny it was hard to tell sometimes.

"Rent a car for me, high-powered and comfortable, all the bells and whistles, and park it outside my house. I'll have Tank make the call to Renzi, give him a script for the girl to follow and have him hold a gun to her head to make sure she sticks to it."

"Sounds good to me," Sunny said. "And then?"

"I'll do the swap tonight, tell Renzi to meet me on Deer Island."

Sunny frowned. "Be careful, Dev. He's a cop. No way will he go there without a gun."

Gratified by her concern, he smiled. "Don't worry, so will I."

He pictured the *Scarface* poster on his bedroom wall, Al Pacino, a sneer etched on his face, brandishing a machine gun. He loved the caption: *Say Hello to My Little Friend.*

"I'll call you before I leave for the meet. Rent a car from a different rental agency and wait for me in the cell phone lot at Logan Airport." He hesitated, then said, "If I'm not there by seven-thirty, get on a plane and get out of here."

Sunny rushed over and put her arms around him. "You'll be there, Dev. I just know it."

Maybe, he thought. Or maybe he'd never see her again. Good luck could bring you wealth, happiness and success. Bad luck could make you miss a plane or have a car accident.

Fate was what the gods gave you when you ran out of luck.

One thing was certain. When he met Renzi tonight, surrender was not an option.

———

12:25 PM – Taunton, Massachusetts

Bridget gripped the wheel as a gust of wind rocked her car, the wipers working furiously to clear the windshield. Route 44, a four lane divided highway, was the most direct route to Providence, but the storm was slowing her down. She was behind schedule.

Twenty minutes ago, one of the west-bound lanes had been closed, cars, vans and trucks inching past a crew of workers with power saws, removing a fallen tree limb.

Now she was on the outskirts of Taunton, a commercial strip with businesses on both sides. No divider, just four lanes of traffic stalled in both directions with traffic lights every other block. At the previous light, she had turned into a Taco Bell, circled around back and ditched her laptop in a huge Dumpster. This time tomorrow, her laptop and everything on it would be buried in a landfill under tons of other trash.

Ahead of her, an F-150 pickup truck with canvas tied over the rear compartment stopped at a red light, the canvas flapping in the wind. She took out her phone and checked the flight info she had downloaded. Would the five-dollar gold piece bring her luck? If she got a seat on the flight she wanted, the plane would take off at 4:55 PM.

Boarding would begin at 4:25 PM. But first she had to get through security. Another worry.

She checked the time, almost twelve-thirty, and did some calculations. A half hour to buy the ticket, another half hour in the security line. She had to get to Green Airport by 2:45 PM at the latest. Even that was cutting it close. She needed to stop at the train station in Providence first and she wasn't even close to being there. Damn this weather!

The F-150 pickup ahead of her accelerated. She dropped the phone in her shoulder bag and concentrated on driving.

Inevitably, her thoughts turned to Maureen. Would Brian let her talk to her father? What if he didn't?

A minute later she stopped at a light beside a Burger King. Not many cars in the parking lot, but there was a line for the Drive-Thru. She hadn't eaten breakfast, but the very thought of food nauseated her.

Tank was at her cottage with Maureen and he had a gun.

Would Brian do the swap at her cottage? Doubtful.

Would he have Tank drive Maureen somewhere else for the swap? Maybe. The alternative frightened her.

Gripping the wheel, her knuckles white, she tried to reassure herself.

Tank had a soft spot in his heart for women. He would never harm Maureen.

Unless Brian told him to.

———

12:45 PM – Plymouth

Maureen sat on the cot with her hands in her lap, afraid to move, barely able to breathe. Cigarman was holding a gun to her head.

"Okay," he said. "I'm gonna call your father now. Tell me what you're going to say."

She couldn't see the gun but she could feel it pressing against her head above her ear. Her heart slammed her chest.

Would he shoot her? Moments ago he'd told her that's what would happen if she didn't say what he wanted.

She took a deep breath and recited the words. "I'm okay, Dad. Please give them the money."

"Very good. When he answers, I'll tap your cheek and you give your speech."

"Okay." She sat very still and gathered her courage.

Moments later Cigarman tapped her cheek with the phone.

"Hi Dad," she said, loud and clear. "I'm okay. Please give them the *seagulls.*"

Cigarman jerked the phone away and jabbed her head with the gun.

"What the hell was that? Jesus Christ! I told you what to say."

He squeezed the nape of her neck with his fingers, a vise-like grip. "You think I won't shoot you? Guess again."

When he let go of her neck, she screamed, "Fuck you! You're a scumbag. And so is your sister."

"Shut your mouth. I ain't got no sister. You're lucky I didn't shoot you."

"What a *brave man*," she said, her voice dripping sarcasm. "I'm tied up like a prisoner, blindfolded, and you put a gun to my head."

Silence. Then footsteps clomping toward the stairs.

"My father's going to put you in jail for the rest of your life!" she screamed.

And heard the door slam upstairs.

———

12:30 PM – Swampscott

Frank pumped his fist in the air and shouted, "YES!" His gamble had worked. Maureen was alive!

Now Devlin knew he had figured out who ordered Mo's kidnapping and his father's assassination, but so what? It was better than waiting for a phone call that might never come.

Overjoyed to hear Mo's voice, he paced the kitchen. She sounded strong, almost defiant, had even slipped in a clue. Seagulls. Letting him know she was near the ocean. That narrowed things down.

He had no proof that Maureen was at Bridget's house, but given Devlin's response to his threat, he assumed she was. He took a laminated map of Massachusetts out of a kitchen drawer and studied the coastline north and south of Kate's group home in Winthrop.

If Bridget drove there from her house, she would likely take one of two routes. If she lived north of Boston, Route 95 was the fastest, but miles away from oceanfront towns like Revere, Lynn and Beverly.

If she lived south of Boston, Route 93, aka the Southeast Expressway, passed through Quincy near the water. South of Quincy, Route 3 went all the way to Cape Cod, passing through seaside towns like Marshfield, Duxbury and Plymouth.

Go down gamblin. If he were a betting man, he'd bet on the southern route. But the most important question remained.

Where would they do the swap?

He got on his phone, accessed the text function and keyed in a brief message. *Where is the swap? What time?*

He hit Send, thinking: *Take that, motherfucker.*

Rain slashed the kitchen windows. Traffic would be bad no matter where the swap was. In any case, Swampscott was nowhere near any of the seaside towns north or south of Boston. But if he left before the afternoon rush began, he could wait in the cell phone lot at Logan Airport, use it as a staging area that allowed easy access to the main routes going north or south.

He put on his windbreaker, locked the house and put his suitcase in back seat of the rental car. Drenched by the heavy rain, he got behind the wheel and called Rafe.

"Yo, Frank, what's up? Did Maureen call you?"

"Yes. Five minutes ago. I just sent a reply asking when and where to make the swap."

No need to mention his threat to talk to Kate. He was operating on a need to know basis. At this point, the less Rafe knew, the better. Plausible deniability.

"Excellent!" Rafe said. "Call me when you get an answer. Devlin left Sunny's hotel in Southie this morning at eleven-fifteen and went to his house behind the Leprechaun Pub. As of now he's still there."

"Thanks, Rafe. Keep me posted and I'll do the same."

But after Devlin texted him the details of the swap, he wouldn't be calling Rafe.

When he confronted Devlin, he didn't want any witnesses.

CHAPTER 38

WEDNESDAY November 2 – 1:20 PM – South Boston

Devlin sat on his bed and laced up his running shoes, the bracelet on his right ankle a revolting reminder the feds were watching him. The slightest mistake could put him back in prison. All-consuming anger churned his gut like a cement mixer. He hated the feds and he hated cops. Hated Renzi most of all, the self-important prick who'd put him in a jail cell for fifteen years.

Renzi knew he was after him. So did his cop pal, Rafe Hawkins.

Kill or be killed flashed in his mind like a neon beer sign in a liquor store window.

Forget the ransom. Put a bullet in Renzi's head and get out of town fast.

His fake documents were already in his suitcase. He went in his closet, opened the safe and took out the two grand Peter Sasso had sent him and a bag of gold coins, thanks to Bridget's tip. Gold holds its value, she'd said. Easier to carry than cash, anonymous, no serial numbers. His were probably worth sixty grand or so.

He locked the safe and put his getaway stash in the suitcase on his bed. The two grand would get him to Houston. He'd cash out the gold coins for small bills, go to the bank, get the fifty grand in his safe deposit box, and be on his way.

The car Sunny had rented for him was in his driveway, a black Audi sedan with less than ten thousand miles on it. His suitcase would be safe enough in the trunk. It wouldn't be there long.

He zippered it shut, went in the office, picked up the burner on his desk and studied the text Renzi had sent him.

Where's the swap? What time?

Renzi was desperate to get his daughter back. Which fit right in with his plan.

Hunting people was a lot like shooting seagulls, a practice he'd begun after Tank gave him his first weapon, a mickey-mouse .22 caliber rifle. There were two ways to do it. Stalk them or ambush them.

Sometimes he hid near the jetty on Carson Beach and waited for a flock of gulls to show up. But an ambush was more efficient. Toss a fish head on the ground, the gulls magically appeared.

Renzi's precious daughter was the fish head. But Renzi wouldn't be getting his daughter. He'd be getting a bullet in the head.

When Bridget got home from work, she would be the one to tell the girl her father was dead. Too bad he couldn't be there to see it.

But his ultimate reward would happen tonight on Deer Island.

By the end of the day someone was going to be dead and it wasn't going to be him.

Renzi was a dead man.

———

1:30 PM – Providence, Rhode Island

Bridget towed her suitcase into the train station restroom and set it beside the sink at the far end. Three women stood at the other sinks, washing their hands or primping their hair. She studied herself in the mirror.

Time for Bridget White to disappear. The thought of chopping off her long black hair sickened her. Her crowning glory flushed down a toilet. But it had to be done. There was only one way to escape.

Get as far away as possible and start a new life as Irene Gillan.

When an older woman left the handicapped stall behind her, Bridget towed her suitcase into the stall and hung her winter jacket on the hook on the back of the door. A diaper-changing shelf was beside the toilet.

She took the necessary implements out of her shoulder bag and set them on the shelf: a sharp pair of scissors, a small hand mirror and a sturdy comb.

With grim determination, she methodically cut off three-inch hanks of hair, threw them in the toilet and flushed. Cut off more hair, dropped it in the toilet and flushed. She ran the comb through what was left and checked herself with the hand mirror. One more round with the scissors should do it.

She flushed the hair down the toilet, put the comb in her handbag and dropped the scissors in the sanitary napkin disposer.

Next step, make herself look like the photo on Irene Gillan's driver's license. She unzipped her suitcase and took out the chestnut-brown wig. Using both hands, she slipped on the wig and checked herself with the hand mirror. Excellent. No wisps of black hair showing.

She put the mirror in her shoulder bag, shut the suitcase and used the toilet. Might as well pee while she had the chance. She might not have time at the airport.

Confident that she could pass as Irene Gillan, she put on her winter jacket and towed her suitcase out of the restroom into the terminal. Her car was parked on the top level of the train station garage. Sooner or later the cops would find it, but not today.

The station was teeming with travelers opting for a train ride due to the storm. Flying in weather like this would not be easy or pleasant. Flights would be delayed and when the plane finally got in the air, it would be a bumpy ride.

Feeling ambivalent about her next move, she towed her suitcase to a secluded corner near the door to the street. After saying a silent prayer, she took a fresh burner out of her shoulder bag and accessed the Text function. This morning she had memorized Renzi's cell phone number.

She typed in the number, then a message. *Maureen is in a basement at 9 Evergreen Lane in Plymouth.*

She hesitated, then typed: *The man with her has a gun.*

She hit Send, and a great weight lifted off her shoulders.

Her guilt feelings about kidnapping Maureen would haunt her forever, but the girl deserved to be with her father.

She felt guilty about betraying Brian. He was her brother, after all. When Renzi found out Bridget White was Brian's sister, Brian would go back to prison. Unfortunately, Tank would also go to jail, but Tank had killed more people than Brian. At Brian's behest.

Damn! Now it was ten past two. If she didn't hurry, she'd never make the flight to Detroit. But first she had to ditch the burner. Renzi might ask one of his cop friends to locate the phone that had sent the text. She removed the SIM card and dropped it in a trash container, stepped outside and buried the burner under some trash in a different receptacle. The workers who cleaned the train station would empty them before the end of their shift.

By then, she would be in Detroit. Provided the rest of her escape went as planned.

She towed her suitcase to the cab at the head of the taxi line. The trunk opened and the driver, a young guy in chinos and a windbreaker got out. She smiled and said, "No need for the trunk. I'll keep my suitcase with me on the back seat. I'm in a rush to get to Green Airport. Get me there before three and you'll get a generous tip."

"You got it, ma'am." He slung her suitcase onto the back seat and got behind the wheel.

She jumped in the back seat, slammed the door, and the cab zoomed away from the curb. Unable to relax, she offered up silent prayers.

Please let there be a seat on the plane. Please let me get through security.

Please let the plane take off on time.

And please God, forgive me for what I've done.

———

2:10 PM – Logan Airport – East Boston

Rain slashed the windshield of his rental car like a bullwhip. Frank drummed his fingers on the steering wheel, parked in the cell phone lot at Logan Airport, hyper-aware of the passing minutes. He'd sent the text to Devlin almost an hour ago. No reply yet. He hated waiting, but Maureen had far more reason to hate it than he did. Held prisoner in a room somewhere, blindfolded, her mouth taped shut.

The thought of it gnawed at him like a throbbing tooth that needed to be pulled.

From here he could get on a highway fast and head north or south. But not until Devlin texted him.

The bastard was toying with him again, making him wait.

Lots of cars in the cell phone lot. Tons of flight delays in this kind of weather. The driver in the car beside him, a guy in his twenties, had conked out, his head back, his eyes closed, his mouth open.

Frank cranked the engine and turned on the heat. He had on black running pants and a T-shirt under his navy windbreaker, but the air outside was a chilly fifty degrees. His suitcase was in the trunk, with his extra ammo, Kevlar vest and his other equipment. His loaded SIG was tucked into the small of his back, hidden under his windbreaker.

After Devlin texted him the place and time for the swap, would he bring Maureen? Doubtful. His primary target had never been Maureen or Judge Salvatore Renzi. His gripe was with Homicide Detective Frank Renzi.

Devlin lived in Southie. Maureen was somewhere else, somewhere near the ocean.

Which meant Devlin would likely come alone, intent on killing him.

That might complicate matters.

During his many years in law enforcement Frank had come to accept certain truths. Among them: Homicide detectives had to deal with the dregs of humanity, vicious criminals, deranged stalkers and murderers.

Sometimes they killed them.

His phone pinged and he grabbed it, hoping it was Devlin's reply. It wasn't. His heart-rate spiked as he read the text.

Scarcely able to believe it, he read it again.

Maureen is in a basement at 9 Evergreen Lane in Plymouth. The man with her has a gun.

Plymouth. South of Boston. He slammed the car in gear and barreled out of the cell phone lot.

Five minutes later he was inside the Williams Tunnel headed for the Southeast Expressway.

Worrying about the man with the gun.

———

2:15 PM – Plymouth

Maureen eased off the side of the bed and stood still for a moment to get her balance. It had taken her a while to get past the terrifying moment when Cigarman jammed the gun against her head and yelled at her, but now that she had, she was too excited to sit still.

Even though it was only *Hello*, she was thrilled to hear Dad's voice.

Thrilled that she'd slipped in the seagull clue. Maybe that would help him find her. The sooner the better.

She couldn't wait to wrap her arms around him. Couldn't wait to get the damn blindfold and zip-ties off, either. Her wrists and ankles were sore, the skin rubbed raw by the plastic restraints.

Extending her arms in front of her, she inched her feet apart and did a squat. Raised herself and did another, and got into a rhythm. Up and down, up and down, counting as she did them.

Fourteen … fifteen … sixteen …

"What the hell are you doing!!"

The voice startled her so much she lost her balance, tipped sideways and fell on the floor.

Footsteps approached. *Thunk-thunk-thunk.*

Cigarman grabbed her by the armpits, hauled her upright and sat her on the cot. "Sit there and be quiet," he snarled.

"I'm sick of sitting here doing nothing. When can I see my father?"

She heard a snick. Felt the gun barrel touch the side of her head.

All the air left her lungs and her mouth went dry as toast.

"Shut your mouth and do what I tell you, understand?"

"Yes," she whispered.

Footsteps retreated toward the staircase. Thumped up the stairs. No door slam.

"Fuck you," she whispered. And thought about how to punish him. It didn't take long, less than ten seconds.

How about shoving a catheter up his penis? Punish him where it would hurt the most. Jam it up there and make *him* yell.

Tell *him* to suck it up and be quiet.

Her neck prickled. Was he standing by the door upstairs, listening to hear if she got off the bed?

When would she see Dad? And where? Would it be here or would Cigarman take her someplace else?

Her heart jerked into a ragged rhythm, pounding her chest. Cigarman had a gun. What if he shot Dad?

She clenched her fists. She had to stop thinking like that.

Dad had been a cop for years and years, ever since she was a little kid.

When she was ten, he had showed her the gun safe in their basement where he kept his SIG.

He hardly ever went anywhere without it.

She had to stay positive. Dad was coming to get her.

When he did, he would have a gun.

CHAPTER 39

WEDNESDAY November 2 – 3:20 PM – Warwick, Rhode Island

The line at the Delta Airlines ticket counter seemed endless, a serpentine maze herding anxious travelers toward the counter. Bridget towed her suitcase around a U-turn. Incessant announcements on the PA system exacerbated her fears: *Attention passengers on Flight whatever to wherever, this is your final boarding call.*

She'd tipped the cabbie forty bucks for getting her here by three, but the departures board showed dozens of canceled and delayed flights. The Delta flight to Detroit was still set to depart at 4:55, but by the time she reached the counter, all the seats might be gone. A man in a business suit left the counter, looking happy.

The line inched forward, only five people ahead of her now. She took out a tissue and blew her nose, preparing her sob story for the clerk at the ticket counter. If she ever got there.

Now it was 3:25. The flight to Detroit would begin boarding at 4:25 and she still had to go through security. More lines, more scrutiny. Dangerous. Renzi was probably halfway to Plymouth by now, and she was waiting in line to buy a plane ticket.

What if Renzi called the Plymouth cops and found out she owned the cottage? What if they put out an all points bulletin on Bridget White? What if they figured out she'd texted him from the Providence train station? Would they give her name to the TSA agents at the airports near Providence? Green Airport was the closest.

What if, what if. She had to stop over-thinking everything.

Pretend she was going on vacation.

She replayed the last one in her mind, weeks ago in California, savoring each frame as if it were a blockbuster movie.

Flirting with a handsome executive at the upscale hotel bar, his dark brown hair flecked with gray at the temples. Inhaling the aroma of his aftershave lotion as she leaned closer, her long black hair draped over the shoulders of her low-cut red dress. He wore an elegant tailored black suit and a white Gucci shirt with gold cuff links. Conscious of his ultra-masculine presence, she smiled at him.

She loved his opening line: "You're the best-looking woman here."

They talked for a while, but she had no memory of what he said. She wanted to run her fingers through his hair and get in bed with him and rest her head on his chest and smell his male scent and hear his voice murmur in her ear. Most of all she wanted to feel his arms around her. Making her feel safe.

Because she never felt safe. Not once in her entire life.

And certainly not now. The woman in front of her left the ticket counter. Bridget parked her suitcase in front of the counter, put on a worried frown and dabbed her eyes with a tissue.

A young woman in a Delta uniform smiled at her. "Hi, how can I help you today?"

She wiped her nose with the tissue. "My mother's in the hospital and I need to fly to Tacoma as soon as possible. My brother said a flight leaves here soon that goes through Detroit and connects to Tacoma." She sniffled and heaved a sigh. "Mom's not doing too well."

"I'm sorry to hear that. Let me see if there are any seats on that flight." The clerk tapped some keys and stared at the computer screen.

She took her wallet out of the shoulder bag. *Please let there be a seat.*

"Delta Flight 4532 to Detroit was scheduled to depart at four-fifty-five," the clerk said, "but there's a ground stop on that flight."

Bridget stared at her, appalled. "Does that mean it won't leave today?" She had to get out of here today! The sooner the better. She felt like an army of ants was crawling down her neck.

"No, but the departure will be delayed. The incoming plane scheduled to fly passengers on Flight 4532 to Detroit has been delayed due to the weather."

"How long of a delay?"

"I can't be sure. Could be anywhere from a half hour to an hour." The clerk smiled. "The good news is, I have one seat available on that flight. It's in the last row at the back."

"I'll take it," she said. "Will I be able to make the connection in Detroit to Tacoma?"

"That depends on how soon Flight 4532 departs." The clerk tilted her head back and forth. "I can't guarantee that the flight will arrive in time to make your connection to Tacoma."

Bridget hesitated, then thought: Get out of here now, worry about the connection later. "Okay, I'll book the Tacoma flight too. If I miss it, I'll just take the next one."

"Certainly," the woman said, busy with her computer, tapping the keys. "Will that be round trip or one way?"

"One way. I might have to stay in Tacoma until Mom gets out of the hospital."

The clerk nodded but said nothing, staring at the screen.

Bridget opened her wallet and put Irene Gillan's driver's license on the counter.

"Can I pay cash for the ticket? My credit cards are maxed out."

The clerk studied her license, frowning now.

Her heart slammed her chest, pounding her ribs like a drum. The Irene Gillan DL was good enough to get her into a federal prison to visit Brian. But ever since the 9-11 attacks, paying cash for a one-way plane ticket was suspect.

She didn't want to use Irene's credit card. She wanted a clean getaway. No paper trails. If the cops found out about Irene Gillan, they would hunt her down like a dog.

At long last, the clerk nodded briskly and handed back the license. "Will you be checking any bags?"

Relieved, she said, "No. All I have is a roll-on suitcase."

"Okay. A one-way ticket on Delta flight 4958, connecting in Detroit to Delta flight 2888 flying to Seattle-Tacoma International Airport costs two hundred-forty dollars."

Bridget took five crisp fifty-dollar bills out of her wallet and put them on the counter.

The clerk counted them and gave her the change. "I'm printing your boarding pass for the Detroit flight now. The boarding pass for the flight to Tacoma won't be available until you get to Detroit." The clerk smiled and said, "Good luck. I hope your mother will be okay."

"Thank you," she said. "So do I."

She took the boarding pass, put it in her wallet and towed her suitcase away from the counter. So far so good. But she still had to get through security. Another ordeal, fraught with danger.

An hour ago she's been worried about missing the flight to Detroit. Now she was worried about the delayed departure.

By then Renzi would be in Plymouth.

———

3:30 PM – Route 3 – Duxbury, Massachusetts

Alert for puddles in the high-speed lane, Frank kept his eyes on the road. A squall line had recently passed through, dumping several inches of rain on the highway. Buzzed on adrenaline, he was speeding down Route 3 toward Plymouth, wondering who had sent him the text.

Devlin's sister, Bridget? Who else could it be?

He'd considered contacting the Plymouth police department to find out who owned the property at 9 Evergreen Lane, but then he'd have to explain why he wanted to know. If he told them, they would go there, the last thing he wanted.

Maureen was there, held captive by a man with a gun.

Nine hours since he got up this morning, but it felt like a ninety. Use the shooting range, drive home, text his threat to Devlin. The phone call from Maureen. Wait in the cell phone lot at Logan.

Then, miraculously, the text sending him to 9 Evergreen Lane.

It had taken him fifteen minutes to fight through the traffic jam in Braintree to get on Route 3 south, a two lane divided highway, separated by a stand of fir trees, lashed by wind gusts.

Pushing ninety mph, he passed a sign that said, Duxbury, and moments later a billboard advertising Plimouth Plantation, a living history museum near Plymouth. Forget history.

Maureen was in mortal danger. Held captive by an armed man.

He'd put the flasher Rafe had gotten him on the roof. He wasn't worried about civilians, he was worried about State cops. He had no time to stop and explain why he was driving like a maniac.

So he could save his daughter from the gunman at 9 Evergreen Lane.

Fortunately, traffic was light. He blew past a car in the right lane, and spotted a State Police cruiser hunkered down in the grass beside the slow lane up ahead. Damn! He passed the cruiser and kept going. Checked the rearview to see if the cruiser pulled onto the highway to chase him. It didn't.

Relieved, he stomped the accelerator.

The last time he'd talked to Rafe, Devlin was in his house in Southie. The bastard still hadn't told him when and where to meet.

So who was the man with the gun?

He took the exit for Plymouth, took the flasher off the roof and drove through dreary streets with olive-green trash bins at the curb. He pulled over for a moment and checked the map he'd downloaded to his cell phone.

Two minutes and he'd be on Evergreen Lane.

He touched the SIG under his windbreaker.

He didn't know who the man with the gun was, but his days were numbered.

———

3:40 PM – South Boston

Devlin stood in his bedroom, admiring the Remington 700P bolt-action rifle. Not a sniper rifle but damn close. Forty-one inches long with a 16-round detachable magazine, the Remington weighed nine pounds. A lethal weapon, loaded with .308 Winchester cartridges.

Perfect for his confrontation with Renzi.

A Leupold Mark IV 10x40 mm telescopic sight was attached to the barrel. A Glock loaded with fifteen 9mm rounds was in his gym bag.

He glanced out the window. Rain hammered the rental car in the driveway, bouncing off the roof of the black Audi and cascading down the windshield. The storm was supposed to let up around five, but he'd better leave soon to avoid the traffic.

He had a stop to make before he went to Deer Island.

He hadn't sent the text to Renzi yet. Why give the bastard time to set a trap for him?

He opened a laminated map to plan his getaway route.

Sunny would meet him at Logan, but they wouldn't be flying anywhere. He traced a pen along the Massachusetts Turnpike. No. Bad idea. All the toll plazas had cameras. He wanted a clean getaway. The cops would be sure to check the tapes after he shot Renzi.

He traced the pen along a different route. It would take a while to get to the Route 128 train station from Deer Island, but so what?

No security lines at the train station.

Ditch the Remington. Pack the Glock in his suitcase with the cash and the gold coins, take a train to New York and tell Sunny to fly down and meet him.

———

3:55 PM – Warwick, Rhode Island

Bridget hoisted her suitcase onto the conveyor belt, took off her jacket and put it in a plastic bin. Removed her winter boots and put them in another bin. The TSA agent at the first checkpoint had studied her driver's license, then her boarding pass, scribbled his initials and waved her through. But this was the real test.

Her heart-rate zoomed into the stratosphere.

Beyond the X-ray machines, standing beside his TSA handler was the biggest German Shepard she'd ever seen, its big pink tongue lolling from its mouth, exposing its gleaming fangs.

What if the dog smelled bits of powdered coke on the fifty-dollar bills? What if the dog was trained to sniff out large amounts of bills?

She watched a young man in scruffy jeans and a soiled white T-shirt pass through the X-ray scanner.

The dog snapped to attention. Raised its muzzle, nostrils flared. Suddenly sat. The cop immediately put out a hand and took the man in the T-shirt aside.

She didn't dare look at them, didn't want to see what would happen.

A female TSA agent beside the conveyor belt said, "Any electronic devices?"

"Just my cell phone. It's in my shoulder bag."

The woman frowned at her. "Take it out and put it in the plastic bin beside the bag."

She took out the burner and set it in the bin beside her shoulder bag.

"Okay," the agent said. "You can go through the X-ray machine now."

Her heart pounded and her hands grew sweaty. The TSA agent on the other side of the machine beckoned her into the X-ray machine. "Hands over your head, don't move."

She stepped inside. Put her hands over her head. Waited as the infernal machine revolved around her.

"Okay," said the TSA agent. "Step out and collect your belongings."

She went down a short ramp and waited by the conveyor belt.

Her suitcase came through, then the plastic bin with her boots and jacket, followed by the bin with her burner and shoulder bag. She put on her jacket, then her boots. Collected her handbag and burner.

Thinking she was home free, she turned.

Five feet away the huge German Shepard stood beside his handler, staring at her.

Her gut twisted and her heart clenched in fear.

Don't look at the dog. Dogs can smell fear.

Pretend you're going on vacation. She towed the suitcase out of the security area and headed for her gate.

CHAPTER 40

WEDNESDAY November 2 – 3:30 PM – Plymouth

Frank slowly drove down Evergreen Lane, ten mph tops, high on adrenaline. He wanted to charge into the house at the far end and rescue Maureen, but that was only the first step. Always have an exit plan.

He had to get Maureen out of here before any cops arrived. If he didn't, they'd be here for hours. He knew the drill. The cops would separate them and ask Maureen what happened, force her to relive the entire ordeal. They would also ask Frank Renzi why he had come here with a loaded weapon.

No way could he let that happen. Get Maureen out of here fast, worry about the cops later.

He studied the houses, looking for lights and parked cars, signs that people were home. People who might dial 911 if they heard gunfire. Because shots would be fired. No doubt about that.

The man with her has a gun.

No one packs a gun unless they plan to use it, and he might not be the only gunman inside 9 Evergreen Lane.

The wind had died down, and the rain had slackened to a drizzle, but the sky was black with clouds. If people were home, they would have lights on. Evergreen Lane was a cul de sac, odd numbers on the right, even numbers on the left.

Lights blazed in the windows of the first two homes on the right, no lights in any of the even numbered houses on the left. Numbers 5 and 7 on the right were also dark, no cars parked outside.

His pulse quickened as he drifted past #9, a one-story cottage with white vinyl siding. In the driveway to the right of the house, a black van stood in front of a detached one-car garage.

Frank assumed it belonged to the man with the gun. He drove around the circle, parked left wheels to the curb and studied the cottage.

Was someone watching?

Facing a gunman inside an unfamiliar house was dangerous. He wished he had a flash-bang to flush him out, but that was one item Rafe hadn't gotten for him. Either way, there would be risk. His Kevlar vest was in the trunk. He'd been too frantic to get here to stop and put it on.

He pulled on a pair of thin cloth gloves, took out his SIG and jacked a round into the chamber.

No lights to the left of the front door, bright lights to the right. He left the car, trotted up an incline and crept along the left side of the cottage. Pine cones littered a muddy path between the house and a line of towering fir trees to his left.

The cottage was built on a slope, no basement windows on this side, but near the back of the house, the cement foundation was higher. He eased around the corner and flattened his back against the foundation. The backyard was a square, enclosed on three sides by thick stands of fir trees. The one-car garage bordered the right side of the yard.

In the foundation six feet to his right was a small basement window, no light showing. Dropping to his knees, he peered inside. He saw nothing, but he smelled heating oil, the furnace room probably. He rose to his feet. No lights showing in the house above him.

He crept along the foundation to a slanted bulkhead. Many homes in New England had walk-out stairs to enable easy access to the basement. Facing skyward, two metal doors opened outward. He tried one door, then the other. Both were locked. He kept going.

Beyond the bulkhead, a basement window had lights showing. He sank to his knees and looked inside. His heart surged with joy.

Maureen sat on a narrow bed, hands in her lap, facing a man dressed in jeans and an over-sized sweatshirt. No weapon in his hand, but Frank could see the bulge of a handgun under the sweatshirt near his hip.

He saw Maureen's lips move. It seemed like they were talking, but he couldn't hear them.

His heart ached for her. Blindfolded, her wrists bound together with plastic restraints. His beloved daughter, imprisoned in this basement room for a week. Unable to see. Alone and defenseless.

White-hot anger exploded inside him. He had never known such rage. He sprinted toward the garage, ducked around the corner of the house, mounted three steps and looked through the window in the door.

A kitchen. No one in sight.

Maybe the man downstairs was his only adversary.

He tried the door. Locked.

He rammed his elbow into the window, reached through the broken glass and released the lock. He opened the door and plunged inside, his SIG up and ready.

"Police! Drop your weapon and show me your hands!"

Silence. Then, "He's got a gun!" Maureen screamed.

Gripping the SIG in both hands, Frank advanced through the kitchen. Ahead on the left was an open door. He crept closer.

"Police! Drop the gun and show me your hands."

"Nooooooo!" Maureen screaming.

Bam-bam-bam. Three rapid shots pierced the left-hand wall of the stairwell.

He ducked back. Heard the sound of thudding feet, but not on the stairs. He stuck his head around the corner and saw a large man lunge through the bulkhead doors, average height, but wide-bodied.

He couldn't see the man's face, but he saw the gun in his hand.

Frank raced downstairs to the open bulkhead and heard footsteps outside. Someone running! He stepped through the door to his right and saw Maureen on the bed. No one else in the room.

"Sit still and be quiet, Mo. I'll be back in a minute."

He charged upstairs, opened the front door and burst outside. He ran toward the driveway, gripping the SIG in both hands, his finger on the trigger. He saw no one and ducked around the corner of the house.

Twenty yards away, the gunman was running toward the black van.

"Police! Stop or I'll shoot. Put the gun down!"

The gunman spun around and fired at him. Bam-bam.

Two wild shots that didn't come close to hitting him.

Frank aimed for the kill-zone and fired twice.

The man staggered forward and stopped, clutching his chest with one hand, a look of surprise on his face. The gun slipped out of his hand, his legs wobbled, and he dropped to his knees.

"Huunnh," the man grunted. He toppled sideways to the ground on his back, his chest heaving, his sweatshirt soaked with blood.

Frank swallowed the coppery residue of fear in his mouth, slowly regained control of his breathing and approached the gunman. He appeared to be in his fifties. If he was related to Devlin, he didn't inherit the handsome gene. A short thick neck, pockmarked cheeks and receding dark hair.

He picked up the man's weapon with his gloved hand and heaved it into the backyard. Time for the reckoning. He stood over the man, who grimaced in pain, nostrils flared, his breath rasping.

"Did you drive the car that forced my father off the road?" Watching the man's eyes. If he lied, he would look away or close his eyes.

The gunman opened his mouth, but one round must have hit his lungs. Blood and spittle dribbled from his lips.

Unable to speak, the man silently shook his head.

"Who drove the car? Sean Whelan?"

The man clamped his lips together and shut his eyes. That was answer enough. Wiseguys never rat on each other.

"I don't know who you are," he said, "but you made a big mistake, kidnapping my daughter."

The man's body twitched violently for three seconds and went still, his head lolling to one side.

Frank whirled, ran to the bulkhead and charged down the stairs.

"Mo! It's me! You're safe now."

Trailing mud and grass, he rushed into the room, grabbed Maureen and held her close. She buried her face in his neck and said, "I knew you'd come for me, Dad. I knew you'd find me."

"I thought about you every minute you were gone, Mo. I love you so much, more than you could ever imagine."

"Love you too, Dad. Thinking about you kept me going. Can you take this damn blindfold off? And the zip-ties?"

He felt her trembling and realized how cold it was in the basement. He took off his windbreaker and tucked it around her shoulders. "Hold on while I do the zip-ties." He took out his Swiss Army knife and cut off the zip-ties, appalled by the raw skin on her wrists and ankles.

She threw her arms around him. "I was so scared when I heard your voice. I mean, I was happy and scared at the same time. Because of the gun. I heard shots outside. What happened?"

"Tell you later, after I get you into my car. Can you walk?"

"Yes, but can you take off the blindfold?"

"Not now." He didn't want her to see the basement room or any other part of the house where she'd been held captive. If she did, she would see it in her dreams forever.

He took her arm, guided her to the stairs and put her right hand on the handrail. "Okay, one step at a time, I'm right behind you."

When she got to the top, he said, "Now we're in the hall. My car's right outside."

"Can you wait till I pee? Where's the bathroom? The first time I get to use a toilet in a week."

"Okay, but be quick. We need to get out of here." He guided her to the bathroom down the hall and said, "I'll wait in the kitchen."

He shut the bathroom door, went in the kitchen and took out his cell phone. His heart jolted. A new text message.

6 PM tonight, Deer Island cemetery.

Six o'clock. Damn, he would have to hurry.

He typed, *I will be there,* and hit Send.

I will be there because I'm the baddest motherfucker on the planet and you are a dead man.

He punched in Gina's number and waited. She answered right away.

"I've got Maureen," he said. "I can't talk long. Just wanted to let you know she's okay."

"Fantastic!" Gina exclaimed. "Did you get the guy?"

"Not yet, but I will." He heard the bathroom door open. "Gotta go, talk to you later."

Wearing his windbreaker, Maureen came in the kitchen, holding a pair of manicure scissors. "I found these in the medicine cabinet. To cut off the blindfold."

"Good, but do it in the car. We need to leave, pronto."

But then he noticed an electric bill on the kitchen counter, addressed to Bridget White. No wonder they couldn't find Bridget Devlin. Her last name was White. Many more questions remained. To be answered later.

He jammed the bill in his pocket and took Maureen out the front door to his car.

Damn! Sirens in the distance. Headed this way.

He settled Maureen into the passenger seat, ran around the hood and jumped in the car.

More sirens, closer now.

He started the car, slammed it into gear and raced down the street. Stopped at the corner, turned left and kept going. Two blocks later he reached the main street and accelerated, thinking of the mud and grass and his footprints inside the cottage.

But Maureen was safe. That was the important thing. He'd deal with what happened here later.

He saw flashing lights ahead, a Plymouth PD cruiser approaching at high speed. The cruiser zoomed past them, one cop driving, another riding shotgun, no doubt headed for Evergreen Lane, because someone had heard shots. When they got to #9, they would find a dead man in the yard with two gunshot wounds in his chest.

And start hunting for the man who'd shot him.

"Cigarman is dead, isn't he," Maureen said.

"Yes." He wasn't going to lie to her.

She heaved a sigh. "That's what I wanted, I guess. But … it's hard to think about it."

"Then don't. These people kidnapped you and mistreated you. But now you're safe, that's the important thing."

"Did my seagull clue help?"

"Yes. Good thinking. I knew you'd be near the ocean."

"He held a gun to my head when I was talking to you."

"Jesus!"

"He got mad when I said seagulls and yelled at me. But he didn't shoot me." Maureen laughed. "I was pissed, too. So I fantasized about punishing him. I imagined shoving a catheter up his penis as hard as I could and asking him how he liked it."

Frank burst out laughing. "Wow. Remind me never to piss you off!"

She slapped his shoulder. "Geez, Dad. Like I'd do that to you. How did you find me?"

"Tell you after we get on the highway." So they could get to Boston fast before the cops put out an APB on this car.

He dug the flashing light out from behind the passenger seat and drove up a ramp onto Route 3 North. Not much traffic, no State police cruisers in sight. He lowered the window, slapped the flasher on the roof and accelerated into the high-speed lane.

After a moment he said, "Bridget sent me a text and told me where you were."

"That's her name, Bridget?"

"Yes. Her brother runs an Irish gang in South Boston." *But after tonight he won't.*

He kept an eye on the rearview, looking for police cars, didn't see any.

Maureen got to work on the blindfold with the manicure scissors, carefully cutting away the fabric, inch by inch.

He looked over and said, "Be careful. Your eyes need to get used to the light gradually."

Mo laughed. "I know, Dad. I'm the doctor, remember?"

"Good to hear you laugh."

"Good to be able to see," Maureen said as she slowly opened her eyes, squinting at first, blinking in the dim light.

"Bridget wasn't very nice to me at first. But I used psychology on her, got her talking, and she started treating me better. She said she had a disabled sister. Is that true?"

"Yes, but that doesn't excuse what she did."

"She said they needed the ransom money to take care of her sister."

Rage blossomed inside him again. "Bullshit! This was never about the money. Her brother had it in for me, personally. That's why he killed your grandfather."

"What??"

Damn! He'd forgotten she didn't know about that. "Sorry, Mo. I never got a chance to tell you. Grampa Sal didn't have an accident. Someone forced him off the road into the tree."

"They killed Grampa Sal? What monsters!"

"Correct, and then they kidnapped you." He reached over and gripped her shoulder. "It's a long story. I'll tell you about it soon, but right now I need to call Rafe and tell him you're safe."

Driving one-handed, he hit the speed dial for Rafe and waited.

"Yo, Frank, where are you?"

"Driving north on Route 3 in Plymouth. Mo's in the car with me."

"Great! That's wonderful news. Is she okay?"

"Yes, but there's a dead man in Plymouth where they were holding her. Can you meet me at Logan and take Maureen to your house so Marcie can get her some clean clothes?"

"Sure, no problem. How'd you find her?"

"Bridget sent me a text. Last name White, not Devlin. Can you put out a BOLO on her, check the nearby airports and train stations? I need to take care of the other thing."

"Devlin told you where and when?"

"Yes. Tonight at Deer Island cemetery, but don't send any cops there. It might scare him off."

Silence on the other end. "Okay, but wait till I get there. What time do you meet him?"

Avoiding the question, he said, "Rafe, I need you to handle the mess at number nine Evergreen Lane in Plymouth. See what evidence they've collected, maybe blow some diversionary smoke up their asses.."

Another silence. Then, "Okay, but be careful, Frank."

"I will," he said, and ended the call

"What's the other thing?" Maureen said.

"Nothing you need to worry about. You're safe. That's what matters."

That, and nailing Brian Devlin. He didn't intend to capture the motherfucker.

He intended to kill him. And he didn't want any witnesses.

CHAPTER 41

WEDNESDAY November 2 – 4:35 PM – Winthrop

"Hello Mr. Devlin," said Sister Mary Margaret. "Nice to see you to-day." Smiling at him as he signed the visitor book.

The lovely Irish lass being flirty, still a virgin probably, feeling safe thanks to the silver cross hanging around her neck.

Employing his customary charm, Devlin gave her a warm smile. "All this rotten weather, I thought I'd come see Kate and cheer her up."

"I'm sure she'll be happy to see you."

He didn't reply. When the cops came here later and questioned Sister Mary Margaret, the devout Catholic girl who always obeyed the Ten Commandments would tell them the truth. Brian Devlin had been here.

But by then, it wouldn't matter. He'd be long gone.

Loathing the stink of overcooked food, he lugged his gym bag down the hall and ducked around a corner. Seeing no one, he stopped at a restroom near the end of the hall, UNOCCUPIED showing above the door knob. He went inside, locked the door and set the gym bag on the sink.

The room smelled of disinfectant, a spray bottle of pine fresh Lysol on a shelf above the sink. Better than boiled eggs and burnt toast.

He removed his windbreaker and long sleeved flannel shirt, dropped them on the floor and took a Kevlar vest out of the gym bag. It was heavy, weighed more than five pounds, but his weapons man said it would protect him from shots fired by most handguns.

Renzi would no doubt be armed when he came to Deer Island, but cops didn't carry shotguns or AK-47s. They used handguns.

He put the vest over his head, settled it over his T-shirt and twisted his torso left and right. The rigid ceramic panels inside the front and back pockets sewn into the fabric restricted his movement a bit, but far better to be protected than not.

Renzi might shoot first and ask questions later.

He pulled the Velcro straps tight, put the flannel shirt on over the vest, buttoned it and studied himself in the mirror. The vest bulked him out some, but that wouldn't be obvious under the windbreaker. He put on the windbreaker and zipped it up.

Now he was ready. Showtime on Deer Island.

But when it was over, he would never come here again. He pictured Kate when he gave her the orange Cal Ripkin shirt, her eyes sparkling with delight, throwing her arms around him, saying, "You're the best brother in the whole world."

He wished he could see her one last time, but she'd want him to stay for dinner. Then he'd have to make up an excuse for why he couldn't, and he didn't want to lie to her. Kate was family.

But what about his other family, the men in the Shamrock Gang who'd been loyal to him all these years? Especially Tank, the man who had introduced him into the gang lifestyle? The respect, owed and given, the recognition and fame, the nightlife and hot babes.

He had always felt closer to Tank than to any other man.

More than once he had trusted Tank with his life.

Over the years Tank had killed many men, but he had never been charged, much less convicted, of the murders, a tribute to Tank's skill when it came to eliminating their adversaries.

Unfortunately, that might change.

Devlin considered what he knew, what he didn't know.

Renzi would meet him on Deer Island at six o'clock. No doubt. After some preliminaries, he'd kill the fucker and split.

But Detective Rafe Hawkins was in cahoots with Renzi.

Would Renzi bring Hawkins with him to the meet? Probably not. From the beginning he'd made it crystal clear..

No cops or your daughter is dead.

Tank knew the swap would happen tonight, but not what time. He would stay at the cottage with the girl, waiting for him to call with instructions about what to do after the swap. Kill the girl or let her go.

The big question: Would Rafe Hawkins be waiting somewhere near Deer Island to make sure Renzi got his daughter? That might screw up his getaway plan: Drive to the train station on Route 95, take a train to New York City and have Sunny fly there to meet him.

Renzi knew where Kate lived in Winthrop. Ergo, Hawkins did, too.

They didn't know Renzi's daughter was in Plymouth, but after he killed Renzi, Hawkins would go to Kate's group home and find out where Bridget lived. One phone call and the Plymouth cops would swarm the cottage and arrest Tank.

Tank would never rat him out, of that he was certain. Tank would remain loyal to the end. But this time he would go to jail.

His throat thickened and tears glazed his eyes. Tank was the closest he'd ever come to having a brother. Or a father.

He clenched his teeth and regained control. Always be in control. But the pain of betraying Tank would torment him as long as he lived.

Peter Sasso would see that Kate was well taken care of, but what about Bridget? She'd saved his ass while he was in prison, smuggling in the pills he used as bargaining chips for protection. Even if the cops never found out she helped Tank kidnap Renzi's daughter, they would charge her as an accomplice.

After the kidnapping, Bridget seemed like a different person. Fearful, always complaining. But he hated to think of her going to jail. Bridget was family, after all. And Peter Sasso was a great defense attorney. Maybe he could bargain with the DA and get Bridget a deal that reduced her jail time.

Devlin checked his watch. 4:30. Enough worrying about others. He had to look out for himself.

Time to set his trap for Renzi. Deer Island was ten minutes away.

He took a pair of metal clippers out of the gym bag, put his right foot on the toilet and cut off the ankle bracelet. He dropped the bracelet in the toilet, flushed and watched the water swirl the the bracelet around and around until it disappeared.

He'd read an article online that claimed water screwed up the tracking system. He wasn't sure if this was so or not.

Eventually the feds would figure out he'd cut it off, but not in time to change the outcome at Deer Island.

His pulse quickened. It was payback time, the day he had waited for during those endless days and nights in prison.

His hatred of Frank Renzi knew no bounds. He couldn't wait to kill him. But he'd tease him first. Renzi was desperate to get his daughter back. Make him beg for his precious daughter, then kill him.

He left the men's room, hurried to an exit door down the hall and ran to his rental car.

———

5:20 PM – Warwick, Rhode Island

Bridget clenched her hands in her lap as the Delta flight bound for Detroit raced down the runway. Moments later she felt the wheels leave the ground and they were airborne. She was free!

When she left the security checkpoint, the sniffer dog and his handler hadn't followed her, but when she got to her gate, the board behind the counter delivered the bad news. The new departure time was 5:15.

An hour to wait. An hour for Renzi to sic the cops on her. An hour to obsess over dire possibilities. What if the cops told the TSA agents at every airport in New England to question every female passenger traveling alone before they let her board a plane? What if they stopped every female who'd paid cash for a one-way ticket?

But they hadn't.

Buffeted by the wind, the plane fought its way through the steel-gray clouds beyond the window. Soon she could begin her new life. If the plane didn't crash.

Oblivious to danger, the young woman in the window seat beside her bobbed her head, her eyes closed, listening to music on her ear buds.

Bridget sank back against her seat. She had redeemed herself. Renzi would get his daughter back and Maureen would be safe. But she would never see Kate again. Never feel Kate's arms around her. Never see her beautiful smile.

Other than her student years at Yale, she had visited Kate two or three times a month. What would Kate think?

A dark shroud of guilt engulfed her, darker than the steel-gray clouds outside the plane window.

She had betrayed both of her siblings. Brian would go back to prison. The Prince of Darkness would never forgive her.

She closed her eyes, picturing Brian as a kid, skinny as a rail because there was never enough to eat. Hearing his voice, the first time he gave her money, saying don't give it to Pa, he'd spend it on booze. Truth be told, she was happy to take the money he gave her and not ask questions about how he got it.

Later, when Brian bought the house in Southie, she was thrilled. Overjoyed to leave the project in East Boston. Even when he roped her into helping him with gang business, Brian had always been generous with his money. The bundles of cash in her suitcase testified to that.

But what about Tank? What would happen to him? He'd probably go to jail for a long time. Brian often called Tank the brother he'd never had. Tank had been like a brother to her, too, especially while Brian was in prison. She tried to remember how old he was. Late fifties?

If they sent him to jail, he might die there. Alone.

Tank had no relatives. No girlfriend. Brian was his best friend, and Brian wouldn't be visiting him.

What would happen when Renzi got to her cottage? Tank had a soft spot in his heart for women, but when it came to cops all bets were off. If Renzi challenged him, Tank wouldn't go quietly. And he had a gun.

What if Renzi killed him?

Was that the price she would pay for wanting redemption? Warn Renzi, Renzi gets his daughter, but Tank dies?

A ping sounded and the seat-belt sign went off.

The woman beside her took out her ear buds, looked at her and said, "What's wrong? Why are you crying?"

Startled, she hastily brushed tears from her cheeks and dredged up her cover story. "Just thinking about my mother. She's in the hospital and she's very ill."

"I'm sorry to hear that," the woman said. "Where is she? In Detroit?"

"No, California. I'm going to see her." Lies, lies and more lies.

Many more lay ahead after Irene Gillan landed in Tacoma.

A lifetime of lies. And a lifetime of guilt, because she had betrayed Kate and Brian and Tank.

The ultimate Bridgette curse.

CHAPTER 42

WEDNESDAY November 2 – 5:40 PM – Deer Island

With the Remington rifle in one hand, his gym bag in the other, Devlin pressed his back against the wall, carefully edging along to avoid gaping holes in the floor. One false step and he would plunge three stories to certain death on the stone floor below him. The field-stone foundation of the abandoned hospital remained intact, but the wood frame structure above it was crumbling with decay, stinking of black mold and rotted wood.

More than 160 years ago, Irish immigrants fleeing the Potato Famine, including his ill-fated ancestor Bridgette, had died here.

He stopped at a tall rectangular opening where a window had once been, no glass, no wooden frame. Beyond a steep hill, he could see the narrow two-lane road that ended at Deer Island. When he was a kid, he and Tank used to play here, chase each other around, jump out from their hiding place and yell, "Bang-bang, you're dead."

Tonight there would be no pretend-killings. Renzi was going to die.

A sixteen-round magazine protruded from the stock of the rifle, and the telescopic sight affixed to the top would ensure accuracy. His weapons man had showed him how to dial in his target and put him in the cross-hairs, but then he'd gone on about adjusting for windage, trajectory and drop. At the time he hadn't paid much attention. Now he wished he had.

The wind was howling like a banshee outside. Inside the dilapidated hospital ancient timbers creaked. Ominous creepy sounds, like the sound track of a horror movie.

One night, alone in his jail cell, he'd read a horror novel that scared the shit out of him. The noises here were worse, like some ghoulish corpse resurrected from hell was after him.

The burden of death.

He had ordered many men killed, but others had done the deed. The only man he'd ever killed was Kate's husband, strangling him with his bare hands. He could still picture the bastard: his eyes bugged out, his tongue protruding from his mouth.

Soon Renzi would be dead, too.

He peered through the sniper scope, watching the road, eagerly awaiting Renzi's arrival.

A minute passed. Then another. Devlin shifted his feet. Where the hell was Renzi?

And suddenly there he was, getting out of a dark sedan, fighting the wind, pulling the hood of a windbreaker over his head. Overjoyed to see his hated enemy, Devlin laughed out loud. A windbreaker wouldn't save Renzi from a .308 slug from the Remington. Or a 9mm slug from his Glock, up close and personal. How sweet that would be.

Standing over Renzi's body, savoring his victory.

Damn! Renzi had spotted the black Audi rental car parked on the other side of the street, the nose pointed west for a fast getaway.

The stash for his escape was in the trunk.

If Renzi tried to open it, he'd shoot the fucker.

He centered Renzi's head in the cross-hairs and waited.

———

Frank stood beside his rental car, the SIG in his right hand pressed against his thigh. Rain slashed his face, but the cool air was a relief. His body was overheated by all the layers, a windbreaker, a sweatshirt over the Kevlar vest, the T-shirt beneath it soaked with sweat.

It was a helluva night for a confrontation, the storm raging on Deer Island. He could smell the ocean beyond the two-foot high steel barrier five yards away that lined the sidewalk. Storm-driven waves broke over the rocks like bombs, hurling geysers of seawater into the air. Thunder rumbled off to the west. Seconds later, lightning flashed.

Dull gray clumps of fog scudded westward over the water. Beyond them, an angry sea was raging, laced with foam. Not a seagull in sight. Gulls knew when to take cover from a storm.

Across the street, a man in a yellow slicker was walking his dog, a muscular tan boxer straining against the leash. Rain lashed the man's slicker, harsh pinging sounds. The man wore no hat and strands of lank hair were plastered against his forehead. Frank watched him pass a black Audi sedan, its nose pointed away from Deer Island, the only car other than his parked on the street.

The nearest house was two blocks away. Was it Devlin's car?

He trotted across the street to check it out. The Audi sported a Virginia license plate, looked like a rental. He circled the car and peered into one window. Nothing of interest inside.

His neck prickled, the feeling he got when someone as watching him. Was it Devlin?

He returned to the other sidewalk, intent on his goal. Find Devlin.

Thunder crackled again, louder now. Driven by the stiff wind, he walked along the narrow asphalt path that led to the cemetery, his breath fogging in the cold air. Ten yards in, he spotted a fresh set of shoe prints in the muddy grass.

He had come here early to get the lay of the land. Maybe Devlin had come here even earlier. To set a trap for him.

A minute later he rounded a sharp curve and saw the cemetery, fifty yards ahead. Was Devlin there, lying in wait for him?

A rifle shot sounded, loud and clear. No mistaking that sound. He'd heard it in his nightmares.

He dove to the ground, rolled, and scrambled to his feet, splashing through puddles as he zig-zagged across a grassy area and ducked behind a rectangular granite monument that faced the cemetery.

Breathing hard, adrenaline pumping, he hunkered down behind the granite slab, ten feet long and four feet high. He was trapped, pinned down by a man with a sniper rifle, a long-range weapon. And all he had was his SIG, a handgun with limited range. Advantage, Devlin.

For all he knew, Devlin came here often. Deer Island was only six miles from Kate's group home in Winthrop. The reason he'd chosen it, no doubt.

Frank waited, the wind howling, pelted by rain, his hand on the SIG. The light was fading rapidly. Soon it would be dark. He risked a quick peek around the corner of the granite.

Another shot, the sound echoing off a tall building, the abandoned Deer Island Hospital, he realized. Devlin was on one of the upper floors or the roof. Shooting at him with a rifle.

From here, he could see the eight-foot chain-link fence that secured the abandoned hospital. But fifty yards away opposite the graveyard, the links had been cut, the lower part of the fence bent inward enough to push a good-sized wheelbarrow inside. Stealing metal and copper wiring from deserted buildings could be lucrative for enterprising thieves.

But that wasn't why Devlin was here.

Aware of a fierce burning sensation, he gingerly pulled his left arm out of the windbreaker, then his sweatshirt. Just below the sleeve of his T-shirt, his arm was bleeding. The bullet had grazed his arm, digging a shallow four inch long groove through the skin and the triceps, the large muscle on the back of his upper arm.

Not life-threatening, but he wouldn't be lifting weights any time soon, and the underside of his arm was bleeding badly.

He took out his Swiss Army knife. With gritted teeth, he held the sweatshirt with one hand, used the other to rip strips of fabric from the bottom edge of the shirt. Keeping his left elbow and shoulder aligned, he wrapped a strip of fabric around his arm, then another, binding the wound firmly, but not too tight. That should staunch the bleeding.

The rain had slackened to a misty drizzle that dampened his face, but rolling thunder sounded in the distance. He gingerly inserted his arm into the sleeve of the sweatshirt, then the windbreaker and leaned back against the granite monument.

As a cop, he had faced plenty of life-or-death situations. In a few instances, if things had gone differently, he would have been dead or seriously disabled. The most frightening moments of his life.

He thought about Maureen, and Kelly and Gina. Would he ever see them again? He banished the thought.

Focus on the mission. Get Devlin.

Ignoring the pain in his arm, he shrugged his shoulders to settle the Kevlar vest and got in a prone firing position on the soggy grass facing the graveyard. Beach grass and wild salt marsh surrounded it on three sides, undulating in the fierce wind off the ocean.

Alert for any movement, he peered through the murky darkness, listening for running footsteps. He saw nothing, heard nothing. He got on his knees and looked over the top of the monument.

Suddenly a figure emerged from the shadowy gray mist opposite the graveyard. Devlin, a rifle slung over one shoulder, a gym bag over the other. Moving fast, he ducked through the hole in the chain-link fence and ran into the graveyard.

Frank knew he didn't have a snowball's chance in hell of hitting him from this distance. But Devlin was no longer in his sniper's nest in the abandoned hospital. Now they were both at ground level.

Devlin was a dead man walking.

————

Breathing hard, Devlin raced into the cemetery, angry and disgusted.

From his sniper perch in the hospital, he had aimed for Renzi's chest, certain the bastard would be wearing a Kevlar vest. He didn't want to kill him, not yet anyway. He wanted to knock him on his ass and scare him.

But the wind had fucked up the shot. He'd seen Renzi drop to the ground, then get up and run behind the large granite monument that paid tribute to his Irish ancestors. No telling if he'd hit the bastard.

No telling what Renzi had done while he was carefully making his way out of the abandoned hospital, either.

Still, he felt good. He was on the hunt, on the move, on top of things.

Panting and out of breath, he ducked behind Bridgette's magnificent headstone, the fanciest in the graveyard, the one he'd bought, hoping to ward off the Bridgette Curse.

For all the good that had done him.

The Remington was designed for sniping from an elevated position, but the scope didn't help much in this weather. At ground level, the Glock 9mm pistol in his gym bag would be better for close combat, easy to handle, fifteen rounds in the magazine, one in the chamber.

Where the hell was the fucker? Behind the granite monument?

He got on one knee and peered around the side of Bridgette's marble headstone. Twilight was fading, but there was still enough light to see Renzi if he moved. No way could he hide in the cemetery. The other grave markers were cheap wooden crosses, no cover there.

Three foot high beach grass surrounded the cemetery on three sides, whipped back and forth by gale winds off the ocean. He studied the grass. Renzi's dark windbreaker would be easy to spot in the greenish brown grass. But he saw nothing. No movement, no Renzi.

The bastard had to be hunkered down behind the granite monument.

It was too far away to hit him with the Glock, but there were still fourteen rounds in the Remington. He grasped the rifle in both hands, rose to his feet and fired a long burst at the monument.

Fifty yards away, but he knew he'd hit it, heard *thunk-thunk* when the slugs hit the granite.

Make Renzi think he could see him.

Flush him out and lure him closer.

Tease him about his precious daughter, then kill him.

CHAPTER 43

WEDNESDAY November 2 – 6:05 PM – Deer Island

Flat on his belly in the beach grass near the graveyard, Frank saw muzzle flashes. Flashes that allowed him to see Devlin, standing beside a large gravestone as he fired.

But Devlin was twenty yards away and the light was fading fast. He needed to get closer.

Propelling himself with his elbows, hindered by the wound in his arm, he drew closer. Hugging the ground, he inched through the rain-soaked grass, the dampness chilling him to the bone. The pain in his arm was worse, but every fiber of his being was now focused on Devlin

He paused for breath at the edge of the cemetery, ten yards from the gravestone now, and gathered himself. The moment he'd been waiting for had finally arrived, the moment he had imagined countless times.

Confront the man who had ordered his father's assassination and Maureen's kidnapping.

"Come out and face me, Devlin," he shouted. "You're a coward, hiding behind a gravestone."

Silence. A minute passed. No sign of Devlin.

"You're the coward, Renzi. You browbeat my sister to put me in jail, interrogated her like a pit bull. She never got over it."

"Bullshit! Kate's fine. I stopped by to see her the other day."

"You want your daughter? Show me the money."

"It's in my car. Stop hiding and we'll go get it. If you dare." Hoping to goad the narcissistic bastard into showing himself.

Another silence, longer this time. Ten seconds. Fifteen. Twenty …

Devlin sprang up beside a gravestone and started shooting, with a handgun this time. Muzzle flashes. *Pop-pop-pop.*

Gripping the SIG in both hands, Frank aimed for his knee, squeezed off two quick shots and flattened himself against the ground.

A yelp of pain, then silence.

Frank parted the grass with his left hand, kept the finger of his right hand on the trigger.

No sign of Devlin.

Another wild shot made him duck, Devlin firing blind from behind the gravestone.

He knew he'd hit the bastard. The question was, how badly was he wounded?

"Give it up, Devlin. I know Bridget owns the cottage in Plymouth. Your sister betrayed you. She sent me a text and told me Maureen was in the basement at Nine Evergreen Lane. Now Maureen's in Dorchester. Throw your weapons on the ground where I can see them."

"Fuck you, Renzi!"

Frank fired at the gravestone, sending chips flying off one edge.

———

Fragments of marble stung his cheek. Damn Renzi to hell!

Curled in a ball on the ground, Devlin clutched his left thigh with both hands, bleeding from cuts on his face, agony in his thigh. He examined his blood-soaked jeans. There was a hole above the knee where the bullet hit him, a big ragged tear in the back where the slug had exited. Damn it to hell! He was bleeding like a sonofabitch.

He put the Glock on the ground beside him. Gritting his teeth, he stuck two fingers in the hole in the front of his jeans and ripped the fabric as hard as he could until his left thigh was fully exposed. The entry wound was ugly, a small purple hole oozing blood. The exit wound was worse, much bigger and steadily leaking blood.

He took off his windbreaker, then his long-sleeved flannel shirt. He folded the shirt and wrapped it around his thigh. Maybe that would stop the bleeding. But it wouldn't stop the pain.

Or the pain of Renzi's words. *Your sister betrayed you.*

He didn't believe it. Bridget would never betray him. They were family, joined by blood.

Enraged, he screamed, "You're lying, Renzi."

But doubt crept into his mind.

His plan had gone terribly wrong. When a plan failed, it usually came down to one of two things. The other gang leader got wind of it or someone in his own gang talked.

Tank would never betray him, of that he was certain. But Tank wouldn't give up Renzi's daughter without a fight.

If the girl was in Dorchester, Tank was probably dead.

His closest ally and best friend. The man he loved like a brother.

A torrent of grief overwhelmed him. Tears filled his eyes and his throat closed up.

But reason prevailed, leading him to an inescapable conclusion.

Bridget had betrayed him.

He studied the blood-soaked flannel shirt. The pain was worse now, a blazing inferno creeping up his thigh, his hands wet with blood.

A spasm of fear seized him. Was this how it would end? Dying near the hospital where his ill-fated ancestor had died?

Not if he could help it. Ditch the rifle, keep the Glock.

Everything else he needed was in the Audi. If he could get to it.

Live or die? One thing was certain.

If he was going to die, he would take Renzi with him.

———

Hidden in the beach grass, Frank waited, knowing Devlin had to be in serious pain. Ten seconds passed, the wind howling, the waves crashing against the rocks.

Fifteen seconds. Twenty.

Then, a sudden motion. Devlin hauled himself upright and stood beside the gravestone. He fired a rapid series of shots, his face contorted in pain, lit up in the darkness by the muzzle flashes.

Another burst of shots, longer this time, long enough for Frank to see Devlin's wounded leg, the pant-leg ripped off, his bare thigh wrapped in a bloody rag.

Frank extended the SIG and fired at Devlin's thigh.

Like a slow-motion video, Devlin spun around, his handgun flying through the air, arching over the headstone, his left arm extended toward the ground to brace his fall, his right arm flung skyward. His legs buckled and he fell sideways, a crimson spray of blood spurting from his thigh like water bursting from a bathtub faucet, his right arm slicing through the pinkish vapor.

The sky lit up with a brilliant flash of lightning, followed by deep rolling thunder. A fitting punctuation to Devlin's downfall.

Frank got on his knees and studied the road a hundred yards away to see if anyone had witnessed what had happened.

Seeing no one, he rose to his feet and approached his enemy, the man he loathed and despised.

An evil man with evil intentions.

Devlin lay on his back in a pool of blood, his legs splayed, blood pulsing from his thigh, likely a severed femoral artery.

But his eyes were open, and full of hate.

"You're a no-good sonofabitch, Renzi." A hoarse whisper.

Frank studied him dispassionately. "Why did you murder my father?"

"To make you suffer the way I suffered, spending fifteen years in a shitty jail cell."

"My father never did anything to hurt you."

"Oh but he did." Devlin paused, nostrils flared, seeking air, his lungs no longer working properly. "He fathered Homicide Detective Franklin Sullivan Renzi."

Fury rose inside him like an untamed beast. "My father was an honorable man doing good in the world. You're a worthless piece-of-shit gangster. Soon you'll be dead. Better say your prayers."

Devlin looked away. After a moment he began singing, so faintly Frank could barely make out the tune.

Oh Danny Boy ... the pipes, the pipes are calling ...

The tune interrupted by Devlin's raspy breathing.

Gazing skyward, he managed to squeeze out a few more words.

If I am dead, as dead I well may be, You'll come and find the place where I am lying ...

His body went limp, his eyes staring at nothing, covered with the milky film of death.

"Good riddance to you," Frank said. And walked away.

———

Ten minutes later he was in an ambulance, wrapped in a blanket but still shivering, his body cold inside and out. Rafe was sitting beside him while an EMT bandaged his arm. Two minutes after he'd called Rafe and told him Devlin was dead, Rafe had arrived, trailed by two BPD squad cars. More were on the way. As it turned out, Rafe had been sitting in his unmarked SUV a mile away, waiting for the call.

"You're okay for right now," the EMT said, "but we'll take you to a hospital, have the doc check it."

Frank motioned Rafe toward the ambulance door. "Rafe will take me. We're going to Dorchester anyway." Not to a hospital, to see Maureen and make sure she was okay.

"Suit yourself," the EMT said, watching Rafe help him out of the ambulance.

They walked past Frank's rental car, climbed into Rafe's SUV and headed out. "Talk to me," Frank said. "How's Maureen?"

"Not bad, considering. When we got to the house, she wanted to take a shower and wash her hair. Afterwards Marcie poured her a shot of cognac and got her talking." Rafe looked over. "Maureen went through some serious shit, told Marcie some horror stories."

"Yeah. The guy in Plymouth held a gun to her head."

"And the woman threatened to shoot her."

Surprised, he said, "Bridget?"

"No. I figure it was Sunny, but I didn't get the full rundown. By then I was hightailing it down to Plymouth, called Marcie on my cell to see how Maureen was doing."

"How'd it go in Plymouth?" Frank leaned back against the headrest. He didn't want to think about it.

"I gave them the mini-version. Someone kidnapped Maureen and sent you a ransom demand. Nothing about your father. I said you left in a hurry to get Maureen checked out at a hospital."

"Good. And they said?"

"They want to talk to you ASAP."

"Not tonight. I'm taking Maureen home to Swampscott so she can get comfortable and relax. If she feels like talking, fine. If she doesn't, that's okay, too."

Rafe nodded. "Figured you'd say that. I told the the State police detectives you'd talk to them tomorrow. At some point, they'll want a statement from Maureen."

"I'll go down there tomorrow and explain what happened. Tell them Maureen's under observation in the hospital or something."

"Sounds perfectly reasonable to me." Rafe held out his cell phone. "Your daughter's worried about you. Call her and tell her you're okay."

———

7:35 PM – Logan Airport, East Boston.

Sunny stood outside the terminal, smoking a cigarette, shivering in the chill damp air. She'd been waiting here for an hour, depressed by the dismal weather and a growing realization.

Dev wasn't coming to meet her.

She didn't know what happened at Deer Island, didn't know if he was alive or dead. Tears flooded her eyes and she choked back a sob. They had shared so many good times together, lots of laughs, a few tears when he got sent to prison, and a fabulous reunion after he got out.

Dev was one of a kind. A tough gangster, a lover with a gentle touch, and a sharp mind when it came to business.

Years ago, he'd bought the Seaview Hotel for her and had his lawyer, Peter Sasso, set it up as a trust and manage it. The hotel was a goldmine. She skimmed twenty percent off the top each month and sent the cash to Peter, who deposited the money into an offshore account for Dev.

What would become of the money, she wondered. Dev had never mentioned a will, and she'd never asked if he had one. She assumed his estate would go to his sisters: Kate and Bridget. Kate deserved it.

Bridget didn't. All she did was cause trouble.

She took a deep drag on her cigarette, considering what to do. Dev also had good instincts when it came to survival. He'd told her to get on a plane and leave if he wasn't here by seven-thirty. She would miss him, but dead or alive, Dev wasn't going to help her.

She had to look out for herself. Get on a plane and leave Boston in case Detective Rafe Hawkins decided to cause problems.

Maybe she'd fly to L.A. and set up a new brothel, like the Hollywood Madam. Plenty of horny rich men looking to get laid out there. Sasso would send her enough money to get started.

She took a final drag on the cigarette, tossed the butt on the ground and towed her suitcase into the Departure terminal. No line at the Jet Blue ticket counter. That looked promising.

She headed for the counter and stopped short. Two Massachusetts State Troopers were marching toward her, grim-faced.

The air left her lungs in a whoosh.

"Sunny Jensen," said the taller State Trooper, "we have a warrant for your arrest. You have been charged with reckless endangerment, forced imprisonment for the purpose of obtaining a ransom, and accessory to kidnapping. Anything you say can and will be used against you."

CHAPTER 44

From his table in the Crab Shack lounge, Frank watched distant lights twinkling in the darkness, airplanes taking off from Logan Airport. Tomorrow he would fly back to New Orleans. Vobitch had told him to take as much time as he needed, but he wanted to get back to work.

His usual tactic when he wanted to avoid thinking about thorny issues. Keep busy.

Over dinner, he'd given Gina the sanitized version of what had happened on Wednesday: the shootout in Plymouth to rescue Maureen, the confrontation with Devlin and the inevitable fallout that followed.

On Thursday, he had spoken to the State Police detectives in Plymouth. Fortunately, they'd found enough evidence inside Bridget White's cottage to prove that she and Thomas "Tank" Nolan had held Maureen prisoner in the basement for several days. That, and the fact that Nolan's gun had been fired multiple times convinced the Plymouth County DA to rule his death a justifiable homicide.

No charges would be filed against Frank Renzi.

Ninety percent of what happened at the cottage had yet to be told. Citing the sensational aspect of the case, the DA had imposed a media blackout and declined to identify the hostage. But that might not last.

Some enterprising reporter might persuade one of the Plymouth cops to talk. Bridget was well known in Plymouth. Already there were lurid rumors that the college professor and her gangster boyfriend had imprisoned a young woman in the basement.

Frank gingerly flexed his left arm, a constant reminder of what had transpired on Deer Island. Visible proof that Devlin had shot him. Multiple shots had been fired from Devlin's Glock 9mm pistol and Remington rifle, which seemed to indicate a clear case of justifiable homicide. Vobitch would call it a righteous shoot. But was it?

He stared into the darkness, ruminating over his actions. As a police officer, he had shot other criminals. Most had survived, a few had not.

This much he knew for sure. When you took a person's life, even a man as evil as Devlin, you paid a price.

Years might pass and he would still see the bright red blood spurt from the severed artery in Devlin's leg, still see the hate in his eyes, still see light fade from those eyes when he died.

Enraged by Devlin's brutal acts—ordering his father's murder and Maureen's kidnapping—he had gone to Deer Island knowing full well he intended to kill the man.

Not that he would mention this at the hearing two weeks from now at Boston Police Headquarters. Or to the Boston Police Union rep Rafe had gotten him, an experienced cop to advise Frank what to say at the hearing. And what not to say.

He looked up as Gina returned from the restroom and slipped onto her chair. "What's up, Franco? Thinking deep thoughts?"

He smiled at her. "Yeah. Deeper than Einstein."

No sense telling her about the ugly sounds and violent images that jolted him awake at night. Tank's bloody forehead and vacant eyes. The shots from Devlin's sniper rifle, echoing off the abandoned hospital. The blood gushing from Devlin's thigh.

Perhaps worst of all, the faint strains of music replaying in his mind. *Oh Danny Boy ... the pipes, the pipes are calling ...* Devlin's last gasp before the milky film of death covered his eyes.

Gina stirred her Irish coffee and took a sip. "How's Maureen doing?"

"The hospital gave her six weeks leave. She's staying at the house in Swampscott for now. Last night she asked me to drive her to Milton to see her mother. Evelyn's older now but no wiser when it comes to dealing with Maureen, kept asking if they molested her.. Evelyn's code for rape. Mo said they didn't, but they were very bad people."

"She's right," Gina said, gazing at him, her dark eyes full of concern. "After you called and said you had Maureen and you were going after Devlin, I was freaking out. How's your arm?"

"A little stiff but it's healing okay. Mo said the wound could get infected and made me go to the emergency room. They gave me a prescription for antibiotics." He sipped his ice water and pulled a face. "No booze for ten days."

"A small price to pay. He could have killed you!"

She didn't know the half of it. He'd left out the part about Devlin sniping at him from the abandoned hospital with a high-powered rifle.

278

"But he didn't, and Sunny's in jail. Rafe thinks they planned to run away together after they got the ransom money. Not that there was ever any money. Attorney Peter Sasso, Devlin's mob lawyer, is trying to get her out on bail."

"Will they charge her with Sean Whelan's murder?"

"Too soon to tell. Boston PD got a warrant for her cell phone and found enough texts and emails to charge her as an accessory to Mo's kidnapping. Rafe wants them to exhume Whelan's body and run some tests. Maybe they'll find enough evidence to charge her with murder."

"Still no sign of Bridget?"

"No. The State Police put out an APB to every airport in New England and got nothing. They tracked the text she sent me to a train station in Providence. They never found the phone, but they found her safe deposit box in Plymouth. The only thing in it was a bag of gold coins. A logbook entry indicates she was there Wednesday morning, probably took whatever else was in there and split."

"I'm glad she had a change of heart," Gina said, "but that doesn't excuse her part in the kidnapping. Will they keep looking for her?"

"Probably. After she left Yale she legally changed her name to Bridget White. No evidence she ever had a husband. For all we know, she might have a fake ID under a different name."

Gina set aside her Irish coffee. "Have you talked to Kelly?"

The elephant in the room, the one that he didn't want to talk about. But there was no avoiding it.

"I called her Wednesday night after I got out of the emergency room and told her everything."

Gina raised an eyebrow. "Everything?"

He smiled faintly. "Well, everything about rescuing Maureen and settling the score with Devlin. She said I was stupid to go after him by myself."

Gina laughed. "Better her than me." But then her eyes grew serious. "She loves you, Frank. Don't tell her about us."

He sipped some ice water, expressionless. "I haven't decided about that yet."

"It's your call, Franco, but why screw up a good thing? Kelly loves you and you love her. Same with me. My husband loves me and I love him. You and I got together because horrific things happened to members of your family. Things that will never happen again."

She gazed into his eyes. "But we'll always be best friends, won't we?"

His throat thickened. He pulled her close and hugged her. "Best friends forever. You can count on it."

———

5:59 PM – Tacoma, Washington

Bridget blew her nose, wadded up the tissue and dropped it in the wastebasket beside the bed. She poured more Glenfiddich over the ice in a plastic cup, took a hefty swallow and leaned back against the pillows propped against the headboard.

Located on the outskirts of Tacoma, the cheap motel was a far cry from the posh hotels where she stayed on vacation, but it had an ice machine and a good-sized color TV with cable news.

The cause of her migraine headache, copious tears and sour stomach.

CNN had run the story at five o'clock: **The Wiseguy Who Wasn't.**

Tank was dead. Her eyes welled with more tears. She'd loved Tank like a brother. He'd always been good to her, treating her with kindness and respect. If Tank hadn't gotten her the fake Irene Gillan documents, she wouldn't be here, she'd be in jail.

According to the CNN report, Tank had died in a gunfight. With Frank Renzi, she assumed.

Her biggest worry: Did Tank tell Renzi about Irene Gillan?

A Fox News banner flashed on the screen. The local Tacoma stations weren't following the story, but CNN and Fox News were, reporters gazing into the camera with wild-eyed fervor but dispensing very little information. She used the clicker to unmute the sound.

The anchorman announced the upcoming stories. Their report on a Massachusetts gangster shootout would follow a story about a Canadian dentist, who'd bought John Lennon's tooth.

Jesus! Did people actually care about those things?

She took the plastic cup in the bathroom and dumped it down the sink. Before she checked into the motel, she'd had the good sense to stop at a liquor store and buy a big bottle of Scotch.

She returned to the bedroom. The John Lennon tooth story was still running. She scooped ice into the plastic cup, added Glenfiddich, took a healthy swallow and sank back against the pillows.

Brian was dead. She still couldn't believe it.

On Wednesday, Brian had met Renzi at the Deer Island cemetery, no doubt intending to kill him. Instead, Brian had died there.

The Gangster Shootout headline flashed on the screen. Her stomach clenched. At five o'clock CNN hadn't mentioned the wiseguy's sister, Bridget. Would Fox News?

The anchorman said they had team coverage on the developing story and cut to their reporter in Plymouth.

Her heart jolted. Damn it to hell! A reporter was standing outside her cottage to give her report. The gist of the story: Brian Devlin, a mob kingpin recently paroled from prison, was the mastermind behind a sleazy kidnapping. His associate, Thomas "Tank" Nolan, was shot and killed when police rescued the hostage. The reporter wrapped up by saying, "Massachusetts State Police have imposed a news blackout on the incident and have not released the name of the hostage."

Bridget gulped some scotch. Renzi must have convinced them to keep it quiet. But people in Plymouth knew the cottage was hers. Apparently no one had interviewed her employers yet, but soon they would. Then they'd be talking about Associate Professor Bridget White. Married to the mob, thanks to her brother.

Jesus, Mary and Joseph! They would put her photograph on TV.

Her heart pounded and her palms dampened with sweat. The cops would find nothing incriminating in her safe deposit box, but they would keep looking for her. And her photograph would be out there.

Right from the get-go, she'd known Brian was asking for trouble, messing with a cop and his family. But when Brian made up his mind, there was no arguing with him.

The anchorman introduced the next report and the picture on the screen switched to Deer Island. An establishing shot showed the shore line, then the cemetery, roped off with yellow crime scene tape. The Fox News reporter stood in front of a granite monument, saying it commemorated the Irish immigrants who had landed at Deer Island after fleeing the Potato Famine and died there. "Some have speculated that Brian Devlin's ancestors were among them."

Bridget gasped and stared at the screen. Goosebumps rose on her arms and a shudder rippled through her. The Bridgette Curse.

But no one would ever hear about their long-dead ancestor.

Kate couldn't tell them, and everyone else was dead. Except for her.

Gesturing at the cemetery where Bridgette was buried, the reporter said, "During a fierce rainstorm, mobster Brian Devlin was shot dead in a gun battle with an as yet unnamed police officer. Recently paroled from a prison where he was serving time for murder, Devlin was well known to Boston police. They describe him as the longtime boss of the Shamrocks, an Irish gang based in South Boston."

The anchorman cut to a taped segment, another Fox News reporter interviewing residents in Southie. Many of them praised Brian Devlin, saying he had done a lot for the community.

Bridget sipped some Glenfiddich. Did a lot for the community? Maybe. But mostly Brian looked out for himself, amassing large sums of money from his multitude of gang activities.

But who was she to talk? For most of her life, she had enjoyed the benefits of that money, some of which was inside her suitcase.

To her relief, the Fox News anchor introduced another story.

No mention of Bridget Devlin or Kate Devlin. Or Sunny Jensen, the bitch from hell.

Where was Sunny, she wondered?

No doubt about where Brian was. Laid out in a coffin at a South Boston funeral home.

Poor Kate. At the funeral Kate would be all alone.

Wondering where her sister was.

The Bridgette Curse exacting its final revenge on the Devlin family.

CHAPTER 45

TWO MONTHS LATER

THURSDAY January 5, 2012 – Boston – TD Garden

Flashing lights on the JumboTron high above the court urged fans to GET LOUD. Along with the rest of the sellout crowd Frank screamed GO CELTICS. The Celts were down by one at the end of the half, but the Garden was alive with energy, the fans as raucous as ever.

He stood up to let people in his row pass him, the usual mass exodus at halftime. Anticipating this, he'd bought two cups of beer before he claimed his seats, one for himself and one for his father. In absentia.

A deep longing rose inside him. How he wished his father could be with him. Their seats were five rows behind the Celtics bench.

The tickets had cost a small fortune, but he didn't mind. A small price to pay to fulfill the vow he'd made at his father's funeral in the Swampscott church. Almost twelve weeks ago, but it seemed like yesterday, his sorrow still palpable.

Time does not banish grief so quickly.

On the other hand, so much had happened since, it felt like an eternity ago. Finding out his father's car accident was an assassination, Maureen's kidnapping and his frantic attempts to find her.

After spending a week in South Carolina with her high school chum, Maureen had come to New Orleans and stayed at his condo for a week. He took three days off and they had a great time.

When he brought up the Jeremy issue, Mo said, "I am soooo over Jeremy. When I stayed with Caitlin at her family's beach house, I met an interesting guy." Flashing her mischievous grin, she said, "Good-looking and smart. He's an investigator for a big insurance company and we hit it off right away. He works out of the office in Scranton, Pennsylvania. Only 200 miles from Baltimore by car, or two hours on a plane."

So he didn't have to deliver the speech he'd prepared and tell her it was better to find out Jeremy wasn't the right guy before she married him. Now she was back to work at Mercy Medical Center in Baltimore, but he still worried about her. She'd put on a brave face, but she had suffered a serious trauma. He had urged her to get counseling, talk it out with someone. She said she'd think about it.

Even his ex-wife seemed content these days. Evelyn had bonded with her cousin in Hartford and asked her to come visit her in Milton.

A roar from the crowd drew his attention to the half-time event on the gleaming parquet floor. A three-point shootout for kids from a local middle school. A little girl had just made a three pointer to win the contest, throwing her arms up in victory, grinning from ear to ear. Frank joined the applause and drank some beer.

Turned out he didn't have to deliver his speech to Kelly, either. When he flew back to New Orleans after the shootout, Kelly was waiting when he came up the ramp to the terminal, all smiles, looking as sexy and gorgeous as ever.

She gave him in a hug and said, "You're alive! I was so worried about you." She drove him to her house and they sat in the kitchen like they always did, and he told her what had happened in Plymouth and at Deer Island. Then they went in her bedroom and made love and it was just as wonderful as it always was.

Maybe Gina was right. *"Don't tell her. Why spoil a good thing?"* The horrible events in Boston would never happen again. That was a one-time deal, and so was making love to Gina. Maybe he'd tell Kelly about it someday and maybe he wouldn't. But he was sure about one thing.

No matter what anyone said, he knew it was possible to love two women at the same time. If Gina needed something, he would always be there for her. And if Kelly needed him, he'd be there for her, too. That's what love was about.

A loud buzzer sounded. The Celtics and New Jersey Nets players were finishing their warmups, Paul Pierce taking a shot from one corner, Kevin Garnett going for a trey on the other side of the court. In two minutes the third quarter would begin.

Frank rose to his feet to let several Celtics fans pass, sat down and chugged some beer. Two months after the horror show in Massachusetts, vivid memories remained etched in his mind: names and faces, brutal events and treacherous meetings.

Like the Boston PD investigation into the death of Brian Devlin. After a tense three hour interview and many questions, they concluded Frank had acted in self defense, and the Suffolk County DA declined to file charges against him.

When the DA asked if he wanted them to continue their hunt for Bridget, Frank said he didn't. If they found her, there would be a trial and Maureen would have to testify. He didn't want that. He wanted her to forget about the kidnapping and everyone involved in it.

But that didn't mean he had forgotten about Bridget. Somehow, she had gotten away. Not knowing her whereabouts would nag him forever.

Despite their best efforts, State Police detectives had found nothing to indicate where she might be: no laptop, no phone messages, no papers. After the sordid details of what transpired at Bridget's cottage hit the national news, officials at Anna Maria College were eager to forget they had ever hired Associate Professor Bridget White. Her name no longer appeared on their website or promotional materials.

The third quarter began and Frank focused on the game, cheering like all the other Celtics fans during a thrilling 18-to-3 run led by Paul Pierce. When a referee called a questionable foul on Pierce, the crowd booed loudly. Frank smiled, imagining Judge Salvatore Renzi's reaction if he were here, hurling a choice epithet at the referee probably.

Inspired by the bad call, the Celtics widened their lead. At the end of the third quarter, Frank set his empty beer cup aside and picked up the full one in front of his father's seat, contemplating the recent events in Boston. A week before Christmas, a raging fire had broken out in the wee hours of the morning at the Leprechaun Pub. Two hours later the Pub had burned to the ground.

Arson squad investigators determined that someone had broken a window and tossed Molotov cocktails inside. The Pub was insured, but the insurance company refused to pay, saying it was a clear case of arson. Attorney Peter Sasso was fighting tooth and nail to get the money, saying someone had a grudge against Brian Devlin. He'd even been forced to pay a man to live in Devlin's former home behind the Pub, fearing someone would torch the house.

Sunny Jensen was in jail, awaiting her murder trial. At Rafe's request, Boston PD got a warrant to exhume Sean Whelan's body. Tests on his hair revealed he had been drugged, first with GHB, then with a paralytic. Rafe had called last week to tell him the results. "Not a fun way to go, Frank. Imagine it, wide awake but paralyzed, Sunny Jensen standing over you? She's a hard woman, got a face like a brick wall."

Gina had sent him a copy of an article she'd written for the *Boston Herald*, saying it won her a $500 bonus; the first edition sold out and they had to do another print run.

Frank loved the title: *Was the Kingpin's Moll a Madam?* He was glad she got the extra bucks. Gina had gone the extra mile to help him, digging up information about Devlin and Sunny.

The crowd roared as the fourth quarter began and Frank focused on the game. The Celtics continued their magnificent run and beat the Nets by nineteen points, led by Paul Pierce with 24 points.

Reluctant to leave, Frank let the fans in his row pass him and settled into his seat. The seat beside him was empty, but he could almost feel his father's presence. He missed him badly.

He would miss his father every day as long as he lived. Most of all he would miss talking to him, seeking his counsel.

Would Judge Salvatore Renzi approve of what he'd done?

Thinking back on it, he should have suspected his father's accident was no accident. If something looked like a coincidence, it probably wasn't, but at the time he hadn't put the clues together. Maybe he didn't want to go there. His mother used to call this willful ignorance, chiding him for his risk-taking tendencies, worried that he took too many chances while he was chasing dangerous criminals.

But he wouldn't trade places with anyone. He loved being a cop. Despite the flashbacks that tormented him. Shooting Tank outside the cottage in Plymouth, the coppery smell of blood, Tank's eyes wide open in a milky death-stare. Tank had shot at him first, but did shots fired in self defense make it okay to kill him?

And what about Devlin? Like Al Pacino in *The Godfather,* taking revenge on the men who tried to assassinate his father, Frank had gone to Deer Island intending to kill him. But in the film, Pacino played a gangster. He was a cop, sworn to uphold the law.

Years ago when he watched the film with his father, Judge Salvatore Renzi clearly disapproved, saying this would be the gangster's downfall. Frank disagreed but didn't dare say so, thinking, *I'd have done the same thing if someone tried to kill my father.*

And then someone did kill his father, with malice aforethought.

He looked around the TD Garden, almost empty now. Most of the fans had departed, a few straggling out the exits. The cheerleaders were gone, and workers were cleaning the parquet floor.

Then, as if his father were sending him a message, he remembered the conversation they'd had when he was a high school senior. His basketball team had made it to finals in the State tournament, to be played at Boston Garden.

Before he left for the game, his father had taken him into his library to give him some advice. "I'll be there rooting for you, Frank, and I hope your team wins. But win or lose, here's what's important. Always do your best, on and off the court. Others may not know if you did or not, but you will know. If you don't give it your best, it will stay with you forever like the stink of a rotten egg."

Frank thought about what had happened since his father's funeral.

The man who had ordered his father's assassination was dead. His top lieutenant, the man who had held a gun to Maureen's head, was also dead. He had killed them both with malice aforethought.

Had he done his best? In his mind, the answer was yes.

Would Judge Salvatore Renzi agree? There was no way to tell.

But if his father knew about Maureen's terrible ordeal, held captive for days, blindfolded, threatened with a gun, Frank felt certain he would.

He could live with that.

######

SUSAN SAYS ...

Hello to all my readers and Frank Renzi fans! If you'd like an email alert when my next Frank Renzi book comes out, sign up at http://eepurl.com/ExkX9 I promise never to share your email. No spam, just a fun newsletter now and then from Susan Fleet with the latest Frank Renzi news.

If you enjoyed *Payback,* please consider posting a review on the Amazon site where you purchased it. Believe it or not, authors depend upon reader reviews to spread the word about their books, and I would love to know what you thought of it!

ABOUT THE AUTHOR

In her travels, Susan Fleet has worn many hats: trumpeter, college professor and music historian. While teaching at Brown University and Berklee College of Music, she discovered her dark side and began killing people. Fictionally, of course! In 2001 she moved to New Orleans, the setting for her award-winning crime thrillers featuring NOPD Homicide Detective Frank Renzi.

The Premier Book Awards named her first novel, *Absolution,* Best Mystery-Suspense-Thriller of 2009. Feathered Quill Book Awards named *Natalie's Revenge* Best Mystery-Thriller of 2014.

Susan still plays her trumpet every day but spends most of her time dreaming up new ways to terrify and enthrall her readers. She now divides her time between Boston and New Orleans. See more on her website: http://www.susanfleet.com

Crime fiction by Susan Fleet

ABSOLUTION
DIVA
NATALIE'S REVENGE
JACKPOT
NATALIE'S ART
MISSING
NATALIE'S DILEMMA
SNIPER
PAYBACK

289

Non-fiction by Susan Fleet

Women Who Dared: Maud Powell and Edna White
At a time when most women stayed home to raise children, these women thrilled millions with their performances. Maud was the first instrumentalist to record for RCA Victor in 1904. Edna played the first ever solo trumpet recital in Carnegie Hall in 1949. Their personal lives were tumultuous. Maud ignored her mother's disapproval to marry the man she loved. Edna left her first husband to marry an opera singer. See http://susanfleet.com/womenwhodared.htm

"Fleet is an expert on female musicians who deserve wider recognition in the history of jazz and classical music."— Matt Morrell, Jazz at WGBH, Boston, MA

"Fleet's heroines were successful, artistic performers, attracting and enriching broad audiences."— Howard Mandel, music critic, *Billboard*

DARK DEEDS: Serial killers, stalkers and domestic homicides
Twelve Twisted Tales of True Crime
DARK DEEDS, Volume 2: Serial killers, stalkers and domestic homicides. Twelve more twisted crimes!

"Well researched and well written. The inner world of these killers is vividly and psychologically portrayed. "Well researched and well written. A 5-star recommend!" – Arthur Smukler, MD, psychiatrist

ACKNOWLEDGMENTS

These days when we think of Irish mobsters, Whitey Bulger and his South Boston gang come to mind. But *Payback* takes place in 2011, when Whitey was still on the lam. Although some events in *Payback* take place in Southie, I deliberately invented fictional places and created a fictional mob kingpin, Brian Devlin and his ill-fated family.

Several scenes take place on Deer Island, near Winthrop, MA. I went to Deer Island one dark stormy day and walked along the shoreline. A monument commemorates the 2400 Irish immigrants who disembarked there and the 800 unfortunates among them who died there. The hospital where they died and the cemetery where they were buried are no longer there. However, for dramatic purposes, I recreated the cemetery and the now-demolished hospital in order to introduce the Devlin family and the fictional Bridgette Curse that plagued them.

Likewise, my descriptions of locations in Southie, the Catholic church and the parochial school are the product of my imagination.

My beta readers prefer to remain anonymous, but I thank them for their insightful and helpful comments. My deepest thanks go to John Amaral, who proofread the manuscript and offered suggestions that greatly improved the book. His technical comments about firearms, ammunition and weapons terminology were invaluable.

Thanks also to members of the crimescenewriters group for answering questions about technical points like burners and drop boxes. My heartfelt thanks to the NOPD homicide detectives who listened to my scenario and answered my many questions about police procedures. However, the events and actions that take place in *Payback* are fictional. In some instances I have taken a certain amount of dramatic license. Any errors or inaccuracies are mine alone.

And finally, a huge thank-you to all my readers! Without you, my work would be in vain. I get comments about my books from readers all over the world. I love reading them and always answer them, so send me an email: susan@susanfleet.com

www.ingramcontent.com/pod-product-compliance
Lightning Source LLC
Chambersburg PA
CBHW070837250626
47159CB00003B/822